GW00454905

DAVID PALIN

PARALLELS

Three Dark Psychological Tales

Copyright © 2023 by David Palin

All rights reserved. No part of this publication may be reproduced, stored or transmitted in any form or by any means, electronic, mechanical, photocopying, recording, scanning, or otherwise without written permission from the publisher. It is illegal to copy this book, post it to a website, or distribute it by any other means without permission.

First edition

ISBN: 9798856562025

*This book was professionally typeset on Reedsy.
Find out more at reedsy.com*

Preface

We are surrounded by parallel worlds; universes waiting for us to create tears in the fabric of space and time, so we can step through.

What would we find there? That depends on what has caused those fissures to appear. Will we view things differently if we are grieving, angry, excited, confused – guilty? What if something or someone decides to push through from the other side and seek us out, or hunt us down?

They say the ones we love never leave us when they die. What about the ones we don't love? As Shakespeare wrote in Julius Caesar:

> *The evil that men do lives after them;*
> *The good is oft interred with their bones.*

Then there's the conscience - it is a world like a negative from old-fashioned photographs, presenting us with something we know, in the same detail, but in much darker, and somehow spookier shades; familiar, but different.

If the above rings any bells with you, then perhaps you will enjoy this collection of novellas. If you're not sure, but are prepared to think about the possibility of these other worlds walking step by step with ours, then why not read them anyway and make up your own mind?

In 'A Conversation with Cain', one man's grief, and his fear of the void that he believes follows death, creates one of those aforementioned fissures and draws to him someone who has lived with a troubled conscience from the very beginnings of recorded time. Both are in pain, but neither is aware of the danger each of them now faces as a result of their interaction.

In 'After-Image' the appearance of a stranger attending an evening event in a small town's art café unsettles everyone. Memories are set loose, which might better have been left undisturbed, and consciences are shaken by the knowledge that there is a heavy, potentially fatal price to pay for an ill-conceived prank played many years before.

'In the Laptops of the Gods', finds the past and the future merging with disastrous, viral consequences. Three ancient gods cross paths with the wannabee business deities of a software giant now controlling society and the battle for power begins.

If you read these works, you will recognise much – and not simply *The Shard*, a needle-like structure overlooking the City and created by me many years before the current version was built! That is when fear strikes the hardest; recognition makes us question the link between truth and fiction. I have seen things in the hardware of history, which made me realise I would never have to fear overstepping the boundaries of belief. We will always be moving in parallel.

I

A CONVERSATION WITH CAIN

Death follows all men – some longer than others

Copyright © 2012 David Palin

The Beginning

H e stood on the heat-blasted promontory, looking across the great emptiness of the world, or what he knew of it thus far; a vista of brown wasteland, the far reaches of which shimmered in a deceitful haze. Was this void his sole reward for enduring the aching loneliness? Could that really have been his father's plan, or indeed *his* father's before him; that man should inherit such arid nothingness? It made him strangely grateful for the vague shapes lurking on the horizon, with their intimations of something different out there. Not better, perhaps, but he would settle for different.

And truly, there was nothing for him here; just the rumour and the stench of brotherly betrayal and a father's foolishness.

Still, in the face of despair he'd learnt to find hope; knew where to scratch for it in the dust of life, like the frogs and insects he dug from beneath the sand. Though he had never seen it, he had heard stories of the sea that brooded beyond the distant plains and on some nights could even have sworn that he picked up the scent. Out there lay a chance to escape the ignorance of others; shun them as they shunned him. He wanted to leave behind forever this soil that was poisoned in

3

permanence by the blood of his family.

How to cross that great body of water when he reached it? On his travels, at the few festering sores of civilisation encountered so far, there were tales of men with boats who caught fish along the coast. He would work a passage with them, learn how to build a boat of his own perhaps, and then see how far from land his courage took him. Would he brave enough to lose sight of the coast? Would his anger give him the strength?

He looked back in the direction of home, though he hesitated to call it such, unless your definition of home was a place of silence and sorrow that held you to it by a single, stubborn thread. He had seen the agony of broken faith in his father's eyes and watched how it consumed him from within. How did you live with the knowledge that you had condemned one of your own flesh and blood to carry with them for the rest of their long days the guilt of killing their own brother? Surely it was a burden too far for both father and son.

He wondered whether he would return one day, but already the place of his birth lay many days distant and soon it would be nothing but a memory; a slight hollow in his story where once there had been a puddle, now dried up. With every step he had traveled away from it, his sense of purpose had grown stronger, fed by the need for revenge; not for the murder, but for the desolation and wasted years. He knew his destiny lay across the sea; felt it in his blood – and another's.

Chapter One

"Don't worry, my sweet." She placed a frail, diaphanous hand on his bowed head and her voice was now a ghost of a whisper. "I have my faith – I'm not scared to die."

"But I have nothing," he sobbed, his words muffled as he pressed his face into the blanket, "if not you." He burned with shame at his weakness; her sickness had brought her to the very edge of eternal darkness, but still she was strong enough to comfort him.

She stroked his hair gently, wires and catheters trailing from her hand and arm – webs of death already spun around her - while his head shook. Then the slight pressure of her fingers lifted. There was only silence. No high-pitched keening of an ECG monitor; just a simple passing away – for her.

But not for Troy. For him, death was a smothering thing and in his grief he couldn't breathe. The lights of the world went out; on the monitors and in his head. He'd watched in horror as cruel cancer had allowed the dying flame to burn ever weaker, to the very end of the match, leaving the ashen stalk, which had once been his guiding light. And now, at last, he understood why people lit candles in churches; to carry that flame forward. It had little to do with faith; rather with disbelief. How could it be possible that someone who had filled a space in the universe with uncomplicated joy had left it a paradox; full of unutterable emptiness? Those flame-bearers were replacing blindness with blind hope, darkness with light, but also confirmation with denial.

She was gone. That was it.

He didn't want to follow, because there was nowhere to go; and the thought of not being – not existing any more - filled him with terror. Though he despised himself for the innate selfishness of it, his desolation at the snuffing out of her existence was as nothing compared with his black despair at the thought of his own.

* * *

Thus began Troy's obsession with living on. Not for him the aimlessness of prayer, nor the pointless fight to prevent the plum becoming the prune. His was a new alchemy, seeking everlasting life from the base metal of existence.

Casting aside all things that burdened the time he had – his job as a software engineer, friendships, sleep – he consumed *life* from countless thousands of pages in hundreds of books, preferring old-fashioned late-night libraries to the potential distractions of the internet; the light of his world now a reading lamp as he studied into the dead hours. Long forgotten tomes welcomed him to their musty universe. The shadows beneath his eyes became as one with the gloomy corners he inhabited.

Much of the fruit on offer in this vast garden of knowledge

was rotten and he assumed it must have been some strange cerebral nausea, or fever, that prompted him to look up from his labours one night at the library to find a figure standing there, whose approach he'd not picked up. Of indeterminate age, the man had blonde hair tied back in a ponytail and a goatee. There were furrows between his dense eyebrows and down his cheeks that deepened in the soft wash of the lamplight. He had thoughtful eyes and an urbane, if not ready smile set in a pale face. His sudden presence both startled and excited Troy, as if he'd sprung from the pages he was studying.

"What do you seek?" asked the man, his precise tone and manner out of keeping with his dude-like appearance.

"Who wants to know?"

A broad smile. "Ah, you're a man with a revolutionary idea, but a terrorist's trust. It is an innocent question, my friend. My apologies; I've observed you here many times, studying assiduously."

"Strange; I always believed I was here alone."

"We're never alone." Troy frowned and the stranger gestured around at the shelves. "Not with all these gathered friends and their collected wisdom."

"Or madness," said Troy, his barb directed at the book still clutched in his hands.

"It's only madness if you recognize that it's nonsense but choose to believe it - just as wisdom is only wise in an open mind, or a way-marker only as true as the surrounding roads. Otherwise...they're all just words on a page."

Troy shook his head and turned back to the book, though not with conviction. "Yeah, yeah, I know, if a tree falls in a forest and no-one hears it etcetera etcetera. It's all just aphorisms and sophistry. If you don't mind, it's late and..."

The man seemed unperturbed by Troy's curtness. "The lateness of the hour's never bothered you before and I assure you, your work will never be finished."

Troy gave him a sharp look. "Have you been watching me?" He found the possibility unnerving.

"I asked the first question. What do you seek? Perhaps I can help."

Troy looked down again. "I doubt it." Silence reigned for a few seconds. The stranger stood motionless. Realising it was pointless trying to continue and unable to deny his own grudging curiosity – besides, it was a lonely road he'd been traveling – Troy lifted his head and waved his hand across the open book. "I seek the same as every man – eternal life."

"Ah, that old chestnut."

Troy pulled a face. "Old chestnut? How can you dismiss it like that?" He noticed how the merest flicker of annoyance deepened the brown of the stranger's eyes, turning them from arid, baked soil to mud.

"Better to dismiss it than seek it in books. Have you found it yet? Is it there in the spores and the motes of dust that circle above those pages beneath your lamp?"

Troy leaned back in his chair. "I'm not looking for some formula."

"You'd have more chance, believe me." The voice was dismissive. "What *have* you found?"

Troy sighed. "I've found the words *everlasting life* create a vortex that pulls in the weak and stupid." He picked up one side of the book and slammed it shut against the other, sending a tiny storm of particles to blow itself out beyond the lamplight. "And maybe that includes me."

The stranger tilted his head to one side. "I doubt it, considering that very possibility has already rasped at your mind. Like the man who questions whether he is mad, your words are your shield and salvation. But back to your research: have you found no leitmotiv; no thread in the labyrinth?"

"Well, I suppose if you believe that there's no smoke without fire..."

No light without life. The words caused him to break off for a few seconds and when he reconnected, he was surprised to find his audience still waiting; patient; unmoving.

"...then the one clue I have points to Eastern Europe."

The stranger grinned. "You mean vampires, porphyria, Countess Elizabeth Báthory, the *strigoi* and all the usual suspects."

Troy gestured in resignation with upturned palms. "There, you see – hobgoblins and demons; your grin says it all."

The man shrugged. "Well, if that is what you have, then that is what you have. What you don't have is anything to lose by checking into it. And after all, there are more things on heaven and earth...That part of the world is shrouded in history and mystery. Cynicism is a sharp axe, my friend, always ready to chop things down," he paused and leaned forward, "but roots run deep."

Suddenly, Troy burst out laughing. It was an uneasy sound, even to his ears and he realised it might have been the first time he'd heard it since she'd gone.

"What's so amusing?" asked the other.

"It's just occurred to me that I'm sitting in a library at nearly midnight talking, in homilies, to a complete stranger in a tie-dyed T-shirt about going to Eastern Europe to seek out some vampires. Maybe I did find something, after all, in my search — I'm just not sure what." Just as suddenly, his laughter stopped; the new bloom withering in the intense gaze of the other man.

Silence descended on the library again. "Follow your heart," said the stranger at last. "At least until it stops beating." There was such coldness in those final words, Troy could have sworn he saw the man's breath turn to vapour.

His mysterious visitor turned and walked away, the hollow *tock* of his Cuban heels echoing, causing Troy to wonder how he had failed to hear their approach. He shivered slightly, felt tired all of a sudden and decided that his thirst for knowledge had been quenched for the night.

Chapter Two

Despite everything that had been written and reported about the opening up of Eastern Europe after the fall of the Iron Curtain, Troy felt he was traveling in a time capsule as the train took him further from his comfort zone. A measure of how much he missed her was that her absence infected even this vast landscape, though she had never graced it.

It was late afternoon on the fourth day since he had shrugged on his rucksack like some Bohemian apprentice of old and set out. The comforting lights of dwellings had dwindled in inverse proportion to the discomfort of the trains and now the aching loneliness of the Carpaţii Meridionali, the Southern Carpathians, offered the perfect setting for the stone that he wanted his heart to become. It was apparent that some of the views from the window had changed little since medieval times; or rather, man had changed little, with the result that there were few signs of that sometime blight called progress. He looked up at the sweeping slopes of pine clad mountains.

"The Transylvanian Alps," he whispered. Until he'd seen their looming bulk, the myths and clichés had been exactly that, but the neglected air of some of the villages, the remote farms, the profusion of horse-drawn carts and the men wielding scythes in rough fields made him believe that here, at least, was somewhere in keeping with his desire to stop the cogs of time's clock from turning.

As his head jolted forward with the halting of the train, he realised that he'd fallen asleep and resented that little wedge of death that fate had driven into his limited stay on Earth. Glancing out of the window, he saw the sign *Vatra Dornei* – his stop. He'd chosen the town for its position in the heart of legend-land. It was only on disembarking that he realised, although the town was relatively small, it was still larger than his misanthropic mindset could tolerate for now. The irony did not escape him; here was a man who wished to live forever, yet shied away from humankind. Finding a tourist information office, he enquired after cheap accommodation in a quieter location and soon a taxi was dropping him in what appeared to be a non-descript village just outside the town.

Having found a suitable hostel just as the evening was starting to close in, Troy dumped his things and wandered around the village. It was illuminating; though he'd believed that nowhere could ever feel welcoming again without her by his side, he'd not realised that there were degrees of loneliness. Here, at nightfall, knowing neither the language nor the ways, he was an outsider in what felt like the remotest latitude on the planet. So, despite his earlier misgivings, as he walked by some lit windows, and heard what might have passed for the hubbub of chatter in those parts, he took his courage in both hands and went inside.

Troy expected all conversation to stop, chairs to scrape back and a pianist to stop playing, as if he'd pushed open the bat-wing doors of a Wild West saloon; *there's a stranger in town.* Yet maybe four days of beard and the dark circles under his eyes gave him the demeanour of a local – more likely the inn was used to travellers from the hostel – and he was able to wander in without drawing too much attention. His next surprise was that the barman spoke some English, enabling him to order stew with dumplings, bread and beer. He sat in a corner, took a swig of the ale and pulled out a map. As conversations picked up momentum around him, it was enough to sit there and not feel lonely, or at least to allow the cessation of pain. Still, the space beside him remained as empty as ever.

Not for long.

He sensed the newcomer was making for his table and willed the feet to walk on by – he didn't need someone in her space – but staring at his map didn't appear to convey the message well enough, because the feet paused.

It was the strangest thing; he shivered just before the man spoke to him.

"Is this seat taken?"

That voice. And now he thought about it, the hollow *tock* of the heels. He looked up, but said nothing – or rather, couldn't speak – as the figure in cowboy boots, jeans and a tie-dyed T-shirt made to sit down at the bench.

"You!" It was a choke more than a word. The figure gestured for him to stay silent. Troy glanced around, but no-one was taking any notice of the newcomer. Maybe his seventies garb still passed for high fashion in these parts, though the blonde ponytail was less de rigeur.

"Don't talk to me – or rather, don't let anyone hear you doing it," said the man. Troy continued to sit with his mouth

13

hanging open. "Well, that's one solution. You'll fit in nicely with some of the locals looking like that."

Troy tried to gather his wits. "How...I mean...why can't...?" he whispered.

"They can't see me. So if you talk to me, you'll come across as insane rather than inbred, and you wouldn't want that." He shrugged. "Then again..."

Troy glanced around and whispered: "What do you mean, they can't see you? And who are you?"

"I'm Cain."

"OK, but *who* are you? And why are you here?"

"Please, keep your voice down."

Troy took his beer, swallowed a long draught, and then looked again at his companion. "It must be the drink; you're still here."

Just then, the barman came over carrying a steaming plate of goulash and dumplings. Troy watched his eyes intently, but the man showed no sign of acknowledging there was anybody else at the table; just left the food and walked away.

"Ah, the ubiquitous dumpling," said Cain. "I don't think the five-a-day has ever caught on here somehow – although you can always rely on cabbage as one of your units at some point."

Troy's appetite was certainly on hold for now. He nudged the plate towards Cain. "Knock yourself out."

"I'm sorry?"

"Help yourself."

"Actually, I will." The visitor took a chunk of meat, popped it into his mouth, and Troy watched as a wistful look darkened Cain's eyes. "I'd give so much to be able to taste that. Still, it will help to restore the strength this crude flesh needs on this side of existence." He gestured towards his body, continued to eat and indeed, the blood did appear to return to his cheeks.

Troy sat back in his seat, looked around again and then, pretending to study his map, said in a soft voice: "OK, what the fuck is going on? Why did...why...oh, just tell me what I need to know, including why you followed me here."

"I'm here because you wanted me to be; not in Vatra Dornei, but here in your world – although it's my world too."

Troy paused. "Well thanks for clearing that up," he said at last, looking away in frustration.

When there was no response he looked back, to find Cain staring at him, unsmiling, as if weighing up something before speaking again.

"You'll lose that schoolboyish sarcasm soon enough." Something in the tone, some shadows of intention moving behind the veil, made Troy's blood run cold. "I can't always choose my companions, but in your case, I see enough grief and anger to allow your disrespect to pass this once." Now he smiled, to Troy's relief, who was not, by nature, impolite.

"My apologies. I'm listening."

Cain took a piece of bread while Troy, imagining the food floating in mid-air above the table, watched for inquisitive stares. There were none; just voices becoming increasingly animated as the local beer washed away restraint and the dust of toil.

"I came because you searched so hard for me and with such intensity – wanted so much to find me – that you shook the very fabric of existence and created a rent in it; a schism in the structure of things. So, I stepped through. And believe me, it's not often I get the chance."

"To do what? I'm sorry, I'm still completely lost."

15

"To interact through choice. Oh, long ago people under-stood better. They controlled things; called by means of their rhythms and their chants and I answered their summons, though sometimes they wished I hadn't. But as time went on – and we're talking serious time here; I mean, millennia – they got confused and started calling for things they couldn't possibly have; things I could never give them. After all, I'm not a superhero from some comic-book – and I include the Bible under that heading – just the oldest man alive." He twisted his mouth in a peculiar grin. "Well, I say *alive*; what I mean is *dead*."

Troy felt his body give an involuntary jolt, glanced again at the other customers to ensure no-one had seen, and then said: "Oh my God, are you Death?"

"Were you seeking Death?"

"No; just the opposite, as you know."

"Then how can I be Death?" He sighed with mild impa-tience. "You know, there are very simple rules governing our universes, most of them pretty logical." Troy made to speak, but Cain raised his hand to stop him and said: "One of them is that a man talking to an invisible stranger in a superstitious part of the world is asking for trouble. Look, there's an interesting ruined castle about an hour to the east of here, at the top of the Tihuta Pass. Its name disappeared along with most of its stones, but they call it the Witch's Teeth in these parts because of its silhouette. Let's go and sit there."

"What, now? In the darkness?"

"Did you have something else planned? What are you afraid of?"

"Nothing."

"Nothing? Not even the finality of death? I would have thought the kind of clichéd Transylvanian fate you're imagining – eternal life granted by the prick of a vampire's teeth – would have been preferable. But don't worry..." He broke off as Troy gave him a thin smile. "What?"

"The Tihuta Pass? If my research has brought me anything – apart from a visitation from the other side – it's been a wealth of facts about, shall we say, the more commercialised, tourist-orientated aspects of this region. The Tihuta Pass; otherwise known as the Borgo Pass, made famous in Bram Stoker's *Dracula*?" Now Troy grew angry. "Is this meant to be funny? Did someone put you up to this? If they did, are you happy going along with it; playing with another man's grief – his need to find some answers?"

He became aware of the silence and looked up to see the entire inn looking back, stony-faced; turned again to see Cain doing the same, except the latter raised his eyebrows. They were probably all in this together; some sort of practical joke.

"Oh, go to hell!" shouted Troy to everyone and no-one in particular. Jumping to his feet, he threw the payment for the food on the table and stalked towards the door.

Cain replied, without humour: "If there is such a place, I've been there. I might even have invented it."

All around, eyes stared at Troy. Now grim mouths started to mutter behind beer mugs and Lech Walesa moustaches.

Cain continued: "They're too simple – too dull-witted – to see me; to feel your pain. They do not question; they accept death. It is in their upbringing; in their lighting of candles; in their Sunday best clothes. Were they to see me, it would both cement and shatter their beliefs. They are meek; perhaps then they are blessed."

Troy knew it was time to leave.

* * *

Whatever his angry protestations, he knew he'd only been raging against his own fear and ignorance. That night – the irony didn't escape him – when he sought sleep at last, it eluded him. He'd become such a creature of the night, through his relentless search for the truth and his shunning of the sad reflections and memories of daylight, his soul seemed to have moved across already to the world of the *nosferatu.*

Chapter Three

All through the following day he played over in his mind the words and events of the evening before, till there was no other choice – or so he liked to pretend – than to head out of Vatra Dornei on a borrowed bicycle in search of the castle of the Witch's Teeth.

Sure enough it was easy to find, silhouetted against the late afternoon sky on its jagged promontory, but he could tell that starting his ascent now – a climb of at least three thousand feet – would bring him to his goal after sunset. He couldn't help but grin; wasn't that how it was supposed to be?

He paused from time to time during the tortuous climb; to catch his breath, but also to take in the stark majesty of the surrounding lakes and wildness. He caught himself feeling at peace, and had to remind himself that life was an Indian giver, which had left him with nothing.

The oblique sunlight on the mountainsides was both a thing of indescribable beauty and a stark reminder that the sun was setting; there'd be no chance of finding his way back down in the darkness; he would have to spend the night sheltering in the ruins. What had seemed an adventure from the bravado of sea level became a dreadful prospect that almost robbed him of his remaining strength now that night was falling on these

19

exposed and lonely heights. Yet not to carry on would have been an insult to her memory. This was the fundamental flaw in his life; the contradiction from which he fled; the reason he feared to sleep: he wanted to live, even without her, more than he wanted to die.

At last he rounded one final false summit and reached the top; a short flat approach to the remaining black stones of the ruin. All that was left was scattered stonework and the crumbling central tower; the weathered fang of an extinct beast.

He wandered through one of the remaining arched entrances into the tower - all the upper floors had rotted away leaving just a shell – and straight out again moments later. It was perhaps five or six degrees cooler in there and had frozen the sweat on his body immediately. Troy sat with his back resting against the outer wall, took a grateful drink from his water bottle and devoured a Mars Bar, while the palest of moonlight provided a fading memory of the sun.

At first he thought his stomach had cramped from the water, but then he realised that something else had inveigled his subconscious; footsteps – *inside* the tower; a light, sinister scurrying of feet.

His first thought was wolves, though surely he would have seen them; there was nowhere for them to hide and unless they were extremely agile, they could not have made their way up the sheer rock faces that surrounded the rest of the castle. Perhaps he'd been mistaken and they had been watching him, assessing him as they hid in the crumbling brickwork, ensuring he was alone.

He could not afford to allow his thoughts to wander down that road. Let common sense prevail. Cain had probably

20

followed him here.

He might have laughed out loud at that leap of faith, if he wasn't so scared. Hadn't he rejected Cain as someone's idea of a cruel practical joke just the day before? Now, suddenly, a visit from a parallel universe was his preferred version of the truth.

A truth apparently reinforced when a voice spoke from the tower:

"You came."

"Cain?"

"Yes."

He breathed a huge sigh of relief, pulled up the zip of his fleece – the temperature seemed to be dropping by the minute - picked up the rucksack and wandered in.

Cain was a vague silhouette some distance away on the far side of the tower against the deepening night sky.

"Why did you tell me about this place, knowing I would have to come?" asked Troy, "To bloody scare me? Because you've succeeded."

"Fear is always good," came the light reply. "It sharpens the senses."

He took a couple more steps forward and heard a light footfall behind him. Swinging round, he perceived another silhouette standing in the archway, blocking the exit. Being much closer, he could see that this one was clothed in rags. On an instinct, Troy spun back towards Cain...and let out an involuntary shriek as he found the first figure standing just a step away from him, also in rags. It wasn't Cain. The dim light revealed a blade, which, in pure reflex, he swung away from as it arced towards his neck. Fleeing across the tower towards a breach in the wall, he stopped himself just in time and stared down the thousand or so precipitous feet that would have marked his final journey. Turning back, he saw other figures moving out of the shadows; dying stars drawn from a corrupt heaven by the onset of night.

"Please...please..." he stammered, "take my money, my rucksack, my clothes...I don't care."

"Oh, we can't do that." He could hear now that the voice was female and realised it had only ever spoken in a whisper before to deceive him, though its sibilance had carried to him with dream-like ease. "Much as we'd like to change from these rags, you'll need something to cover your modesty for the next – what's it been, ladies – six hundred years?"

His eyes were adjusting to the dark and as the figures approached, which they did with a sinuous, slow, continuous movement, he heard girlish peals of laughter that might have been seductive if they hadn't issued from lips curling in murderous anticipation.

"Six hundred years for you perhaps," said another voice; "only a couple of centuries for some of us."

The faces were awful - beyond description – ageless but ancient; worse because clearly they had once been beautiful. In a moment of hysteria he entertained the lunatic thought that blood was the Botox of the vampire world. For he knew now what these things were; not a band of robbers, but something much older.

His breath came in tiny puffs, not even gasps, and as the terrible hostesses drew ever nearer, he tried to understand:

"But...you're...carrying knives."

"Yes," said the eldest one, "and you're welcome to examine our teeth." She bared her lips. "Not a fang amongst them. In fact, some of my sisters don't have many teeth left at all." Even in the night he could see the icy, vulpine quality of her eyes. "You've read too many books; watched too many of your talking pictures. Of course, we carry knives!" She brandished it in threat. "Let me guess; you expected some beautiful, but cruel-eyed seductress in a floating silken dress, gliding towards you several inches behind her voluptuous cleavage; sending you into a lover's swoon while her lips and teeth brushed your neck before taking a delicious bite. Well, I am sorry to disappoint you, but we will make the following concessions to your fantasies; this is Transylvania, we were once beautiful, we will drink your blood to keep us alive, but not drain you, which will allow your body to live on." She gestured around her. "If you can call this living."

Troy knew he was close to losing his mind when he found himself questioning how he could understand her. Was he in fact dreaming? When the creature spoke again things were no clearer, because she appeared to have invaded his thoughts.

"Who knows?" she said in an almost casual manner. "One of life's little mysteries; or one of death's."

Her powers were far greater than she pretended, because the eyes and voice had held him hypnotised and the pack were almost upon him. He turned towards the open archway.

"Go ahead; jump – if you dare." She laughed as he stood shaking. "Even now you cling to what you call life. I've seen it all before. Man is so weak; refusing, even when faced with the inevitable, to believe that it may not be the end; failing to see that it can signal a beginning – not of life again as he has known it, but of something different; perhaps better, perhaps worse, but how will he know unless he has the courage to try? Two foolish young girls, including one of my sisters, stood where you now tremble and made their choices. Both had

23

the courage of their convictions in their separate ways, as women do. Unfortunately for one, the fall didn't kill her." The vampire gestured behind her towards the darkness at the far side of the tower. "She tends not to emerge too often from the shadows, for we still drank her blood and her broken body lived on. So, if you must be a vampire, why not give yourself a chance to live it to the full – at least in the early centuries. Do nothing that will cause disfigurement or leave you hiding in the shades of night; disabled, drinking the blood of vermin and contemplating once again whether to end it all – this time by stepping into the light – though believe me, you would cling to this new life with the same tenacity that you display now." Her tone changed; became almost sympathetic. "Come; one swift slice to the neck and we can all live happily ever after."

"Enough," said one of the others, "we must hurry. He called to Qayin."

The vampires stopped in their tracks for a moment – every one.

"He knows Qayin?" asked a tentative voice.

"Indeed, you are right," said the leader, "let us hurry."

In the second or two he had left to live, Troy felt as though he had indeed plunged from the archway, and passed his life on the way down. He found himself wondering whether the simple folk at the inn had it right; hold onto your faith, accept your lot, or else pollute the Earth like rotting vegetation. All at once he was prepared to take his chances; braced himself for the backward step and the rush of a thousand feet of air past his neck.

Except...except perhaps it could be different for him; a

vampire of the modern age; one with courage enough to leave the crumbling ruin that was his life. Of course, he would be a killer. A cancer. A snuffer-out of lights. Would that end his pain?

"Stop!"

That word, spoken with authority, might have been aimed at him, preventing him wandering down the path he'd been about to tread. But the vampires froze.

From the archway, through which Troy had entered, stepped Cain.

The effect on the vampires was immediate and striking. The light in their eyes went out, replaced by frustrated acquiescence.

"Qayin!" said the leader. "It has been a long time."

"But not a moment too long, it would seem."

Her tone verged on coquettish. "How can you say that? We do what we do; cannot help the beings we are, any more than you can."

"Except I am no killer." She snorted at his response. "Only of necessity; in self defence."

"Qayin, not a killer. Oh, the delicious irony! And is it not necessity for us to feed?"

"Lilith, my dear, your presence on this earth – in this universe – is, unfortunately, an abomination; a mistake."

The vampire looked hurt. "Well, you would know."

"Besides, he does not seek you or what you have to give – at least not in the way he might think."

"He was about to embrace his fate; I saw it in his eyes. Why else would he be here?"

"Ah Lilith, you can be very persuasive and you cannot help

trying to deceive. He is here because I, in many ways, I told him to meet me."

"You told him...?" She laughed in incredulity, and the sarcasm dripped like blood from her lips. "That was benevolent of you. Could he not have met you in a pit of vipers instead?"

Suddenly, Cain seemed to lose patience. "I would suggest you leave now. My friend and I have much to discuss."

"For one kiss I will go."

Cain sighed. "Very well."

Troy, who clung still to the stone arch, watched in trepidation as the vampire stepped forward, with the wicked blade still glinting in her hand. But she stood on tiptoes and planted a lingering kiss on Cain's lips, then looked at him, the sorrow in her eyes a reflection of the softening in her voice.

"Oh Qayin – do you remember?"

With that she bowed her head and backed away into the shadows, followed by the other vampires. Soon the tower had been returned to the wind.

"Are...are they gone?" Troy's voice trembled.

Cain seemed to cock his head and listen. "Yes."

Troy stepped away from the arch; then his legs gave way and he sank to the floor. "You were right...you came...just in time."

"No, I was always here."

Troy looked at him in horror. "And you let them..."

"I must admit there was a moment when I thought it might have got out of hand."

"A moment?"

"Yes, but she'd put all her ageing energies into that one spell."

26

"Spell?"

"When she crossed the space between you quicker than the eye could see. Had she been five hundred years younger the knife might have been in you before you'd realised. But it drained her, and you escaped; well done to you."

Troy contemplated what he'd heard and breathed out shakily. "Well done to me," he agreed.

"You see – your sense of irony returns. You'll be fine."

Troy slipped off his rucksack, opened it with trembling fingers and took a long swig of water.

"Well," said Cain, "I would say you have now officially, well and truly checked things out; ticked the Eastern European legends box – though let me tell you, you only scratched the surface."

"I can imagine." Troy sat with his arms crossed over his knees and stared through the archway into the night.

"No, you can't," corrected Cain, "but it doesn't matter." He sat down next to Troy. "A scratch on the surface was all it required. I wanted you to experience this for yourself; to see that it was not what you seek. I know it scared you, but there is no substitute for reality. And did I imagine it, or were you tempted at one point by what they had to offer?"

"They were..." Troy looked around for inspiration, "...like this castle; ruins of something that was once beautiful and powerful."

Cain put a finger to his lips. He, too, looked around, but in caution. "Be careful what you say. Despite everything, they have feelings – and good hearing. If you anger them they might return and take you, even though they fear me. I could not fight off so many."

Troy was surprised and not exactly comforted. "So they

could kill you?"

"No – but they could kill you; or rather, turn you into one of them."

"Why not you? Are you already one of the Undead."

Cain laughed, but it was a sound of scorn. "A ridiculous word dreamt up by writers of pulp. If you're undead, you're alive. And I'm definitely dead."

Troy put a hand on Cain's arm. "You feel alive."

"Oh, in the corporeal sense I am – or rather this body is. But the thing I am now – you might want think of it as a soul, for ease of reference – does not belong to this machine; this marvellous, but very fragile thing of flesh and blood. I provide it with the light it needs to survive as a sentient being and it provides me with a means of moving around this particular part of the universe, where crude matter is so paramount. But those…" he paused, "…ladies cannot take my life; I am dead already."

Troy frowned. "I don't pretend to understand – at least not fully. But I did notice that, when you called the leader an abomination, she said *"you would know"*. Did you create them?"

Cain shook his head with vigour. "First, let me correct you; I did not call her an abomination, only her presence on the earth."

"Still sounds pretty harsh, from someone who told me to be careful what I say."

"I told them only what they know already; what they know they are. Secondly, I am no creator. Let's just say the creative force is strong in me, but there is only one of me – can only ever be one." Cain smiled. "They made a film and a song about that."

"Why were there only...females?" *If you could call them that,* he'd been about to add, but this time remembered the warning and his manners.

Cain smiled again and pointed across the valley. "This benighted ruin is just the deep shadow of that world out there. Male vampires are more ambitious and overreach themselves, trying to live amongst the living, you might say. It brings only sorrow, for they are reminded by everything they cannot do – including sharing the daylight – that they belong no more. There follows despair, or impatience, or anger, all of them bringing death, sometimes at their own hands. The women, on the contrary, know how to survive."

Troy looked around him. "Is it worth it?"

Cain lifted a finger for emphasis. "Don't be too quick to judge, for in this they are only following the oldest of instincts. Once they accept what they are and surrender to it, they live a life like any other predator. And are they worse or more evil than robbers and thieves? – at least they can give something in return for what they take. You might even say they are perhaps less corrupt in their visceral need."

Troy met this answer with silence. "I know," continued Cain, his tone altering, "I feel your confusion. So many questions; so little time. And that's the essence of it for you, isn't it? Too little time. Your poor heart can't bear to think of it. You seek either life or a meaning to its ending, but in a way quite unlike countless billions of your fellow sufferers. It was the particular, desperate intensity of your need to know – to defy the universal laws – that created the fissure through which I stepped."

Now Troy turned to face Cain and the latter was almost overwhelmed by the unuttered cry of pain in his companion's

29

eyes and the stark simplicity of his question: "Who are you, Cain?"

"In some ways, I've almost forgotten. But such a beautiful, far-reaching question deserves a simple answer. I've been around ever since my brother passed the first breath of creation to my care."

"Your brother?"

"Yes. You can call him Hebhel."

Chapter Four

He was a strong man and in his opinion, despite the nature of things at that time, a lucky one. That morning, he gazed out from his home across the plains, which rippled unbroken in the baking heat as far as the eye could see. It was already an ancient world; vast, but as yet sparsely peopled; one where every deed still carried the scent of birth and discovery.

At first, the few inhabitants of this empty land had followed his lead. Now that respect had been replaced by fear and it grieved him to know this. He had accepted it as the will of the universe, for the suspicion in the eyes of his fellow men resulted from the gifts he had been granted, and sunshine will always cast a shadow. His crops grew, even in rocky soil. His sheep and goats were numerous and healthy. From ideas that seemed to come to him in his sleep he invented tools that worked. And his sons; his sons were healthy and loyal.

His sons.

He shielded his eyes from the glare and squinted into the distance - even his sight seemed keener than other men's. On a distant ridge he could just make out Hebhel, sitting watching the flock. Probably dreaming as usual, but he was a good, diligent boy.

The father's eyes clouded over.

Swiftly he withdrew his gaze to a piece of land much nearer to the homestead, where a more heavily-built young man with a broad back and mop of black curls tilled the soil with a heavy wooden plough – one of the father's dream-inventions – and made light work of the unwieldy tool, though it required great strength. He handled his burden well and without complaint.

It played no part in the man's thoughts, that this embryonic civilisation did not yet have a word for murder.

A movement in the house distracted him and, once again, he found himself pondering the double-edged blade of fortune, as he thought of the beautiful woman who had chosen to be his wife; someone whose eyes often seemed to reflect his own moods; the magical mirror-image of his own stark bluffness.

He knew that the few men who had once populated this sometimes hostile plateau had envied him his luck when she had arrived, exhausted and afraid, at his door one sunset. Her tale was one of misfortune, having been separated from her family's nomadic caravan by a sandstorm, but as they said in those desolate parts, it was an ill-wind that blew an ugly woman to a lonely man.

What had struck him, apart from her feral beauty – her eyes were the only splash of green in his sun-blasted world back then – was the manner in which his luck changed from the moment he gave her shelter under his roof of animal skins.

She spoke in the common tongue and they had spent much of that first evening talking. Then suddenly she stood and fixed him with her eyes, before saying:

"I can lie no longer. It was no storm that drove me here.

I am the last gusts of the wind that raged at the creation of this earth, and am destined to lose all strength and die; to be nothing more than a stirring in the desert dust. But I could not accept that fate. I still have much to give, yet feel the strength in me fading as I try to hold this human form – that is my punishment for defying the natural order of things. Share with me what is left of my powers; let them grow strong in you and in your children. Keep what remains of that elemental force alive, for the sake of mankind."

With that she allowed her robe to fall to the floor and the man was lost in the wonder of her body – the first woman he had ever known. She woke in him such desires and sensations, that he scarcely recognised himself or his actions. He named her *Evening,* in honour of that time and she likened him to the good earth of that place in which her powers were now planted; *Adamah* in the common tongue.

And from that day, he had been like a man reborn; a husband, a provider and a creator – Eve carried their first child as a result of their passion. The only blot on his happiness was the increasing isolation from his neighbouring farmers. They envied him everything. Yet he was content; his days were filled – and his nights too.

Despite their jealousy, his tenuous relationship with his fellow men might have survived, but for one last gift bestowed by his wife to celebrate the child growing in her womb. She had withheld it at first, not understanding fully, or perhaps knowing only too well, its implications for mankind; would it be wise to give this little piece of creation to such a fledgling species? But she loved her husband, he was a good man and she trusted him to wield fire wisely. This he did, but understanding how a man could control this natural force

33

that banished the night was beyond the other simple folk of that plateau and they retreated to the neighbouring lands, leaving these gods on earth to their fields of plenty and their flames. The blazing torches that guarded their farm at night formed a boundary that others were unwilling to cross.

He felt rather than heard her approach and a delicate hand rested on his arm as she followed the direction of his gaze.

"What are you watching, my husband?" They both knew she had the answer already. "The boys?"

"They are men now; this world does not allow the distraction of youth for long."

"Qayin is certainly a man already." There was qualified agreement in Eve's response. "But Hebhel needs more time."

Adamah looked over his shoulder at her. "Indeed, he labours. He is not strong. Strange how the gift – or is it a burden? – passed over the oldest boy."

Eve chewed her lip in thought. "There was no choice in how things happened. It seems the wildness – the sheer unstoppable forcefulness – of early creation hewed Qayin and the first shuddering breath that gave it life passed into his brother."

"Young Hebhel struggles to contain it. It weakens him. I fear it might kill him."

Gripping him, she said with certainty: "No, it cannot." Then her fingers loosened and she stroked his arm. "I pledge to you now that he will not die."

Adamah's eyes grew dark. "But my wife, I have seen how his strength already fades."

She turned him to face her. "It is true; the first breath of creation is now a part of him and he of it. It is indeed a load

34

to bear." Her eyes started to glisten. "He will never be free of it."

"Never? So he will live forever."

"In a way, yes."

At that moment they heard a shout and turned to see Qayin waving a greeting. They returned that wave, he turned back to his plough, and then Adamah said: "And Qayin?"

The shadow returned to Eve's features. "He will die – as must we all."

"How can you know these things?" There was a hint of impatience in both his voice and the grim set of his mouth. He turned and sat down on a stool.

"I just do. And I understand your fears; your frustrations. You love both your sons, but I know that Qayin is the better companion for a man like you."

"That is not my care, woman."

She was stung by his tone, but kept her voice calm. "My husband, I do not tell you these things to vex you and I do not always understand where my knowledge comes from, any more than you know why you wake some mornings with the ability to make tools, or objects," she pointed to the stool, "or knowing what seeds to scatter where." She came and knelt in front of him. "But I know, as surely as I know I love you, that nature will not allow the first breath of creation, or its bearer, to die." She put a hand to her breast. "I am not like other women. In here, I am sure that, as long as I think of Hebhel with love at some time during the day, he will endure, no matter how weak he might be."

Adamah took her hands. "My wife; surely that will be a burden – for him and for you. Is there no way he can pass that breath to Qayin, who is, in nature and perhaps in mind,

35

a stronger man?"

Eve sighed. "I do not pretend to know all that is to come; but the breath is a gift – for better or for worse – and may not be given up. That is the law of the universe. Even when my eyes close and you are gone, and there is no-one left to think a loving thought for him; even then, Hebhel's body will only fade. As moonlight compared to noon he will be, visible only to the wisest of seers, but the breath will live on, in a way and a place beyond the understanding of men. Only a violent death could part them – and then the breath will seek a new home; perhaps elsewhere in the universe, or here in another body on this earth."

"Perhaps then, it will pass to Qayin."

Eve looked down. "Come that day, I fear Qayin will have passed into the dust, for I know he will always protect Hebhel. And as long as Qayin lives to bear a loving thought for his younger brother, Hebhel will not die."

Adamah turned eyes full of regret towards the plains again, lost in thought, before saying:

"I mean to travel beyond the hills in the coming days and down into the far valley. I am tired of losing some of our herd to the cold of winter and want to see whether there is good grazing on the valley floor. This plateau is a cursed place in those bleak months. If it is possible to move the flock and ourselves at that time, we may prosper."

"When will you go?"

"At first light. It will be a long trek and I don't think we will be back until the following evening."

"*We?*"

"The boys and I?"

Eve put both hands on his arms. "You would take Hebhel?"

36

"I will need him to drive the flock when the time comes, so he must come to see if the way is passable. He is a good shepherd."

"Can you not see for yourself whether a few sheep and goats can be moved across the land? You just admitted he is not strong. Is such a long journey a good thing?"

"It may strengthen him. Whatever happens, I cannot allow Qayin to feel that only he must labour."

Eve could see in her husband's eyes that the decision had been made. She wanted to roar her disapproval – to rage – but it was no longer a choice for her from the day she had chosen to be mortal.

* * *

"We will lay our heads here for the night. Gather wood for the fire. Tonight, once more, we will thank the stars for this gift that banishes wild animals and darkness."

"Yes, father," said Qayin, dropping his pack to the ground and immediately searching amongst the sand and rocks for any signs of tinder.

Hebhel threw himself to the floor instead of his pack. "I must rest first, father. How far we have travelled today."

"Nonsense, lazy-bones," said the older brother in a light voice. "Come, I think if we climb to the top of this rock, we will still be able to see the fires of our home."

The younger brother pulled the water-skin from his bundle and drank before saying: "You climb, Qayin. You have such a way with words that I will wait for you to tell me what wonders you see. It will make a good tale by the warmth of the fire, even though I know you will make it all up – for as far as I can tell, we have passed nothing but soil and scrub today."

"I will come." It was their father. Both sons looked at him in surprise. He threw down some kindling, which he had brought with him. "Hebhel, start the fire as I have shown you. After a day crossing the plains, I feel in need of fresher air on my face and some exercise for my arms."

With that, Adamah set off to climb the rocky outcrop by which they had settled for the night. Qayin looked at his younger brother, shrugged and smiled and then, with a final ruffle of Hebhel's hair, set off in pursuit.

Adamah was a man whose back had bent into everything he'd done – that was the way of the early world, when strength came from toil and nothing came from nothing – so his bulky arms hauled him swiftly to the top of the outcrop. He was joined just a short time later by Qayin who, despite his muscular build, was panting as he stood respectfully at his father's side.

"Join me," said Adamah. The boy sat. "You were right." He pointed. "See there, that flicker is our home. Your mother has the fires burning. How vast this world must be, when we have travelled from sunrise till sunset and yet have covered such a tiny part of it. And how small man must be. We should know our place in nature's plan; not question what must be, just accept that we are shown a way to follow."

They sat in silence for some indeterminate time, staring into the darkening night, before Adamah's voice broke the stillness.

"Your brother grows weak."

"He will gain strength, father, as he grows."

38

"No, he will fade." Adamah felt, rather than saw, Qayin's head turn and his eyes question. "But he will not die. He bears a burden that he may never put down. It should have come to you. And so, despite the universe and my own words just now, I can accept nature's plan no longer – I *do* not accept it. I will question. And I know you will too, after hearing what I am about to say."

"No, I cannot do this!" Qayin had listened in horror to his father's words.

"It is the only way to ensure this gift is not lost to another bloodline or forever. We have been given the future of mankind to our care."

"I will look after him, no matter how sick he becomes." Qayin was on his feet, pacing the summit of the rock. Man and youth spoke in desperate whispers.

"And what sort of life will that be for him? You are strong in body and mind. What if someone evil hears of the thing he carries and takes it from him?"

"I will protect him. But it was given to him. Surely that is something we cannot question."

Adamah grasped his eldest son by the arms. "But I do question. You are meant for better things. You are not your brother's keeper. One day you will understand. I want this precious power to be in the best hands. I know you are strong enough to take care of it."

"I am not strong enough to do the terrible thing you ask."

Adamah's gaze fell. "It is a terrible thing. But something tells me this is what we must do."

Qayin wept as he spoke. "Mother will never forgive me."

"She will not know. You are not coming back." Adamah

did his son the courtesy of looking him full in the face as he uttered those awful words. He made a point of not flinching from the pain in Qayin's eyes. "Look across these lands. They may seem endless, but they are barren; arid. Beyond our tiny plateau must lie a huge world, I am sure, and it is yours to explore."

Qayin sank to his knees and sobbed. "I want to go home. Why can't we just stay there and look after this breath of creation of which you speak; take care of Hebhel and live our lives."

His father turned and stared into the night across the plains. "Because I know in my heart, that is not how it is meant to be. I can explain it no better – I am a simple man with no great skill in words. The home I have made to the best of my abilities will not last forever. I believe I have been chosen for a reason by the universe; to make this decision for all mankind. It is not chance that your mother arrived at my door."

"But..."

"Enough." Adamah drew himself to his full height and though Qayin had never seen a bear, he would have recognised in it the strength of his father's physique. "My lot will be worse than yours. I will lose both sons and spend the rest of my days comforting a mother who has suffered the same fate."

Suddenly he grabbed his son and pressed him to his chest. On releasing him he said: "Go now; be strong. I know it is a terrible thing I ask, but I believe such trials, both yours and mine, will be the way of this world. Creation and discovery are violent acts. Go out and light the way for mankind to follow."

Qayin, his eyes full of tears and horror, swallowed hard.

"How will I know whether this breath of which you speak has passed to me?"

"I do not know. Just be with him at the end."

"Father, why should I do this? Why would I want the sort of life that you ask me to spare Hebhel from? And my life will be so much worse for having taken his and carrying the death of my brother with me always."

"You do not want it. But you have been chosen. Now go my son. I will wait here till you are done and have gone. Then I will find a fitting place for the body of Hebhel."

Chapter Five

J ust as he imagined Cain must have stared at his father on that primal night above the wilderness, so Troy found himself staring at Cain.

"Cain rose up against Abel, and slew him," he said in awe. Like so many biblical sentences, the spare wording did little justice to the immensity of an iconic moment. "My God!"

"Certainly not mine. He abandoned me to my fate."

"That really *was* the beginning of civilisation as we know it, wasn't it – unfortunately."

"Are you not repulsed by my act?

"Who am I to judge? If posterity chooses to draw a picture of me, it will be of someone who could feel only sorrow for himself while the person dearest to him in the world, despite weakness and the imminence of death, still found the strength to comfort him."

Cain continued to stare out into the night, but who knew what he was seeing out there; what ghosts?

"The deed still hangs heavy on me," he said, "even after all of time as man knows it."

"And did you feel that first breath of creation pass into you?" Troy was fascinated.

"I didn't just feel it; I saw it."

"What was it like?" whispered Troy.

"Beyond our ability to describe, my friend. If you have the words to frame a fragment of a storm, a piece of history, an echo of stardust, then become a writer, Troy, and live eternally through your work instead."

"What happened afterwards?"

"They say Cain was reviled by mankind." He rubbed his chin. "Yes, one of the good book's many contradictions. For there was no mankind; just as there was no-one to tell of my deed."

"Then how do we know of it, eons later?"

"Who knows?" said Cain. "Perhaps the earth did cry out, as they say, at the shame of what I'd done in the name of all things. Or perhaps St. Cuthbert did listen to me after all. His yearning for everlasting life – admittedly of a more spiritual kind – and the strength of his belief once gave me a chance to step through into this world, fourteen hundred years ago. But I am part of Old Testament lore and his strength lay in the New, so I'm afraid he might have taken me for something demonic.

"Or perhaps my mother didn't believe my father's story, feared his intentions and found Hebhel's body. But she would have hidden my misdeed from the world. She was a strong enough woman to carry another heavy burden, having already defied the universe. I know either she or my father lived a long time, because it was at least a hundred years before my physical form started to fade."

"I'm sorry, I don't understand."

"Weren't you listening before? Only when a full day passes without someone, somewhere, sparing you a loving thought, does a person truly die. And for the bearer of the first breath, that is when the body can no longer sustain its existence in this world and it retreats to the reaches of the cosmos where the crude valencies of atoms and molecules hold no sway. But for even the lowest forms of life, the universe allows the paradigm that as long as there is love or the possibility of it, the energy lives on." He looked at Troy with a wistful expression. "Not in any way that you will ever know, I'm afraid. She has gone from your world – the love of your life. Don't allow any medium or other charlatan to tell you otherwise. It is empty in the places you inhabit. A ghost town without the ghosts."

Troy's stomach had lurched at the mention of her, in part because he couldn't believe his thoughts had wandered from her more than once in the tension of the last hour or so. It felt like betrayal. As if sensing his discomfort, or perhaps to digest his own memories once again, Cain stood and wandered over to the crumbling archway. Beyond the sea of darkness which had swallowed the sheer drop and the other side of the valley, the odd light twinkled in a small town or isolated homestead; the last coals of that day still smouldering. The oldest man alive spoke into the night and his words floated back to Troy.

"This much I do know: a hundred years of wandering that empty earth prepared me, like no-one else, for Armageddon. I stood many times looking across a world largely devoid of man; a scene of unutterable loneliness. There was that impulse, even then, to share, before the word or the deed ever existed."

"Is that why you take life, as you said to the vampires, of necessity? So that no human other than you must face that final emptiness of the earth. I can't even begin to imagine how desolate that day – the end of humankind - will be, when the loss of just one person can leave me so bereft." Cain said nothing in response. "Is that why you will kill me?"

"Your death is neither foretold nor decided. Such magic tricks don't exist except in the minds of men." He turned to look at Troy. "But yes, I have killed, though I'm neither a willing nor a brutal killer. Unfortunately, there's no denying, the life taken does refresh my spirit – recharge the battery, so to speak."

"And the change of clothes must be welcome," said Troy, trying to lighten the topic; never an easy task where killing is concerned. "It can't be easy materialising in an outfit that's two hundred years out of date."

Cain smiled, appreciating Troy's attempt to lighten the mood, but then a strange look came into his eyes. "There was one occasion when killing was necessary for the greater good. He was a man of such overreaching ambition, he would have destroyed many lives to achieve his goals. The strength of his desires practically tore the subatomic world apart. Like many men of power, I think he almost wanted to die; as if one world – certainly this one of clay – was not enough to contain or satisfy his appetites." Cain paused, as if remembering that moment for the first time in ages. "I suppose I startled him," here he took up Troy's theme, "it's not every day a man in fancy dress materialises from thin air – and he reached immediately for his gun. I got to him first."

Then Cain squeezed his eyes shut at the unexpected force of the memory, until at last he felt ready to continue. "I've witnessed many deaths; so many. Sometimes I've stood helpless behind people who are about to become victims of murder or an accident, screaming warnings as death

45

approaches, though of course my shouts have remained unheard from beyond the two way mirror that divides here from now. But still; taking life is hard – though never more so than that first time." He shook his head. "My poor brother."

"What happened?"

"I got to his throat before he got to his gun – I had no choice. He would have killed me otherwise and then the precious gift might have passed from me to him."

It was not the answer Troy had been seeking, but he realised just how insensitive his actual question had been and accepted Cain's digression. "Who was this guy?"

"Honestly, I can't remember. All I know is that I stopped him before his star had risen fully. I guess for you it's a bit of a non-story, as if someone chopped off the head of Genghis Khan when he was a boy. If I remember correctly it was in America during the Great Depression. Anyway, I avoided absorbing his energy – it was pure negativity - though I could feel the spectral fingers of his ambition still trying to reach out across his fading kingdom, then clawing back towards me, even as he died. I would never have considered moving my life force into his body; it would have faded soon, as I'm sure even his mother struggled to think lovingly of him." Then Cain smiled, just for a moment. "He had a nice suit though.

"One thing did strike me as I looked out from that pent-house across the vast cityscape; my mind was taken back to all the terrible doubts on that rocky summit where my father and I discussed the future of civilisation, as yet a blank map, without signposted paths. And while I marvelled at how far our species had come, though in which direction I couldn't say, I questioned again, Troy. As I saw the scab of that city covering the infected wound of man's progress, I questioned

46

whether my father and I had done the right thing. Worse, as I thought of all those times I'd looked out upon an empty world, I wondered whether it had been a better place back then; if Armageddon really would be such a tragedy."

Troy looked at Cain and his heart went out to him as he saw the anguish re-emerging and heard a voice struggling under the weight of memory.

"Most men have doubts in their lives, but few are stepping into the complete unknown. They have the known facts to guide them; a touchstone, if you like. When I placed my first tentative foot upon the path meant for me, my doubts were seminal, and the place from which I set forth had no name. For all I know, I was the creator of uncertainty. How do you recover when you see the depths to which your action – a vile deed committed in innocence – has led the world? The question is rhetorical, of course; I will never recover. And as for whether my father and I did what was best? - I travel always in hope of finding the answer to that one. It is all that keeps me going. I think I won't know till the end of days. I see acts of great kindness and love along my way, but all of them stem from a rotten seed; from a boy who killed his brother and a father who gave that deed his blessing. Sometimes I choke on the word *humanity*."

They sat in oppressive silence for a while. Then Troy took a long draught of water and handed the bottle to Cain, who took a sip – and grimaced.

"Hard though my life was in my early exile," he said, "and though I can barely taste food any more, I know when I have drunk poison compared with the virgin waters of the Euphrates or the Nile."

"Typical old moaner," said Troy, "always going on about

47

how things were better in your day. The trouble is, every day is your day." He managed to coax a grin out of his companion, lifting the veil of Cain's black mood long enough to scuttle in and continue: "Another question; forgive me, but as I don't know whether I'm about to die there are a number of things I need to know. How does it work – this killing; this mutual absorption society?" He plucked at the sleeve of Cain's T-shirt. "I doubt if tie-dye was all the rage to the east of Eden and -" here he pointed to Cain's blonde pony-tail "- you spoke before of a young man with black curls. Again I don't imagine Babylis straighteners or hair dye were around in the land of Nod." He misread the look on Cain's face and raised a hand in apology. "I'm sorry for being flippant. It's just that creation is rather heavy to take in."

Cain shrugged. "No need to apologise. You're trying to absorb several millennia in one night." Then he laughed. "Perhaps I'll have another T-shirt made: *Creation is Heavy Shit.* It's the sort of thing he might have said."

Chapter Six

The breathing and sighing of the sea brought the paradoxical peace that comes with their perpetual sound. Some distance off to his left, the light from the campfire threw occasional sparks, which were the far-off reflections on the faces and beer bottles of his surfer friends. From time to time a squawk or squeal carried on the wind, or the thud of a volleyball. For them, *drunken* would be the adjective to the rest of the night's nouns, whether *stupor, copulation,* or *vomiting.*

He wanted more than that; man, he wanted so much more. So a few minutes before, he'd lifted the arm of that evening's Guinevere from his chest, where it lay in post-coital sleep, pulled on his clothes and taken himself off down the beach. Sitting cross-legged, he lit a joint and started, yet again, to search for some answers. For once, he decided to meditate with his eyes open, because closing them, by one of life's little ironies, had brought everything except closure. And the stars were so beautiful this night.

He'd been growing disenchanted for some time now. His companions were dilettantish; not beach-combers, but beach-bums; as fucked-up and shallow as the society they claimed to have left behind. They were pissing away their time like Faust. Not one of them even tried to come to terms with the simple stuff; like why was the sea - which never held its shape for even an iota of a fraction of a millisecond – taken as the ultimate symbol of immutability? Man, that *was* a simple one. Anything that man couldn't get his head around – couldn't control, didn't understand – was labelled unchanging. Was that why so many natural phenomena were referred to as women?

He had a little laugh at that, took another puff of the reefer and stared at the sky.

"It's out there, man. The universe. Damn!" It had fascinated him, ever since he'd seen it reflected in the chaotic order of the minds at the psychiatric hospital where he'd been completing his studies. They knew; they got it. There was no chaos; there was no order. Infinite possibilities but no possibility of infinity. Who decided that there was genius in trying to cage some of the complexity of creation in a little jumble of symbols – $e=mc2$ – when the oxymorons and inverted clichés of the humble, with as much balance and more logic than any equation, were considered the lingua franca of the insane? Insane? They were chaoticians, with their awareness of the impracticality of laws in an expanding universe.

They'd done his head in at the last, but they'd asked him questions and he'd moved on seeking answers. Except there were none to be found, just one more big, rather worrying question spawned by a string of others; did his volleyball-playing, humping, puking friends down the beach have it right? Were you woven into just one layer of things, and did looking below it reveal only a jumble of stitches and cut ends, destroying the breathtaking intricacy of the design on the other side? And if that design was an illusion, did it matter? Wasn't there a place for simple beauty in the grand scheme – assuming the latter existed?

This was more like it; at least he was thinking, even though his head ached with the millions of partly-formed thoughts and incomplete answers falling around him as he shook the tree; leaves that danced away from him even as he grasped for them.

He looked at the spliff. Boy, this was good gear, because now he could have sworn that the air a few feet to the right of him had shimmered for a moment, like a blood vessel floating across his vision, and a man in a sharp, but dated pin-striped suit had stepped into view.

Dwight closed his eyes, started to hum the first few bars of *Good Vibrations,* and then opened them again. No, they were still there; the black lace-up shoes and the well-pressed creases of the zoot-suit. He put out a hand, touched the shoes – they were solid beneath his fingertips.

"I feel your pain, Dwight. Feel mine."

Now that was some voice; resonant; a thing of substance and as multi-faceted as any of the thoughts he'd been trying to crystallise, as if they'd now been compressed by a weight of history and time into the tough prism of a diamond. It promised knowledge, to be dispersed in all the shades and hues that light can offer.

That was when he noticed the drops of warm liquid falling on the back of his hand. He saw the arm drop; the hand level with his eyes holding a bloody blade that glinted in the starlight. Dwight sprang to his feet and ran his hands over his body. He'd not felt the blade – shit, it must have been sharp!

But then he saw the knife fall from limp fingers and the visitor fell to his knees, his eyes losing their life-lustre beneath a mop of dark curls. The left side of the man's jacket also glistened in the moonlight, thick now with his own blood as he collapsed. A surreal, night-shadow formed around him on the sand, growing steadily. Dwight crouched by him.

"Shit, man! What've you done? Hey, stay with me, stay with me!" Dwight tried pressing his hands against the man's neck to stop the bleeding. He turned and yelled down the beach. "Hey, you guys, hey, anyone, help me!"

Then he turned again at the touch of the man's hand on his arm. "Forget them. Come with me."

"What do you mean? Where are you going, man?"

It was the strangest thing. Dwight saw the answers even as he asked - despite the lifelessness of the sockets, he saw things in the man's eyes - but, being human, he couldn't resist throwing questions into the metaphysical hole opening up in front of him; trying to shore it up.

"Why did you do this?"

The dying stranger released a series of short exhalations, and Dwight realised he was trying to say something. It must have been the effect of the dope, because it seemed to him the words were taking physical shape in the night air. He leaned in.

"One more handful of dirt in a lost cause," said the man.

"What you say, man?"

"Your question...just dust that will be swallowed. A black hole can't be understood, because it has no meaning. Do light and knowledge collapse in on themselves, or is it the darkness growing?"

Perhaps it was the incomprehensible words, or the surreal

situation; at first Dwight even put it down to the joint, but he started to feel light-headed; sinking, but not drowning. It was his final rush; a river of memories flooding into his veins. Someone was saving him – passing their breath into him. And actually, he couldn't remember who he was any more. Such things he saw; he was filled with joy to know that they would be a part of him forever, and he of them – whoever *he* was. So many things; too many to take in. Every structural imperfection in the surface of time; every conscious or unconscious thought; every flicker of an eyelid in REM sleep. He was the restless bubble in a spirit level held between the hands of good and evil, joy and sadness, hatred and love, love and self-love, war and peace.

His mind couldn't take any more and he passed out, but not before giving the faintest of smiles, knowing that he had the answers – *who needed drugs?* – knowing that he was...

"Cain?"

"Uh-huh?"

"You'd gone silent." Troy paused. "So, I take it that Method 1 is: you take your own life and pass it to someone else."

"Correct. However, you have to have the ultimate trust to do that; and in Dwight I saw a good and enquiring mind; an intellect on the cusp of changing from pupa to butterfly. It was the one and only time I felt able to risk all. He was so desperate for knowledge, rather like you."

"But I thought you said you alone were the best-equipped to handle the loneliness waiting at the end of things."

"So I am; and as you can see, I am still me. I moved into his being and body because there were elements of it that could strengthen me. He had a strong brain with enough knowledge to equip me for the modern world. Make no mistake; I am a parasite. I took what I needed from him, but essentially he is me. Unfortunately, he must have dropped right out of the everyday lives of those who loved him – maybe disappointed some rich, shallow father – because no-one has ever come up and said *'there you are'*; not even the beach-bums."

"He had them sussed, hey?"

"I'm sorry?"

"Oh, maybe that wasn't Californian surfer-talk back then. Anyway, it is a pity; he seems to have been a thinker. Maybe he pissed off his parents by rejecting the career they'd selected for him." Troy remembered for a moment the barely-concealed look of frustration on his father's face when he had chosen IT over the FT.

"Well, whatever the truth, it is sad that the body didn't remain on this side of the universe for longer." Cain grew wistful. "Perhaps his mother died of a broken heart; otherwise their love usually outlives mere unfulfilled expectations."

"That raises an interesting point. What happened when your mother finally passed away? How much warning did you have? And back then, when the world's population was so sparse, when there wasn't necessarily a suitable replacement for you to inhabit, how did you stop from simply fading away?"

Cain said nothing and Troy didn't press the matter at first. Again the words of the vampire came to him: *"you would know"*. In desperate times, had his companion, still a callow being in a new-formed world, struggling to contain the elemental force within him, done what was needed to survive, for the good of all creation? Was self-defence a relative term when the stakes were so high? Was Cain indeed no different from Lilith, giving life by taking it? It was no good; he had to ask. In fact, with his own fate in the balance, he had a right.

"Tell me, Cain, what do you give in exchange for all you take away when you are forced to kill?"

Cain stared across the valley. "The memories - a not-so-brief history of time - and the chance to share in history unfolding."

"You mean the chance to help you share the burden."

"No; that I do alone, as always. As you know, the first breath of creation can only be carried by one. But in the case of Dwight, at least his body and his mind get to feel the universe in motion; experience the movement and wonder of creation."

"You mentioned memories; I take it from that, you can't travel back in time."

"No, I am not a time-traveller. My time is always now, perhaps because the universe is still expanding. If I could fill the empty hours by re-visiting some of the great events of history it would make some of my days more bearable. Perhaps when the universe starts to contract – which it will one day – I may be able to surf that kinetic wave and travel back through creation. But for now, it is almost a curse; despite living beyond the laws of man's restricted cosmos, I'm able only to see what's before me. It might be that the most significant event of the twenty-first century is happening somewhere on this planet at this very second, but my place right now is here with you." He turned and put a comradely hand on Troy's arm. "Still, though you may find it hard to believe, I would rather be nowhere else, strangely enough. This night has been illuminating.

"But at least there is an element of sharing for the chosen one who falls to Method 1, unlike the people involved in Method 2; those who try to take the gift – or is it a poisoned chalice? - from me. Usually they start out as lonely souls, crying out for answers; for companionship or consolation."

"People like me, you mean."

"No – you sought life. You decided what positive action was needed and set out to find the way, by hook or by crook. That is why I have seen fit to share my story with you. Others seek a guiding hand in their time of need, but then they bite it; become ambitious; see everlasting life as a trophy, which will help them to achieve power. So they try to take my powers from me. I have no superhuman abilities. I cannot even read their thoughts. But I have seen so much evil in my time that I recognise it in their eyes and am prepared." He shuddered slightly at some part-exhumed memories. "And then yes, I kill, though only in self-defence. Afterwards, if I can find it in me to believe that the positive energy in them outweighed the negative – that their greed was a temporary aberration - I absorb it so that it can sustain me a while longer. Let's just call it the chi equivalent of the goulash I ate yesterday. But I cannot stay. Once they are dead I have no choice but to return to my limbo. I can remain a lifelong companion for anyone whose cry opens a doorway for me, but when the light goes out, their world is no longer mine."

"Would I be right in assuming that Method 3 would be if someone succeeded where all have failed so far and killed you."

"Indeed. But once I have been summoned, I can come and go between the parallel universes these aspiring gods inhabit, so it would be wise to succeed with your first attempt at killing me, otherwise I am likely to return when least expected – and there can be no mercy. When a man has been forced to kill his brother, he will not hesitate with someone who betrays him. Indeed it would signify the biggest betrayal of all – an affront to the memory of Hebhel – if I allowed the villain to live." Cain shook his head. "Another of life's prolonged games at my expense; that I am allowed to live forever, even though I brought the act of murder into this world.

"The fact is, I have travelled a long, long road, which still stretches out way beyond the horizon. There is no hope upon that road, except the hope of wandering. There will never be an end because the mark of Cain is pain and weariness, and I will not pass that burden to another. And the irony is; I have been, and will remain, far lonelier than any person who has dragged me to them in their hour of need; yet I am far stronger than any of them."

Chapter Seven

They stumbled out of *The Rose That Blooms* – which was either a name of ancient origin or an attempt by the pub chain to create an olde worlde ambience – into the chill night, leaving the stale air of the crowded bar behind. He wanted her so much, but his idea of getting her drunk enough to screw seemed to be backfiring at the moment, because she'd tipped over into that zone where everything was funny; where a slight stumble provoked gales of drunken laughter. And for him, sex wasn't a funny business; it was something you took seriously. He wanted her active and excited, not giggling like a stupid teenager – although that's what she was; a schoolgirl with the body of a whore. He needed her to be writhing and filthy, not lying in the back of his car like a comatose slag while he banged her; just coming round long enough to throw up all over his upholstery at the key moment. That was why he'd suggested they come outside. Of course there was a risk that the fresh air might finish her off completely, but staying inside wasn't an option; she'd have just downed one vodka Red Bull too many and that would have been an expensive waste of his time. And he was horny; boy, yes. He'd even settle for a hand job from her, but one way or the other something had to give before his flies did.

"Where's your car?"

"Over there."

She focused on the place he was pointing out, looked at him and said: "Ooh, it looks a bit dark over there." With that she took his arm and pulled in closer to him. "Are you sure it's safe?"

"I'll look after you."

She giggled and touched the end of his nose with her finger. "I'm sure you will. But what about once we get to the car." More giggles. Still, things were sounding more promising.

"I'll be a perfect gentleman."

She pulled a face of such mock disappointment that it sent a huge surge of lust through his already hardening length. "Oh, and I was going to be such a slut."

He pulled her to him and forced his mouth onto hers, which responded with a wet hunger that, combined with the cloying taste of the alcohol and the smell of her sweet breath, had him reeling. He broke off before his need burst in his pants. They looked with absolute understanding into each other's eyes and headed down the riverbank towards his car.

Clearly her previous laughter and general silliness had been what passed for modesty; a cloak masking her need to fuck. Now that the disguise was off, she started the bigging-up ritual, meant to make him feel enough of a man to give her the seeing-to she craved.

"Aren't you scared?" she asked.

"Of you?"

"Of the dark." She sounded strangely serious.

He laughed at the irony. "Here you are walking along the canal path with a man you met a couple of hours before who wants to have sex with you in his car, and you're talking about the bogyman."

She pushed a bit closer to him and said nothing. Likewise he remained silent as they walked on.

"BOO!!"

She almost fell, clinging onto his arm till she recovered, and then hit him on that same arm with surprising force before pulling away from him.

"Not funny; so not funny!"

He laughed, but it sounded hollow already, even to his own ears.

She continued: "I was attacked on my way home one night."

"Hey, calm down. How was I to know?"

"Fuck you!"

"I thought that was what we'd decided."

She was stalking back in the direction of the bar. "No way, Jose; you can forget that."

He was starting to get irritated now. "It was just a joke." No response. She wasn't stopping. "Hey, Lisa, c'mon!"

She turned. "It's Laura!" She zapped him the middle finger, pulled open the door to the bar and disappeared inside, dissolving into the sounds that faded back to nothing. It was as if she'd never existed.

"Fuckin' bitch," he mumbled under his breath and wandered, angry and frustrated, back towards the water's edge. Obviously she'd not been bigging him up after all. Well, if he couldn't have the sex, at least he could have a cigarette. These new laws really killed, but he was used to freezing his butt off now when he needed nicotine on a night out. He took out a packet, patted his pockets a few times and was just about

60

to swear because he'd left his lighter somewhere, when he felt a small, flat square in one of them. Frowning, he pulled out a book of matches. He'd picked it up off the table where someone had left it.

It was as he opened the book to tear out a match that he noticed it was advertising the bar. The logo was a bit creepy – a bunch of dead flowers with one healthy rose amongst them. Strange image for a strange name. *The Rose That Blooms.*

Starting to feel a little drunk himself now – Lucy...Laura... whatever...could certainly knock them back – he reached the canal, still muttering the name of the bar under his breath like a mantra; enjoying the sound of its meaninglessness. Perching a cigarette between his lips in a way that made him feel like Marlon Brando, he struck a match.

It flew from his fingers at the sight of the face next to him in the night, which bloomed in the match's flare.

"Shit!"

He stepped back in shock and trod on air before plunging into the icy water of the canal.

Though he knew he was going to die – could feel the life being sucked from him by the freezing water – he called for help; whispered it rather, as his throat had constricted. Yet he was caught between the devil and the deep blue sea – or at least the black polluted water of the Grand Union Canal – because the thing standing on the bank looking down at him didn't extend a hand and he wasn't sure he'd have taken it. But still he called in reflex.

"What do you want?" he spluttered, thrashing in the water.

"The same as you – answers. What do *you* want?"

"To live."

"It's not all it's cracked up to be, believe me."

PARALLELS

"It is..." he gasped "...from where I'm looking now."

"Why did you summon me?"

"I didn't. I don't know what...look, for God's sake get me out of here!"

"Tell me the word – and I will."

"What word?" His aching muscles were struggling and his head slipped below the surface till he clawed his way back.

"The one you used to bring me here."

"I don't know what you're talking about." He looked around in desperation. "Help!"

"No-one will hear you right now. You've slipped into my world as much as I'm in yours." The figure on the towpath crouched down, which made it seem more menacing - somehow feral – and the features, which had so startled Ken, came into clearer view again; or rather their absence.

That was the terrifying thing; that's what had caused Ken's plunge into the canal. The figure had no face. There was a void – a space for Everyman's monster – though at times it seemed myriad expressions flitted across it.

"You must have said something," said the figure. "I've been summoned like this before. Yet to me it's also a myth. I am my own legend. What did you say before I appeared." Silence. "Tell me!"

Ken could feel his strength seeping into the water by some inverse process of osmosis. He looked around, but the book of matches was nowhere to be seen. And hypothermia was setting in, because he couldn't think. What was the word? What was it? Did it matter? "Something...written...I can't remember."

"Where?"

"Matches."

62

Ken continued to thrash in the water, but his movements were increasingly laboured. "Give me your hand," said the figure, reaching out.

"I can't."

"The cold will kill you."

"Just leave me alone."

"That, I'm afraid, I can't do. You brought this on both of us. Call me what you want; call me the bogyman or bugaboo for all I care – but you're stuck with me now, and I with you. Only death can part us. And I assure you, I do not intend to spend my life following you."

Large mouthfuls of dirty, freezing water had started to fill Ken's lungs. The figure stood looking down at him and shaking its head. "Come with me and share the loneliness of eternity, or just let it go. Those are your choices. I'm sorry."

A final spark of something caused a little flame of black humour to gutter in Ken; he must have been slightly delirious. "Well...as you put it like that...I think you sold me. You said life wasn't all it's cracked up to be."

With that he allowed himself to sink, turning his gaze away from the faceless man – he didn't want that to be his last image. As the wavering lights of *The Rose That Blooms* dimmed – a reminder of the sordid night he'd planned – it occurred to him that he might be leaving life a better man.

* * *

Not for the first time, Troy looked in amazement at Cain.

"So you don't know how or why this happens?"

"How? - to some extent yes; why? – no. It's like a curse; a

63

joke at my expense, as if the ongoing one was not enough. I've entered mythology in various guises. Repeat the monster's name and it will appear. Except it's not my name; at least not in a form I recognise. There are tribes whose incantations must have contained the key, but in their own tongue of course, so when I've arrived I've struggled to understand."

"And how can you tell the difference between, say, that summons and one like mine."

"Because it *is* a summons, whereas yours wasn't – as I've said before, you didn't seek me directly. But if that weren't enough of a clue, there's always the fear in people's faces. I'm being called upon as some goblin - some incubus – and I have no control over my appearance. It's one of those laws that exist purely for balance in the universe, like the so-called Murphy's Law; random, but demanding and inexorable. Those who seek me expect a monster and that is what they get – a faceless mannequin on which to hang their nightmares.

"Who knows where knowledge starts – the concept is so unfathomable that someone came up with the image of biting an apple just to make it comprehensible to the common man - but there is often more dark truth in a nursery rhyme or playground chant than in a host of horror stories. I've appeared at drunken teenage parties where, for hormonal youngsters, the dare is everything." Cain's head dropped. "And the worst thing is, though they never seem to know what they did to summon me, I can't let them live."

Troy's eyes widened. "Why not..." he paused "...ah, I get it. If they call you once, they'll call you forever. You'd be a puppet, pulled at a whim from universe to universe. Or they'll kill you out of pure fear. So once more, in a way it's still self-defence."

Though he said nothing, Troy was beginning to understand why Lilith had responded with such pique to Cain's comments.

Cain remained silent.

Then Troy felt his insides turn cold. He looked across the valley, at the far side of which appeared to be the first strands of dawn light. "Which brings us back again to a conundrum; the question of me."

Chapter Eight

Half the world was shutting down – or half was powering up; it depended on your point of view. *The Sunset Hours* bobbed lazily out at sea in the twilight of the darkening hemisphere.

He leaned back against the rail and for a moment – *but what defined a moment?* – might almost have believed he was at peace; that the glass was half full, like the one in his hand. The margarita was perfect; so was its provider, who lounged in the deck-chair, the fluid, subtle muscularity of her tanned legs revealed all the way to the hips by the split in her dress. She watched him now, alert and sensual like a nocturnal beast; and doubtless he was her intended prey. He would allow the illusion for a while longer. Again, what was *a while?* It might be days, weeks, months, years – or just the time it took to finish a margarita.

How many of her sort had passed on through his life on their migratory path to richer pastures? Which number wife was she? Yet he couldn't bring himself to hate any of them. He didn't miss the money; the cash-cows of his software empire just kept on lactating. Besides, between the burnished legs of these very polished whores was one place where, for a few moments at least, he could forget everything. However, there was always cruel irony and a cold reality in the post-coital isolation. It showed sex for what it was – the false summit of human passion.

Far off, the lights of North Africa twinkled. How strange it had been, when he'd returned to his first love; the sea. Now that was a passionate mistress! How much she had changed, yet how little. As always she asked for nothing and gave the same in return. For someone who had been alone so long, he found a peculiar sociability in the solitariness out here; part of what he saw as the natural contradiction and disorder of things; the same chaos that meant you were loneliest in crowds. Perhaps it was the atavistic comfort in the distant presence of humanity, represented by the glittering shoreline; a nightlight for the children of the sea.

Suddenly, despair caught him off guard; the rogue wave of an unfulfilled life, bringing with it the knowledge that he'd never found what he was looking for, nor had the faintest idea where to begin. Yet he was driven to search; impelled by a universe that seemed to taunt him. Was that why he'd gone back to living on a boat; because once, long ago, as a pilgrim in exile, he'd believed hope might reside here?

Now the dark side of him resurfaced – the one that had guided him to his coruscating yet shallow financial successes – and he felt the usual process begin again; melancholy and self-awareness were filtered from his despair, leaving a distillation of hatred. He'd never had control over this.

Could it really be that the one person in all of creation who mattered knew nothing of him; had picked up none of the signs or calling cards; – not observed his success? As he'd beaten the drums and the grass, had he somehow driven away the tiger as well as the snakes?

Strange, but he *could* hear drums now. He looked back towards the distant coastline, surely too far away for him to hear anything. Perhaps it was a trick of the wind. Africa, Africa – always drums; whether warding off or summoning the spirits. So much was dark beyond that little line of lights, which was the pale skin of the demon, or the flashing of its eyes, but the drums were the heartbeat that dictated the rhythm of its movements and its inexorable march towards destruction – or triumph; rather like the sunset, it depended on your point of view.

Suddenly, something broke the surface, glinting – a flying fish of an idea. It was worth trying. After all, nothing else seemed to have worked. But the drums - they were the opiate of the heaving masses. Drugs and drums. And if he was powerful enough to hear them at this distance, who else might be? It would be a gift possessed by few men.

Then he groaned inwardly; she was choosing the wrong moment. What he most definitely didn't need right now was the distraction of Helena, but she'd risen from her chair and weaved – *slithered?* – across the deck towards him; a sinuous serpent coming to poison the purity of his focus and his new idea.

Her hand was on his face.

"Baby, are you ok?" Her eyes suggested power; she believed the answer to whatever was bothering him lay between her thighs. "You look so sad."

"I am, Helena; I am."

"Why? Tell me. What makes you sad?" Her words were punctuated by repeated kisses on his neck. This was her answer to everything.

"Because it is a terrible thing that only one woman has ever

68

deserved my respect and, as a result, I have never been in thrall to beauty."

She frowned. He'd known she wouldn't understand. It wasn't really her fault. There was certainly nothing behind the lights of her eyes; as the saying went, no-one was home.

It made throwing her over the side much easier. Then, without a backward glance at her thrashing body, he went to the bridge and started the engine. Time to head back to the places he knew best and try again. His idea might have germinated in the distant shadows of the home of ancient civilisation, but to bloom, it would need a different darkness; the one beyond the lights of the greatest hotbed of febrile humanity on earth; London.

Chapter Nine

"You seem fixated on this idea that somehow, I'm going to kill you. It's getting a bit wearing."

"Well," said Troy in response to Cain's dismissive comment, "people who encounter you do have this unfortunate habit of ending up dead."

"Yes, I set off early down that path." It was a retort tinged with anger and perhaps a hint of self-pity.

"I'm not talking about your brother and you know that." He could see Cain wasn't yet prepared to drop his petulant stance, but Troy didn't want to fight. "OK, maybe I phrased it badly. I suppose it is in the nature of things now that you're too deeply connected to the patterns of this universe. And they're nothing if not fundamentally tied to creation and destruction, attraction and repulsion – life and death."

He sensed, rather than saw Cain's guard drop. They sat again in silence staring towards where they knew the other side of the valley lay, somewhere beyond the oily pitch of night. Troy realised it must have been the last vestiges of the passing day he'd seen earlier, rather than the dawn, because all was blackness now. It had grown cool; he glanced around the ruins again, fearing the preternatural Amazons might have returned and be sneaking up on them even now, but only the deeper darkness of the castle's stones showed against the night sky. At last he felt he could tread onto old territory again.

"So, at the risk of annoying you – and please forgive me, but as you know from my nights in the library I have this fear of a little matter called death – where do we go from here?"

Cain continued to stare at nothing. "I don't know, my friend – and that is how I see you, by the way; as my friend." Now he reached across and put a hand on Troy's arm again. "You cannot know how it feels; that moment of physical contact – of kinship; comradeship."

Troy felt multiform tears start to prick his eyes. "I lost someone so dear to me, that I can still feel her fingertips on my scalp if I stop to think for too long."

"But her blood is not on your hands. In my worst moments, I look down and still see red on mine." He shook Troy's arm to make him look round. "Imagine if the last time you felt an embrace that came from the heart was before the Flood. I grieve for you for your loss, but it is recent. The danger would come when the pain ends."

Troy's eyes widened. "How can you say that? I would give anything to be free of it."

"Yet you sought eternal life. Do you wish to mourn forever?"

"Now you're contradicting yourself; you said the pain passes."

"I never said it passes; I said that *would be* dangerous – it would signal your physical or spiritual death. Because I am forever travelling, I'm reminded constantly of the reason I set out. It's a strange man who steps out on the road each day without remembering why. So each day I think of Hebhel. But do you know the worst thing? I remember why I set out, but I have forgotten where I'm going." He paused. "Troy, think hard on this question; does the idea of dying really terrify you so much that you would have my existence instead?"

At first Troy gave no answer. The thought of that cease-less wandering through the shadows constricted his chest, smothering him till he felt claustrophobic. He thought of the first nights after she'd died, when he'd had to sit up in bed and switch on the lights to dispel the idea that he was the one in the coffin, or in limbo, or worse. That was part of the reason he'd abandoned those little slices of death called sleep, as far as his body would allow.

He turned to Cain. "Do you ever sleep?"

"For me, or at least in the worlds I inhabit, the concept has no meaning. During sleep, as you understand it, the body does not cease to exist. It merely enters a dimension of alternative creativity in which you also exist." He saw Troy frown. "For an oversimplified analogy, which is nevertheless accurate as a concept, think of the brain as a sun, with the other dimensions orbiting it as planets. Just because night falls on the only planet you recognise – your own life – doesn't mean that it isn't daybreak elsewhere. However, those other planets are – in relative dimensional terms – so far away you can't see them without the power of a massive telescope. Scientists, psychiatrists, psychologists – all they can do is study a few solar flares and sunspots, or the effects of them, to know what life on the other planets is like. If anyone ever constructed such a telescope, it would blind them, or drive them mad. Many of those you would call insane have seen the other side. That is why the universe prevents you from existing consciously in those far off places. Occasionally images slip through; you know them better as dreams. "

"If the telescope were ever built, what would it be made of?"

Cain thought long about that one. "Death."

"Sorry?"

"The single most significant material in the cosmos – and its most insubstantial. Everything stems from it, whether the avoidance of it, the journey towards it, the remembrance of it, the celebration of it. Remember, creation started with the single biggest act of destruction known to...I was about to say *mankind*...whatever existed in the nothingness that preceded it – whatever your ideological or existentialist view might be. And we are all made from the debris."

"Whoa!" Troy passed his hand over the top of his head. "I might need some time to digest that."

"You still have time – even though my hands are itching to kill you."

Troy looked across to see Cain's broad smile and he, too, laughed. Then his mind jumped on to something with which it could deal more readily. "Hey, you mentioned the Flood. So that really happened? I saw a documentary once where these guys found the remains of a boat on the mountains of Ararat, which matched the Biblical proportions of Noah's Ark..." He trailed off at the sight of Cain's face. His companion stood and cocked his head as if listening. "What is it? Cain?"

The latter seemed puzzled. "I hear something."

Troy strained, but all he heard were night breezes.

Cain continued. "This is strange."

"What do you hear?"

"Someone is calling me."

In the silence, Troy thought he understood. "You mean,

like the guy at the canal; causing one of these...rifts?"

Cain looked concerned; thrown off balance. "Yes..." he hesitated, "...and no. It's different from before, as if there's something ancient at the core of it. As I said, I don't travel through time and this is definitely coming from now; from this world – and yet something else is at work. Something much older."

He started to sway.

"Are you being summoned?" Troy half expected Cain to disappear into thin air. Instead, the latter put his hands to his head, as if concentrating.

"No...and yes."

"You're not making much sense, talking in riddles like this."

Now Cain looked at him and Troy was relieved to see that his companion hadn't gone into some sort of trance. "Well, it doesn't *make* much sense."

"What exactly is *it*?"

Cain shrugged and gave a helpless smile. "At the risk of speaking with forked tongue again, it's drums, but not drums; primitive but modern. The message is very confused. Normally there's a cry of need – your howl, for example, might have split the skies. But this - it's like nothing I've experienced."

"Sounds like it might be worth avoiding."

There was a strange light in Cain's eyes. "You haven't travelled my road; seen it reaching on forever across a featureless wasteland, straight as a die. You'd take any diversion the fates offer you." He reached out his hand. "Let's go take a look."

Chapter Ten

Talk of the coming gig was on everybody's lips. '*Be there; be at the square*' ran one of the tag lines on the myriad posters that had appeared all over London. That was partly a play on words, of course, but it was also a reference to the venue: Somerset House.

This gig was to be the climax of the usual summer season of concerts at that revered London landmark. The clever use of a colon on the posters – *Somerset:House Thunder* – linked the place to a type of music and to one man in particular; the enigmatic Nick Black; DJ, club owner, man of veiled history and origins. As much as people knew about his upcoming shows, they knew nothing about him.

He was legendary in an old-fashioned sense; not the overworked, tired use of the word that prevailed in the shallowness of modern times. It was rumoured that he was wealthy beyond counting. He'd not advertised the latest gig through any of the usual channels – the press, TV, radio – nor issued any tickets. '*Entrance free*' said the posters; who could afford to do that in London? His music – an insistent, throbbing fusion of trance, acid house, heavy rock and African-influenced drum, merged with astonishing expertise – which he called S&G, wasn't for sale in the shops and could only be downloaded, again free of charge, from certain websites by those in possession of Mandrake software. It was played only on selected radio stations; few broadcasters had the necessary licence; others held it to be the sounds of the devil and refused – a standpoint that has always guaranteed the buy-in of the youth of every generation.

All of this added to the iconic status of the gigs themselves, as did Black's unavailability for comment. He was never seen or papped anywhere. Word had it that he was a master of disguise. Others claimed that he wasn't human at all, though these were usually concert-goers who hadn't come down fully from mind-enhancing drugs.

There was undeniable mystery surrounding the man, who had simply appeared on the London scene, purchased a defunct power station and turned it into a nightclub called *House Thunder*. His star had risen swiftly and almost as brightly as the kaleidoscopic LSD-trips that were his light shows, bursting from the chimneys of the iconic power station. His clientele were clubbers of all ages, genders, leanings and proclivities and were usually ecstatic in every sense of the word.

And that was another rumour about the coming concert; the typesetters for the posters had deliberately put the capital *E* at the end of HOUS*E* and the stories went round that there would be free drugs at the gig. Regular fans spoke of women wandering through the crowds at Black's concerts dispensing more than sexual favours. They were bare-breasted in tribute to Far Eastern drug factories, where people worked naked so they couldn't steal the product.

And if anyone wondered why the authorities – police, councillors, Members of Parliament – didn't investigate this hedonistic state of affairs, or how Nick Black had permission to hold gigs into the early hours in heavily populated areas...well, it was better to keep such naïve questions about oligarchs to yourself, and clearly you weren't enough of a mover or shaker to be listened to anyway.

Only the Christian extreme right was missing from *House Thunder's* guest list. But Black loved to play a particular piece of film as a prelude to his gigs, projecting onto a huge screen at the back of the stage footage of an impassioned evangelist at a Christian gathering called *The Mission*, which had taken place in Hyde Park shortly after Black had materialised in England:

"Sisters; brothers; the need for prayer is greater than ever; for the devil is amongst us. There, beneath the Satanic chimneys, in a latter-day Nineveh, he gathers to him his armies of the corrupt, indulging their appetites as they worship him in the darkness or by false light. And what is this unholy incantation to which they sway and swoon?He tries to hide its true meaning, but we see that his so-called music – this S&G – is nothing other than a devilish code thinly disguised; Sodom and Gomorrah. In other words, anything goes in that dank pit. And like those places of dissolution, it will be destroyed by the anger of God!"

Nothing seemed to set the good denizens of House Thunder up for getting down as much as that rant. As Black said to his own followers during one of his gigs: "The Christian Right; don't you love 'em? But tell me – is there a Christian left?"

As far as the event on 24/7 was concerned – the date revealing once again the man's playful side – there was only one question worth asking: how the hell could an intimate venue like Somerset House accommodate the number of people expected to attend?

* * *

On the night, the question answered itself – it couldn't. Thousands were crammed armpit to face to armpit into the courtyard itself; the embodiment of hysteria as the mass swayed and pulsed in unison; sweating and groaning as one; a sick beast with sides leaping to its febrile heartbeat. Many, both men and women, had stripped down to their underwear – or indeed turned up in it, more or less - in the summer heat, which led to misplaced questions to some of the women about the availability of happy pills.

People also hung, fists pumping, from the windows of the building overlooking the main quadrangle; not the usual office workers hanging back on a Friday evening for a free Amy Winehouse or Kasabian gig. Now, bodies swayed and arms waved; human barnacles and anemones moving in powerful, invisible currents, driven by a wall of sound, which would have had Phil Spector waving the white flag of submission or genuflecting to the new master.

As for the overspill, it partied into the streets beyond; the density of the sound and the sheer scale of the light-show, the latter entwining in an ethereal snake-orgy, meant that the gig could be enjoyed by a large chunk of the surrounding square mile - and, given the availability of chemical supplements in that same area, enjoyed it was.

For one man, it wasn't yet enough. The synchronised mayhem needed to be cranked up a notch or ten. It needed to split the universe.

He'd been controlling events from behind the decks; cold-minded; laughing at their weakness and the way they'd come crawling from their pits to offer him their unwitting help with his plan. He thought back to that night on the boat. Once the timeless pulse of drums had reached his ears from the impassive shores of Africa, and Harry Mann had decided what needed to be done, things had been so easy to manipulate. If this latest attempt to call Cain was going to fail, it would do so in style.

He'd grown wealthy enough to become invisible – money could buy you that, no matter what the publicity-craving, paparazzi-hunting celebrity parasites of the modern era protested. Yet some things remained ludicrously cheap and simple. He could put together his own credit card advert; blonde hair-piece, prosthetic enhancements, contact lenses – three fifths of fuck-all; new identity in an old city – priceless. Nick Black was born at a cost of less than five thousand pounds. The services and confidence of a notable prosthetic surgeon, great session musicians, lighting engineers and deck-masters had cost a lot more – though like his ex-wife, it was the proverbial drop in the ocean.

He'd laughed out loud when that throwaway line had come to him.

Then, contradiction though it was, he'd needed massive publicity. Empty iconic landmarks were ten-a-penny in London; it was the planning proposals that threatened to delay things, but he'd managed to reduce the waiting period to the time it took to write several large cheques. Now all he'd needed was an accomplice – an audience. And if two things drew clubbers, they were free drinks and free drugs.

He looked out now across the seething mass. Fools; puppets, all of them; but they might help him to achieve something

79

that, till now, had proved beyond him on his own.

He stepped forward.

The reaction was instantaneous and – even to him – startling. There was a scream and a tidal surge forward; one mind, flowing with the same poisoned blood. He saw – no, more than that, he almost tasted - how it could be; his empire. He stood at the front of the stage, dressed in his trademark black, arms folded, and started to pick out individuals; hear their pleas. Women and men were offering themselves to him. He signalled to the bouncers to allow through one beautiful girl – lust in physical form – whose *House Thunder* T-shirt stretched in sweaty anticipation across a pair of proud, defiant breasts. She clambered onto the stage and sank to her knees before him, her greed and need apparent through her semi-conscious drug-haze. But he lifted her up, gave her a lingering kiss, allowing his hands to wander where no decent man or woman should on a first date, before lifting her up and hurling her back over the heads of the heavies into the crowd. The people cheered. It was ridiculous. But they were ready. They were his.

He took a microphone. Almost immediately, most of the strands of the music snapped off, leaving just a pulsing, but subtle beat. And he could see the anticipation in the eyes of the crowd – Nick Black was going to speak. He knew these pictures would also be seen on the big screens he'd had set up at various locations in the vicinity.

With ridiculous speed – given the circumstances – it fell silent.

"Howya doin'? You feelin' good?"

A roar of approval.

"Are you havin' a good time?"

"*YEEEES!*"

"Are you havin' a great time?"

"*YEEEES!*"

"Are you freakin' out?"

A word of indeterminate structure.

He dropped his voice to matter-of-fact: "Fuck."

Shocked laughter from thousands of throats.

"That ain't good enough. I quit."

"*NOOO!*" Then silence again, through which a lone female voice was heard. "I love you Nick!"

"I love you too, baby."

Another shout: "Where ya from, Nick?"

He looked straight at the man, even though he was part of a mass of sweating faces, which he could see unnerved the guy. "From inside your head, my friend; from inside all of your heads. I'm what you want."

Another huge roar. He silenced it with down-turned palms; arms outstretched towards his audience. In the background, soft but insistent, the beat continued.

"Well, if you're only having a good, great or freaky time, then I'm letting you down."

Another chorus of disagreement. He pointed to them. "Don't be too quick to say no, because if I'm your creation, then you're letting yourselves down."

Silence greeted that one; perhaps they were too stoned to understand.

"Now any of you who've been to my gigs before – shall we say any attendEEs –" there was much applause at his pun on Ecstasy, "will know that at this point of the night I like to take things up a level." *More roars.* He gave a signal with his hand and the music level started to rise; a gradual, but inexorable thing. "I'm telling you all, this one tonight is gonna be the best yet. This is gonna be unique. This is gonna split the sky!"

A primal yell.

The music's volume and intensity continued its upward trajectory.

"We're gonna do this together. Are you ready?"

Of course they were.

"I said are you ready?"

Pandemonium with a capital 'E'.

"This is gonna be the one to end them all."

They didn't know how true that was. He could feel the ground shaking.

"Ladies and gentlemen – and others – on the count of one let's make Somerset House Thunder!"

From the darkness at the side of the stage flew a guitar, which he caught with all the cool showmanship he'd planned.

"Three!"

Now forward stepped two of the session musicians, dressed as if they were auditioning for *The Matrix*; long, black leather coats, short black hair and fly-shades.

"Two!"

Below him he could see a woman vomiting through a combination of tension, booze and drugs. His mind flicked back for a moment to Helena; a moment's regret for having swatted her like a fly when there were so many more disgusting members of her gender waiting to crawl out from under stones – especially here in London. He'd be so glad to escape this; leave it behind. The stark featurelessness of the Rhub al Khali was preferable to this mass of sickness.

He started to clap his hands in time with the bass, then made a whipping-up motion while chanting in syncopation:

"SOM-erset HOUSE THUN-der! SOM-erset HOUSE THUN-der! SOM-erset HOUSE THUN-der!"

The crowd took it up and he could hear the surreal echo on the square mile beyond. This was sound as a physical thing and he could see people losing their way – their minds even – in the charged particles of that sonic sandstorm.

He and the guitarists lifted their plectrums and then, as he screamed "ONE!" they chopped their hands down across the strings, in a riff made for nose-bleeds and permanent tinnitus. They sawed at the guitars, filling, roughening and counterpointing the beat, while the chant continued: *"SOM-erset HOUSE THUN-der! SOM-erset HOUSE THUN-der!"*

Now, guitar slung round his back, he returned behind the decks, leaving the other guitarists to keep the crowd penned in; compliant; chanting. And the lights, which had kicked in on the first riff with double the lux of aircraft landing lights, sent pulsing, flaring, twisting columns into the night, again confusing the senses till it seemed the ululations of the tribes of dark continents had become visible. Thousands of disembodied faces caught in the glare, each one contorted in the hellish passion of the moment; dancing till Judgement Day.

Black stepped back from it all with a bitter taste in his mouth and looked at the screens he'd set up beneath his decks. On one he could see satellite imagery revealing that this gig was now visible from outer space. "Eat that, Great Wall of China," he muttered. Other split screens showed news coverage of the event; on Sky, on CNN, the BBC, almost every network. Most of the items showed the name of the gig in the rolling headlines at the foot of the screen: *Raising Cain.*

"If you don't pick up this calling card," he said under his

breath without looking away from the screens, "I surrender."

Chapter Eleven

"**W**here are we going?" asked Troy. In response, Cain gave him a peculiar smile. "What's funny?"

"Well, you'll say I'm talking in riddles again, because I don't know. In some ways we're going nowhere, just passing into another layer of our universe. Quite a polarity between those possibilities, I'm sure you'll agree. Imagine stepping off the surface of the earth and coming back down again; you haven't actually moved or gone anywhere, but everything around you has." Troy opened his mouth to speak, but Cain decided now wasn't the time for the complexities of it all. "Anyway, whatever you do, stay in physical contact with some part of me as we pass through, otherwise you'll be left here." He looked at the surrounding shadows. "And then I won't be in a position to save you again from our thirsty vixens."

Troy took hold of Cain's sleeve. Then, even allowing for all that had happened to him since his search began, what followed was surreal.

They started to walk towards the arch leading from the ruins. It seemed to Troy that his eyes were playing tricks. He'd been into photography once, and remembered watching pictures taking shape in the development fluids. Something similar was happening now. Images and ghosts started to soak into the air around him, except this time there was movement and sound; the drum beat of which Cain had spoken, but something else too, as if a swarm of locusts was approaching. It grew louder, and suddenly, it was just loud; deafening, in fact.

He stumbled, in part because they had reached their destination on the trans-universal escalator, but also because their journey appeared to have ended in Bedlam Hospital; the old lunatic asylum in south London. The image was more appropriate than he knew.

Now Troy grasped Cain's sleeve in his fist, seeking reassurance, yet confusion and panic was all he saw in his companion's face. Around them, half-naked bodies jumped and lurched, pumping their fists, their faces reflecting a trance-like state of ecstatic agony and a hellish interplay of light and shade from the pulsing lights; while booming beats struck at the internal organs like an inflamed, enraged heart. Troy put his hands over his ears and looked around in astonishment.

"My God!" he yelled. Cain didn't hear him above the chaos and he shook his shoulder. "I recognise this place."

Cain turned to him and Troy could see in his bewilderment that it was beyond even his experience; or rather, that it disturbed Cain more than anything he'd ever seen. Troy was shaken; that was quite something to contemplate in a man who'd seen the beginning of this species' inexorable crawl towards civilisation, then on through its terrible apogee towards inevitable destruction.

"What?" was all the ashen-faced Cain could manage right now.

Troy had to bellow right into Cain's ear to be half-understood. "I said I know this place. We're in London. Somerset House, I think. Looks like some sort of rave."

Cain looked around in despair. "You were right – we should never have come. Let's get out of here. This is awful. I knew I might live to see Armageddon – but it's worse than I imagined." He grabbed Troy's arm and closed his eyes.

Nothing happened. The pummeling and jostling from the heaving bodies around them continued. Cain opened his eyes again and Troy saw blind panic in them; and even though he himself had been in the mosh pit at many a rock concert, he understood why; this was at a different level – an altogether more disturbing one.

"I can't get us back like this," said Cain. "I can't clear my thoughts." He shook his head. "I witnessed the mayhem and panic at the fall of Jericho, and when the seas and rivers reclaimed the earth, but this is just hateful. Get me away from here."

Troy put his arms around him, and noticed that suddenly Cain seemed frail; drained by the burden of the longest life. He made to lead him away, but the pressing wall of bodies didn't give. He tried to push a way through, but the man next to him turned.

"What's your problem, buddy?" he screamed.

The words shocked Troy, until he remembered that it was only Cain they couldn't see; he'd assumed universe-hopping had made him invisible too. It hadn't been a friendly enquiry; the guy was built like a wrestler and wore some sort of black 'death metal' T-shirt.

Another woman had been staring in their direction; now she pointed and screamed, mainly to be heard: "They're some sort of aliens!"

"They"? It seemed Cain was visible after all, and to every-one, though not everyone was looking; far from it - most of the crowd around them seemed lost in their own nether-world. But still, it had to mean that they'd been summoned by the crowd, just like one of the tribal incantations Cain had described before; a frightening thought. Yet Cain had mentioned that this call was unlike any he'd heard before.

"What you talking about?" yelled the woman's partner.

"I saw them arrive...sort of appear out of nothing."

He laughed. "One too many pills, eh, sweetheart."

"No, look at 'em; they don't belong 'ere." She turned to the man. "And I haven't done any pills...well, not enough for that."

The 'wrestler' continued to block Troy's path during this blaring interchange and still he stood his ground with a stupid grin on his face. He had the sort of muscles that came from working out for the hell of it and though he'd probably never take on anyone with genuine fighting credentials, like all bullies he enjoyed throwing his weight about.

"That right? You guys some sort of freaks from outer space?"

The grin said that he didn't believe it in the slightest, but it was a chance to push someone around.

Now Troy saw a peculiar look enter Cain's eye and he reinforced his grip on his companion's shoulder. "Just ignore it, Cain; let's go!"

He'd had to shout to make himself heard and the woman picked up on his words.

"Hey! His name's Cain. Isn't that what this gig's called: Raising Cain?"

The wrestler turned to a couple of his mates nearby, also muscle-mutts. "Hey, guys, looks like we've done what we were asked to do. This guy's just appeared from nowhere and his name's..."

"Don't be fuckin' ridiculous," said Troy, panicking now on behalf of his friend, whose *rabbit- caught- in- very- bright-headlights* expression wasn't helping.

"What you say, buddy?" The big guy pushed a firm hand into Troy's chest and sent him flying – or at least that's what would have happened if he hadn't crashed into the people behind him, who turned, noticing the difference between drugged-up jostling and violence.

"Hey, man, take it easy," said one of them.

Now Troy saw Cain's expression mutate, the variegation of the light-show making it seem like his mood had changed the colour of his skin. He reached round the back of his waist and suddenly there was a blade in his hand. Now Troy remembered that, of all the actors and posturers here, his companion was probably the only one who could claim to be a killer.

"No, Cain!" he shouted, but, within the confines of the throng, a small arena had opened up around the protagonists and the scene was set.

"He's got a knife!" warned another female voice.

There were a few more screams; their pitch still audible above the continuing thump of the bass and rasp of guitars.

"Hey, fuckhead, you sure you want to do this?" said the wrestler, but he'd backed away towards the edge of the small circle and there was panic in his eyes in response to the darkness in Cain's. All around this knot of rage the gig thundered on.

89

And suddenly, the big guy fell backwards. People stepped back out of his way.

"Oi, Reg, geddup, you fuckin' great poof!" laughed one of his meaty friends. "Geddup and put the little cunt's lights out."

During those few seconds, while everyone's attention was on the prone figure, Troy and Cain felt strong hands grab them and pull them back into the crowd.

"Hide the knife – now!" hissed a commanding voice. "And smile – it can cover a multitude of sins when no-one knows what the hell's going on."

And now they were surrounded by other drugged, dancing people who were clueless as to what had happened just a few feet ahead of them. The companions turned, to find themselves being pulled along by a muscular yet lean figure in jeans and a white T-shirt.

"It'll take them a few seconds more," he said, "to realise he's dead."

Chapter Twelve

He'd noticed it straight away from the stage, despite the chaos of the gig – a peculiar shimmer in the air – and because of that, had seen them arrive. But even he, whose eyes had witnessed so much, had needed to blink and stare again. There was no denying it; they just looked so...out of place. It wasn't so much the clothes, though certainly one of them, in his tie-dyed T-shirt, seemed a complete misfit. Yet it was more the look on their faces – a mixture of alienation, horror and panic – that caught his eye; plus the fact that they did seem just to materialise.

As they looked around, clinging to each other like young monkeys, he just knew. He had an eye for these things after so long. The only thing he couldn't work out yet was: which one was Cain? Which one was the oldest man in creation?

This was it; goodbye Nick Black. Mind you, it would have been after tonight anyway.

Now the problem was, how to get to them. There was no way Nick Black could simply walk through this crowd without being overwhelmed. But he'd planned for this and congratulated himself for never having surrendered to fate, leaving himself without a contingency. *Prepare; don't despair.* A clever mantra. He made a mental note of it, then laughed as he realised that, if all went well now, he'd never need a mantra, slogan, acronym, catchphrase or other stupid fucking gimmick again.

With the frisson of possibility and discovery still shivering through his limbs, he disappeared backstage; so, too, did his black shirt and trousers – revealing a white T-shirt and jeans – along with his goatee and prosthetic nose. He didn't take his leave of the band; didn't need to of course; he owed them nothing and they'd rocked the world for a time as a result of him. It would have been a pointless gesture anyway, as they'd never fully understand the events of which they'd been a part. Men never did. Besides, farewells would have become the incidental music of his life if he'd ever started saying goodbyes.

The courtyard of Somerset House might have been packed, but it wasn't that big. He fought his way round the edge and then started to cut in. No-one recognised him; why would they? He'd never been seen off-stage, even in disguise. As he pushed past people, the look in his eye and the sight of his sculpted torso beneath the white T-shirt brooked no aggravation; received the odd admiring glance, in fact.

Before he reached them he knew something wasn't right and arrived at the edge of the small clearing in time to hear that this black-eyed knife-wielder was, indeed, Cain.

He'd expected to feel such overwhelming anger if he ever, finally, caught up with this man. Instead, he was filled with wrathful indignation at the humiliating treatment this father – this protector – of civilisation was being forced to endure at the hands of the lowlife-form known as modern man. And he'd not waited all this time – all *of* time – to have the prize snatched away from him by morons.

In the general melee, nobody noticed the muzzle of the gun, the silencer pointing at the muscle-bound oaf.

* * *

"Relax – you're in good hands. In that ludicrous T-shirt, even once they've noticed he's dead, they won't see straight away he's been shot."

"Shot?" said Troy.

"Smile!" The sibilant command came through teeth clenched in a grin.

Having seen where Cain kept his knife, Troy looked at the back of the man's belt; there was no bulge beneath the shirt.

"Looking for my gun?" asked their new-found guide, amused by the startled response this elicited. "I ditched it back there. Don't worry – they won't find my prints on any of their records." He looked around. "I like the irony; Somerset House used to be where all the family details were kept." He reached up and pulled from his head a blonde hair-piece, complete with pony-tail, and threw it to the floor. "And now they definitely won't find me." He looked at Cain's hair. "And hopefully they won't think you're me," he said with a sardonic grin, before addressing Troy. "Give him your fleece to cover up the tie-dye."

He appeared able to part the sea of people, none of whom, there at the back of the courtyard, knew what had been going on. The three men heard the start of the ruckus behind them, but were already heading out through the archway that led from Somerset House onto the thronging Strand beyond.

"I'm afraid we've got a way to go before we're clear of

people," said Nick, "but we'll be safe now – I'm sure of it."

Something about the stranger's black locks, which had tumbled from under the blonde hairpiece, made Troy look at him and Cain by turns. "Who are you?" he asked.

"There'll be time for explanations once we're clear of here," Nick responded, "but for the moment –" he looked at each of them, "– Nick Black at your service."

"*THE* Nick Black?" said Troy.

At one stage, as they were heading through the thinning crowds, they heard sirens and stepped aside with the other onlookers to allow an ambulance, flanked by police cars, to pass along Victoria Embankment.

"Well, at least some of those brainless, drugged-up idiots had enough presence of what's left of their minds, to call the emergency services. But it's pointless. I shot him through the heart. Those mighty pectorals won't have saved him from that bullet."

Troy said nothing. He looked at Cain, but the latter still seemed almost catatonic from his ordeal and was moving on autopilot.

At last, after a circuitous walk, they were wandering along Tooley Street in Southwark. Troy heard a chirrup, saw some indicator lights flash and realised they were at the stranger's car.

"Can I offer you guys a lift?"

Cain didn't respond.

"Not unless you're heading through Transylvania," said Troy.

"Transylvania?" The stranger frowned and grinned at the same time. "Is that where you..." he paused, "...arrived from;

not outer space – though it might as well have been?"

Troy narrowed his eyes. "I'm picking up that you already know more about...let's just call them *things*, than you let on – including perhaps the answers to your own questions?"

"Oh, undoubtedly," said Nick.

"Do I know you from somewhere?"

Nick shifted a little and then started to get into the car, which Troy noticed was a top-of-the-range Mercedes Sports. "Well, I *am* Nick Black – if that doesn't sound too up-my-own-arse."

"Yeah, but there's something else."

"Well look; why don't you let me offer you both a shower, a drink, something to eat; maybe even a good night's sleep. It's not far from here and it's the least I can do after the welcome this city's given you. Then we can talk."

"I'm from this city."

Nick looked out through the passenger window at him. "Then you'll know how expensive food and accommodation are."

"You have a point." Troy wasn't fooling anyone, least of all himself. There was no way his curiosity would allow him to back away now. He pulled forward the passenger seat, allowed Cain into the back, and climbed in. Cain seemed as dazed and confused as Robert Plant; an open book to Troy's closed one.

Nick fired the ignition and looked at Troy. "Besides, you might be from London, but we both know we've all reached this place, this very moment, via somewhere else." Cold, dark eyes observed Troy, barely thawed by the wink that followed.

The car rumbled away.

A few minutes later, across the Thames from the cannibalistic darkness of the Isle of Dogs, huge electronic gates topped by barbed wire were opening before them.

"UK Petroleum Ventures Ethanol Plant," read Troy from a dilapidated sign above them as they drove in. "Rolls off the tongue."

"Arbeit macht frei", said Cain, who had rediscovered his voice but wasn't exactly brimming with good humour.

"Yes, it does have an air of Auschwitz about it, doesn't it?" agreed Nick, "There's a certain frayed grandeur to this tough old bit of London, isn't there. But it suits my purpose."

"Namely; anonymity," said Troy with a disingenuous smile.

"Interesting oxymoron." Nick pointed at him playfully. "You're sharp."

"I am," said Troy, continuing to look at the driver. At length the latter nodded and said:

"OK, look; I'll give you your explanation once we get in."

"Where are we going?"

"My place. No-one comes here – it's disused and derelict with a demolition application against its name as far as the outside world's concerned, but hopefully you won't find it wanting in comfort."

And he was right. They parked up, made their way to an old, creaking industrial lift, but when they stepped out of it, they entered a world of luxury in the shape of an oak-floored apartment, both futuristic in its open-planned immensity, yet traditional with it's central copper-flued fireplace, works of art and spiralling iron staircase. The heavens were visible for 360 degrees through the angular glass ceiling and the apartment was high enough that beyond the twisted, tortured pipework of the ethanol plant , the lights of London were visible.

Nick looked west: "I see the gig has stopped."

"Not surprising, with a murder to investigate," said Troy.

Nick laughed; an easy sound. "If every one of my gigs stopped whenever a crime was committed..." he paused, "... but it would have ground to a halt anyway, once my band realised I wasn't there."

"Your do's are legendary – though I've never been to one."

"You have now; the last one, in fact." Troy's mouth opened in surprise. "So, legendary is what they'll remain. Nick Black is gone. No-one will ever know where. His purpose is fulfilled." He turned towards Cain. "His purpose stands before us."

"Getting cryptic." Troy felt a shudder of comprehension, which sat uneasily amidst all the unanswered, indeed unasked, questions.

"Can I offer you guys a drink?"

"You can offer us an explanation first," said Troy. He looked at Cain for support, but his unease grew as he observed the way his companion was staring back at Nick and nodding.

"I don't understand why," said Cain, the sound of his voice startling against the preceding silence, as if his soul had just returned unannounced, "but I do understand that it was you who called us, or at least arranged for it to happen. I'm not sure how to feel about that - and there's something else I don't get."

"There's plenty I don't get," said Troy.

Nick replied, though without looking at Troy: "Well, if you'd seen the name of the gig tonight – Raising Cain – you might *get it.*" There was a hint of something in the last two words that fell just short of contempt.

Troy saw the disturbing uncertainty of hope in Cain's features; he was a man who didn't want to believe the mirage in the wilderness, but couldn't help himself, and he, too, had eyes only for Nick. For Troy, there was an awful sense of foreboding; compared with this luxurious, but somehow soulless apartment, the Transylvanian ruins suddenly felt like home from home.

It was as if Nick read his mind. "You're home, Cain." The dappled shadows moved on Cain's face, sunshine interchanging with shade. "I'm your brother."

"You can't be." Cain's open mouth turned the words into an incredulous whisper.

"You know I can; I am. Who else could have called you – would have known you were there to be called?"

"Hebhel?" said Troy, equally astonished.

"No," said Nick, the words addressed to Cain, "the brother you never knew you had. My name is Seth." Now he walked across and put his arms around Cain. "Welcome home, brother; you are no longer alone; never were, if only you'd known."

Troy could see that Cain was almost lifeless in the other man's arms. The only sign of life was the sobbing – the silent heaving that squeezed the tears from him.

Chapter Thirteen

The fire was lit in all senses. They sat around the central blazing hearth, whiskies in hand, both Cain and Troy silent for their own reasons; one wanting to believe, the other refusing to. But now the fields of stubble were ablaze – remnants of the countless harvests of Cain's ancient life – and Troy could see no way that the racing flames would burn themselves out till everything was consumed and life could start afresh. He watched the two of them – the siblings – knowing that one of them was only too aware of Troy hovering above them like a bird of prey; riding the breeze that fanned the flames; waiting for the smoke to clear and the vermin to appear.

Now Nick – or Seth as he preferred to be called – raised his glass. "To absent - or should I say ancient - brothers."

As Troy raised his glass he nodded, but it was a gesture intended for himself alone. He could see now what had struck him earlier on the way out of the gig; when even in the few words exchanged, there had been something in Nick's intonation – the delivery, the inclination of the head, a peculiarity of the accent – which was redolent of Cain. It must have struck him at a subliminal level first. And again, now, something else about Nick still nagged at him, but he couldn't place it and the breeze took it away.

It was as if Seth had read his earlier thoughts: "I suppose there is a strange symmetry to this. While hiding behind a blonde ponytail and goatee, I find you...hiding behind a blonde ponytail and a goatee."

Except Cain wasn't hiding, thought Troy.

Cain shook his head. "I still can't believe it; that you found me against all the odds in this enormous universe."

"Never underestimate the powers of attraction," said Seth. "Everything and every one of us on this planet are made of the same basic building blocks as the rest of the universe. Then bring brotherly love into the equation."

"Strange," said Troy, "one of the laws of the universe seems to be that opposites attract. Maybe that's where sibling rivalry comes from."

Seth flashed a look at him and a broad smile. Troy was no more fooled by it than a man looking across a hostile desert is fooled by the beauty of the sunrise. He inclined his head in silent acknowledgement.

"Still, Troy has a point," said Cain. This was stated like the opening of a philosophical debate, in a voice devoid of irony or aggression, rather than one of support. "Genetically, we're the same, I presume, but you had no reason to seek me out – to love me. Rather..." He stopped.

Seth was still looking at Troy. Now he turned back to Cain and raised a hand. "I understand your hesitation, but it's okay. Our mother told me everything."

Cain looked astounded. "Everything? If she knew what act had been committed in the name of humanity, I'm surprised she ever allowed father to conceive another child with her, after he'd taken her two existing sons and ruined their lives;

taken them into the wilderness and made one..." His throat seemed to block and once again he stopped.

"Don't punish yourself. He never told her directly, but I think she guessed. I'd worked things out a long time before that. She and I only spoke about it after I'd buried my father."

"Did you...?"

Seth looked affronted. "No I did not; he lived a long life and died of extreme old age." He stared into his glass, seeming to find memories in the reflections of fire. "I was bound to them till their lives ended."

"Bound?"

"I could not take my mother's third son from her." He looked up and into the distance. "It was a long and lonely childhood." The strain of reeling his thoughts back to the present was almost visible, and he looked at last at Cain. "And through it all, the thought that out there somewhere I had a brother kept me going."

Troy looked at Cain and saw that his companion was troubled; those words had triggered a thought, which remained a secret for the moment.

"What, for more than one hundred thousand years?" Troy picked up on Seth's comment. "That takes more than will power."

Again Seth wore the ready smile of a shark. "It's OK, I understand. This must be difficult for you. You've been my brother's friend for some little time – perhaps forming a fraternal bond. It must be tough to discover that there is a real brother wandering the earth," he paused, "with a bond of blood."

For the first time, Troy was lost for a reply. Was that it? Was he jealous and in denial? Had Cain slipped almost unnoticed into part of the gaping breach that death had left in his own universe, and now he couldn't bear to lose him too?

Cain glanced at him as if he could feel Troy's pain – now he saw sympathy and defensiveness in that look. "Again, Seth," said Cain, "he has a point. How did you live so long?"

"I was with her at the end. To you she gave something precious – the first breath of creation. To me, she gave the last – her dying breath; as powerful, it would seem, as her gift to you."

Troy felt those words – intended for someone else – reach out for him from the darkness, till he could feel frail, dying, but loving fingers resting on his head. He was now the one driven deeper into his silence, whereas Cain was doing the talking: "So that means...all those wasted years."

"See it, rather, as the glass being half full, my brother. We have found each other now, and time cannot keep us apart. In fact we can protect each other; watch each other's back and allow nothing to drive a wedge between us." He was clever enough not to bother even looking at Troy as he spoke those last words. "But you look sad."

"I can't help it; it's the thought of their lonely deaths – mother; father. Already, while Hebhel and I still lived..."

Seth interrupted: "You speak as if you died."

"In spirit I did – for a time. Even back then, when we were a family, the few people of that bare world had already distanced themselves in fear."

"Our parents had each other – and me. Yet there were times that I felt I had no-one; those countless nights when I sat and looked across the emptiness to the horizon, and the world seemed but sand and rock. And unthinkable though it was – except I *did* think it – I wanted them to die so I could escape; find some as yet unimaginable adventure. I didn't know what I sought and mankind was still too young for any call of the wild to exist in my heart. So tell me, Cain, where did those longings of mine originate, if not from the pull of our common blood and bond, reaching across the universe?"

"Sometimes," said Cain, "I think the universe must be made of smoke and mirrors. I, too, sat gazing across the desert wishing I were not alone; trapped in that same adventure you couldn't imagine. Who has been playing with our fates for all this time?"

Suddenly Troy stood. "Gentlemen, obviously you have several millennia of reminiscing to catch up on – and I mean that without a hint of irony – so I will take my leave." He looked at Cain. "Maybe tomorrow we can meet again?" Then he smiled. "I never thought I would hear myself uttering the following words – they just sound too surreal - but I left my rucksack at the top of the Borgo Pass. I'm sure Lilith has probably helped herself to the contents by now, but I wouldn't mind reclaiming the pack. Besides, my passport is still in Vatra Dornei and as I haven't paid for my room, nor can I return to Romania without my passport, I'd appreciate your universe-hopping help to get me back there."

Cain stood. "Let me come with you now."

Troy tried to keep any peevishness out of his voice. "Frankly, I'm worn out. I'm sure I can find a cheap hotel for a few hours' sleep."

Seth joined them in standing. "Don't be ridiculous; what sort of host would I be? There are spare rooms a-plenty here. Enjoy my home."

"D'you know what," said Troy "I really appreciate the gesture, but being on my old stomping ground tonight has made me realise that I've missed good old London while I closeted myself away in self-pity. I lived in Greenwich for a time. So I'm going to take a chance; take a stroll; find a nice café tomorrow for a bit of breakfast and then come by."

"But..." Seth was thrown.

"Listen," said Cain, "I can't let him wander the streets of east London on his own at this time of night."

"It's not safe," agreed Seth. "There's a knife culture the old city never had before, but then I don't think, under the circumstances, that you wandering around with a blade is a great idea either. I can give him a lift."

"I'd rather walk," said Troy. "I need to clear my head."

"To be honest," said Cain, "I need some time too. There's a lot for me to digest." He wandered across and put his hands on Seth's shoulders. "I'd like to take my farewell from my friend; drop him back where he needs to be. And then you and I have, well, to the end of time and beyond that to catch up; to be brothers. I'll return once I've seen him down safe from the Borgo Pass."

Seth shrugged. "Very well." He hugged Cain. "Go careful, my big brother."

Chapter Fourteen

They weren't the only two people on the streets of east London, even at that hour, but their particular dilemma was probably unique. Troy couldn't be sure who could see Cain and who couldn't - he would be visible to anyone who had helped to summon him to Somerset House – but he didn't try too hard to keep his voice down; there were enough folk talking to imaginary friends, found mostly in the bottom of a bottle, for him to feel in good company.

"What's the matter?" asked Cain, as they walked along. "Did I make you feel somehow excluded? If so, I'm sorry – I apologise. But I can't help it; he's my brother, who I didn't even know..."

"Exactly," said Troy, aware that he looked and sounded petulant with his eyes-front demeanour. "Just because he's your brother shouldn't automatically earn him your confidence. I just don't trust him."

"But he has earned the chance to be heard; anyone who's lived that long has. And he saved our lives."

"Did he? That whole gig was set up with the express purpose of calling you. He *put* you in danger and always had control of the situation."

"So, do you not think he's my brother?"

"Oh, I think he's your brother all right. There's no denying his logic there." Now Troy stopped and turned to his companion. "But think, Cain; you, who have seen how black a man's heart can be – what did you see, once the scales had fallen; once the knowledge that you were no longer alone had finished dazzling you; had finished searing its after-image on your retina?"

"You have no idea how lonely it's been." Something plucked at Cain's vocal chords. "You've been grief-stricken for a few months only; you chose to be alone. I did not. I was hurled face-first into the dirt of a world still screaming with its birth pains. Young and gullible, I allowed myself to be convinced that killing my brother would help that world. I've carried the burden of that mistake forever, along with the whole of mankind's fate and revulsion, and the knowledge of my parents' grief; so much worse for not being able to share it with them. And now to find that I'm not alone and need no longer be..." he clicked his tongue in irony "...well maybe it does cloud your judgement a little, but then at my age I don't mind a few clouds. And have you stopped to think of how it was for him, growing up with the sadness and shame of that deed hanging over him too?"

The two men stared at each other as a capricious breeze whipped a polystyrene drinks cup past them. Then Troy softened his stance. "I understand. Believe me, I was prepared to leave you with him tonight. You chose to come with me – why?"

Cain reached for the olive branch and put a hand on Troy's shoulder. "I've grown fond of you. I want to help you collect your things and say a decent farewell."

"Well, out of that sense of kinship, will you do me one more favour?"

"For sure."

"I need no sleep tonight - I know you don't – but I do need the internet and I know a twenty-four hour café not far from here. So, the favour I ask is; please bear with me and keep an open mind. Let's do a little bit of research together."

Chapter Fifteen

The coffees were surprisingly good; the skinny mochas a speciality. The café owner might have wondered why this one man ordered two, but his surprise manifested itself in the mere lift of one eyebrow; as an all-night café owner in London he saw much and asked few questions.

Even before the caffeine, Troy felt wired. He logged-in to two screens in the furthest corner of the café, the silence of which was endowed with a surreal patina by the sparse scattering of tired lives at its tables. Despite the intensity of the matters in hand, he still found himself grinning at Cain's child-like fascination with the information highway to which he'd just been introduced. As another pair of breasts flashed up on the screen Cain gave a soft whistle. "I might just be tempted to merge with you after all, Troy. Being a – what did you call it? – a software programmer seems to have plenty of advantages. Who is this Lucy Pinder? I'm sure Lilith would like to meet her – her tastes run to, shall we say, the exotic." He shook his head. "Poor old Dr Faustus; I understand now only too well how you let the years slip by in waste."

But Troy was no longer listening. That was it; the key – or keystone. *Software programmer!* Yes; the trail had been warm at best, but suddenly a voice from the past had shouted *HOT!* He remembered the life, which had been his before death left its gargantuan footprint.

He started scribbling; circling letters. Now he searched with new vigour and purpose for certain websites, making more notes; more circles. "Oh my God, yes!" He slapped the pen down on the pad loud enough to make Cain jump and cause the café owner and customers to look across in mild irritation. Having raised a hand of apology towards the former, he whispered to Cain: "Come here; oh, and click on that little 'x' in the top right-hand corner first; you don't want to leave that image on your screen."

Cain came to sit by him. "Well, what is it?"

Troy lowered his head, as if this would somehow aid secrecy. "I believe the multi-layered universe of which you speak so fondly has been playing a little game with our friend Seth."

Cain frowned. "Is that what you've been doing; finding ways to continue driving the wedge? You're like some fanatic, trying to find an outlet for his hatred through a loophole in the Koran."

Troy kept calm. "Just bear with me. Be the one with the open mind, if you like. I tell you, something's been staring me in the face, as if I've been toyed with too. But somehow I don't think I'm the intended target.

"I'm sorry if it seems I have a suspicious mind and I admit there is something about Seth I mistrust. I suspect his motives – I believe it's what we mere mortals call 'gut instinct'."

"OK, I'll go along with you for the moment, as you re-quested." Cain stared at the wallpaper on Troy's screen; a picture of a path passing through an autumnal forest. "I've wandered into a storm that's been brewing since the dawn of civilisation; of the things I first knew, there's not much left standing – particularly my wits. Go ahead. I've been around long enough to know that fools rush in."

Troy turned back to his screen. "Right; it was when Seth spoke about the symmetry of both you and him hiding behind the blonde ponytail that the thought flashed through my mind; you, Cain, weren't hiding. Something struck me – and it wasn't just the look he gave me when I said opposites attract; he knew I was onto something. I started thinking of those universal laws; that for every action there's an equal and opposite reaction. I remembered the Star Trek of my youth, when they entered anti-matter universes, which existed as mirrors of our own. And I wondered – what if Seth's place in the universe is to counterbalance you?"

"Well then he must represent good; because I was the first murderer – at least the first one that history recognises."

"But Cain, you followed your father's edict; meant for the good of mankind. And as for your blonde ponytail; as I say, you weren't hiding. You were trying to blend into the modern world; to develop. You'd seen something in Dwight that made you trust him as a vessel for carrying you forward, and the creative force with you. Seth's disguise was all about concealment."

"OK, but this is a pretty tenuous argument."

"Agreed; but it prompted me to wonder whether something – call it what you will; fate; the cosmos – was both toying with Seth and warning us. Remember - you said the call that brought us here today felt different from any previous occasion."

Cain shifted in his seat. "I guess that's because it was my

brother. Maybe I felt it in my blood."

"Perhaps; but then again, perhaps he was calling you for the wrong reasons. You don't yet know his intentions. All those years alone; you'd think he would have grown to hate you for the barren life he was forced to lead. It's a point you just stopped short of making yourself."

"This is all supposition."

"What I'm about to show you might just be coincidence – but what is coincidence, if not a point at which the infinite threads of possibility, even probability, coincide? I want you to look at a picture."

Troy moved the cursor and clicked on a minimised tab. Onto the screen flashed a photo-archive image. Cain blinked, craned his neck forward and then his mouth opened. "It's him – on the front page of The Times."

The archive was dated 11th July 1985.

"He never made a lot of public appearances," said Troy, "which was why I barely recognised him. The persona of Nick Black was a mask for more than just Seth. I knew his face was familiar in more ways than one."

He scrolled the screen down.

HARRY MANN BUYS KOMPUKRAFT

"Harry Mann," said Cain, short of anything to say

"Let's face it," said Troy, "Seth is Harry Mann."

Cain whistled softly. In a far corner of a café, the owner's Jack Russell terrier lifted its dozing head from its paws and looked briefly for whatever had caused its hackles to rise. "Wow! So he's a billionaire." Cain frowned. "Kompukraft; weren't they the ones involved in that huge virus scam?"

"Oh, so you do get to be in some of the right places some of the time – and understand a bit more about IT than you let on." Troy grinned, but then returned to his theme. "Anyway, Seth had sold Kompukraft by then. But how's about this? – the Mann Corporation owned Fish-net, the company I worked for, and we once did some sub-contracted development work on software for Microsoft Operating Systems. It was for a password recovery tool." Cain looked blank. "When people log into computers they have a confidential password. Sometimes there might be a need to know what those passwords are, or people forget them and need to recover them. The software we worked on helped to sniff them out and decode any that were encrypted." He saw Cain's eyes glaze over again. "Ones that were wandering around in the computer system in fake blonde ponytails and goatees; hidden. Anyway, guess what this software was called: Cain and Abel."

Cain, who was still staring at the screen, swivelled his head through ninety degrees to look at Troy and was speechless for the second time that night.

"Wait," said Troy, "the best is still to come. Really, it's as if somebody out there," he pointed to the heavens, "is wearing a shit-kicking grin and saying: *you own a company that made software meant to find scrambled passwords, yet you haven't seen this.*"

"Seen what?"

"As I said, if my guess is correct, something or someone is leaving us cryptic clues, possibly warnings."

Now Cain pursed his lips. "I'll be honest; my mind is still creaking on its hinges with the effort of not closing – but carry on."

"Look at this other newspaper article." Troy clicked again.

MYSTERY FIRE DESTROYS OLD PRINTWORKS

At 5am today, firefighters finally contained the blaze that destroyed Offset House – the 150 year-old lithographic printing works in Wapping. The building still housed several small independent printers. Most recently, it was in the news as the headquarters of CASH (Christians Against Slave Houses); a religious organisation campaigning against child labour and sweatshops, which had targetted, amongst other organisations, the Mann Corporation. CASH accused Mann of paying obscenely low wages in the Far East for the manufacture of circuit-boards, and of providing unfit working conditions for employees in India who recycle raw materials for the production of copper components. CASH printed its flyers at the old printworks.

The Metropolitan Police has said it cannot comment at this time on the cause of the blaze.

"I remember this – it was in 2000," said Troy. "Some of the mud that was flung stuck. It was around that time that Harry Mann seemed to disappear from public view altogether. But do you notice something?"

"Go on." The dogmatic edge had retreated from Cain's voice, but remained a presence.

"Run together the words – OffsetHouse – and what do you find hidden in there?"

Troy could almost hear the flicking of a switch inside Cain's head. "Oh…" he drew out the word to an indecisive ending, "…I don't know. That might be a coincidence too far."

"OK. Then what about a concert held at Somerset House?"

He looked at Cain "Alright, alright, what about this? What was the name of that pub where you appeared; where the man drowned in the canal?"

"Oh," Cain clicked his fingers, "yes, that...what was it? The Rose That Blooms?"

"See anything familiar?" Cain was turning quite pale. "Are we being left warnings? Or is the great IT guru in the sky developing a sense of humour? I think we're hiding from the truth if we ignore things like this."

With that he clicked on another tab; another archive shot appeared. Again it was Seth - looking different, but unde-niably him – on the deck of a boat, folded in the arms of a sultry beauty. Troy nudged the headline into view:

BILLIONAIRE'S WIFE DROWNS
Police search for missing
software magnate

"The paper dates from a year and a half ago," said Troy, "just around the time a certain Nick Black emerged on the nightclub and DJ scene. Look at the picture. Can you make out the name of the boat?"

Cain peered closely: "The Sunset Hours". Now he did blanche.

"There's more. Until...I was left alone I was a bit of a music buff. I remember the excitement when Black's particular brand of music burst onto the collective awareness; house music, but somehow much more elemental – both raw and sophisticated. The press labelled it with the name of Nick's club: *House Thunder*."

At first Cain said nothing, as yet another poorly concealed

crossword answer confronted him, but then he turned on Troy with eyes blazing.

"Has it not occurred to you that Seth himself might have left these as calling cards; signs for me to pick up?"

"Why would you pick them up? You never knew he existed."

"What – you think I've never read the Bible?"

"Have you?"

"Wouldn't any man in my position, out of morbid curiosity, peep inside the covers – just once. I said you don't listen. Back in the ruins I told you I knew Cain was reviled by all mankind. How did I know? That wasn't just my conscience talking – though it might as well have been for all the trust I have in man's version of God's word."

Troy was astonished; frankly, he wasn't sure what to believe.

"And what would you have seen there," he snapped, "except that Seth was born, lived, and died?" Cain fell silent, to Troy's sudden shame. "I'm sorry. I'm just amazed you said nothing before."

"You said it yourself; I have seen into the hearts of men – but sometimes I just want to believe I'm wrong. Maybe you're right. Perhaps Seth has hidden his true identity from the world for so long he's forgotten who he really is. Act mad for long enough and you will go mad. Call yourself anything but Seth since the beginning of unrecorded history and eventually you'll cease to recognise yourself. So maybe he would have failed to see the clues."

Troy decided that he, too, needed to back down; after all, this was hard on his companion. "Listen; maybe you're right and I'm wrong, though that means you should be all the more careful of his intelligence. And he is certainly capable of playing games. He commented on the irony of playing Somerset House, the home of all family records in this country, even as he led his own brother to safety." Troy placed a compassionate hand on Cain's arm. "I do understand what it must have done to you to discover after so long that someone of your blood, who you thought was dead, lives. Believe me, if...*she* were to walk into this café now, no matter how much you might tell me I'm dreaming or looking at some doppelganger, I would hate you for destroying the vision and the hope. But please don't hate me. Other things here," he pointed to the screen, "have made me wary. I remembered my Ancient Egyptology."

"You speak of Set."

"Yes. The God Set..."

"...also called Seth," – Cain took up his companion's words, as if this were a story he had heard so often he could recount it better – "seen as the father, amongst other things, of evil, destruction, drought, storm, desert; first worshipped, then feared. They say that he tore his way out of his mother's womb; such was his appetite for life." Cain's throat seemed to become dry as he recalled the legends of a dead civilization and the seed of doubt grew again from its parched soil. "He was rumoured to be jealous of his older brother. There were myths about him cutting up his brother's corpse and flinging the parts throughout Egypt – or maybe that's just what he told someone he would have liked to do. The stories about his powers, longevity and anger are as varied as you might expect of someone who has been stalking the surface of the earth in disguise since forever."

"And you of all people must have witnessed something of that cult."

"But a man's body and the head of a creature..." Cain shook his head.

"...means he was feared, but an enigma. And man has forever created monsters for his own peace of mind; to encapsulate the things he can't understand; anthropomorphised and yet disfigured, so he can grasp them – even fear them – yet feel superior somehow, even in his dismay."

"I never saw the man on whom the myth was built."

"The very basis of most religions, wouldn't you say? Certainly shades of Nick Black in modern times."

"I had already passed through. The dynasty of the pharaohs was in its infancy and, as one of the race hated and enslaved by the Egyptians, I didn't wait around. I've never stayed anywhere for long, even on those occasions when I have bonded with someone. Funnily enough, people grow suspicious of you if you neither age nor die."

Troy smiled at the deadpan remark. "Who knows, maybe you're the inspiration for one of their enigmatic gods. And maybe Seth is the bogyman of legend, having passed through the ancient world trailing fear in his wake." Troy puffed out his cheeks. "These are the knotted threads..."

"*A jumble of stitches and cut ends.*"

"Quite. Very poetic."

"Not my words; just the thoughts of someone very close to me."

"Maybe your brother is the inspiration for the biggest bogyman of all. It's just a small step from Set to Satan. Evil is not beyond him. Do we really believe his wife simply fell into the sea and drowned? And you felt the atmosphere at that gig tonight; it wasn't pleasant." Suddenly, Troy sat up. "Hey, wouldn't it be the biggest irony of all if Seth's name

117

itself was the code for calling you across the universe?"

Cain's eyes narrowed. "Explain."

"Well, it would certainly fit in with the circularity of everything we've seen and then we'd know life really was playing with your brother. Perhaps those people who've summoned you – I don't know; unknown tribes in the rainforests or Satanists in Middle America or whoever – were calling to him. His name seems to be the key to so many things, yet it would be the best way to keep the two of you apart. Perhaps the universe has been protecting you. After all, Seth would hardly call his own name in his attempts to find you - and as we've said, perhaps he'd even forgotten it." Troy grinned. "I can just picture one of his many conquests calling out to him in her ecstasy; '*Harry, Harry…*' In hiding his true identity he removed the slender chance of finding you."

Cain's shoulders slumped. "But he found me." The grin faded from Troy's face; there was no denying that fact. "He wins. So I must confront him. Clearly it's been written in the stars for a long time."

"Who says you must? Just come away."

There was such desperate sadness in Cain's eyes as he turned back to Troy. "You know I can't."

"In that case, let me tell you what I believe will happen if you go back. My research…"

Cain interjected. "You've done a lot of research." The cynicism had returned to his voice.

"If you remember, it had become my speciality around the time you found me. Listen; you're both characters in the biggest-selling story of all time."

Cain managed a wry grin. "If it was eternal life you were seeking, you certainly found it."

"With a bullet, as they say. In the darkest hours of my searching, I disregarded with contempt all of the things I saw as religious mind-fucking…"

"Mind-fucking? That's a new one on me."

"OK, try clap-trap."

"Right, I'm with you now." Cain ran his fingers through his hair. "Mind-fuck," he repeated. "Interesting. Extreme; but interesting."

Troy gave a theatrical sigh and continued. "Whatever you want to call it, it explains why I never remembered that you had a brother, or thought to mention it to you. But even toiling under the weight of grief, the brain is an incredible machine. It has retained details, like Seth living till he was over nine hundred years old." He turned to the screen and tapped on it with a pen. "I checked it all out again; look. According to some histories, when Adam was dying, he instructed Seth to go the Garden of Eden and collect three seeds from the fruit of the Tree of Life. Seth was supposed to put these in his father's mouth before burying him." Troy looked at Cain. "My bet is, he didn't. Your mother gave the first breath of creation to her son; a precious gift and a unique one. Your father commanded you to guard it for the sake of mankind. There was no *last* breath. Which loving mother would give her dying breath to her child? That is what Seth wants; to take that first breath from you – in my humble opinion."

"But why would he? He has overcome time, like me; lived history."

"Well, if you believe your bedtime stories – which I now do, if only as allegories – the power given by that seed has become corrupted. He has knowledge and power, but without

119

the force of pure creativity it's merely superficial." A thought struck Troy. "*A propos* nothing, doesn't it seem strange to you that by acquiring knowledge in its earliest, purest form, when it was just an elemental force – when there was nothing to know – man became corrupted? If evil is just the absence of God and good, in those earliest times, when all around was goodness and God, how did evil even begin to exist?"

Cain sighed. "I shall miss our philosophical ramblings...till we meet again."

They sat in silence for a while, and then Troy mused: "I wonder what happened tonight that allowed his cry to reach you across the schism between your world and ours."

"That monstrous show; the lights, the people; Seth's need to find me."

"Maybe." Troy was unconvinced. "But he's chased you across all the ages of man. There must have been times when the screaming in his mind was so intense as to be almost a thing of colour and shape; at least as much and probably more than mine was when you found me. And when the two of you were most likely to find each other – in the emptiness of a fledgling world, when your mutual need for companionship and understanding might have brought you together - you felt nothing."

Now, suddenly, Troy clicked his fingers and put his fingers to his chin in thought before continuing: "Of course! When you heard the call tonight, you said there was something unusual about it. It wasn't lights or loudness. There are aircraft with lights that split the darkest skies; others that crack the heavens with a bang as they break the sound barrier. But what if – and please hear me out on this one – he knew he had to disguise his real intentions. So thousands of drugged, ecstatic or hedonistic minds, all bent towards destruction – of themselves or the civilised order of society - were used to channel his polarised energy, hiding his powerful and corrupt mind from you; swathed in the fog of those hallucinating, frenzied brains?" Troy slapped his hand on his thigh. "That's why the people in the crowd could see you tonight. They'd all been involved in calling you. And you answered; just like those occasions when you're summoned as the bogyman – except there, you're compelled by the power of some incantation that we're unlikely ever to discover. It's ironic; my feeling is, the devil summoned *you* tonight."

Suddenly, Cain stood. "Do you know what; it doesn't matter."

"Cain, I didn't mean..."

"Don't worry; I'm not angry with you. Really, it doesn't matter; whether I was called, whether I jumped, whether I was pushed, whether he was leaving me a trail of bread- crumbs in the shape of *Seth,* whether the Fates were warning me. The fact is, I will seek him out. It is my destiny; perhaps mankind's. I will not sleep tonight, so I might as well go and get this over with."

Troy stood. "I'll come with you."

"No, that's certainly not how it's meant to be. Besides," here he patted his belt, where the bulge of the knife-sheath showed, "I can look after myself. Plus, I have surprise on my side. He will not expect me back tonight."

"But he has evil on his side."

"We don't know that."

"OK, but *if* he has evil on his side, it is a powerful weapon."

Cain put his hands on Troy's shoulders. "Don't you think I have witnessed evil in all its extreme shapes during the thousands of years of my weary life? As you pointed out, I have learnt to see it in the eyes of men and I have always beaten it. Rest assured, Troy, I have no intention of entrusting the gift I hold to anyone, unless they be truly worthy of it; and the man masquerading behind the name Nick Black and a culture of drugs and violence is not worthy – even if he is my brother - for he has not spared a kind or loving thought for me his entire life."

Troy was astounded. "What makes you say that now, all of a sudden?"

"If he had, then the Cain I was – the physical form I was born into – would never have died; yet it did. When Seth told me the thought that he had a brother out there kept him going all these innumerable years, I found myself wondering what type of thought that might have been and it hit me, just like that." He clicked his fingers.

Troy gave a knowing nod. "I knew something had disturbed you earlier, I just couldn't think what it might be. And all your protestations and counter-arguments have been..."

Now it was Cain's turn to nod. "...the simple need to be sure. Rage against the unfairness of it all." He sighed. "Well, our insight, and his lack of it, will be my shield tonight. Clearly, he possesses a great power, but it is a crude one; his longevity is all about the crude matter of his body. In his eternity love plays no part. It may yet prove his weakness instead of his strength. We shall see."

Those last three words didn't fill Troy with confidence.

Chapter Sixteen

To Cain's surprise, the gates of UK Petroleum Ventures Ethanol Plant slid back as he approached.

"So, I'm expected," he said to himself. "He knows me better than I thought."

He looked up at the company name above the gates.

"Ah, there's a *SETH* you missed, Troy."

He wandered through and the gates swung shut behind him; more forcibly, it seemed, than they'd opened, though that had to be pure imagination.

The dead arches of old sodium lamp-posts hung down, devoid of any glow; whale-skeletons in a fishing port that time forgot.

"And there was darkness on the face of the ethanol plant," said Cain, seeking solace in humour, puffing out his cheeks and contemplating the fact that, although he'd wandered into recesses of the universe where shadows were the brightest spots, this place gave him the good old-fashioned creeps.

He spoke out loud again to disperse the phantoms: "Is this how it might all end for me – as it began; with the murder of a brother?" Looking towards the stars, he added. "Please, do not make me use my hands in that way again."

He found his way to the industrial lift. A deep black gleam

in the shadows revealed the shape of the Mercedes. Seth was still at home. Every alternate beat of Cain's heart took on a different resonance as he entered the lift.

And out he stepped again into the apartment.

Seth stood in the middle of the room, back towards him, staring into the fire. He didn't look round as he spoke. "Welcome brother. Couldn't sleep?"

* * *

"He's a bright guy, your friend Troy; misguided, but bright." He paused. "But have you wiped him finally from the soles of your shoes?"

Cain was taken aback. "He was a man in need when I found him."

"More than me? More than you? I've lost count of how many millenia it's taken me to travel my road; to walk my circle. Him – how much grief has he endured? One visit by Death maybe?" Cain looked up sharply, but said nothing. Seth's face remained averted, the air around him a striking and seductive foil for the harsh glint of his anger. "Mortal men are so wrapped up in themselves. What do they know of grief? I've seen so much of their pathetic hand-wringing; scratching in the dirt; writing '*woe is me*' in the sand, then staring out misty-eyed at the horizon even as the tide rolls in to wipe away their miserable words, as it always will. They forget that, as the sun goes down, it rises elsewhere." Seth turned at last to face Cain. "Angst in their pants, eh brother." He grinned and it was as if the eloquent anger had never been; as if it, too, had been swept away by the sea.

He had a glass of whisky in his hand and he held it up,

his fingers a plinth. "Half-empty or half full? I could have chosen the former; after all, I was the afterthought son, given as compensation to the dying shell of a woman containing the broken laws of the universe and a man who had hacked at the bonds of kinship; I was the forgotten sibling of a fratricidal brother. But you know, I chose neither. My credo is, whichever way you choose to view the glass, you should be emptying it." With that he poured the whisky down his throat and gestured with the glass. "Join me?"

Cain ignored him. "So, wherever you've gone, you've drunk the cup dry. What did you use to wash down the seeds?"

Seth threw him a knowing look. "Been doing a bit of research this night, have we? I said that Troy was a sharp one." Seth poured another drink and came over to stand opposite his brother. "But you've looked at the wrong legend. I did bury the seeds with our father. You see, back then we still feared God and fulfilled the dying wishes of our parents, as if they were a diktat from heaven itself.

"But if we're talking myths and legends, and as you couldn't sleep tonight – or any night for a long, long time, I imagine – I have a bedtime story for you. Come and join me by the fire, for this story, I guarantee, will chill you. Oh, it doesn't strictly have mythological or legendary status yet –" here Seth fixed his brother with his eyes, "– firstly, because no-one knows this tale and secondly, because it's true."

* * *

That evening, the knock on the door shocked them both, breaking, as it did, several days' worth of silence. It was a stone dropping into a pool of water; a misshapen, ugly rock causing ripples that

125

would be felt for all time. Its immediate impact was that all the events, which had led to that silence, were stirred from the mud at the bottom of the pool.

Eve put down her bread with a shaking hand - for days, it and the broth had tasted like so much ash to her – and looked at Adamah, who mirrored her expression. She saw fear in his eyes for possibly the first time in their life together. At the dawn of civilisation, when your fellow men avoided you as if you were cursed, or capable of cursing, a knock on the door was a singular event; one that could not possibly portend anything good.

Adamah rose, took up the wooden club he kept in readiness in case wild animals threatened the flock, and after much indecision pulled open the door with a swift movement.

Eve saw the club fall from his fingers, watched him step forward, stagger and then step backwards, dragging something with him; a heavy load; the heaviest a man could bear – the body of his dead son.

Only a mother possessed of Eve's powers could have remained standing.

The figure lay now on the crude wooden bed where it had lain throughout it's childhood nights. They had covered him with all the animal skins they had. So strange how in many ways his face looked healthier than before. But Eve was a mother unlike any other; she had sensed immediately the change in him, and though at first there was just joy at the sight of the son she thought she had lost, there were other matters at hand here, which could not be ignored. As she dabbed his forehead with the wet cloth, she drew back the animal skins once more to take in the livid marks on Hebhel's neck. Despite everything, this was no happy ending.

Dragging herself away at last from the bed, she went outside to *where her husband stood staring into the distance. For a moment she was taken back to the happier times of...was it really just a few days before? – but when he did not turn to her she knew that things had changed forever; likewise she did not reach out to him.*

"He sleeps," she said. "His recovery is good; in fact it is remarkable. He seems stronger somehow. I wonder how that could be."

Adamah stared out in silence, avoiding her gaze.

"What are you doing, my husband?"

"Looking for Qayin."

"You would do better to set out and find him, rather than wish for his return."

Still Adamah averted his eyes. "Why do you say that, wife?"

She continued to reel out the rope. "Well, you sent him to find Hebhel when he disappeared in the night. Perhaps he, too, is in the same danger from the monster that attacked his brother."

Adamah turned his head sharply. "What do you mean attacked?"

She turned on him, ice and flame vying for her eyes. "Though I have held my silence, do not take me for a fool. My powers are weaker, yet still I am stronger than you. Do you think I have not felt your lies in my stomach."

Adamah dropped his gaze and almost as swiftly Eve's anger was gone, condensed in the tears she saw running down his cheeks. She almost staggered as it left her; a remnant of the great storm that marked the beginning of the cosmos.

She put her hand on Adamah's arm and felt him shiver beneath her touch. "Just tell me what happened on that terrible night. One son has returned; I am already happier than I ever thought I would be again. Tell me why – be truthful with me – and I will forgive you.

Halfway through the next day, as Eve pressed yet another herb-soaked cloth against the brow of her son, his eyes opened.

"Adamah. ADAMAH!" she cried. Her husband came rushing in. "He wakes."

Their son looked at both of them, frowned and smiled by turns. It seemed to Eve that the eternal battle between darkness and light waged within him; his muddy waters had been stirred. She placed a comforting hand on his face, knowing now the full horror of his final memories; how terrible they must be as they seeped into his awakening mind.

Then he shocked her by smiling broadly at last and speaking – except his words drove a dagger into her heart:

"Whoever you are, thank you for your kindness."

She'd never seen him eat so heartily or look so healthy. Only now did she see for the first time just how much the gift had weakened him before.

As they sat across the table from him, watching him eat, Adamah's relief at Hebhel's loss off memory was palpable; but still they could not put off forever the dreaded question.

He looked at them and smiled: "Are you not eating?"

Eve pushed her plate in front of him. "Eat, my s...my stomach is not so well today." It was not yet time – would it ever be? – for him to know the truth.

But clearly Adamah could wait no longer. "So, tell us your story."

Hebhel looked up from his broth and smiled, then shrugged. "Truly, I cannot." He looked down at his body. "I see that I have lived some years." Suddenly his face darkened and they could almost see his thoughts drift. Eve felt her husband tense.

Hebhel continued: "It seemed to me that a sudden rush of air into my lungs woke me and I was in darkness. And a great weight was on me. I pushed against it and felt it move. Stones; I was covered in stones." There was an audible crack in his throat as he swallowed, struggling with the smothering image. "In panic I threw them from me and sat up gasping. And now my neck pained me terribly. The weight did not appear to have lifted from my chest and I realised some black memory still sat there, though it remained out of my reach.

"I looked up and around me, and tried to piece together my story."

Eve saw Adamah reach across the table for his water-cup as Hebhel continued.

"Above me was a rocky height and I could see that I must have fallen from it, injuring my neck. Then someone – perhaps a companion, perhaps another traveller in that desolate place – must have found me and buried me beneath the stones. Looking out into the gathering darkness, I could see why; there were eyes watching me and doubtless those wild animals would have fed upon my body if I had died. Someone wanted to spare me that fate."

"It was I." Adamah's voice; Eve tried to hide the shock that passed through her. "I buried you there. I was...herding my sheep across that plain when I found you; poor abandoned soul. It was the least I could do."

Hebhel reached across the table and took Adamah's hand. "I thank you for your care." His brows furrowed. "But that was not yet the strangest thing. There was a single plant growing near where I had lain and from nowhere the thought came to me that all of my life before – all my memories and experiences – had been drawn from the soil by the roots of that plant. For a moment I was tempted to pull it from the ground, but something stopped me. I think it was the thought of the madness that would surely follow if my thoughts proved true.

"Now I decided that if I had indeed fallen from that rocky outcrop, I must have been up there for a reason, and I found the strength to drag myself to the top. There was no enlightenment up there – I couldn't think of a single reason for being there – but there was light; yours. I saw it in the distance. Strange the ways of the world. If I hadn't climbed, I might have set off in some other direction and perhaps died alone in the wilderness after all. But the flames from your farm led me here."

Now he shrugged again. "That is it."

As Eve went to speak she realised that she was barely breathing. But before she could say anything Adamah found his voice.

"Your coming here tonight is a blessing. We had a son, but he has gone."

"Gone?"

"He wanted to find his own way in this world and I need a pair of strong arms and a broad back to help me with this land. Will you do that? Will you be my second son?"

Hebhel stood, came around the table and embraced his new family. When he took his place again he saw that both of them were on the verge of tears.

"Gladly I will be your son. I have no memory of another life." He paused. "But what if someone comes knocking one day and says that I am their son?"

Adamah gave a grim smile. "Well, we will slay that beast when the time comes."

Hebhel's eyes opened wide with excitement. "And I will need a name."

"Yes," said Adamah, as he and Eve exchanged looks, "a strong name. We will call you Seth."

* * *

Seth had gone to the well.

"Adamah, I am afraid."

"Why, my wife?"

"What if someone sees him and calls him by his true name, so he starts to question? He knows he has a past. What if Qayin returns?"

"He will not return."

"I'm sure you thought the same of Hebhel."

"If Qayin returns, I feel this would be the least of our worries." Then he shook his head and put his hand on hers. "My dearest Evening, let us try to see this as a happy day. Our son has returned; stronger; freed from the burden that was killing him. Yes, our first-born has left us and that will always be a sadness that hangs over us, but he is in possession of the greatest gift a man can have and follows a path towards a mighty destiny in which we can play no part, other than to think of him with all our love every day, to give him strength. The future of mankind is in good hands. Seth will stay here with us. He is strong, but not the questioning kind. People stay away from us now and we, dear wife, must make sure that it remains that way. Forgive me please for the solitary life that we will now lead; harder to bear than before, because there is no hope of friendship, but blessed by a healthy son. And who knows, there may be more."

Eve's eyes opened wide, and then she pointed to the third empty bed.

"Oh no, my husband, I have forgiven you, but some things

131

cannot be as they were. You make that bed – and you lie on it."

To ensure that no-one ever came too close to their home, and knowing the superstitious nature of folk back then, Adamah, with the help of Seth, put posts around the furthest reaches of his territory, making sure, of course, that he enclosed a vast tract of land. It might almost have been called a kingdom, except there were no subjects and he was no king. On each post burned great beacons. No-one ventured near and the legend grew that their home was guarded by angels of fire.

Chapter Seventeen

"As you can imagine, I came to hate you, my brother, until enough millennia had passed to allow that particular fire to burn itself out. Then all I wanted to do was find you and not be alone anymore."

Cain was a statue, unmoving, perhaps hoping that he would remain impervious to everything if he just stayed still. He was staring at and through Seth. For the longest time he said nothing – what *could* he say? At last a single word fell from his lips. It might have been '*Hebhel*', but was too faint to make out. Realising his brother was lost for the moment, Seth continued:

"My wait didn't end with my father's death. I couldn't leave our mother. She'd wandered away in the night, many years after my return, for she had found no peace in all the years since. There was a terrible cry, which travelled across the desert to my father and me, turning our blood to sludge. We set out; I know now, of course, why he found the way so easily. There we found her clutching that strange plant, the roots of which were shaped like a man, and beside her was the broken, stony grave of her lost son. They used to say that anyone who pulled that plant – the mandrake – from the ground would go mad if they heard it scream. They are wrong of course; in two ways. Firstly, the scream doesn't come from the plant; it is our mother's cry from the restless place she inhabits now. And secondly, if they hear it, they are already mad." Seth followed these last words with a laugh that raised the hairs on Cain's neck.

"We brought her home," continued Seth, "but her mind remained wandering in the wilderness, lost for all time." Seth raised one finger. "Except...on her death bed, she seemed to recover her wits, as if the perverse universe wanted her to suffer at the end for her betrayal of its laws. It was then she told me everything you know already and parts of the story I have just passed on to you.

"So yes, as you seem to have discovered, I lied about her dying breath. But she gave me something far greater.

"She told me such secrets, and instructed me. On her bidding, I waited for the seeds, which I had planted with my father, to grow. She passed away – the earth grew dark for a full day. Still I waited. I started to resent every furrow I ploughed, every seed I sowed, every sheep I sheared and every pull on that thread that bound me to her; our deranged mother, who had done me no wrong, but still had longed every day for your return. Every minute had been like an hour in that loveless house and now, with both of them dead, I lost all track of the years, while time sat like an egg in the palm of an idiot's hand. The years passed; the seeds grew. Then, when I had almost forgotten what it was to be a man, the trees bore fruit - just once, exactly as our mother had predicted; only one tree and one piece of fruit. This I ate. I'll never forget the image of our mother's face, seeming to hover before me bidding me to take that first bite. It was bitter, but its reward has been sweet. If you can even remember where home is, you may find the trees still growing; old and gnarled; black and twisted – a wonderful metaphor for the souls of men who have lived too long. My long interaction with the most powerful species on this planet has given me great insight into the rotting putrefaction at its core." He took a swig from the glass, sucking through his teeth to cool the bite of the grain. "Yes, mankind is a dying tree, forming a heroic yet defeated silhouette againt the sunset. Doubtless it will continue to stand there for some time till someone decides to hack it down." He raised a hand. "Oh, not you of course. I've seen inside and through you already. You, my poor brother, despite your deep-seated disenchantment with man, still believe in hope, even though you know there will be no redemption, just Armageddon. If anyone has a circle to complete, it's you; certainly not me and not even Troy. But I know, all that's left for that dead wood is to make a magnificent blaze.

"By the way, did you notice while you were doing your research tonight, some stories say the trees which grew from our father's grave provided the wood for the three crosses on Golgotha?" Seth started counting on his fingers: "God creates life; man takes life; man kills God; man creates gods; God abandons man; the new gods destroy life. Now that's what I call a circle."

Suddenly, Seth placed a hand on Cain's shoulder. His eyes seemed to soften. What was this curse of blood that weakened Cain, as if his veins ran through Seth's fingertips? "I feel your pain. Let me take it away – by forgiving you for what you did to me. Between us, we can complete creation's work, as it should have been. I know it was wrong that the breath of creation came to me – it should have been yours as the

135

first-born. But better still now, we can put it to its proper use. Believe me, mankind is not worth saving – you must have seen that. You know what a stinking mess he has made of his chance. Yet if you have been charged with safeguarding his future, then surely the best thing you can do is start again. From the ashes of the fiercest volcano life grows afresh. You were chosen, so make the rules. Do it your way. Let us join forces; father new children – a stronger species. You have the universe's creative force and I have its immortal one."

The argument was compelling. Forgiveness. A fresh start, freed from the burden of believing he had his brother's death on his hands. It was almost unbelievable. Perhaps too good to be true. Beyond his brother's shoulders Cain saw the lights of the city winking in conspiracy from the darkness that hid its many vices; a mass of humanity that day by day seemed to grow more uncontrollable and sinful. And he was responsible for it all.

Now Seth winked like those lights, once again seeming to have read his brother's eyes – except his words suggested he had misread the hesitation in them. "But hey, no need to rush things. Take time to think; to enjoy not being alone. No harm in indulging ourselves in the meantime; all those things you've been denied or have denied yourself out there on the flipside of the cosmos. Mankind might be doomed, but it has still produced wonders to be marvelled at," he grinned, "some of them in human form. You owe it to yourself to live a little before the task ahead."

Cain looked into Seth's eyes and saw what needed to be seen. Then he gave a curt nod. "Perhaps you're right. Though I hate to admit it after all I've seen, neither Troy nor any man could ever be to me what you are, my brother; flesh of my flesh. And, as you say, perhaps we have been chosen to do what we must. But I tell you now, an eternity of hedonism is not the way it was meant to be. The world is in this mess precisely because man has broken, or failed to understand, the laws of the universe. If we are to blaze the trail again it must be different."

Now it was Seth's turn to look him long in the eye. "Very well, Cain, brother, we'll not just blaze a trail, we'll scorch the earth behind us; leave nothing visible of the wrong paths people have taken. I'll drink to that. Will you?"

Cain nodded.

As Seth turned back towards the drinks cabinet, Cain saw his hand moving towards his pocket. He tensed, readying himself. Seth turned again to look at him and said: "It must be our shared blood. I sense your fear. No need, brother. We must learn to trust."

With that he revealed the hankerchief he had pulled from his pocket. He winked again. Cain gave a rueful smile and cast his eyes downwards in shameful reflection.

It was enough – that tiny moment when the guard was down.

The movement and strike were viper-sharp; the piece of cloth no hankerchief, but a treacherous serpent in the form of a silk scarf with coins weighting one end. It coiled around Cain's neck and Seth was on him, the weighted end now back in his free hand and the cloth already pulled tight. In an instant he was behind Cain, twisting the improvised garotte. "Useful trick I taught the Thugee sect centuries ago," he hissed through teeth clenched in vicious concentration. "Shame on you brother; you of all people. Did you think I'd forgotten that the breath couldn't be surrendered willingly, after all we went through together that cruel night beneath cold stars." He jerked on the cloth, trying to subdue his victim's struggles. "Or had you forgotten that you are dead; that I'm the only one who could really function in this world you pretend to despise, yet long to return to?"

Unable to breathe and the room turning purple around him, Cain fumbled for the concealed sheath where he kept his dagger. Before he could lay his hands on it his head was jerked to the left and held, forcing him to look at a small table on which lay his knife.

"Is that what you're looking for," said Seth. "I'm afraid I betrayed you with an embrace when you and your friend were here earlier. I'd seen where you hid your blade at the gig. Oh I'm truly a master at various forms of deception. You thought you'd seen the truth in my eyes earlier, didn't you. And you had. I warned you it was wrong to believe in redemption."

Cain tore at the garotte, but despite the extremity of his fear and desperation, his mind took him back countless millenia. Silver specks danced in his blood-engorged vision; the night sky above a new-born world, where the stars were so bright in the unpolluted heavens, the joy of them would have been enough to overwhelm a boy, if he hadn't been sitting cradling the body of his dead brother while a primeval force, newly consumed, raged in his chest. That same force was stirring again; a slumbering beast, which had been awakened and was preparing to emerge from the back of the cave. He knew he would be powerless to prevent it. It would mean the end of the world at the very least. The power itself was incorruptible – the beginning of everything – but blood from corrupt hands would stain it forever. How could he have let this happen?

It was no consolation to know that the possibility of love

had weakened him.

It was nearly the end of all things for Cain now, but Seth's words came to him through the roaring in his ears. "So here, dear brother, as it all starts again, I want you to know that I have already created a new universal law, which is that one pair of hands is better than two. One pair can steer the wheel of the boat in the new storm." Cain thrashed from side to side; the useless flailing of a hooked fish; a reflex grab at a passing life. Still, in his desperation he forced Seth to jockey for a firm hold. Ornaments flew from tables as they crashed into them. "I suppose if this is a fresh start for the world, then it's appropriate that it begins with brother murdering brother and relieving him of his burden. Talking of which, I have limited experience of this. What did you do when you killed Abel? How did you take the breath from me?"

Just for a moment the purple fog of death was replaced by the red mist of rage and Cain threw himself back against Seth with all his might – but all his might didn't amount to very much now. Seth staggered, but kept his feet and tightened the garotte, whilst saying through gritted teeth: "I'm afraid this noose is the only circle you'll be completing after all."

Suddenly, though he wasn't yet dead, Cain's struggling ceased. He went limp.

* * *

Assuming, like any man whose conscience has atrophied, that it was a trick, Seth didn't yet release the garotte; but then he saw it, and both his hands and his jaw dropped in wonderment.

This was the moment he'd both longed for and dreaded

– since forever. He had no control over what was about to happen; no pre-conception of what to do or expect; no memory of it. Behind it all had lurked the fear that there might be nothing; that countless millennia of fermenting bitterness might end in a disappointment so immense it would swallow the void containing the future and leave him with an eternity of everything he had already; again, nothing. And the only sound in the ensuing emptiness would be the cry of his mother; that awful, screeching wail. As with all legends, facts grew as tangled and confused as mandrake roots, even to the protagonists.

Yet as suddenly as these things can happen, his search appeared to be ending right now.

It came forth, issuing from Cain's mouth. Cain seemed to see it too, and even in the dying of his light it made him smile. Seth, too, smiled now and whispered in awe: "And he saw that it was good." He swore to himself then, never to try to describe the elemental purity and perfection, or the delicate strength of that vapour, fecund with the possibility of life and just one missed heartbeat away from death.

Except a sharp pain told him he would never have that chance, or any other chance, ever again. He looked down to see the tip of Cain's dagger protruding from his chest. He stared at it with almost, but not quite, the same wonderment and slumped to his knees.

The breath was now rising beyond his reach in all senses. His arms strained towards it. He just wanted to touch, to run his finger through the earliest...what? They weren't even molecules. This predated the crudeness of atoms. It preceded everything. Was it God? Of a sudden, he felt something akin to peace, maybe for the first time in his troubled, fretful

140

existence. Just for once, the fabric of his life did not feel overstretched. Even to a wretch like him, with a soul shaped by the barren, shifting sand of his early days, creation had given something precious at the end. It shimmered like the horizon he'd viewed from that promontory on the day the sea called him. He saw now the truth; that he could never have controlled it. What had he done by destroying Cain?

He slumped forward, dead like so many other things since the beginning.

Troy stared for a moment in horror at his handiwork, and then stepped over Seth's body, lifted Cain's head and cradled him. "Looks like I came just in time and just too late. If I'd only followed a little closer behind you. Fuck!"

Cain frowned at that; he couldn't speak, but his eyes motioned upwards while one hand tried to point. Troy, who'd had eyes only for the two brothers struggling as he'd entered the apartment, followed the dying man's gaze and saw it for the first time, floating there, almost invisible, yet so powerful in all its diaphanous beauty. In an instant, he regretted that last word, as if he'd uttered blasphemy in the vastness of cathedral.

He looked back at Cain, but Cain was dead.

Despite the violence of his end, there was peace on his face as there had never been in the short time they'd known each other. Troy laid down his companion's head with gentleness and then stood, staring into the vapour, which was the very first exhalation of the universe. It was waiting for something; perhaps for him. Mesmerised by it, he was a man held by the most bewitching of sunsets who nevertheless fears the darkness that must surely follow.

When at last he could break away, he looked down at the body of Seth, encircled by a spreading pool of blood, and then at Cain, the ravages of his end showing on his neck if not on his face. The only one missing from the trinity was Abel.

How peaceful had been Sarah's end compared with these unhappy brothers?

The sound of her name in his memories shocked him, as if into waking.

"I think I've found what I was looking for," he said to Cain. "You know, I meant to ask you if you had ever been in love. It's hard to think I'll never know the answer. But in a way it doesn't matter. You had your wonderful gift and I had mine."

Taking a deep breath, he blew, dispersing the vapour. "Let's see if mankind gets the ending it deserves."

THE END?

II

AFTER-IMAGE

You can hide – the past will seek

Copyright © 2016 David Palin

Chapter One

She couldn't really remember how she ended up in the loft. It might have been that, despite the medication, she was having one of her 'bad days'. That was the problem with her condition; you were never really in much of a position to self-diagnose. The big clue was finding herself now in a dark space. For some reason, 'bad days' seemed to awaken her inner troglodyte and send her retreating to the back of the cave.

She wasn't completely barmy, of course; far from it. There would have been a purpose to her trip up the aluminium ladder. It was never a conscious decision to seek out hidden corners, any more than moths had much control over their kamikaze rush towards the light. But right now, she just needed a memory jog, stooped here as she was in the cramped space, looking around at assorted tins, crates, cases and...that little carved wooden box.

A strange thing indeed - memory. In so many ways it was the bedrock of conscience, so she would always be grateful to the great god Hippocampus for allowing her such latitude in that area. The tests on her frontal cerebral cortex, agreed to years ago by her concerned parents, had been most revealing and the issues of memory loss had always bought her a bit of freedom; a touch more room for manoeuvre than some other kids back in her schooldays. But she never forgot the good things; or rather the bad things - which were the ones she tended to define as good.

But that little carved box in the corner – she was at a loss now; couldn't remember seeing it before, though it must have been there all along, as the patina of cobwebs would testify.

She picked her way across the joists to the object of her curiosity, wiped away most of the cobwebs with a confident hand and made the huge mistake of lifting the lid.

Chapter Two

When she first caught sight of the dark figure sitting in the shadows at the back of the cellar and once she had recovered from the shock, Joanna might have assumed that it was Charlie - the long, dark coat; the black, wide-brimmed hat that hid the eyes - if it hadn't been for the chill spreading through her stomach. Next, she took in the brittle paleness of the skin and the gaunt hollows that spoke of the sharp overhang of cheekbones.

And there was that silence. Charlie – bless him – her would-be resident tortured genius and attendee at all the café's various artistic events, loved the sound of his own voice too much, and preferred to sit holding court upstairs. Not for him a life spent skulking away from public gaze. She would not have failed to notice his entrance. Not in a show-stopping way; genetics had rendered Charlie incapable of making a woman lust or swoon. Despite his long leather coat, he was – what were the jokes amongst the other café enthusiasts? - more spreadsheet than Matrix; more Jack Lemmon than Harry Lime. But he was a regular and for that, as the owner of a small business, she was grateful.

However, if this presence, coiled here in the darkness, was thinking of making Jo-Jo's Art Café its usual haunt – the word seemed appropriate somehow – gratitude would not be Joanna's overriding emotion.

He must have been sitting there all the time she'd been preparing the tables for that evening's event; a poetry night in support of the Christian Blind Mission. How and when had he come in? The thought of him watching her without a sound made her shudder. And was that the faintest of smiles now, dragging one corner of his unwilling mouth towards the cave of his cheek? Had he sensed her unease; had she failed to suppress it? She could not yet see his eyes, but doubted much humour lit them in the darkness.

At last a frisson of impatience with herself sparked her engine back to life. She remembered who she was - the owner of the Art Café; her baby, her own little environmentally-conscious, low carbon-footprint, fiscally-challenged cottage industry, tucked away in deepest, darkest suburbia. As such, the onus, sometimes burden of hospitality lay with her. Yes, her regulars were her lifeblood, but each of them, apart from the quorum of school-chums of course, had once been a first-timer here, perhaps enticed in for a cup of coffee by the old building's eccentric half-timbered frame, and then enchanted by the rustic, lantern-lit interior, which in turn awoke some artistic impulse from the shadows of its slumber. An energising sip of Fair Trade espresso, and they shook off the cobwebs; freed the muse within them.

Sure, there was no denying, some particular dire recitals weren't so much freeing the muse as exorcising the dreadful demon of a teenage angst poem, or a middle-class protest song, or not-short-enough short story.

Whatever; she had a duty. Her guest might have been just too shy to mix in the familial hubbub upstairs; or too pale and gaunt to feel relaxed, surrounded by banter which suggested, perhaps, a coterie. Who knew? Maybe he was truly bohemian and saw through the facade of some of their urban pretensions. Who was she to sit now in prejudgment?

Who was she indeed?

Yet her gut feel was that none of these scenarios applied to this newcomer and though she never entertained the idea that he might be other than flesh or blood, still her heart raced as she wandered over to him.

"Hello, can I get you anything?"

From the lack of response she assumed, at first, that he was either deaf or asleep, and was about to repeat her question when she saw a movement from one of the hands resting in his lap.

Many things about those hands made an immediate impression, perhaps because, apart from his lower face, they were the only parts of him which were exposed. First there was that paleness again; the porcelain whiteness. Then, to her horror, she saw that he had no nails, giving the bulbous fingertips an almost amphibian quality. He was holding a piece of folded paper, which looked as if it had seen the seasons come and go, and this he twisted and rotated, as if the contents themselves were restless. For a moment, Joanna was almost sure he was going to hand it to her.

Last, strangest of all, given the latent strength of his hands, she saw that they shook as, in apparent response to her question, a raised index finger waggled from side to side. It was evident that the man wished to be left alone and though Joanna might, under other circumstances, have felt the indignation of any hostess at being dismissed in this peremptory way, she was grateful to move along; to leave this – *what was the right word?* – this presence.

****

Kate observed Joanna cradling the coffee. Her friend was a hard-working woman with her own business, a very hands-on affair, but still there was enough of the well-heeled Roedean ingénue about her to render the Halloween novelty mug crude and incongruous in her slim hands, which seemed made to carry bone china. She was looking down into the coffee; silent, as if she saw things floating just below the dark surface. Something was stirring.

"Typical," said Kate at last, breaking the silence. "The one time someone windswept and interesting turns up I'm not there." She paused for a moment. "OK, I admit – I'm not normally there at all."

In her peripheral vision she caught the look of admonishment from her other visitor, Diane. But there would be no apology; just the opposite. She turned to Diane, who as usual froze in the headlights of Kate's frank gaze.

"Oh come on," she continued, "you know very well why I don't come along to most of the café *events.*" She parenthesised the last word with air-commas. "All those would-be hippies and middle-aged peace-quilt seamstresses; and the bright young things with their light minds and heavy consciences. God, there are so many virgins there I wouldn't be surprised if our mysterious friend *were* a vampire, come to feast on their blood." She paused for a moment to light a cigarette and send out an ostentatious jet of smoke. "He would have been disappointed; can't think of any worth ravishing among those plain Janes."

"Really, Kate!" protested Diane.

"What?" Now an arch smile did settle on Kate's lips. "Just telling it as I see it." She inhaled another lungful of smoke and her words came out as vapour-ghosts. "Look, you know my tastes run a bit more to the..." she paused.

"Kinky," said Diane without humour.

"Gothic," corrected Kate.

Now at last Joanna looked up. "It's alright, Di; Kate's entitled to her opinion, however..." she too grasped for the right word...

"Truthful; harsh?" ventured Kate.

"You know, it's weird," continued Joanna. "Whoever he is, he certainly has a gift for creating tension in the air. I mean, look at us now; different from last night at the café, but it's there nonetheless."

"Joanna, I'm sorry, ok? I know how hard you work at trying to make something of the Art Café; something of your own; not a leg-up from the folks. And you know I'll always support you. It's just...well, you also know I've always been cut from a different cloth from the two of you."

"Yes." The curt response said many things. Kate watched Joanna's thoughtful, wary eyes take in the artwork on her walls; nightmarish paintings and sketches by Gerald Scarfe, Peter Greenaway and Bruegel, posters advertising theatrical ghost stories and horror movies old and new – *Nosferatu, Vampyr, A Nightmare on Elm Street* and *Hellraiser* among them – and it was clear her friend was uneasy with them. The Art Café did not aspire to the edgy or avant-garde. Joanna was uncomfortable with shadows and sharp edges, evidenced as she broke off from her observations and concluded. "Yours was always a dark soul."

"I don't believe in the soul." Kate drew deep on her

cigarette. *And that's always been the problem, hasn't it? Time to move on.* "But I do believe in the power that remains in the darkness when the light goes out. I'm intrigued. What was that you said about the tension?"

Diane took up the thread, folding her legs beneath her as she spoke. "It was disturbing. We were all trying, in that very English way, not to turn and stare, but it was as if the shadows in which he sat at the back of the room spread; seemed to reach out and touch you on the back of the neck, so you couldn't help but take a little nervous peek over your shoulder."

"I bet Charlie's nose was put out of joint," said Kate. "That's exactly the effect he's always wanted to achieve, but he doesn't know when to shut that chubby little mouth. Doesn't he know that dark silence in a man is so much more..." she crossed her hands in theatrical manner over her breasts, "...thrilling."

"Well our guest was certainly silent," said Diane. "I didn't like to look closely. Seemed that every time I risked a glance in his direction he was looking at me."

"Yes, ironic that," said Joanna. "I did – and didn't – want to see what was beneath the brim of his hat, but when at last I did catch sight of his eyes..." She stopped.

"What," said Kate, "were they icy? Dead, like a shark?" Her whispered delivery reflected anticipation, not fear.

Joanna looked out of the window and sipped her coffee. "No. I mean they were a clear, clear blue, almost unnaturally so, and there seemed to be a smile playing in them," her shoulders convulsed slightly, "although there was no movement from any other part of his face to suggest any emotion. But there was knowledge." She was groping for the words.

"Something flitting in the back of a cave," ventured Kate.

A sudden squall of rain hit the French windows. Now it was Joanna's turn to smile as she said: "Did you organise that? Will the windows blow open and the curtains billow as if disturbed by some preternatural force?"

They all laughed, though Kate heard nervousness in her companions; a lack of conviction in the merriment. She stubbed out her cigarette, while Joanna continued:

"Then, to cap it all, when I decided enough was enough and I was going to talk to him, he'd disappeared." She looked down again, as if uncertain, and then back at Kate, who was intrigued, indeed encouraged by the fear she observed. "The worst is; it was as if I knew he'd gone, yet I didn't see him go."

"Like the finest filament of thread had been connecting you all evening, so delicate you didn't even notice except for the tiniest release of pressure that told you he wasn't there anymore." Kate looked up at the ceiling. "How exquisite?" The others were silent; for once they were inhabiting the same world as their hostess and weren't finding it a comfortable experience. "It's no good; I'm going to have trouble keeping my hand from between my thighs tonight." Now there was tutting and sighing from the other two, but also a snort of laughter. "I must meet him. No more 'Cooking for Peace' evenings; make your next gathering... I don't know...a tribute to Edgar Allen Poe or something. Hopefully the raven will alight."

"Shame," said Joanna, "I was hoping I'd never see him again."

"Don't be ridiculous," said Kate. "He's the Dark Man. Few are lucky enough to meet him in their pathetic little lives."

153

"Who is *he*?" asked Diane, sounding nervous.

"It doesn't matter." Kate leant forward, gesturing for emphasis with her cigarette. "Whoever he is, he's timeless. His identity is immaterial. He's not one person – he's everyone. They say he's often drawn to wrongdoing."

"Are you trying to scare me?"

"No," Joanna interjected, "she's right. I felt something the moment I saw him. Damned if I know what. But the thing is I know I'll see him again. I believe I won't have a choice."

Chapter Three

THIRTY-FIVE YEARS BEFORE

The flame of the day was almost done; the residual light fought its usual hopeless battle on the horizon. Mary O'Connor stood in the doorway watching, sensing other changes in the air; there was more than one storm coming. She was dwarfed by the monolithic doors, which stood open – an exception at this time of evening. She didn't hear the soft footfall approaching from behind her, so was startled by the voice:

"A bad night coming. Oh sorry; I didn't mean to make you jump."

Mary patted her hand on her chest. "That's alright, Agnes, my nerves have been on edge all evening. I know why – I'm ashamed to say."

Agnes looked sidelong at her. "You mean you're not sure whether you're worried that he hasn't come back, or that he might."

Mary crossed herself. "May the Lord forgive me. Sure, isn't this why I wasn't able to go through with taking holy orders in the end, being such a sinner?" She looked towards the heavens and recited: "Have mercy upon me, Oh God, according to thy loving kindness."

Agnes put a comforting hand on her shoulder. Her West Country burr was always the anodyne to Mary's Irish Catholic angst. "I prefer to call it an awareness of your own frailties."

Mary rested her hand on the other woman's, but continued to stare at the horizon. "You can dress it up how you want, but the fact is, though I should pity him as an abandoned child, though I should love him more for his...other problems," she turned to look at Agnes, "I can't stand him; can't bear to be near him." She looked back at the threatening bulk of the cumulonimbus clouds still visible against the last vestiges of the sunset. "Heaven help me; I don't want him to come back."

Agnes squeezed her shoulder. "You're not alone, y'know. There's somethin' about him gives me the right creeps as well. It's nothin' he does; more what he don't do. Don't speak; don't play with the other children, just stands starin' at them..."

"Well now, that's not exactly his fault, is it? They're all repulsed by him, as we would be at that age." Again Mary crossed herself, looking at the floor as she whispered: "As we are now, may the Lord Jesus forgive me for saying so."

"Well, it doesn't help that we know nothin' about him; a foundlin' like that. At least if we knew his parents had been killed in a crash or somethin'...all we know is, heaven help them, they didn't want him."

"But Agnes, what if they ever change their minds and come looking for him."

"I think you're lettin' your fears run away with you now. There's no record he was ever here; well, no record that can't be destroyed very quickly – tonight even."

Mary looked in shock at her colleague. "You can't be sug-gesting...surely we have to tell the authorities he's missing."

"Says who?"

"What if something's happened to him and they find a body?"

Agnes' lips pursed with slight impatience. "I'm tellin' you, there's nothin' to link him to us. Old Mrs Winsford, the benefactress, has passed on – God rest her soul. We just deny all knowledge. But it won't even come to that. This isn't some chick that's fallen out of its nest and you just have to look up to see where it came from. It won't be a case of denyin' all knowledge; there'll be no-one to deny it to."

"But if someone does come knocking," Mary raised a hand to stave off the protest forming on Agnes' face, "just say they do; won't the other children talk?"

"Not if they know what's good for them."

Mary watched the darkness fall in Agnes' eyes. It always frightened her when she saw it, so the Lord only knew how it made their charges feel. She never questioned its provenance; never would, for fear of what she might uncover. Now there was a slight shift in Agnes' tone, in both voice and shade. "Plus he gives all of them the creeps. None of them willingly has anythin' to do with him. There's a difference between noticin' someone's gone and missin' them. Besides..." Here it came again; Agnes made an old-fashioned gesture with the back of her hand. "The wonderful thing about the little loves in 'ere is that they all understand a bit of discipline." She stopped and looked out into the night. "That was one of the other things about him that unnerved me; nothin' I did or threatened to do seemed to make a difference. No, my dear Mary, just like you I'm glad he's gone and hope it's for good."

Mary dropped her hands to her sides in frustration. "Then why in the name of all that's holy did we ever raise him here?"

Agnes had started to pull shut the first of the big oak doors. "Well, as they say in my neck of the woods; one way or the other, it never harms to keep a light burnin' when the devil's abroad." She slammed the bolt into place and then pointed out into the coagulating shadows. "C'mon now. Even the way he is, we wouldn't see him if he came wanderin' up the path now. And if he does, a night in the rain will be his punishment for wanderin' off."

Mary shook her head. "We'll go to hell for this."

"Well, it's a saintly person indeed who thinks there's only one reason why they might go to hell." Agnes put her hands on Mary's shoulders. "Look, he might turn up in the mornin' - but let's hope not, eh?"

Chapter Four

She had never known anything like it in the ten-year history of the Art Café, but ultimately, while the takings were a huge consolation, it seemed that the evening would end as a disappointment in a perverse way.

None of the weekday gatherings had ever drawn such numbers, so she had to assume word had got around about the mysterious newcomer. The plethora of long-absent, but familiar faces seemed to support this. She knew some of them lived as far afield as Wembury, so they couldn't have just happened to wander past and popped in for a cuppa. Besides, more of them than usual had come prepared. Stories, poems and songs abounded, dedicated to that evening's theme, *The Night.* So someone had been spreading the word about 'the dark man.' One could assume it wasn't Kate; misanthropes weren't keen gossips! It was clear the whole incident had tapped into that vein of darkness intrinsic to all mankind and with the capriciousness of a cinema audience that knows it will be watching most of a film from behind fingers, they had come along in the hope of a harmless fright. Indeed, what did it say about her that, despite herself, she had listened to Kate's insistence on a theme that might trigger mysterious or spooky responses?

Looking around the crowded cellar before the start of proceedings, Joanna had observed how people hid their latent fascination with the occult in plain sight. The reaction to the rumours had been akin to the response associated with alien sightings. In the event of reported UFOs, the sci-fi junkies typically came out in force, from those with a genuine '*ology*' to their name to those who just like to wear robotic silver and say *"Klatu barada nikto"*. This evening she had seen respectable goodwives come through the door, drawn by idle curiosity and feigning insouciance. Then there were the serious but frustrated 'Edgar Allen Poets', within whose memory banks her flyer email had triggered a remembrance of bleak stanzas; their moment in the moonlight had arrived. There were young Goths for whom this was an opportunity to wear their nihilism with pride and throw down the challenge to society.

As usual, this was also the perfect excuse for the weirdoes to turn out in force, dressed appropriately for the arrival of one of the Undead; worn copies of Bram Stoker and Anne Rice their badges of honour. Joanna had almost started to feel some sympathy for the dark man. Perhaps he had seen this motley crew arriving and headed for the hills. When Charlie looked the picture of sobriety in his black ensemble, you knew something was afoot.

And then there was Kate.

Only God, or perhaps some darker deity, knew to which category she belonged. Joanna looked at her now. The current performance occupying the small wooden pallet that passed for a stage in the café cellar held no interest for Kate at all – not that Joanna could blame her for that; the young lady's acoustic version of Patti Smith's *Because the Night* would have doubtless become a YouTube classic for all the wrong reasons if attendees had not been requested to switch off all mobile phones. Kate had chosen to sit at the back of the room and her tension was palpable as she waited in hope for the stranger to arrive. Yet there was something about her bearing that set her apart from anyone else; a different aura from the other audience members, as if she was the keeper of some eldritch secret. A few of the attendees were nervous, as borne out by their furtive glances towards the stairs that led down from the café; others were eager or evincing the frustrated nosiness of rubberneckers. Their attentiveness and mood had not been helped by some of the less-than-inspirational offerings from the pallet. There had been few atmospheric moments; the odd poem or reading which had provoked shivery suspense, but goose-bumps were in short supply.

Yet earlier, when Kate had stood up to read one of her own compositions, the temperature in the musty room seemed to drop by a few degrees. Joanna had looked towards the other musketeer, Diane, and seen her own surprise mirrored in her friend's face.

The intensity of the poem marked it out as very personal, and that might have been the reason Kate – the only person with an emotional buy-in to it – had kept if to herself up to this point, rather than allowing the uninitiated to give it a critical mauling. It had managed to convey desires in which warmth played no part. Rather, it was a thing of cold passion. That Kate had chosen to air it in public at this time said something about her state of mind, but it was beyond Joanna's powers to decipher the psychosexuality. Still it had given her an insight into her friend which she had not been granted in nearly forty years. She had jotted down as much as time and memory allowed both during and straight after the reading; the beginning was lost for now.

At midnight, as I paced the empty streets,
The striking clock impelled my marching feet
To flee the dark that ghost-confused my path;
To stir love from the ashes of my hearth.

Joanna had been unable to write fast enough at this point, but there was something about fears being unleashed as someone unlocked a door to find:

A single chair and forms that firelight
Sends scurrying over ceiling, walls and floor.

Only now, reading back through the lines - as Patti Smith continued to be immortalised in a way she had never intended - did it strike Joanna that the frightening thing about these words was the loneliness leeching from them.

This was further illustrated by the last lines; a sense that, for Kate, the sexual act was a moment of extreme isolation:

This time is unforgiving; it is cold.
It falls with a malevolence of old
Like dusk-sheets on a widow's dusty world.
Together we will come and limbs unfurl,
Here, underneath the covers of the night.

Joanna wasn't yet sure what these fragments told her about Kate; these pieces of clay unearthed from the desert of her friend's soul by a scouring wind. Unlike Kate, Joanna did believe in the soul; in its potential to be arid, but never beyond the reach of redemption. Often, through the years, she had feared that Kate's amoral universe would never see the rain. This poem gave her renewed hope. She was fascinated by the unexpectedness of the creativity.

Although they had known each other since school, there had always been something withheld by Kate; a few seconds' delay when you knocked on the door of friendship – a faint, secretive shuffling before the invitation to enter was extended. Theirs had been more of an accidental relationship, forged by the fires of circumstance and time, rather than a bond between kindred spirits. To a degree they shared an appreciation of the arts – they had all been educated at the same school - but it seemed to be the black arts that fascinated Kate. She would devour anything by Edgar Allen Poe, Stephen King, Henry James, Clive Barker, John Carpenter, but there'd been no stroke of pen or brush, no click of a shutter, no act of creation through the years. Or at least so Joanna had thought, till now. She had her Art Café; Diane her gallery; whereas Kate seemed to fritter her time like Faust.

What made the fact of their friendship stranger still was Joanna's belief, until tonight, that if Kate had a heart it was made of obsidian. She lived in financial comfort as the result of a cold, calculated act of marriage, at which they should have handed out divorce vouchers during the wedding service. Joanna remembered Robert well; wealthy, but stupid. She and Diane had watched with detached and fascinated dismay as he'd blundered into the web. Since then, no other mate had even begun to get close to the black widow – except when she required a meal.

Which rendered this poem all the more illuminating. It did not quite represent a soft underbelly, but rather the beauty of a great white shark breaching.

She was dying to ask Kate whether it was pure fantasy or based on experience. On the other hand, if it related to some past event, that might be territory from which Joanna would do better to steer away.

With all this going on in her head, it was no surprise that it took a few moments to register that the music had stopped. One was grateful for small mercies! But then she frowned. It was unusual for the Art Café crowd not to applaud a performer, however stale or dire. Once, they had even applauded a fire juggler who set himself alight, till it dawned on them they ought to try to extinguish the flames.

But now the room was silent.

Joanna looked up and then turned to follow the gazes of everyone else. Although no-one seemed to be moving, there was a frisson of activity. One of her customers was pointing towards the steps.

Now Joanna saw the object which had become the focus of their attention - and it might have been considered an anti-climax were it not so bizarre.

There was an envelope on the floor, lying in the soft pool of light emanating from the café above. No-one had noticed it before, or seen it float down, so of course it could have been dropped by one of the attendees.

Except no-one believed that for a moment.

Kate stood – the first person to break the spell – wandered over and picked up the envelope. She turned it and read:

"For the attention of the Three Witches." She scanned the

gathering, then glanced at Joanna and Diane in turn, before grinning. "Ordinarily, I'd have said that must mean us, but looking around here tonight, I can't be sure."

The remark drew faint laughter – the circumstances were crying out for a touch of comic relief – until it dawned on people that Kate might be delivering a veiled insult. Nevertheless, the three friends were the cynosure of all eyes.

Kate handed the envelope to Joanna, who felt her hands start to shake as she withdrew two sheets of paper, one of which she recognised as the piece the mysterious visitor had been holding a few days before. It was distinctive and appeared to have been ripped from a notebook. Joanna chose to put off reading this for the moment and turned her attention to the other piece, which was a sheet of letter paper. She read it and felt the blood drain from her face.

Kate turned and ran up the steps; a few seconds later she returned, to be met by expectant faces. She shrugged. "There are still a couple of customers up there and they saw nothing."

A whispering breeze seemed to ripple the attendees. A few people stood now, pointing at watches, offering perfunctory apologies while muttering about buses and baby-sitters. Joanna felt aggrieved. There had been no such move during the performance of Patti Smith's nemesis. Why had these people bothered in the first place? Most had been drawn by the prospect of something out of the ordinary, but seemed to have changed their minds when it showed up. Then again, maybe her irritation was, in part, directed at herself for wanting to join them.

The little flurry of activity had caused enough air movement for the candles to gutter, shadows to dance and the remaining audience to glance with unease at the unlit corners of the cellar. Words flashed into Joanna's head: *forms that firelight sends scurrying over ceiling, walls and floor.* She looked around for Kate and saw her sitting on the steps, watching. At first Joanna wondered why, but then Kate made the slightest of gestures with open palms which indicated: *read the letter.*

Seemed like a good idea; the only one right now.

Joanna cleared her throat:

"*Good evening. My apologies for the late arrival of my letter. Please continue. I hope my humble words may still contribute to the evening's fun. Do not worry about those who are making their excuses and leaving. This is not meant for ignorant or insensitive ears.*"

There was a collective intake of breath. The room had grown colder – it wasn't her imagination. Perhaps it was just the smaller number of bodies. Joanna paused. Unbidden, the image of those powerful white hands sprang into her mind, because they had reminded her that day of a puppeteer; a conceit which now seemed appropriate, as he had them all dancing to his rhythm and movement. And he was clever - who would now dare to get up and join the exodus? She suspected he meant what he said – there was no place here for those who could not listen.

Why the intuition?

It was time to read on.

"*I am sorry I cannot be present in flesh and blood, but I hope you will appreciate my offering. Might I ask that it be read out first before the rest of my letter?*"

"Well in that case," Joanna looked around at wide-eyed faces; fish watching the heron at the edge of the water. "I'm sure we're all happy to take a moment to listen."

Chairs creaked. Again Joanna looked across at Kate. In

166

many ways her face was its usual mask - expressionless, if one didn't know better - but the metaphor was more appropriate than before. Joanna could tell that all manner and shades of questions and desires flitted behind the disguise; the eyes were a study in latency. As at the height of the dissolute grandeur of Venice, behind the decorative and disturbing masque hid, by turns, companion, conspirator and courtesan.

Joanna unfolded the paper; noted where its texture had become fibrous, having absorbed microscopic particles of grime and oils from human fingertips. It was almost reassuring to feel the evidence of that interaction – until she remembered yet again the amphibian hands.

She was about to start reading when Kate spoke:

"On the pallet, Joanna." It was a command; one Joanna found herself obeying. "It is where everyone should strut and fret their hour?"

A voice from the back: "If you are a poor player – or a walking shadow."

Kate turned to the speaker. "Well said – you know your Shakespeare."

What was it about Kate's voice? To Joanna, it sounded misplaced in that space. In many ways, it was as if the Kate she had known at school had reappeared – the dominant, remote ringleader. The memory was uncomfortable; a parchment lying face down at the bottom of a trunk waiting to be turned over. It passed for the moment.

"This is called 'The Owl'.

A mole was cursed with blessed sight,

And as he looked up at the beauty of the night,
A spinning wheel that pulled a silken skein of blackest silk
Across the tapestry of skies,
He longed to leave the life of mud,
Which nature with her blood of poison
Had consigned to him as home.
But as he clambered up
Towards the airy freedom of the higher world,
Whose myriad twinkling stars moved him to weep
And bid him turn his back upon the deep,
He saw the owl
And knew at once his fate and his domain.
He turned back to the darkness whence he came
And cursed the world that he would never see again."

Absolute silence followed – graveyard stillness; tactile. Upstairs, a cup clinked on a saucer. It took an eternal moment for the audience to realise that Joanna had finished. Then, with some apparent discomfort at first, there was the pattering of applause.

Joanna had been standing with head bowed over the piece, but at last she looked up. Struggling to contain her emotions, she said: "I believe that does now conclude the evening. I want to thank everybody..."

The scraping back of chairs on the floor drowned out her next words, but she just raised her voice: "I'm sorry – I just remembered; there's the rest of the letter.

The jarring of wood on stone stopped and all looked at her in surprise. She swapped the sheets over in her hand.

"I have a further request. I wish to suggest a topic for discussion

for another event night. It can certainly be applied to broader themes." Joanna paused, wishing now that she had allowed everyone to slope off into the night. *"Mole or Owl – who is the true master of the night? There are deeper philosophical questions here. Was the mole indeed cursed, or blessed, to have seen the Promised Land? Would it have been better off blind? Did it turn its back on the stars, or flee from them? Did it fear the owl or freedom? Interesting topics for debate, do you not think?"*

The paradox in the conversational tone of the letter was disturbing; somehow it and the absence of the writer were combining to enhance his presence. Something deeper was at play here, though Joanna hadn't yet worked it out. She felt as if she had just held a séance rather than a themed evening.

There were other, perhaps more prosaic, but no less imminent matters swirling in the flotsam of her thoughts; as she looked at the confused faces around her, most of them female, she became concerned for her business. True, some of her regulars – especially the distaff element - might have welcomed the debate; hijacking it; forcing it towards the minefield of feminism in the time it took to down a cappuccino. For others the moral compass would have turned towards racist issues. However, the bulk of her customers liked nothing better than a light-hearted natter and the chance to knit for peace. With this in mind, she cursed her decision to read the remainder of the letter. Why the hell had she? What had been the compulsion? Again, words from Kate's poem came to mind: *The striking clock impelled my marching feet.*

Joanna folded the piece of paper, looked at the remaining customers in despair as they pulled on hats and scarves in silence, and then turned towards Diane and Kate for support.

169

The latter had disappeared as if the dark man had swept her up in his coat on his way out.

Because he had been here tonight.

Chapter Five

The doorbell of the gallery rang its old-fashioned chime; a homely sound, but startling Diane, who just managed to catch the glass sculpture she had been straightening before it tumbled to the floor.

"Your nerves seem in the same state as mine," said Joanna, stepping in.

Diane put her hand to her chest. "I think I'm just tired. I didn't sleep well."

"Bad dreams? Moles...owls...white hands?"

"Not quite so specific, but a disturbed night anyway." Diane raised her eyebrows. "I shouldn't be jumping like that – the bell has been ringing off its hook. I tell you, I've never had so many people through the door as I had this morning, yet sold so little. All they want to know is: *who is he?* It's the question on everyone's lips. That and: *what is he?*"

"They probably homed in on you because I didn't open the café this morning." Joanna paused. "Then again, I'm sure there were several people who left Jo-Jo's for the last time last night, thanks to Kate's dark man turned postman."

Diane pursed her lips. "Yes, what was he supposed to be again?"

"I don't know. The dark equivalent of the green man?"

Even to her own ears, Joanna's humour sounded weary, fragile and forced.

"Talking of Kate, she's the one person I would have expected here this morning who hasn't shown up. Any idea where she is?" asked Diane.

"Probably sleeping with him." It was another throwaway line. "Seriously though, I don't know when exactly she disappeared last night." She watched Diane continue to straighten the abstract glass sculpture on its plinth. "You'll break that in a minute if you don't find another outlet for your nerves."

Diane shot her a glance. "I said I'm not nervous, just tired."

"Oh come on; you're as edgy as a turkey in November – and I recognise myself in that."

"Would you like a coffee?"

"And make myself even spikier?" Joanna chewed her lip for a moment. "Actually it's a good idea."

Diane transferred her fidgeting to the preparation of two Nescafes, passed one to Joanna, and they sat down on the dais that passed for an office at the back of the gallery.

"So what *did* you make of it all?" Diane's question verged on rhetorical.

Joanna took a sip of coffee, sighed and then cocked her head to one side. "You know, maybe we're the moles and we're making a mountain out of this," she laughed, "or have I got that metaphor all scrambled?" She paused for thought. "I mean, after all, he's done nothing wrong; just turned up at the café and submitted a poem..."

Diane gave her a knowing look. "Spectral Delivery. Gave everyone the shudders. It's not just us, you know."

Joanna continued to look thoughtful. "But still, we might

172

be over-reacting to first appearances; I mean, the other night. The dark clothes; the hat. Charlie dresses exactly the same, as we've said before, and we don't recoil from him."

"Speak for yourself." Diane chuckled.

"But I guess Charlie doesn't look like he might be carrying a scythe, as if Death has decided to drop by for a latte and a spot of reaping." There was a pause as both of them sipped at the coffee. "And the poem was..."

"Sinister?" suggested Diane.

"Elegiac."

Diane stopped nursing her coffee mug for a moment. "What are you hiding from, my friend? What's scaring you?" Joanna looked at her and said nothing. "Because whatever it is, I admit it – I'm scared too. I saw what you saw in his eyes the other night..." she considered, "... knowledge. You had that absolutely right. And I hear it in his words. That letter – it was as if he had read our minds and actions in advance of the event."

Joanna noticed with detachment that, once more, her hand was shaking. She rested her cup in her lap.

They sat in silence, the only sound the ticking of a bomb somewhere, hidden in the gallery. Was it waiting to blow their world to fragments?

"But why?" asked Joanna, before realising that she had voiced her thoughts.

Diane answered nevertheless: "I don't know."

Strange that their minds seemed to have taken tentative steps along the same overgrown track.

"Do we know him from somewhere?"

"Absolutely not," said Diane. "You wouldn't forget some-one like that."

173

"Look, perhaps his appearance is just – what do the Americans call it – grossing us out." Joanna resumed studying her coffee. "But I don't think so. He seems too – I don't know – sensitive. Is that the right word? I mean, going back to the poem; it was moving."

"It was – though I'm not sure that doesn't make it worse."

"It struck a chord somewhere."

"Yes, a discordant one." Diane looked embarrassed and seemed to be summoning up the courage to say something. "I needed a man last night."

Joanna opened her mouth in surprise, before giggling. "Well, well! Do you mean...did you let your fingers do the walking?"

Diane returned from whatever memory she had been revisiting and her forehead cleaved with denial. "Good God, no! For some reason I remembered a boyfriend...from way back."

Joanna had never understood her devout friend's reluctance to acknowledge carnal needs. Not that Joanna herself was in any hurry to share – each to their own proclivities. OK, the power-crazed hierarchy of the traditional Church had tried to strike the fear of their God into men lest they succumb to masturbation, but as women had no seed to waste on stony ground, what possible harm could it do to release the building pressure?

Diane's eyes returned to the here and now. She reddened. "I'm sorry – I don't know why I shared that. I needed some comfort. It's not like I find him or the thought of him sexy or anything..." She trailed off, as did the momentary smile. "But it is strange, isn't it; the three of us – lucky in so many ways, but not in that."

"Well, Kate's had her share."

174

"Do you think that counts?" Diane gave her friend a frank look. "One money-making project and a few bangs. That's not happiness; feeding primal hunger."

And then, as so often since the beginning of their forty years of friendship way back in the mists of the prep school playground, they looked at each other and gave a tinkling laugh. The sound had altered little through the years.

"Look at us," said Joanna. "Anyone would think we had something to hide."

The smiles faded again. *Tap tap tap.* An uninvited guest had arrived – the Ghost of Christmas Past. They just hadn't let him in yet.

Chapter Six

THE NIGHT BEFORE

T She had to get away from everyone, so had slipped off from the café. She needed to be alone with her thoughts – with him – so he could become everything she had imagined and she a Christine to his Phantom; a Lucy Westenra to his Transylvanian Count. Had he been there tonight, his eyes would have scanned the room upon finishing his poem, looking deep into her and seeing nothing but cold fire and desire; finding no encumbering soul. That hunger was still there, in the swelling of her loins and the aching of her breasts.

No matter what world he inhabited, this was her neck of the woods and had been since childhood. She loved just to drive through the night. As she swung left into Polzeath Lane and plunged into the darkness of the woods, the beams of her headlights threw the trees on either side into stark relief and it seemed she was heading down the nave of a vast cathedral; one where she wanted to worship on her knees before a dark saint, the fact or fiction of whose credo or mythology didn't matter. It would be a dreadful, unholy tryst!

An objective part of her acknowledged that the evening's events might have been viewed through the prism of her obsessions, which didn't split the light, but merged the spectrum back into black. And yet, could it really be explained that easily? She smiled; thanked the stars for small mercies and big mysteries. She would live this here and now. Too many people went to bed dreaming of tomorrow. For her the night was always open to possibility, such as this very act of driving alone to commune with her thoughts; maybe beg forgiveness of the dark man for having ever let him slip from her mind.

She knew where she was heading, even though that place had been driven from her thoughts for many years.

In due course she reached a T-junction, to the left of which lay the road back to Bixham. To the right, about a mile further on was Highhill – and it was this way she headed. Her beams caught a reflection way up ahead, which she knew was the sign for the village.

Now she scanned the left-hand side of the road with anxious eyes, needing somewhere to dump the car. Her destination lay just beyond village sign, before the modern urban development began and Murphy's Law being what it was, she knew a car parked in the immediate vicinity might attract attention, even at this hour.

There it was – the bridleway! She'd known it was around here somewhere; had just never needed to find it at this time of night. Turning into the muddy opening, she drove down a few yards and parked up. She killed the lights and was almost overwhelmed by the darkness. It placed two cold hands around her heart and she couldn't help but shudder.

Perfect.

Kate got out of the car and waited for her eyes to adjust to what meagre light there might be. There was none beneath the trees. She remembered a phrase – *as black as Newgate's knocker* – an expression she had always loved for its brevity and the way it conjured a stark image of that cold iron object on the entrance to a hellish prison. Nonetheless, it was not without misgiving that she set out with extreme care back to the Highhill Road.

Save for her pulse and a counterpointing breeze, all was silent as she hurried along the pale strip of unlit tarmac, passed the village sign and saw her destination to the right.

She'd never been past St. Martin's Church, Highhill at this hour without the benefit of headlights, but still was struck by how unthreatening the graveyard felt, neat and well maintained as it was by the local residents. The tombs seemed tended and the grass between the plots was free from moss. It wasn't as creepy as it should have been. More to the point, it seemed a bit exposed. She had never really noticed that it wasn't overgrown. Part of her was disappointed that there weren't more Celtic crosses and crumbling crypts.

She knew on instinct where she needed to go, passing first the looming bulk of the monument that guarded the Trelawney Mausoleum.

The Trelawneys had owned the biggest tin-mine in the region and most of the village population had worked for them through the centuries one way or another. But they had been a rare breed; enlightened pharaohs who had ploughed money back into the community, with the result that their name was revered still, hence the immaculate condition of the graveyard where their dynastic remains lay and over

178

which, standing in heroic pose on top of the massive plinth, towered the statue of Sir Philip Trelawny, chief founder of that dynasty.

Kate rested her back wearily against the monolithic stone, not realising till that moment how tension had drained her of strength.

And now, if a prod were needed to rouse her and set her adrenalin racing again, the sound of footsteps approaching along the road provided it. She spun behind the mausoleum and risked a glance around the corner, though she felt as if the tiny portion of her head thus exposed threw a huge deformity into the smooth silhouette of the stone's lines.

Her eyes had adjusted well to the night, but still the strip of road danced to the beat of her heart. But there could be no doubt; someone was coming, making their way with an odd, uneven footfall.

He lurched into sudden view. Not the tall, edgy shadow of the dark man, but the lumpy, staggering form of a tramp. She heard him muttering imprecations against the night and as he waved his arms, there was the slosh of a half-empty bottle – or half-full of course if he were an optimistic fellow.

Kate was both relieved and disappointed – and hadn't expected to experience either of those emotions. Then she tensed again. He had stopped. He turned towards the cemetery - seemed to be looking straight at her. Of course! This piece of land, with its open gate, well-kept lawns, smooth stone surfaces and, indeed, benches would be the ideal location for most drunken tramps in need of a good night's sleep.

"Damn!" she hissed.

179

It was strange. He continued just to stand and stare – that was, until he raised and flapped his hands as if warding off something. It might have been a giant moth for all she knew, except now he crossed himself and, giving a little yelp, gave as good an impression of running away as the alcohol in his legs allowed.

Kate puffed out her cheeks with relief.

There was an audible screech as the air stuck her throat, throttled by the sound of a voice, both alien and yet aching with familiarity.

"I believe that means we're alone."

Chapter Seven

Both women sat upright, their hands folded but restless in their laps.

"Do you know, I haven't thought of that in years," said Diane, her voice thick with the dust of a forgotten memory dragged from its ancient storage place, "at least as far as I'm aware."

"And I can't remember many details," said Joanna. She reconsidered her statement. "Well, when I say that, I mean I can see a picture, but it's too big; and too dark for me to make out. And I have no idea what drove us to..." She looked out through the window. "We were so young." Her eyes scanned the horizon. "The people we were then - the children - are still running around out there. They never followed us home." She winced. "Sorry – bad choice of words."

Diane's shoulders hunched as she pushed her hands deeper into her lap. "And you think this incident has some bearing on what happened lately?"

Joanna shook her head, with perhaps a touch too much denial. "No, no, no; I just think that the poem has sparked a random memory; one we'd succeeded in shutting out."

"Or thought we had." Diane chewed her lip. "But Joanna, you said it – we were just kids. We didn't know what we were doing. No point in beating ourselves up about it."

"No, I guess you're right." Joanna fidgeted in her chair. "But then again, isn't the cruel wisdom of children..." she hesitated, seeking an analogy, "...almost the opposite of the Emperor's new clothes; most definitely there, but people choose not to see it; don't want to believe in it?" She bowed her head, weary of a sudden, and fearing what she might find if she looked her friend in the eye.

Now it was Diane's turn to stare out of the window. "I wonder whether Kate remembers; whether she has carried any baggage into that world she inhabits – the one she never lets us into."

Joanna looked up sharply. "I wonder where the hell she is."

Chapter Eight

The voice came from above her. Kate felt a trickle from her bladder and stumbled backwards as her legs gave way. On a night of uncertainties, she couldn't be sure whether she blacked out. Whatever the passage of time, on opening her eyes at last and looking up, she saw what she assumed had caused the tramp to make the sign of the cross and run.

On top of the mausoleum, forming a deeper shadow against the night sky, stood what might have been taken for another statue, so still did he stand, with pale hands crossed in front of him, white face looking down. Though smaller than the figure of Trelawney, his aura was palpable and terrifying.

The monolith was perhaps fifteen feet high and smooth sided. Kate was almost sure he had not been up there when she arrived. "How did you...?" It was all her constricted throat would allow.

"Get up here?" She could hear jollity in the voice, rendering it all the more threatening. "I'll leave that to your febrile imagination. Or are you perhaps wondering how I knew you would be here?" He looked in the direction of Bixham, already a million heartbeats away in another life. "Oh, your eyes told me everything I needed to know about you back at the café, when you came running up the steps to find me. Except I was there all the time, in the audience. Easy to hide in plain sight tonight amongst such a collection of ghoulish freaks – and then there were those in costume as well." His laugh went through her. "You are cut from a different cloth from your two friends, aren't you? Black lace to their tweed."

That was somewhere between wonderful and creepy, hearing her own words, her own description of herself not days before, echoed by him.

He continued. "And when I saw you leave I knew you would be looking for me. I saw you emerge from the woods, frozen by time and doubt - I know you did not see me – and it wasn't difficult to guess your destination." He looked down at her again. "I know a lot about you, Kate."

That single word – her name from his lips – aroused such unnameable emotions in her, and he seemed to sense it. Oh, he knew everything; hadn't he just said so?

"It is Kate, isn't it?"

And then, with a single spring he landed, soundless, beside her and extended a great pale hand in her direction. As she took it she felt its phenomenal latent strength; as hard as stone, it's toughness akin to crocodile skin.

The moment's silence held her firm in its embrace, as had the darkness, just minutes ago in the woods. He, alone, had the power to break that silence. He used that power.

"What is it you seek, Kate?"

She found her voice. "Your story."

"You know my story, because it's your story too. That can wait. Once you remember it, you may no longer want me or what I can offer you." His eyes were just hollows in the night, but she knew they were searching her face. "Unfortunately

184

for you, by the time you hear my tale, there may be no choice in whether you want me or not."

He continued to hold her hand and she didn't try to resist him, fearing both that she might succeed and that she might not. She was terrified and thrilled in equal measures – though terror still held sway – and wasn't this how it was supposed to be; whatever *it* was?

He made an all-encompassing gesture with his free hand. "But right here, right now, what is it you want? Is it to remember?"

Without waiting for an answer, he started to guide her away from the monument towards an older part of the cemetery, hidden from the road by the church, where ancient trees spread their gnarled arms to shelter graves, which were not as well tended as those near the mausoleum. They stopped by a particular mound. There was a headstone, but it bore no words.

"Sad is it not?" His question was rhetorical. "Unknown; unloved; unoccupied perhaps. This is where you were heading, wasn't it?"

"I..." Kate looked down at the grave, her mind as bare as that headstone for a moment.

"Or is it this you were seeking?" He took her hand and placed it against his groin. "Somewhere along the line, isn't it always this?" She swallowed hard - and she'd thought his *hands* were big and hard! "The devil always gives one a gift as compensation for one's soul."

Now Kate gave a nervous smile, allowed her fingers to take a grip and heard his breathing change, which gave back to her some semblance of control.

"I have immortal longings in me," she whispered.

185

"You certainly do know your Shakespeare," he acknowl-edged.

Her words again from that evening. He had been there! Or was he just omniscient?

"Why did you come here?" She had to know; boy, did she! "Not to this cemetery, but to this place – this time?"

"I have always been near, but the time seemed right to come. I have been waiting my moment. We need to talk – about so many things."

"I'm listening."

He lifted her hand and started to lead her away. "I have somewhere more...intimate in mind."

Kate saw that they were heading towards a crypt, further back in the less well-tended section of the graveyard. She could see that part of the carved memorial had fallen away and not been repaired by the townsfolk.

The Stygian gloom lurking within shook her. It looked like a huge smashed-open box containing the birthplace of night itself, grown ancient, cobwebbed and mouldering through uncountable years. The first tingle of indecision played with her.

He was watching her. "Not scared of the dark, are you?" The tone was mocking.

"I feel like my life has been heading to this moment and yet pulling me away from it."

He re-applied the pressure on her hand; drew her towards him. "There are steps here. Come; I'll show you things you've never..." he hesitated, and then gave a wolfish grin, "...actually, I suspect you probably *have* dreamed of this. Are you dreaming now, Kate?"

"One thing..." *what was the matter with her?* "...you gave

186

me a fright earlier on, and I had a bit of an accident, as they say at school."

Now he threw back his head and laughed. The sound was neither pleasant nor mirthless, though its echo from the hollow of the fractured crypt was unnerving. He turned his white face to her.

"For a woman who would surrender her body in a graveyard to someone whom she believes may well have had conjugal relations with the daughters of Satan, you've picked a strange moment to have concerns about hygiene."

Now it was her turn to try to laugh, but once again she found the air stuck in her throat as she stared at the opening of the crypt. It was calling her, drawing her, the blackness. She drew closer to it and felt it swallow her.

Chapter Nine

Diane's quintessential English rose complexion was paler than usual, and Joanna knew it was more or less a reflection of her own face. There were mirrors aplenty in the gallery, some with faceted or bevelled edges, so that as she looked around she seemed surrounded by a congregation of lost souls.

Doubt and all its attendant shadows crowded in on her. This man – she would continue to think of him as that, not some other distorted truth – was her nemesis. Whether he knew this was another matter and, in the grander scheme, irrelevant; his arrival had awakened the ghosts. His footfall approaching her door was enough – opening it to find no-one there was somehow worse.

The women looked at each other and no words were needed, just like all those years ago.

How long had it been - three decades? - when they had...

...looked away from the TV screen and at each other, the three of them, their relief tangible, but unspoken. Even Kate, their de facto leader, tough as old boots at the age of fifteen, puffed out her cheeks.

"Well, that's two nights now and nothing on the news," said

Kate at last. She lowered her voice, glancing upstairs in a gesture that signified 'parents' even at six in the evening. "You'd think someone would have reported something by now." She caught Joanna's nervous glance through the window towards the back garden. "Don't worry," the tone was dismissive, "It's not here. I dumped it yesterday in the old quarry. Told you I would."

"Sorry." Joanna looked down, ashamed.

As if she sensed the other two might be at breaking point, Kate stood: "Let's take an oath."

"You said that before, but you don't believe in God," said Diane, with a stroppiness alien to her – clearly nerves were giving her some desperate strength.

Kate didn't hide her derision. "You don't have to swear to God, you know. You can swear to..." she spread her arms for dramatic effect, "...the powers of the universe." Then it seemed something occurred to her and she shot a keen, sparkling eye at them. "Like the Red Indians, we can swear with our own blood; a bond that will never be broken."

Joanna wrinkled her nose. "Ooh no, I'm not doing that!"

"What's the matter?" taunted Kate, tilting her head to one side. "You afraid of a little cut?"

"No," she replied. Yes, she thought. But at this time there was no denying they needed strong leadership.

Kate went to the door, looked out into the hallway and then disappeared. There was the sound of rummaging in a cutlery drawer and then she was back, closing the sitting-room door with exaggerated care, before making her coltish, slightly knock-kneed way, wielding a small, but wicked-looking knife with a black handle and a tapered blade of perhaps four to five inches.

"Right; who's going to be first?" Diane grimaced and tucked her hands under protective armpits. They looked at each other

and Kate raised her eyebrows. "Always the same."

She huffed and sighed. Then, without apparent hesitation, she drew the point across her left palm. Some nameless emotion flickered on her features – no more than the shadow of a passing butterfly – and she seemed to watch with as much fascination as the others, as a tiny part of her essential force issued through the cut.

Kate's unflinching performance gave Joanna courage, though not enough to inflict the wound on herself. She held out her hand, eyes squeezed tight, and was astonished when Kate announced that it was done. This in turn brought Diane round and as she held out her hand, Joanna thought it wise not to tell her that the pain had now kicked in.

Soon the three of them stood with upturned palms, one steely and determined, one biting her lip and thinking of plasters, and one with tears rolling down her pale face and a sob brewing in her wobbling chin. But just as the ordeal with the knife had helped them to forget for a moment, so sudden remembrance of its cause made them disregard the pain.

"Now all we need is a suitable oath," said Kate...

... at which point Diane burst into tears: "I'm scared."

Joanna put her clean hand on her shoulder. "We'll be all right." How she wished she believed it.

Kate stood with eyes shut and head bowed. Now she opened them again and said:

"I have it! Hold hands." She raised her eyes in frustration. "The bloody ones!"

The sticky, disturbing intimacy seemed to make things worse, but by the will of Kate they persevered. She stared at them by turns and then intoned with as much eldritch power as her youthful voice could summon:

By the pricking of my thumbs
Something wicked this way comes
By the cutting of our palms
Comes the blood of friends that calms.
Of the bad deeds of that day
There is nothing left to say.
To our silence we all swear;
Break this circle – none will dare

They stood with hands still clasped and heads bowed, each lost in thoughts they believed would never leave them.

At last Diane broke the silence: "Can I wash my hands now?"

Kate and Joanna burst out laughing. Soon, Diane joined in. They were going to be ok.

* * *

As Joanna emerged from her thoughts and blinked in the daylight, it was to find herself rubbing her left palm with the thumb of her right hand. Looking across, she saw Diane doing the very same thing.

"It's strange," said Joanna.

Diane looked up. "You can say that again."

"No, I mean about last night. Kate's poem - I'd convinced myself that she hadn't a creative bone in her body, and now twice in the space of a few hours I've seen, or remembered, a different side to her."

"Her oath."

"You remember it too? Even in the darkest corners of our universe there's creativity." She stopped on seeing Diane's

bottom lip tremble. *Echoes; echoes.* "What's the matter?"
"Joanna, what's happening to us?"

Chapter Ten

She knew she was screaming, only because the sound echoed back to her from the surrounding stones of the crypt. Otherwise this was almost beyond perception; beyond anything she could have imagined in her most intense dreams – and she knew they were set in places where even the shadows feared to tread.

Despite her visceral longings, the tattered remnants of Kate's dignity had reached back towards the night air as she had descended into this place. As the air had grown musty and the stars had disappeared, she'd woken up to the fact that an eternity sleeping in a vampire's coffin might not be her thing after all! It was a conceit for those to whom it could never be a reality.

But they had descended to the depths of the crypt; an unexpected, high-vaulted hall of the departed. From somewhere, her host had produced a single candle and lit it. She found herself wondering whether he had been spending time here, but dismissed the idea, or rather, did not want to entertain it in this dreadful place – too many awful images were disturbed by treading that path. The flame did not dance in the still air; a relief, as it might have set the stones into unsettling movement. Then he'd gestured towards the light:

"In tribute to your poem, with its firelight and shadows."

That had shocked her. "How did you...you were really there?"

He had ignored her. "And for the part of you that has reawakened tonight."

She'd shuddered, but before her misgivings could send out tentative roots, he'd doused the candle again and she was thrown into total darkness.

Now the air around her came alive. She couldn't see the hand in front of her face, yet images seemed to flash and sounds brushed past her ears before she could identify them. There might have been water, screams, birds, whispers.

She had stood cold, vulnerable, but stationary, fearing that any attempt to move would disorientate her further, though she couldn't help turning her head this way and that as she discerned movement around her.

And then powerful hands grasped her and bent her backwards. She felt breath, warm and sweet, first on her cheek and then tracing its way down towards her neck, on down to her breasts. Lips brushed against her and then the tips of teeth – which was when the screams started, continuing till the crypt was lit by lights behind her eyes. A hand forced its way between her legs, one finger making its serpentine way to where she felt the pressure building. She fell onto the damp stone floor of the crypt, legs trembling with the force of her orgasm.

A flame flared and seemed to explode into the after-image that was his face in the darkness.

Her head turned a slow, painful path away from the light and there was soft fabric beneath her cheek. Familiar objects came into focus. She turned back towards the light and recognised her own bedroom lamp. A sense of place, if not time, was returning to her limbs – which was when she realised where her hand was and withdrew it in haste. Other memories flooded in with the wakening. In shock, she put her fingers to her neck – no puncture wounds. But she did ache. She pushed herself up onto the edge of the bed. It couldn't just have been a dream, could it?

One look at herself in the mirror disabused her of that notion. She was still wearing her shoes, which were streaked with mossy stains. Blades of grass clung to them and to the hems of her jeans. There were damp stains on her elbows and knees, and rolling up her sleeves she uncovered bruises.

Her heart pounded as she limped across to the window and it raced faster when she saw her car glinting beneath the streetlamp in the dark. She had no recollection of driving home.

Kate wandered over to her dressing table, took a deep draught from the glass of water standing there, then sat with a thump and looked into the mirror. She stared at herself and wondered which world was the true one; the one in which she sat or the back-to-front one inhabited by her other self. As if in response, images seemed to stir behind her; flitting in and out of view, raising dust-ghosts, which retreated as quickly as they formed.

Some of it was coming back. He had stripped her bare, also held the mirror to her and forced her to decide, one way or the other. She looked at her neck again and heard his voice, mocking: *"Surely a would-be hellcat like you is not scared of a little vampire's bite. I do not think even you know what your expectations were when we met tonight. Perhaps you thought I would suck your soul from your veins."*

He was right. She could not help but admire how he had played her. He had read her doubt; scented it. By taking away the poisoned chalice, he knew she would want to drink from it more than ever. All of her privileged middle-class life she had longed for something delicious, corrupt and otherworldly to come to her, offering dark knowledge in return for her surrender, but perhaps she had placed too heavy a reliance on the extreme unlikelihood of it ever happening. It had been her shield; perhaps crucifix.

She closed her eyes, opened them again and could see him in the mirror. He came close behind her, leaned in and whispered; words she recognised as having been spoken earlier that night:

"I despise those simpering couples who talk about togetherness and creation. We are never so isolated and selfish as when we are about to climax. But you and I, we have something here – something shared; something deeper, darker, more intense and worth holding onto. In fact I know you cannot let go now. There are acts in our lives that live with us forever and the mind returns, even when the body cannot, like an addict; a recidivist criminal." His eyes flayed her all over again, exposing flesh, bone and a black heart. "How wonderful did it feel to cast aside your judgemental soul, which is nothing but a manifestation of everything that society demands of you, and abandon yourself to the darkness? How ironic it is that, in these times when anything goes, we seem more intent than ever on holding kangaroo courts of moral judgement, condemning as selfish those who wish to end the suffering of another, or defenders of justice who mete out the punishments the courts are too lazy or scared to impose? It's A.D. that turned *decent* to *decadent*. But tonight, Kate, something died here - or rather, something was born to darkness – and that is a state of being, which can make you feel so powerful.

"Do you want to play that game, Kate; the Game of Death?"

Now Kate closed her eyes again, leaning on the dressing table for support, swaying as the faintness started to over-whelm her once more. When she opened her eyes again, his face, the memory of it, was nothing more than a shimmering in the mirror.

He was right; what had died tonight was her need for the supernatural. But it had been replaced by something all the more powerful and dreadful for being within reach; the knowledge that death *is* forever - that it would come and all that mattered was finding someone in your pitiful short life to share your nightmares. In the absence of punishment there was no sin; in the absence of sin, no punishment. But what if the line between sin and crime became blurred?

That was why he had taken her into the crypt tonight; to drive from her mind all that nonsense about the Undead and eternity? Yet if he had chosen to drink her blood, was he not still a vampire? It was only through popular literature that the tradition of returning to a coffin and eschewing the daylight had entered the public consciousness. She couldn't begin to imagine – a unique circumstance for her – how and where he spent his nights or days, but really it didn't matter and she didn't care. If his ability to climb onto a vertical mausoleum was down to a rock-hard ueber-muscular physique and gymnastic training rather than eldritch powers, was it any less wonderful? He was flesh and blood; an eerie, magnificent, controlled version of it, but a version nonetheless. She had even felt part of that flesh and blood grow glorious and huge in her hand. Bread of heaven! She would take a hard-on over preternatural flesh any day.

She stood and turned, hoping to catch him before exhaustion stole him from her once more. He had gone. She called out to him, benighted and confused. Though the order of that night's events was beyond her - a puzzle she was incapable of piecing together for now - one thing came back to her with clarity; one request she had made to the dark man: "The Game of Death," she had whispered, "show me."

Chapter Eleven

J oanna glanced towards the street and saw only her own reflection in the window. When had the nights drawn in? How had the late autumn crept up on her? Funny how the last couple of days had affected her perceptions. She looked at the clock again – eight-thirty. It had been half an hour since she'd shut the café. Only on activity evenings did she stay open till eleven.

She heard the reedy voice and realised that the phone had slid down from her ear.

"Sorry, Di, what was that?"

"I said you seem a bit distracted."

"Yes, I'm sorry." She flicked the kettle switch yet again – the water would boil away if she wasn't careful. "I'm just going to have a coffee; maybe that'll rouse me from my stupor."

"You should get home."

"Perhaps." It was a nothing response; a filler word devoid of meaning or conviction, and in that sense appropriate to her life of late. "To be honest, it's not somewhere I take much pleasure in being right now. Can't seem to switch off, so I might as well be here."

She glanced over her shoulder at the steps leading down

to the cellar. Was he down there? She wouldn't put it past him. Now she shook her head, to clear it of that and other ridiculous thoughts.

"Hello?"

"Ah, I'm sorry Diane. Maybe you're right; maybe I should go home." She put her palm against her forehead. "Oh, I don't know. Everything feels wrong at the moment. My life as I know it is in pieces. I don't want to be at home; I don't want to be at work; I want to be in both places, but whichever one I'm at I want to be at the other one. Business is doing well, but I'm taking no pleasure in it."

"So your regulars haven't been scared off after all."

"Oh, some of them have, for sure, but ironically, I have a new, younger clientele. This has suddenly become a trendy place to hang out. I get a lot of the university students in here. I've had to set more of the tables in the cellar as people keep asking me whether the place is haunted. *Would you prefer one or two manifestations with your espresso, sir?*"

The laugh that followed sounded hollow.

"Well, to some extent it is haunted, I guess," said Diane, "depending on your definition of haunting - a presence hanging over somewhere."

Joanna stared at the poster on the front door that advertised forthcoming events. His aura was certainly there, in the blank space under *TUESDAY*. She didn't know what to do. If she didn't put up his suggestion for a theme night, would he turn up and question the ethos of her café? If she went with it, would she frighten away her regulars – though she might attract her new demographic?

All of these issues were symptoms, rather than the cause of her unease.

Diane was saying something and Joanna lifted the phone back into place once more: "...going to come over tonight. You sound like you need someone there." A pause. "And, if I'm honest, so do I. I'm going through a bit of a lonely phase."

"Lonely – or alone with your thoughts?" There was no response. "I know mine are making my head spin."

"For example...?"

"I'm sure you can guess some of it." Joanna moved across to the window and looked out onto the twilight of the empty street. Behind her the kettle clicked off for the fourth time. "There's a part of me that can't shake the feeling, whether by chance or not, that I'm paying for my sins; being punished for them – for having forgotten them." She gave a little snort. "I know it all sounds very melodramatic, but there must be some significance to the appearance of this...dark man; some causality. Tell me honestly, Di, did you ever think back on those days before he turned up?" Silence. "Di?"

"Sorry, I am here. I was just trying to remember."

Joanna understood. The conscious brain had its limits. She had read a story once where the subconscious mind was described as comprising the miscellaneous details captured in the background of a photograph while you focussed on the main subject, and they emerged as dreams. Who could tell how many times her memories had crawled unseen from their shadows? Perhaps it was a bit like subliminal advertising? The danger was, if you could record it and advance the images frame by frame, what awful thing might suddenly confront you? Better, perhaps, to let it flash by after all.

"And Kate's worrying me too," said Joanna. "Have you seen her since the last time in the café?"

"No, I haven't. I went round and knocked on her door

yesterday – no response."

Joanna turned away from the window and headed back to the kettle, all the time casting little glances in the direction of the cellar. "Coincidence that there's been no sighting of *him* either during that time? I'm wor..."

There was a thump behind her - soft.

Horrible.

The phone fell from her fingers and Joanna spun round.

Nothing.

That single thump had been replaced by the thundering in her chest.

The window; was that something? She tried forcing her legs forward, but they wouldn't move. In the distance there was a tinny squeaking, which forced its way through the rushing in her ears and she realised it was the phone again - Diane shouting:

"Joanna! Joanna!" She picked it up. "Are you ok? What happened?"

"I don't know...a sound."

"Call the police, Joanna."

"No - just stay on the line. Besides, what would I tell them – I heard a sound at quarter to nine in the evening? "

"I'm coming over. You stay put."

"Just standing here terrified is also not an option. Hang on the line a moment – I need to take a look outside."

Great! Wasn't that the exact thing that made you scream 'STUPID!' at the movies, as the frightened girl – who, of course, was the only person unable to see the *'victim'* stamp on her forehead - decided to leave the relative sanctuary of four walls to take those ill-advised steps into the surrounding night?

When her legs at last obeyed – or disobeyed - her brain and she approached the window, Joanna saw a shape on the glass, or rather the ghost of one. She reached out to touch it, but it was on the outside. It was indistinct; perhaps nothing.

Against her better judgement, she unlocked the door and leaned out.

She gasped and slammed it shut again.

Straight away, she regretted not looking to see whether anyone was out there. How she would have reacted if she had found someone was another matter altogether.

Diane's voice was calling her.

"Well, that decides many things," said Joanna, as much to herself as to her friend.

"What's wrong? Look, I don't care what you say, I'm coming over."

"Yes, please do; that would be a good idea."

"What happened?"

"I'll explain it all when you get here. But do hurry. Oh, and bring some warm clothing; a fleece or something - and some walking boots. We've got some ground to cover."

"Meaning what?"

"We're going back?"

"Where?"

"A long way."

* * *

At last, Joanna got round to making that coffee; a flask of it, as well as an espresso for herself. During that time, not a minute passed when she didn't glance towards the cellar or the window.

Chapter Twelve

Although Diane was someone for whom life's glass often appeared to be half-empty, her arrival that night gave Joanna immense strength and she acknowledged that with a big hug.

"So what's this all about, Jo-Jo? You've really turned the thermostat down."

Joanna collected an archive box which stood on the café counter and placed it on the table where they were drinking their espressos.

"I managed to pluck up the courage to go outside again."

She lifted the lid. Diane shrieked, her chair scraping back on the stone floor as she put her fingers to her mouth.

"The poor thing," she said when she had recovered. "What happened?"

"It must have flown into the café window."

Diane looked in that direction; saw the pale smudge, the spectral snapshot of the bird's unfortunate end. She frowned. "There must have been something wrong with it already. Of all the birds I'd have expected to avoid that fate, the owl would be high on the list."

Diane was right, of course. Joanna forced herself to look into the box again. The bird's staring eyes and twisted neck were a grotesque parody of its natural state.

And then it seemed the penny dropped, because so did Diane's fingers from her lips. There was an out-of-character flash of impatience in her timid eyes.

"OK," she said, "I see the significance..." - she lifted a finger again to correct herself – "...the coincidence of this; and I can see, in the light of our conversation and recent events, how it spooked you; the owl and the mole and all that." She looked long at Joanna. "How I wish I didn't know the answer to these questions, but...where are we going and why?" She turned her finger now and pointed at the owl. "And what does this have to do with it?"

"Don't you see?"

Diane shook her head. "No." It was clear to Joanna she was in denial.

"We're being sent a message."

"Oh, pur – LEEEZE!" There was anger now; quite unlike Diane, but driven by fear.

"Look, Di, I'm not saying it's anything supernatural; in fact yes, it probably is nothing more than coincidence, but does that matter? It's woken us up to something. We have to go back – to the moor."

Diane rose from her chair. "No!" She paced across the room. "I thought you were heading this way. It makes no sense."

Joanna, still standing by the table, put her hands to her head and she, too, paced away, before returning to the box.

Diane's laugh lacked any trace of humour. "A weirdo turns up, reads out a poem about an owl. It makes you melancholy and you think about an event we'd all prefer not to have happened. An owl dies, and suddenly we have to return to

Sedge Moor – all because of some freak."

Joanna pointed an accusatory finger – not at Diane, but towards wherever the past lay. "*Freak. Weirdo.* Exactly the kind of attitude that brought us there the first time. And I for one want to face up to my responsibilities; to what I did. Repent, at least, of my sins and then hopefully move forward again."

Diane seemed caught between indignation and shame. "What exactly would we be looking for?"

Joanna bit her lip; shrugged. "Redemption? I don't know." She threw herself down in a chair "I don't know, I don't know. I have no answers. I just know how I feel."

"Aren't you forgetting something; shouldn't Kate be with us?"

"I left a message on her voicemail after you and I finished talking. I'm worried about her too. About all of us. Maybe there's a part of me that believes if we at least show penitence then things may turn out ok."

Diane walked round and put a hand on her friend's shoulder. "I'm sorry I shouted. Maybe I'm just in denial. From the moment I remembered what we did – or didn't do – I've been so restless; ashamed that in thirty years I could actually forget; feel no regret." Of a sudden, she turned pale. "But Joanna, what if we find something other than redemption?"

Joanna did her best to smile. "I can't answer that either. Let's go and find out."

* * *

The beams of the headlamps drilled an empty path into

the night, the shadowy featurelessness of the surrounding landscape providing a suitable metaphor for what lay ahead. So much of the past is a black foil for the present, lurking unseen and forgotten, waiting for the light to turn its way.

They had rested for a few hours, or at least lain down in sleeping bags in the café and given it as good a shot as you can when your bloodstream is full of espresso, and both pulse and mind are racing. Joanna could not remember whether she slept – though who can? – or whether indeed at any stage she'd been able to draw her eyes away from the entrance to the cellar. But she assumed that exhaustion had overtaken her at some point, because the alarm on her mobile phone had startled her when it went off at 4 a.m.

They had agreed to set off early, in hope of reaching their destination to coincide with the first flickering of dawn's eyelid. This was a time of low physical ebb, so perhaps not perfect for what they had in mind, but they did not want to be disturbed or raise suspicions. There was little in the way of traffic, so when they did at last pass a vehicle, a muddy Landrover, doubtless on its way to some market, it flicked to full beam, irritated by Joanna having forgotten hers were on and blinding her as retribution.

There was nothing more than a rumour of light in the east, but it was enough. This was no horror flick, where they would set off, against all wisdom and advice, at the peak of the witching hour. So it was that they had driven for more than an hour in silence; tongues and spirits weighed down by the knowledge that this landscape was once again their stage, but they didn't know their lines.

Sedge Moor, even at those times when it benefited from the dappling wonder of oblique sunlight and the latency of spring, had at best a sibylline beauty; feared, respected, enslaving, but never loved. At this time of day it offered no respite, just slumbering, monumental gloom. So, it was a relief to see a sign of civilisation at the side of the road; an actual sign that caught in the headlights. That comfort gave way to foreboding as the car drew nearer and Joanna read the words. An arrow pointed down a lane, which had barely time to lead anywhere before the shadows swallowed it:

Harriet's Grammar School for Girls

At times during the silent drive, Joanna could not tell whether Diane was awake, but now the latter spun in her seat to watch the sign disappear behind them.

"Did you see that?"

"Of course; I've been driving," said Joanna with unnecessary testiness. "I wasn't sure whether to stop or not, but decided there's no point. I had been wondering whether my memory was playing tricks, but now at least we know we're on the right road."

"Do you remember exactly where it is?"

"I hope I'll know as soon as I see it."

On they went for another ten minutes, while the condition of the road surface deteriorated, rough tarmac turning to dirt and stones. At least that provided some distraction from what lay ahead, as Joanna took care to avoid the worst of the potholes and bumps; this was no place for her urban Prius to get a flat tyre.

Diane puffed out her cheeks: "We must have had some energy in those days to cycle this far."

"Well, the devil makes work for idle hands," said Joanna. "Maybe he gives strength to the legs as well."

And then she stopped; for there it was. The lane carried

on, becoming single track with passing places, but to the right stood a gate, leading out onto the moor. There were no way-markers. This was not part of an established route.

In almost every sense it was an unexceptional gate; wooden, five-barred. Joanna inched the car onto the patch of ground in front of it, where weeds and nettles showed that there had been no regular traffic for a long time, and killed the engine. She noticed that the old, rusting lever closure had been supplemented by a padlock and chain. At first she assumed that somebody must have acquired the land, but then spotted a sign:

Danger! No admission – coastal erosion and land slippage
Danger! No admission
Danger!

The desolate setting left Joanna feeling exposed. There was no obvious sign of a human presence – or any life form, for that matter. She knew this was guilt talking, but killed the lights nevertheless, fearing that they were advertising her presence. Once her eyes adjusted to the change she could tell that the dawn's reassuring glow was imminent.

"And now?" The impatience of Diane's words failed to disguise the fear, which had pushed them stumbling into the open.

"And now?" repeated Joanna, but without anger. "I think we gird the loins with a cup of coffee."

"Can't we just...you know, get on with it – whatever *it* is?"

Joanna looked at her friend. "No." It was emphatic, but not harsh. "I need to think."

She felt the car rock as her friend threw herself back against the seat, rummaging in her rucksack for the thermos. *I know you get it,* thought Joanna, *despite your irritation.* People dealt with things in different ways, but she wasn't about to try to hide from the memories. She looked at the gate, its worn surface and few remaining scabs of paint becoming more distinct in the meagre dawn light. It looked much the same as she remembered, despite the intervening years of weathering – except now it needed a padlock; as if that was going to stop someone with enough determination from clambering over it.

Someone like her.

But oh my! – how everything had changed since she'd last been here, when the bicycle still leaned there, as anomalous as a saddled horse without a rider.

Oh my God!

The unexpected remembrance of a seeming triviality made her shudder; a disconnected memory.

She'd been walking through Bixham town centre a couple of years before – God knows when – and had spotted a child's bicycle leaning against a lamppost, the owner nowhere to be seen. She remembered now, for the first time since, how that sight had filled her with apparent random dismay, which she could neither relate to nor pin down. Her mother had told her once of having a similar experience; how she had been walking home from the shops one day when she spotted a red rose in a garden, the sight of which had caused her to burst into inexplicable tears.

Now, in spite of everything, Joanna smiled, just because it made sense.

But little else did yet. Nailing one ephemeral butterfly of a memory to the board wasn't going to help her now. A whole flock of them had started their capricious fluttering around her, bringing panic as they brushed her face in the dawn light.

* * *

Diane came hurrying across the playground.

"Bunny boy's here again. It's bunny boy."

She kept her voice down, but not out of consideration for the victim's feelings; fourteen year olds didn't always understand such nuances. In her still-callow mind he looked like a rabbit, but minus cuteness or fluffiness. Then, of course, there was the fact that Kate had come up with the nickname; it wasn't Diane's to own. And any nickname thought up by Kate could be guaranteed to be cruel.

All these things Joanna recognised as she watched her friend scoot across the playground. But also, she knew that Diane was keeping her voice low because it was their secret. It seemed no-one else had spotted him since he'd first appeared a couple of days before. He'd just been there one day, out of the blue, standing at a corner of the playground fence where the triumvirate hung out, away from the main buildings. Such was Kate's reputation at Harriet's – clever but cruel – that no-one wandered into her territory without an invitation, and those never came. She was the one everyone looked up to but nobody wanted to be. Even back then, there had been a darkness to her and it wasn't just because she smoked.

Which made the fact that she had two companions all the more surprising – in particular to them; the chosen ones. Perhaps they were just her two stooges, but if they knew that back then, it was at some subliminal level that made no difference.

Whatever the reason, she'd made her choices and they were in her inner sanctum, which gave them grudging kudos.

Kate spun round on hearing Diane's words: "Again? What's he doing – just staring?"

"I think so."

"We're going to have to do something about this."

"Shall I fetch Miss Bowman?" suggested Joanna.

Kate turned on her. "No! This is our problem; our challenge – our business."

"I think he's got a bicycle," said Diane, her tone timid in the face of Kate's dominance.

"Do rabbits have bicycles?" asked Kate rhetorically. "Maybe he's escaped from a circus...or a laboratory." They sniggered and then Kate's eyes lit up. "Hey, I've got a good idea. We can teach him a lesson."

"A lesson?" It was out before Joanna could stop the words.

Kate glared. "Yes, a lesson...for being creepy. Follow me."

They disappeared around the corner of the brick building where all the gardening and sports equipment was kept, and wandered over to the chain-link fencing that marked the end of the school grounds. Sure enough, there he was, in a copse about thirty yards from the fence, his shock of white hair giving the appearance of an enormous lone dandelion in the shade beneath the trees.

Kate stood just shy of the fence and beckoned for him to approach. His mistrustful hesitation was apparent. Now indeed he did resemble a startled rabbit in the headlights as he stood transfixed. She gestured again and with obvious reluctance he wandered over, blinking, into the sunlight, leaving his bicycle leaning against a tree.

His steps were tentative and he looked around as he crossed the open space, as if expecting treachery, before looking again at Kate for reassurance. She hurried him along, doing her best not

212

to look threatening.

At last he was close enough that the extent of his burden became clear, repelling the other two girls with the whiteness of his skin and his pink eyes, which squinted constantly, so that he appeared half-witted. Joanna and Diane took cover behind Kate, who appeared not to be cowed.

"Hello, who are you?" said the latter. A shuffling of feet marked his response, and nothing else. "What's your name?" Silence. "Don't you know it's rude not to answer polite questions?"

"Tom."

The voice surprised them with its roughness, as if coated with cobwebs from lack of use.

"Peeping Tom, more like," said Diane, her volubility unusual under the circumstances. It seemed she felt the false courage of all who have a human shield.

Kate made a motion with her hand behind her back for Diane to shut up. "Where are you from, Tom?" she asked.

"I don't know."

More sniggering from the girls at the back.

"That's a silly answer," said Kate. "But anyway; why are you here?"

A shrug of the shoulders and again silence. Joanna could feel Kate's irritation; it had not quite surfaced and for some reason she was controlling it. That meant she must have a plan, otherwise she would have been much ruder by now.

Again Kate prompted him. "Have you come here to play?" Another shrug. "Would you like to play?" He nodded. Kate pointed past him. "Is that your bike?"

A moment's hesitation. "Yes."

"So they have bicycles at the nowhere place you come from."
He looked furtive. "Anyway...how's about we meet you at the

end of the lane after school today. I know a great place we can go and play. It'll be a bit of an adventure."

When the smile broke on the boy's face, it was like the brightest shaft of sunlight. So why, then, did it provoke such despair in Joanna?

"We finish at three-thirty," continued Kate. "That gives us a bit of time before we have to be home. Meet us at quarter past four at the end of the lane." He frowned. "Do you have a watch?"

He shook his head. To Joanna's astonishment, Kate removed her watch and handed it to him. "Quarter past four; don't be late." A bell sounded; end of the mid-morning break.

"See you later Tom," said Kate, giving a little wave. If anyone was more taken aback by this display than the boy it was the other two girls. They didn't really understand what was going on and, rather typical where Kate's plans were concerned, they found themselves struggling to stay afloat in her wake; short of breath and just a little fearful.

Before they disappeared round the equipment store, Joanna glanced back. She saw Tom running across the opening towards the trees. His left arm was extended to the side and she could tell he was admiring the watch, which he wore with pride on his wrist. Even at this distance his joy and reverence were palpable.

* * *

Joanna squeezed her eyes shut; to no avail. The tears escaped as easily as the memories now; and no – she would not spare herself.

A peace-pipe in the form of a mug of coffee was held in her direction by Diane. She took it, sipped and then allowed her hands to rest in her lap. Out of the corner of her eye she saw how Diane clutched her mug in two hands, though the car was warm. The coffee's aroma was too comforting, so she cracked open the window and allowed the whistling gusts of wind to thrust her back again to the end of the lane thirty-five years before. It was as if the scales had fallen – she could see that fateful day now, through her windscreen. It was so clear. Her younger self stood out there beckoning and she knew she would have to join her.

* * *

He was waiting for them – was that ever in doubt? – as they approached on their bikes. They must have looked like a squadron of enemy fighter planes; or could that have just been a retrospective projection of guilt? Their tyres kicked up stones and dirt as they ground to a halt, the dust whipped up and away by the gusting south-westerly breeze.

Joanna and Diane sat just behind Kate. Interesting to realise now that she was the only one who had a plan; who knew what was going to happen. Joanna felt exposed in more ways than one. She was aware of the eyes of the universe watching her, which was tantamount to admitting that she was about to embark on something naughty at best, wicked at worst; and if Kate was in charge, the latter was more likely. There was another nuance to that sense of exposure; standing there facing this strange boy, with his white hair, whiter skin and translucent eyes, she found herself missing the chain-link fence of the school playground.

It was Kate who spoke first – it was always Kate.

"Ever played hide and seek?" Tom gave one of those shrugs

that seemed to make up at least half of his vocabulary. "You must know whether you have or haven't." He nodded. "OK, well there's a great place we can play, where we won't have to worry about anyone getting in our way." With that, Kate stood heavily on her pedals and set off west along the lane with which they had intersected. "C'mon!"

Joanna and Diane looked at each other, gave a Tom-like shrug and headed off after her. They were so intrigued, they forgot about their new companion, until Joanna remembered and glanced over her shoulder. He was following at a distance.

"Doesn't look very steady on the bike?" she observed.

Their curiosity soon gave way to misgivings, partly the result of tiredness as they seemed to have been cycling for hours.

"Where are we going?" panted Joanna to Kate, who had set a tireless pace. There was no reply.

"We shouldn't go too far; mum and dad will get worried." Diane's voice shook; a cocktail of exhaustion and nervousness.

Around them, the rolling, verdant landscape so typical of the countryside around Harriet's transformed into the heather and gorse of undulating moorland, and neat hedgerows gave way to untamed brambles. At first their spirits had been buoyed by the occasional passing car, but these became much fewer and further between, until, at last, there were none. From time to time Joanna would glance back over her shoulder; despite her strained expression, Diane, who was often a dawdler and never in the vanguard, had kept up with great determination, perhaps for comfort in the alien surroundings. They didn't chatter, a combination of fear and exhaustion, as if careless talk would cost lives, alerting some beast other than the moor to their presence.

Beyond Diane was the distant figure of Tom; his white hair a will-o'-the-wisp in the grey light. He didn't appear to be labouring, just riding at his own pace; perhaps assessing whether it was wise to continue. He was not alone in that.

And then, at a point where the hedgerows lining the lane grew even taller and wilder, Kate stopped. The girls caught up with her to find her standing by a gate. As Joanna drew alongside she saw there was a path beyond it. 'Path' was perhaps an exaggeration; it was more of a sheep trail overgrown by gorse; not something one would have picked out at a distance. Up ahead, it disappeared behind a hump in the land.

"Where are we?" wheezed Diane.

"Dartmoor," was Kate's sarcastic reply. "Now listen," she whispered, glancing over at the still-distant Tom, "here's as good a chance as any to tell you the plan."

"Plan?" Joanna frowned, even though she had known deep down that this was no random destination. "I thought we were going to play hide and seek. To be honest I don't really want to play it out there." She pointed beyond the gate.

"You're such a scaredy-cat," taunted Kate, still sotto voce. "But don't worry; we're not playing out there – at least we're not." The other two exchanged glances. "When I start counting to one hundred, get going, but come back here as soon as bunny-boy is out of sight. We'll head back." Her laugh was purest malice, untainted by adult conscience. "It'll be so funny; the thought of him hiding out there waiting for us. I wonder what time he'll get home. That's another reason I brought us out here – we've no idea where he's from, so coming all this way is the only guarantee he'll have a long trip home."

Joanna was shocked and, knowing Diane well, could tell she was too, though she didn't dare to show it. "Isn't that a bit cruel... and dangerous?"

The indifference Kate evinced was more shocking than if she had turned on Joanna with a feral smile. "Yes; but it'll teach him not to hang around watching girls."

"I suppose." The response was uncertain; uncommitted. "What if something bad happens?"

"Something bad did happen; he met us." Kate laughed alone. "Look, no-one knows he's with us. If anything goes wrong, we don't say anything. We'll be fine."

"I wasn't thinking about us." But now she was. That was an added worry she didn't need.

"Look shut up, ok? He's coming."

When Tom arrived sweat was pouring down his forehead and running into his eyes, causing him to blink and squint more than usual; it was not an edifying picture. And so the tussle within Joanna grew more violent. Should she side with this boy, whom she reviled and pitied in equal measure, or just go with the flow? At fifteen years old her options were limited.

And then the moment had gone on the breeze, swirling away, still within sight, but skittish and uncatchable.

"Okay, Tom," said Kate, "we'll leave our bikes here and go play on the moor. I'll do the seeking. I'm going to count to a hundred."

Tom looked past Kate towards the moor. "It looks creepy."

"So do you," said Kate, without apparent artifice, "but it hasn't stopped us playing with you, has it?"

The other girls looked at the ground. Tom shrugged. Perhaps the insult had not registered; ricocheting this time off the brittle carapace of one who knew he was always seen as different.

Quick as a flash Kate clambered over the gate. Hands on hips, she stared across the moor. Her short hair just quivered in the gusting wind like an alpine plant.

"They say you can hear the voices of the dead out here," she *said to no-one in particular. As words of encouragement went, they ranked alongside the wisdom that tells you to face down an angry grizzly bear or charging silverback.*

Joanna knew she couldn't go through with this for all manner of reasons; the featureless surroundings seemed to throw the nastiness of their actions into stark relief. So did it say something about her, or Kate's dominant will, that, at the words from her tall friend – "Right, here goes" – and the simple act of her covering her eyes and counting, Joanna scrambled past her scruples, over the gate and headed right. She saw Diane head with even greater reluctance to the left; clever on both their parts as they knew they could simply follow the hedgerow back to the gate.

She looked back. For one merciful moment it seemed that Tom was stronger than them as he stood rooted to the spot. But then, with surprising agility, he was over the gate and running with a peculiar straight-armed, stiff-fingered half-skip north across the moor. Within about thirty seconds he was lost from view.

Joanna turned and raced back towards the gate. Now it was done, she just wanted to be away. She saw Diane doing the same. As they got nearer they heard the count; seventy-three, seventy-four, seventy-five. She looked north, full of fear. There was no sign of that bobbing white head.

Kate was also looking in that direction. She cupped her hands to her mouth and bellowed: "Coming, ready or not!" She turned, her face once again a featureless map. "C'mon, let's get out of here."

Joanna knew there was little point in hanging around and soon they were racing away from the scene of their cruel trick. She began to realise why it had been so tiring coming out here, as they were able to free-wheel downhill much of the way back. As the distance grew, so Kate's mood became jovial, till she was laughing, legs pointing out straight in front as she raced down the slight, gradual incline.

But for Joanna, the absolute opposite was true. The turning chains of her bike might as well have been ratcheting up the tension. As for Diane, she could have been mistaken for catatonic if, driven by her usual fear of being late home, she hadn't said:

"What time is it?"

"Oh fuck!" Kate screeched to a halt, as did the other girls at the sound of the 'f' word. She looked back over her shoulder. "I didn't ask for my watch." She considered something. "Oh well, I can always get another one."

Joanna and Diane looked at each other, chilled by the words, but said nothing. Kate's grown-up language had intimidated them. Under the circumstances she wasn't to be messed with.

They rode on home. For two of them, their hearts sank with the sun.

* * *

Of course, by the time they were back there was nothing they could do. Daylight was fading and Dartmoor had smudged into the horizon. Joanna hoped nothing else was dying with the light.

That night, she lay staring at the ceiling of her bedroom, trying to convince herself that it would be amazing to lie beneath the stars, but she had trouble believing it would be possible for poor, lonely Tom, even before she heard the heavy rainfall. To make matters worse, she had no idea how his parents might be reached.

The next day, the hours dragged to mid-morning break. As soon as that bell sounded, Joanna hurried to the corner of the playground, though she forced herself to walk to avoid drawing attention. Nothing. No Tom; no bike.

Diane joined her. Her bottom lip started to tremble and for once Joanna was no stronger than her friend in starting to cry.

At last, Kate sauntered over to join them. It was hard to tell whether her casual approach was studied or not, but still, her eyes betrayed curiosity.

"What the hell's the matter with you two?" She delved into a pocket, fished out a packet of cigarettes and lit up.

Joanna pointed towards the fence. "He's not here."

Kate shrugged. "Well, I told you it would teach him a lesson."

Joanna continued to stare at the trees, as if their victim might materialise; escaping from the bottle where they had trapped him with their witch's curse. "Poor Tom," she said.

Kate started rubbing her arms as if she was shivering. "Poor Tom's a cold." The girl's looked at her uncomprehending. "King Lear. We're not supposed to read it yet, but it sounded so dark."

"Look, this is serious," said Joanna, fear and guilt giving her unexpected courage to speak up.

"Why; what do you know that I don't?"

Joanna steeled herself. It was unusual to plough on in the face of Kate's displeasure. "Supposing he's come to some harm; didn't make it back last night."

"That's his choice. Nothing to do with us." Kate leaned forward and looked at them from beneath hooded eyes. "Just you remember that."

"Can't we go back and find out?"

"We got away with it once ~ heading out there without being seen...we think. If we go a second time we might not be so lucky and that'll really draw attention to us where there's none now."

Now Diane found her voice and though it was full of sobs, her fear of the consequences of their actions overrode her fear of Kate:

"What if he did make it back and now he's angry with us and comes back looking for revenge? Or sends his parents over to tell the teachers what we did?"

Kate tutted, drew on her cigarette at length, and then threw her hands out in exasperation. "And what exactly are you going to do? Go on – go back then. What if you find his bike, or if you don't find it; how are we better off?"

Joanna, too, still had the bit between her teeth. It wasn't often she stood up to her friend – were they friends? – but this mattered; it really mattered. "Well I'm going back after school today." She held Kate's forbidding gaze; sensed her dilemma. Was this some sort of turning point?

Whether it was or wasn't, she felt relief when Kate shrugged, sighed and, with a theatrical tilt of the head said: "Okay, I'll come with you then." It was all very well challenging the leader, but it wasn't a role she wanted on a permanent basis.

* * *

It was a beautiful, sunny autumnal afternoon, quite at odds with the chill that suffused Joanna as they approached the gate leading onto Dartmoor and found the bicycle still leaning there.

"Oh no!" groaned Diane, whose lip started trembling again.

Kate turned on her, jabbing a finger and hissing: "You'll have to control that if we're going to come through this." But as she turned back to look at the bicycle it was clear, to Joanna at least, that Kate's anger was interwoven with a thread of another colour, visible for a brief moment but now defying the eye once more.

Joanna's thoughts returned to more pressing matters. "We're going to have to look for him," she said.

"No way."

Kate's response brooked no argument and Joanna's new-found steel soon proved to be brittle: "But we have..."

"Think about it, stupid!" There was nothing indefinable or evasive about the anger in Kate's eyes now and Joanna took an involuntary step back. "His parents will have missed him by now. They might not know to look here specifically, but at some point they'll be searching the district. We don't want to be wandering around here, conducting our own search, just in case..." she hesitated, "...just in case something bad has happened. We need to get away from here quickly. Luckily, I don't think many people come out this way – ergo the bicycle still being here; it's too dangerous on this part of the moor."

Both Joanna and Diane looked in shock at her.

"You knew it was dangerous?" said Joanna. For once their companion – 'friend' seemed a misplaced word at that moment – was silent. "What if he's dead?"

That peculiar thread glinted in the sun again as Kate spoke: "Well then it doesn't matter, does it?" The other girls gasped. "I mean there's nothing we can do then; we can't turn back the clock and bring him to life." Her features shifted. "Look, I'm sorry if that's what's happened – really. I only meant to play a trick on him; teach him a bit of a lesson. But what's done is done. If we allow ourselves to be tied up in this, it could ruin our lives." She focussed on Diane, using inherent cunning to apply pressure on the weakest link. "We might end up in one of those borstals."

Joanna felt the whip of righteous indignation being ripped from her hands and she was powerless to resist it. But she knew, even as Kate continued, that if their friendship survived this, it would forever be on a different footing.

"And you know what they do to scaredy-cats like you in borstal, Diane. And after that you'll have a criminal record; won't be able to go to university or get a good job, or travel. Look, there's nothing to connect us to this, so let's just keep it that way. And if anything comes up on the news, if his parents are looking for help, somehow we'll tip them off; put an anonymous letter in the post or something."

It all made sense to Joanna, much as she hated herself for admitting it. Defeated, but still resisting, she asked: "Why did you come out here today Kate; really?"

In answer, Kate pointed to the bike. "To see if this was still here; and to get rid of it. Without it, no-one will ever really know."

"Surely then there's no chance of anyone ever finding him."

Kate looked across the moor. "It's better that way." Her eyes focussed on the bike again. "Besides, I've seen lots of programmes about police forensic work. If they come here they'll find some trace of us. Look at the ground; here are our tyre tracks. There might be a thread of your dress snagged on something. But if no-one sees a bike here, I bet you no-one will stop. I know where I can hide it. I'll sneak out tonight and dump it in the quarry."

"Tonight?" said Joanna, aghast.

"Yes. Some of us aren't afraid of the dark." Kate shuddered in anticipation. "It'll be exciting; my own secret mission in the night."

Joanna felt any remaining nervous energy draining from her, till her legs seemed rooted to the soil, bound forever to this place of wrong-doing. Kate was watching her, and her features seemed to soften, just for a moment, as she addressed her.

"I am sorry, Joanna. I didn't mean it to go this far. But now that it has we must stick together." She turned one last time towards the moor. "You never know, in some ways it might have been

224

the best thing for him. What sort of a life do you think he had till now? I don't think we're the only people who will have treated him this way."

* * *

Joanna could not remember the exact point at which she stopped seeing a white face in the dark, but its after-image grew ever fainter with the repeated blinks of each passing day. There was also some indefinable point at which the sound of a police siren no longer set her heart racing. There was never any news of a manhunt, a lost boy, or at least none that ever filtered its way to her. Then, somewhere along the journey she passed the marker that pointed the way to the rest of her life. Perhaps it was when she first fell in love; the sickness that drives away one set of selfish thoughts and introduces another all-consuming variety. Somehow, a combination of the resilience of youth and the human defence mechanism contrived to bring her to a point of, if not contentment, then calmness; stasis.

Now, of course, thirty years later, she recognised that the demons had just been locked in a soundproof room, not silenced; that there had been an equilibrium in her life, perhaps even happiness, that she would never know again and which had only been the calm before the storm.

Diane's whisper was the precursor of the howling tempest. "Joanna," – her voice was shaking – "what is that in the long grass the other side of the gate?"

Chapter Thirteen

Though both women were paralysed in thought and action, Joanna knew just sitting in the car was not an option.

How had she missed it in the first sweep of headlights?

"Oh God." It was all she could think of to say and the only thing that seemed appropriate, though heaven knew He had played no part in that misadventure of her youth.

Diane shook her head. "Can we just leave?"

Joanna didn't even look at her as she replied: "There's only one answer to that. Unfortunately, it's not the one you want to hear."

Diane was shrinking in her seat. "You go if you want. I'm going nowhere."

"I didn't come all the way out here just to turn and head home."

The conviction in her voice was a lie; there was a game of cat's cradle going on in her guts.

When Diane rounded on her, it was so out of character, it just added to the impression the world was turning the wrong way. "Don't be so ridiculous, Joanna! Can't you see someone is playing with you? The past doesn't work this way. You don't just find it by looking backwards."

Joanna waited, avoiding a knee-jerk response. Getting angry with her friend wasn't going to help. If someone was toying with them, they needed to stick together. "Maybe it's time for me to stop being a victim."

With that, she got out of the car. The wind did its best to wrench any resolve from her, pulling the door in her hand and nipping at her, but she tried to evince calmness and insouciance, in part for the sake of poor, weak Diane, but also for her own.

That determination lasted for as long as it took her to wander across to the gate and look at the old bicycle lying there in the grass. The sight of it provoked a chill that no amount of fleeces or high-tech walking gear could keep out.

Diane had got out of the car. "Is it...?"

Joanna nodded. "Yes, it's the same one. It has to be." She looked across the bleak moor. "Kate...where are you? What's your part in this play?" If ever a sign were needed of the topsy-turvy nature of things now, it was Joanna's growing concern for the safety of her self-assured friend. "I left her a message telling her the time and the place. Maybe she's not as strong as we thought."

"Or maybe she doesn't see the point."

Joanna ignored that. Turning back to the car, she opened the boot and pulled on a thicker fleece, a waterproof and walking boots. Looking up, she noticed Diane had made no move to do the same, but stood rather, with hands thrust into her thin fleece and shoulders hunched against the chill that emanated from within.

"You can stay here if you want." Joanna's tone was sympathetic.

Diane continued to stare across the moor. "What are we

even looking for? Where do we start?"

That did stop Joanna in her tracks for a moment. "Good questions both. I'm really not sure." She thought about it a while longer. "I guess we're looking for Tom, or at least to come to a full appreciation of what we may have done to him. And who knows; perhaps we'll come to a better understanding of ourselves in the process. We need to pay penance for what we did."

"What did we do?" Diane turned to her.

"Forget."

* * *

As they picked their way with care through the tangled gorse of the moor, one thing did become clear to Joanna; things were going to get more surreal before the denouement. When you found yourself at dawn on a blind trail across unwelcoming moorland in the hope of shedding light on a thirty year old conundrum and bringing yourself some peace - or at least clarity – of mind, it was obvious that your life had indeed stepped off the marked path.

But would there be a butterfly on the sole of her shoe? Would she return to the world she knew to discover that it had only ever been a place of fragility; made of ice or wax, where fate had been waiting to hold the flame a little closer? And was it to fate that she owed the prescience of her thoughts from the moment she found that serpent coiled in the shadows of her cellar; the immediate knowledge that the stranger had arrived for a reason; that he was a key in need of a lock? And did that make her just a gatekeeper – or Pandora?

Yet in many ways, despite the physical discomfort of that exposed landscape, she was relieved that the moment was finally upon them.

They carried on for some indeterminate time. The stumbling nature of their route and its gradients had rendered the passing of minutes or hours vague at best. Joanna never looked back - ironic under the circumstances – but not because she feared turning into a pillar of salt. She was heading towards her judgement, not fleeing it. She might have been avoiding looking at Diane, but that was another matter.

Then at last they stopped, just beneath the brow of a hill, hearing the unmistakable breathing of a tidal ebb and flow. For just a second or two it seemed to be the rhythm of the moor, still not roused from its sleep. A few more steps and they found themselves staring at the grey, heaving waters of the Atlantic.

Despite the circumstances, Joanna was moved. "Immense," she said, her hand making a sweeping gesture towards the sea, "and unforgiving."

Diane nodded.

"Just like mankind," continued Joanna, before reconsidering. "No, it's different." She paused. "What am I trying to say? I mean, take us; the reason we're here today. Sometimes we try to suppress our conscience, but can't – not forever. It never gives us a break. With the sea -" she sought the word "- it's remorseless. I mean, it feels no remorse. It feels neither pity nor malice; answers to no higher power; not even mortality."

229

Diane seemed not to be in the mood for lyricism or reflec-
tiveness. The trek appeared to have robbed her of both breath
and will. "What now? Why did we come this way, Joanna;
why?"

"This was the general direction he ran in. I guess I was
hoping we might see some sign he had come this way."

"Thirty years on? Such as?"

She ignored the laconic question – she had no answer.
"Let's walk as far as the cliff edge and, if we see nothing that
sparks any ideas, we'll say a prayer asking for forgiveness
and head home. At least we came; we tried."

"But what were you hoping to find? I still don't really get
it."

Joanna thought for a moment. "I don't know exactly, Diane.
Perhaps just something – some illumination – that would
help me to forgive myself."

They had left even the faintest of sheep-trails behind now and
wings of panic had just started fluttering once more in Diane's
stomach when Joanna stumbled and disappeared from view
over a little eroded verge. Diane ran up and looked down at
her.

"Joanna, are you ok?"

Joanna was sitting, gazing ahead. She didn't respond.
Diane scurried along and down the ledge of land to join her.

"Are you ok?" she asked again.

"Uh huh...yes." It wasn't much of a response.

"Did you take a blow to the head?"

Joanna realised she appeared to be staring at nothing, just
at the lip of land down which she had fallen, so she lifted her
hand and pointed. Now she scrambled to her feet, reached

forward and drew back some of the gorse, wild flowers and deadfall as if they were curtains – which was when they noticed some of the branches were loose.

Both women caught their breath as shapes emerged, alien to that environment; pieces of wood, possibly driftwood, uneven in size, but in a regular pattern. They had been lashed together with discoloured rope, through which were wound pieces of gorse, briar and grass creating a second level of disguise behind the initial layer. Joanna moved the cunning construction to one side to reveal a concealed entrance. Dark and dank, it might have been the mouth of the moor's ancient spirit. Diane shuddered. She pressed against Joanna for both comfort and protection."

"What is this place?" Diane's voice quivered

"An educated guess would be a mine – originally," replied Joanna. "But I fear that it became the repository for something else – or should I say the resting place."

With that, Joanna made to enter.

Diane gave an incredulous snort. "You're joking, of course; I mean about me going in there." She straightened up, feigning the bravado to match her words. "What say we don't? It's bound to be dangerous – the Health and Safety Executive haven't paid a recent call, I would suggest. And if Tom went in there and never emerged…look, no-one knows we're here."

Joanna opened a clenched fist. "I more or less landed on it. I suspect the question of whether Tom went in here or not is no longer up for debate."

Diane looked in dismay at the pink plastic watch in Joanna's palm. Her heart sank.

Joanna continued: "And as for whether anyone knows

we're here..." she looked around, "...oh, I think someone does. You were right about someone playing with us. But I can't turn back now. I need to know. Hope you understand. If you want to stay out here, that's fine."

Now Joanna stooped and entered the black portal. To follow her took reserves of courage Diane didn't possess. Ignoring that fact was an unfortunate lack of judgement.

Chapter Fourteen

They entered what appeared to be a tunnel with a gradual downward slope. Joanna reached into her coat pocket and produced a torch – a Maglite with a candle bulb feature in the handle.

Even with the entrance open, the immediate darkness was so dense they could almost taste it. Their eyes adjusted to the remnants of light and then Joanna flicked on the torch.

"I suspect this was someone's crude attempt at copper mining centuries ago," she said. "The area is riddled with mines. Long ago, this region was the source of most of the world's copper."

"Thanks for the history lesson."

Once again, Joanna ignored her friend's sarcasm. She had decided talking about something in which she was interested was a good distraction; an alternative to the other attractions on this ghost ride: blind panic and horror.

"It was shipped all over the civilised world and made some people extremely wealthy. This was probably someone's attempt at getting rich quick."

"Are you for real?"

"What?" She knew what.

"I know you've always had an interest in local history, but

would you mind doing me the very great favour of shutting up. I'm really not in the mood."

So much for that theory then.

They walked on in silence, which Joanna broke at last.

"You're right, of course. Sorry."

"I'm sorry too."

The place – the low ceiling, the darkness, the presumed recent history - was weighing on them both.

Then Joanna stopped in her tracks, gasping and provoking a sympathetic response from Diane. "Take care now, because who knows whether Tom did."

She switched the torch function to beam and aimed it downwards to illustrate her point.

They found themselves looking into some sort of deep pit.

"Get rich quick, eh," said Diane, swallowing hard. "Or die trying; as that awful song says." "So what is it?"

Joanna just shrugged. "I'm not sure. It doesn't really matter, does it?"

Diane shook her head and continued to stare down the pit. "Probably not."

Joanna swung the beam across the bottom of the hole, sweeping the floor with the light.

"Any sign of...?" Diane seemed reluctant to mention the name in there.

"No, but we need a closer look. The beam is too narrow and the candle-function not bright enough."

Diane pointed a reluctant finger down into the shadows. "You're not expecting us to...?"

"If you want answers, yes."

"What answers? I didn't ask for any answers, Joanna. There are no answers, only assumptions."

"No, Di, those assumptions may become answers, but either way, this is something we must experience for a full understanding. You can turn back now, of course, but I feel if something I did led to an innocent boy ending up in this..." she looked around the pit, shaking her head, lost for words. "...dreadful, dreadful place, then I owe it to him to share some part of that with him. And if I do, so do you."

"Fine, just fine!" *Fine...fine...fine...fine.* Diane's raised voice echoed, mocking both women. She dropped it to an irate whisper. "Pity the main culprit isn't here."

Joanna glared at her. "Yup – we were just following orders." Her dismissiveness left only room for the silence that followed.

Now she spotted something near the lip of the drop and shone the torch onto it, revealing a rope.

"Oh no!" groaned Diane, "I was never any good at rope climbing. I was hoping there might be a ladder."

She gave a pleading look to Joanna, who knew her own eyes said *don't desert me now.* "Don't worry," she said, "the first part is technically rope descending and I'll haul you back up if I have to. It's probably about twenty feet at..."

She stopped and caught her breath.

"What is it?" asked Diane, leaning as far forward as her back-on-heels stance would allow.

They could both see the small rectangular object lying on a small ledge just about halfway down the rock-face.

"Hard to say," Joanna replied, "but it looks like a book of some sort."

"Odd."

"After all we've been through in the last twenty-four hours, it's weird that this seems odd." Joanna gave a sardonic grin and both women laughed – a nervous sound, if cathartic. Again the echoes in the chamber caused them to wince. "Let's see if we can grab the book on the way down."

Needing to keep moving, Joanna looped the rope through an iron hook in the floor, which was hammered deep into the rock. She pulled it with all her might to test it.

"Clearly this has always been the means of entrance and egress," said Joanna. "Boy, they bred them tough back then."

With that, she inched over the drop, having put the torch onto candle mode and left it with Diane. She descended into darkness; the fulfiller of her own prophecy.

She was rather glad to have gone first as she started a gentle swing, hoping to bring herself closer to the book on the ledge. It was terrifying to think of the rope somehow breaking free from the iron hook and leaving her to fall into the pit with no means of escape; no-one up top to save her or go for help. For that reason, she contemplated continuing alone, but that wasn't the cosiest prospect either and the contemplation was stifled at birth.

The rope held firm and at last she was able to grasp the ledge and grab the book, which she stuffed into her jacket pocket.

That part of the mission accomplished, she continued down and called out when she had reached the ground. Next came the torch. Joanna made a safety net for it with her jacket before it was thrown down. The prospect of being here with no light filled her with horror and she was so grateful for having packed it, like all good, experienced hikers, even though she had only expected to be clambering around on the moor, not under it.

Now Diane followed; less confident, but with increasing

assuredness as the ground drew nearer. Although Joanna, just like her friend, had always been poor at climbing ropes, or other such tomboyish activities, she hadn't hesitated, fearing Diane might otherwise panic. Though she couldn't have come out here alone, and despite their exchange of views moments before, Joanna was torn with regret for having dragged her more fragile companion along on this dreadful trail.

Once they were both down, Joanna looked up at the rope, contemplated giving it a tug to check it, but then decided against it and to banish all thoughts of the climb back till they were unavoidable.

In this lower chamber, the sense of isolation and claustrophobia was growing by the minute. They were now truly in the big, strong, inhuman hands of Mother Earth and had to hope that she was in nurturing rather than destructive mode. They could hear the wind and the sea, the latter sound all the more unnerving for being above them, somewhere up in the gloom.

"Where to now?" asked Diane, her tone suggesting the preferred answer would be anything suggesting reverse gear.

Joanna swept the torchlight in a circle. The floor of the cave was damp but they made no gruesome discovery. Directing the beam onto the walls revealed an opening to the left and closer inspection showed it to be a tunnel.

"I don't like this," said Diane. "Not at all."

"Whereas I'm absolutely in my element," was Joanna's ironic reply. She shone the torch into the tunnel. "I can't believe I'm even contemplating going down there, but I have to." Hearing Diane's intake of breath, she pre-empted the objection. "I have one torch and there's two of us. If you want to wait here that's up to you, but..." She could tell Diane

237

got her drift. "This way then," she said and set off.

With perhaps her third or fourth step she slipped, just managing to stay on her feet. Several times in the next minutes, they clung to each other to prevent a nasty fall.

The tunnel proved to be longer than the entrance shaft, narrower too, so that the sound of the sea continued to reach their ears with the resonance of a conch. At last, the pattern of the reflected light and sound changed and the women found themselves stepping into another chamber, from which led further tunnels. Joanna played the beam of the torch across the roof of this inner space, revealing it to be far higher than the tunnels; almost vaulted.

Perfect acoustics then for the screams that tore from their throats as the beam lowered and they saw the thing on the floor. The dancing shadows in the eye-sockets and cheek hollows gave the skull macabre, false life and Joanna wondered for a brief, insane moment whether it was the dark man himself. The skeleton was tucked against a boulder by the wall of the chamber.

"Who is it?" Diane's whisper was hoarse; raw.

Joanna recovered some of her composure. "Perhaps a redundant question under the circumstances, given the reason we're here."

She put down the torch, standing it on end and setting it to candle mode again. It threw a haunting light in the grim surroundings. In the glow they could see that it was a small skeleton rather than that of a full grown man.

Joanna moved towards the figure despite Diane plucking in protest at her sleeve. She squatted down and patted her jacket, looking for the pink watch, intending to place it next to the body. Instead, her hands felt the edge of the book, which she removed from her pocket. "First things first," she said, returning to Diane and the torchlight.

It was a plastic-covered notepad, held closed with a rubber band. As Joanna opened it, she recognised the paper and it was evident that a page had been ripped out.

"The poem?" she whispered as she and Diane exchanged an ominous glance. The exact significance of that possibility, if indeed it had any, escaped them for now.

They turned to the last few pages.

"Oh God!" said Diane, turning away after scanning a few words. "I don't want to read this."

"We must." Joanna was resolute. "These pages can be our penance."

"I can't!"

"Then I will read for both of us."

In Joanna's hand was some sort of journal kept by Tom; a brief, but tragic diary of a boy with no-one to talk to but himself; no-one to react off. Perhaps he kept notes so that when he woke each morning he had some proof that he did indeed exist; fragments of a ruin. And he had kept that journal to the end. Joanna was determined to let him live for a moment through his words.

In pondering Tom's sad life and horrid end, she found herself getting irritated as she looked across at Diane's fraught demeanour; she was like someone desperate to wake from a nightmare. She was withdrawing so far into her carapace that Joanna felt cheated of the moral support she, too, could have used at that moment. Sometimes, pleading insanity was the easy way out. From what she read, it seemed poor Tom – *poor Tom's a-cold* – was cursed with lucidity in his darkest hours. She would free his restless words from the

239

pages.

Her capricious mind took her back for an instant to poetry readings in the café and she tried closing out the image, just as she imagined soldiers had to banish thoughts of home on the verge of battle. That way did lie madness.

My leg hurts. It feels broken. Even if it isn't, I won't get out. There's a rope lying on the floor next to me; old, frayed. It must have come loose from up there.

That caused her a few seconds' pause, given the rope she had found. Perhaps he had escaped!

Way to go, Joanna! So who's this lying dead here?

She had to read on.

I've given up calling; the echoes are more frightening than the silence. And I don't suppose they would hear me, even if they were looking, which I doubt. This must have been a trick. It always is."

As she flipped over a page, Joanna reeled from the unexpected, dignified eloquence of the dead boy. Allowing herself a glance, she noted with horror the greenstick fracture in the ossified bone of the silent witness. She took in, also, more of the dark patches on the floor, which she could see now were seaweed.

"Is it his?" Diane had retreated to the penumbra at the edge of the torchlight.

"Yes. There are no dates - I guess down here that became an irrelevance — but it's his final moments." Joanna delved into her pocket and removed the watch. "The watch appears to have stopped at 6 o'clock; let's assume that's the time of...his fall outside."

She resumed reading in silence:

"They're not coming. My own screaming is just making me scared. Despite the leg, I have to see what's in the tunnels."

Another page.

"I have lights in my eyes from the pain, but everywhere else is black. But now I've seen it will be over soon. There was a rock-fall at the far end of the main tunnel. Perhaps I could move it, but I think there's water coming. It sounds angry. It's coming fast. Perhaps I will be safe back where I fell. If not, I saw a ledge above the spot where I landed. If I can get back to that, perhaps I can stay above the water and try again tomorrow."

She snapped the book shut.

Joanna could have sworn she heard her eyelids squeezing tight.

Despite the immensity of her guilt, Joanna's mind was snatching at other data; seaweed the fact that not only had the sound of the sea not diminished, it had grown in intensity.

A sea cave.

It was from somewhere ahead that the surge of the Atlantic reached her ears, bringing its paradoxical mix of comfort and despair, and providing the most incongruous soundtrack to the scene.

Gathering the tattered remnants of her courage together, she wandered back to the bones and addressed them:

"What can I say when sorry sounds so weak and inappropriate? But it is penitence that has brought me here, not idle curiosity. We were young..." she raised her hands in a gesture of appeasement, "...I know, I know - younger people have leapt into rivers in spate to save a dog," – the last word was spat out with such self-loathing, Joanna half expected to see it glistening phlegm-like on the floor – "sacrificed their ambitions to care for sick relatives." Now her fingers twiddled and tapped at the sides of her thighs. "Youth is no excuse."

She looked at the pitiful pink watch and all strength drained from her. Dropping to her knees, she whispered: "I'm sorry. I'm so sorry."

Somewhere in the distance a wave broke, sounding for all the world like it might spew down the tunnel and swamp them. Both women cast nervous glances, but then Joanna regained her focus:

"My God, what did we condemn you to?" She looked at Tom. "I swear we never intended you to die."

But you knew that he might; that any number of horrible ends might have been his.

Diane had kept her distance, but found her voice and as it squeaked its way from her constricted chest Joanna grew very concerned.

"Have you no mercy? We were young and stupid." She smiled in nervous hope. "We came back, but allowed..." the smile faded as she hesitated "...Kate to talk us out of... whatever we were going to do."

The denial in those words was written large, as if Kate had been their dark mistress.

"Diane, that condemns, rather than condones our actions. We were the ones with consciences that we suppressed. The worse crime was ours."

Each breath of the ocean was accompanied now by a pleuritic rumble. Joanna felt its resonance and wanted to be away from there. Atonement could be a long process; her journey had begun, but she would continue it in the world of light, not down here. She would pay due penance; even return and collect these remains for a proper burial, but first, she needed to escape this terrible place. She got to her feet and said:

"Where there is crime, there is punishment. I will never forget how horrible it must have been to die down here in the darkness and the flood."

The flood! Crime and punishment. The punishment should fit the crime.

"Diane, what date is it!"

Diane was looking towards the tunnels down which the pounding of the ocean was growing in ferocity. She looked tearful, just on the cusp of mild hysteria.

"Um...what...Thursday?!"

"Date! I don't know why I'm asking anyway; it's the twenty-fourth of September."

"So what, Joanna? Please can we get out of here?"

Joanna sprang to her feet. "Damn right we can! It's autumnal equinox, give or take, and that will mean spring tides." She stopped. "Wait a minute – when did we...when would the whole thing have happened?"

It was a rhetorical question, but she could see that the answer had occurred to Diane too.

"You mean we're not safe?"

"We were never safe, Diane, but I wasn't worried like I am now - like I feel there's something at play which is way beyond us. C'mon, let's get out of here to higher ground."

What happened next was not a blur; *that* requires light.

As Diane turned, she knocked the Maglite. It was a robust hiker's torch, but the exposed candle-bulb at the end was fragile and was snuffed out like a life. Through the growing tumult they heard the light tumble somewhere in amongst the rocks. Both women stumbled, screamed and, as if propelled by an unseen hand, landed in vertiginous darkness, all breath gone from them. Sucking in deep, Joanna filled her

243

lungs with air.

"Joanna!"

The scream was a black light in the darkness. As it faded and bounced, other words filled the space: *the echoes are more frightening than the silence.*

"Diane?"

"Joanna, keep talking to me!"

"I'm here." She reached out; waved her arm around blindly.

"Oh God, help, Joanna, help!"

She reached towards the sound and caught a handful of fleece, which brought momentary comfort out of all proportion to the event. Pulling her friend towards her, she felt desperate arms grip her.

"Stay calm, Diane, stay calm." The litany helped her focus, an anchor in the bedlam of thoughts.

"Oh my God, Joanna, oh my God!"

"I think he's lost his torch too."

How very British of her it was, to find time for graveyard humour, but it did help. Her panicking friend would either drag her screaming into the whirlpool of madness or make her be strong for both of them, so Joanna chose the latter.

"Quiet, Di." Joanna clocked how unfortunate that diminutive was under the circumstances – a millisecond's distracted thought before she tried to concentrate again. "We must try to orientate ourselves by listening."

The tidal surges were growing in intensity, resounding in the cavern and making directional sense impossible.

Then it struck Joanna. "The skeleton; we have to find it. Stay with me – we can orientate ourselves from there."

Clinging together – they were almost invisible to each other

- they listened for the next surge of the tide, then turned away from it and headed to their right. They met solid wall.

"This way," said Joanna.

Soon enough her reaching hand grasped the repulsive frame of the dead boy's ribcage. Creeping forward along the wall, the two blind mice came at last to the opening of the approach tunnel, which would lead them up and out – of the lower section at least – to the chamber into which they had abseiled; a place that seemed like sanctuary now. Though she didn't voice her fears, Joanna doubted it would seem that way for long.

How far would the avenging angels take this punishment? Joanna harboured no doubts now – a power beyond her control had driven this. She would not allow herself to believe there had been any supernatural intervention, but there were too many coincidences, the last one being the date.

But for now there were more pressing matters. Would the rope still be there? If not, would they be able to find and reach the ledge in the darkness. These were the only questions that needed answers; the ones that meant survival.

They pushed ahead, cautious and blind, following on the heels of a chimera, while all the time, inexorable and ever louder, a remorseless monster dogged their steps.

Chapter Fifteen

When Kate reached the gate, as per the voicemail instructions, she took in the diffuse light and enjoyed the air blowing through her gills. She pulled off the baseball cap, allowing the breeze to ruffle her hair, kept short for as long as she could ever remember. A strange thing; memory. If she wasn't careful she would soon be finding it hard to remember what a sunrise looked like. The last few days had in many ways brought the peculiar fulfilment of her darkest imaginings, but not in the way they had played out in past dreamscapes. Each dawn found her waking to a world in which her heart, her body and, most puzzling of all, her mind ached.

Last night and the early hours of this morning had been different – the strangest acts she had committed at his bidding. She would deny him nothing; wished there was more of herself she could give, but also needed to understand why she felt compelled and why everything filled her with a sense of dizzying unease? Was it some genetic curse of humankind?

She found herself wondering now about this place. Why was she here? She looked around. There was something; this gate; this gusting breeze, the way it rippled her hair; the whispering as the hem of its coat dragged through the gorse.

The parked-up car looked out of place, like it really didn't belong, but at least she knew it meant she was at the right location. The bicycle – its place in things – was much more disturbing.

As she continued to scan her surroundings, hands stuffed in the pockets of her cardigan, she was startled, despite everything she'd been through, to see a figure standing on a distant crag; a tiny slash in the canvas of the seascape. How long had he been there, watching her? Was it years? She blinked and he had gone.

It stirred her into action. She clambered over the gate and set off in that direction.

Chapter Sixteen

The women stumbled from the tunnel back into the first chamber, to the temporary relief offered by the meagre light which made it down to this level.

The rope, and the climb it offered, seemed twice as long as before.

"I'll go first," said Joanna. "That way, I can help pull you up when it's your turn."

She watched Diane look in terror back down the tunnel they had just exited and assumed her friend would insist on going first. The flow of the distant sea was a menacing roar - a first dummy attack by a lion which was growing bolder and hungrier; each ebb bringing temporary relief before the next advance. Nevertheless, Diane agreed with the decision and Joanna gripped the rope with both hands, hoping desperation would give her strength.

Too much strength perhaps. As she hauled herself off the ground, there was a grinding sound from above and both rope and hook came flying over the lip with misplaced glee, to land twisted on the floor beside her. It seemed powers other than hers had decided it was not to be. She imagined white fingers loosening the hook.

Hadn't she known this would happen? Why didn't she

listen to her instincts? Though Joanna had swallowed her fears for Diane's sake, they came spewing forth now as cries for help. A combination of terror and their recent arduous progress as they'd slipped and slid their way back along the uphill tunnel rendered their first shouts weak. Above all though, they were pointless. Who the hell was going to hear them?

Nevertheless, it wasn't difficult to imagine the dark man, whoever he was, standing somewhere out of sight listening to them, soaking up their panic and pain by some osmotic process; growing stronger for it. Joanna gave up before Diane, though not through despair. It was partly a stubborn streak; she wouldn't allow their tormentor that pleasure. However, her friend's cries soon became too much for her.

"Diane...Diane, stop!"

The sounds were sapping her energy and she sat down, pressing her hands to her temples. Right now she didn't need the added stress of seeing the tear-stained face of her friend; witnessing the hysteria, the breakdown, which she knew was inevitable.

"But we have to do something," remonstrated Diane; a reasonable enough statement. "We have...to do...SOMETHING!"

Joanna dropped her hands and looked across, regretting, but unable to control the anger in her tone. "And we will. Screaming at the top of your voice isn't it. What did..." - she hesitated – "...Tom write in his diary? The echoes, the sound of his own voice, only made things worse." Then her expression softened. "Look, come and sit here for a moment." Diane obeyed, but there would be no arm of consolation around her shoulder. Joanna had enough of a burden to bear; the twofold guilt of the original sin and of having dragged

Diane into this mess through her need for catharsis. She was going to have to support herself for a while before attending to anyone else's needs.

She tried to think it through. "Hopefully someone will see the car."

Diane was sitting with her head in her hands and her voice was muffled. "The punishment should fit the crime, you said. We took the bike away – you think whoever's stalking us won't take the car? And if it's not him...well, what chance anyone caring? Oh look, a car by a gate. There must be two women trapped in a hidden pit after chasing shadows."

Diane might have been on the margins of despair, but her reasoning was sound enough – it would indeed require a peculiar leap of imagination.

"Perhaps he's just teaching us a lesson and he'll come back for us."

From the corner of her eye Joanna saw Diane raise her head and look at her. No words were needed. She clasped her knees and tried just to shut it out for a moment.

And impossible though it should have been, her body's defence mechanism must have allowed her to drift into a sleep. From somewhere in that surreal power-nap she could hear her deep, rhythmic breathing and a voice telling her it would be good not to wake. Was this how it had been for Tom; a sudden calmness and the urge to give up the fight? For everyone the time would come, though they might cling by the tips of their fingers to the edge of the abyss. Perhaps it was best sometimes to plunge into the deep - still whole in mind and body - rather than slide in miserable fear; aged fingers grasping at immutable stone, dystrophic muscles quivering, addled brain regaining awareness long enough to be terrified.

But something was wrong here; discordant. A frantic voice. Her arm being shaken.

"The sea – it's the sea!"

A cold awakening indeed, in all senses – an icy one.

"Oh my God!" Joanna recognised now that there was to be no salvation except of their own making; that the dark man was without mercy. She saw, too - a fragment of insight amidst the chaos – the utter naivety of her previous thoughts. The prospect of dying down here could inculcate into your very bones a frenzy for life with each rising surge of chilling water.

But such reflections could wait. "I didn't think the tide would come this far."

She cursed herself. The damp floor of the pit should have given some clue.

The water glistened in the mouth of the tunnel. The next surge sent it spilling into chamber, already halfway across the floor; a horrible, wet, pulsing beast in the murky light.

Joanna looked up and around, then pointed: "There."

"What?" said Diane.

"The ledge. C'mon, let's see if we can get up there."

"But what if the water comes...?"

"For God's sake, Diane, we must do something?"

"That's what I said before and you shut me up."

"You were just wasting energy." She raised a hand to stave off further protest. "Look, this tide must have climbed a fair distance already, so hopefully it's not going to make another eight or nine feet."

It took just a couple of trial leaps to convince Joanna they weren't going to reach the ledge that way, or if they did they wouldn't be able to hold on.

And the water was coming. Having flooded the other tunnels it had funnelled into the chamber, having nowhere else to go. Already it was around their knees.

"Quick," said Joanna as the cold of that spring tide made aching progress into her joints. "Give me a leg-up."

"Why don't you give me a leg-up?"

"Because I'm stronger than you."

"Well exactly."

"No, I mean once I'm up there I can pull you up."

Diane glanced over her shoulder and then, seeming to realise that it would be futile and maybe fatal to argue, she made a stirrup with her hands and heaved till Joanna could haul herself up and onto her elbows.

Which was where Joanna met the next problem; one with no solution; as intractable as the stone facing her from perhaps a foot away. The darkness had deceived them. There might have been room up there for one person to rest a part of their body long enough for the tide to pass – if indeed it would – but, for sure, not for two.

She glanced down, past her shoulder, at Diane's pale, quivering face and the swirling vortex of water, already up to her midriff.

Chapter Seventeen

He was further away than she'd thought. Every time she looked up he seemed no closer and sometimes he wasn't there at all, till she doubted everything and assumed she was hallucinating. Then he would reappear, but the distance never closed. The undulations of the land hid him from view much of the time. Another ridge crested; another one stood between them. It was starting to annoy her. Was he playing some sort of game? He liked games. Perhaps this was foreplay on a cosmic scale and he was leading her towards some ancient barrow where he planned to have her again. But some instinct, honed by the increasing cut of the wind out there, warned her that this was no tryst. Something was moving in time with her as she trod her way across the damp soil and through gorse soaked by showers and sea air, and though it had never accompanied her before, she recognised it as fear.

There was a dream-like quality to her progress and again, for a moment she wondered whether she were, indeed, asleep, but restless, as so often of late. Yet the discomfort of this place seemed real enough.

At last, after one more Sisyphean effort, she was shocked to find him standing there, his proximity startling her. They stood motionless, buffeted by the wind; a tiny piece of Easter Island transported to the south-west of Britain. The disorientation continued; she felt all at sea – in all senses. The flapping of his coat might have been sails billowing in the breeze and nearby she heard the unmistakeable roar of the Atlantic. She knew how it had to be, so waited for him to break the silence:

"They say you can hear the voices of the dead out here."

There it was again; that unnerving pulse in her brain. Was it triggered by those familiar words or their meaning?

"The moor is full of ghosts," she responded.

He continued to stare ahead in the direction of the sea.

"Yes, but these are the ghosts of the living." Now he turned to her. "The soon-to-be-dead."

He gestured towards some point in the middle-distance. "Listen carefully and you might catch their sound on the wind."

As he looked at her she realised it was the first time she'd seen something cold in his eyes. Oh, there was always cruel humour, as if humanity amused him, or a glint, but she'd taken it for steel, not ice. This was different; a deadness.

"What are they," she asked, "these living ghosts?"

He'd not moved to close the gap between them till now, but took a step towards her. "Don't you know? I say 'ghosts', but perhaps there is only one."

Oh my God! Did he mean to kill her? No, that was ridiculous – she was his...soul-mate, for want of better words.

Foreboding; fear; what was happening to her? She could have used a momentary infusion of anger. Most people were robbed of their innocence at some point; throughout her life she had always enjoyed watching the scales fall from

254

their eyes, considering herself immune, though she had still questioned why she seemed devoid of conscience; why things that set other people in a spin left her untouched. Now life appeared to be having a joke at her expense, introducing her to emotional reflexes which, as far as she was concerned, belonged to the same evolutionary group as wisdom teeth and the appendix; redundant yet troublesome.

She had read once that the brain never loses or deletes a memory, but simply files or misfiles it. Though still unsure of what she was remembering, somewhere a dusty box was opening.

Kate stared at him and was greeted by a knowing smile, along with a playful question:

"Is it coming back to you?"

"I'm...I'm not sure."

Of a sudden, she knew there was one huge, fundamental question she had never deemed it necessary to ask: "Who are you?"

It was the strangest thing.

He put a gecko-like finger to the side of each eye; pulled the skin and, with surprising delicacy, reached between his eyelids to remove the contact lenses.

She sank to her knees as the rolling roar of the sea hurled the memories ashore, knocking her off-balance.

"You." Her whisper was abducted by the wind, likewise her senses. She collapsed onto the gorse .

"I understand this is a shock for you," he said. "I hope not an insurmountable one."

There was no response; how could there be?

"I know it must be hard to process; a man you thought was dead – who repelled you – has become your companion and understands you better than you understand yourself. The problem you have – he is you." Now he came and stood by her. She could not yet bring herself to look him in the face again, so the pendulous hands became the focus of her attention. "Now I invite you to experience something greater still; having played the first part of the game with me, I offer you the power over life and death."

Chapter Eighteen

EXTRACT FROM THE JOURNAL OF TOM AND BONES

It was as if I couldn't stop running. More than the desire to find somewhere to hide, out on that moor I was overcome by the sweetness of freedom. I had thought sneaking away from the orphanage and stealing the bicycle had made for a heady day, but it was as nothing compared with racing through the gorse, the wind driving everything from my ears except the sound of my own breathing. Birds flew up in panic from my scatter-brained steps.

And then, my first ever sight of the sea; glistening in the dipping sunlight. I was lost for a time in the wonder of it all.

At last I decided I had better stop somewhere, so that the seekers could find me - which was when fate decided to play its first trick.

I picked up a few stones and started throwing them absent-mindedly. When one of them made a peculiar clunk I wandered over to investigate. When I found a hidden door it seemed to be turning into every boy's dream adventure. It opened onto some sort of tunnel or cave - an abandoned mine, as it turned out. A perfect place to hide; no-one would ever find me there. That last thought brought me to my senses. After all, I'd just made three new friends and wanted to be found. So I wandered in out of *curiosity, fully meaning to return. But I didn't see the drop in the fading light. I hurt my leg; couldn't be sure whether it was broken or not.*

Then I saw something pale lying a little distance from me in the darkness. Two pale patches in fact. An old piece of rope and the skeletal remains of a person.

My ears had been attuning to the darkness and I could have sworn I heard the sea somewhere ahead of me. Such hope that gave me; ironic, when one considers what a pitiless beast it is. I feel an affinity with it to this day. Its roar kept me going as I took on the huge pain in my leg and fought my way through the tunnels. I longed to confront the monster.

At last, after hours of struggling, the darkness lit only by the flaring pain of my injury, I saw the nature of my prison. I stood before a rock-fall, which seemed to fill the entrance to a cave. I could hear and smell the sea on the other side. Nothing had any meaning now except moving those rocks. But how? The smallest of them weighed several pounds, the largest were the size of a humble dwelling. I was a boy of indeterminate age. Yet hope and anger gave me strength. And strange to relate, I forgot all about hope and anger as my whole being threw itself into the task of moving rocks. It was the purest of deeds.

But the joy, when at last I caught a glimpse of the world beyond that wall of rocks. Twice in less than a day, I felt the overpowering wonder of seeing the ocean. Night had fallen, and I fell in love with the night.

I scrambled through the hole I had made – and then my joy became despair as I turned my head and looked up to see the waves were crashing against a wall of cliffs perhaps a hundred feet high and sheer, There was no way I could climb them.

And mocking me from up there was the moon; my owl; its

pale, round face indifferent to my struggles and waiting for me to decide my own fate while it lit the way to temptation.

For a moment I contemplated trying to climb. Surely it was better to die out here in the open, plunge to my death if necessary, trying to scale the cliffs. But then a strange thought; I remembered the third thing I had found lying at the foot of the drop when I first fell into the cave – a friend. I knew I couldn't abandon him, who had also died forgotten. So I turned, exhausted, bleeding where fingernails had ripped away, never to grow again, and made my way back to that place, which, not without humour, I came to call the pit.

I had decided I didn't want to die and spotted a ledge, just about reachable if I jumped. I managed to scramble up; there wasn't much room.

I waited out the turn of the tide. I defied the monster. He would not have me that day. And up there, I made a discovery; found the answer to a question; a half-formed one that must have been waiting.

There was a crevice along the back of the ledge; a further indentation of perhaps a hand's width. As the water swirled below me I tried to jam my hand in there, to ensure I did not slip off the ledge if I passed out. My fingertips touched something. I managed to pull it out – a small leather bag. Even in the meagre light, as I tipped the contents into the palm of my hand I saw them glitter. Of course I could not know for sure, but I was convinced they were diamonds and gold coins. After all, they were not there by accident.

I guessed my friend must have been a smuggler who took a little share of what had never been his to take, and certainly not once it became the property of certain duty-free shoppers. Of course I will never know whether his partners-in-crime suspected him, followed him and loosened the rope. Maybe they tried to make him tell where he had hidden the booty. He might have maintained a stubborn silence, believing he could get out again once they gave up. Or he might simply have been careless in how he tied the rope and it came loose, leaving him trapped. Who knows? The only certainty is; the end of his life is as much a mystery as the beginning of mine. Together, we made a complete secret history.

There was a small...correction... a huge fortune in that tiny pouch. Had my luck finally changed? I remember looking up in anguish at the wall that separated me from freedom; a much more solid wall than the one that barely separates hope and despair. It had been beyond Bones, as I came to call my companion; that is, if he hadn't died from the fall.

But that was when I determined that luck was to play no further part in my life, nor fate. I would be a victim no longer. When the waters at last ebbed, they washed away the dust of my old life.

My hands were so raw now, it didn't matter what I did to them. I found a way – somehow picked a route – up the remainder of the sheer rock, losing the remaining loose nails in the process, until at last I dragged myself over the lip and back into the real world.

The real world.

Was that where I belonged, or even wanted to be? What had it ever given me, compared with the friend, the fortune and the resolution that I had found in my subterranean universe? Already it seemed an alien and discomforting place as I clambered back out onto the moor, though I was grateful for the darkness.

It was, as they say, a piece of cake to find my way back to the gate after what I had been through. The bike was missing. I saw everything then for what it was. The malice in that real world.

Chapter Nineteen

Carried on the wind came the distinct sound of a whistle.

Something was stirring in her stomach. Her brain had rediscovered where it had filed certain memories; deep in the pit; in the gorge where the bile and the acid did their work. It was rising from that gastric swamp, where it had lain in waiting for just this moment. Kate scarcely managed to push herself up onto her knees before vomiting.

"Tom."

She half expected to see the letters spattered like reflux in the gorse, though not as much as she expected to see him when she turned around. He had gone, leaving her the emptiness of the moor. However, the shapes of his last words still flitted there; moths in her subconscious. It was the only way she could be sure he had been there: *"Decision time, Kate. You can go to rescue your friends; you can save a life,"* he had paused, *"but not your own. That belongs to me. But turn your back on me now and you will never see me again."*

What had she done? She had lost him. How could that be? Had she passed out? Things were blurring, where before there had been so much purpose.

She needed the whistle to sound again; just once more. It

had seemed so close before. She should have known where to head, but all her memories seemed to be emerging from a fog and that same mist had clouded her sense of direction for a moment.

The sun decided to mock her deepening depression, putting on a glorious display against the western sky; wrapping up the strands of the day into a big red ball. But she faced it defiant, refusing to look back for her lost soul, despite the screaming of her nerves.

She ploughed on. The moor extended wet fingertips to pull at her ankles. "Joanna!" she called. "Diane!" The wind ripped the words from her mouth and threw them with contempt back in her face.

Yet that same wind carried the sound of the whistle to her.

Someone was still alive. She might well have been damned for thinking it, but if only one of them had survived, she knew who she wanted it to be.

Another whistle – to the right of her. Now the outline of the makeshift door was visible and obvious. It was open.

She chanced a glance back towards the west. Nothing.

He was lost to her now.

Kate looked into the darkness beyond the door and then on into the much murkier realm beyond that. Perhaps it was the sound of the swirling water ahead that triggered it. Her mind was thrown back with such force she stopped in her tracks.

Standing in the entrance of the tunnel, she recalled inching her way along and peering over the lip, heart in mouth, thirty odd years before – very odd years, it seemed.

She had come back without the others; hadn't expected to lie there the previous night tormented by images of him, alone and in danger. Of course, she knew about the old mine. She sought out dark places, even from very young. She had even been in once, got so far and no further, and then consigned it to the dustbin of memories; or rather, thought she had – until Bunny Boy had hopped into their lives, at which point the bin had tipped over, spilling its rotting contents.

It had seemed like a cruel, but funny trick – until they found the bicycle. She hadn't allowed the others to see, but the impact of that moment – the very real possibility that she had caused his death – had shocked her. She'd been grateful that it was the weekend, because it gave her the chance to come back alone the next day.

The mine was the first spot she had searched. As soon as she had stepped through the entrance, she'd known something was different. The rush of the water transformed the nature of the place and the tincture of the danger.

Looking with horror into the pit, to be met by the sight, sound and smell of that black, swirling mass, she'd realised it might have been easier if she had found Tom's body at the bottom; broken, but recognisable. Instead, there was a monster, which had left no trace of her victim, just the rumour of his fate.

Except...except she had spotted the book on the ledge. It was beyond her reach, but she knew she had to have it.

Her parents had known something was wrong. She didn't dare tell them what, but hid behind a headache and went to bed. There was no sleep to be had and she decided she had to return to the mine. She had to know.

All through that night, the question driving her mad was why? What had triggered this exceptional and very unwel-come attack of conscience? The only conclusion she could reach was that, in some way there had been a surreal kinship. He was an outsider; so was she. He perceived life through a different lens as a result of his condition; so, if her parents and the doctors were to be believed, did she. Was that why she had found herself both repelled and yet drawn to him; as a pale – very pale – reflection of herself?

Whatever the reason, she'd gone back the following day, armed with a rope, waterproofs and bars of chocolate. The previous day had been a harsh introduction into the power of spring tides and she had no intention of doing anything other than grabbing the book. The thought of what the receding waters might reveal had tormented her nevertheless.

Again nature had been perverse and her mind followed. The pit was clear of water, but there was no sign of Tom. She had tied the rope to an iron hook near the lip of the drop – it looked old but felt like it would withstand time itself.

Kate had lowered herself over, manoeuvred her way to a point where she could reach the book and was ready to clamber back up…when a capricious finger had tapped her on the shoulder, suggesting the journey wasn't over. She had looked down, then over at the tunnel leading on from the pit. Perhaps there were other answers down there, even if there were no questions.

What she had found down there was an answer of sorts, mainly to the question of why her parents agreed, several disturbed months later, to her having electroconvulsive therapy. They didn't know why her depression deepened, just that they wanted her to be free from it. She knew that now – in her upside-down world she had been granted a gift of hindsight which had been denied before. She had little control over it, but it was illuminating.

Was this his gift?

A shrill blast of the whistle brought her back to the present.

She lit her torch.

"Hello?" A weak and shaking voice called to her. The torch must have seemed like a searchlight.

"Joanna?"

"Oh God, Kate, oh thank God...! Please be careful, there's a drop."

Kate identified the edge and with the delicious, gravity-daring caution of someone peering from the top of a skyscraper she craned her neck.

"Jesus!"

Kate was curled, shivering on a narrow rock ledge. In the dim light she could still make out tearful, exhausted eyes looking up at her.

"Where's Diane?"

The face below just stared back at her. "Help me, Kate."

Kate leaned over the edge.

"Take my hand, Jo." At first Joanna just reached up from her foetal position. "Stand up, Joanna. I can't reach you."

Joanna got to her feet, hesitant, all the time looking beneath at the eddying, inky water. She reached up. Their fingertips brushed.

"C'mon, you can do it."

Joanna stood on tiptoes, while Kate leaned as far as she could and reached. They were not quite palm to palm.

"Joanna, take off your coat. That's right. Now roll it like a rope. Give me one end. Good. OK. You holding firmly? OK, here we go." She got onto her knees. "I'll pull, you climb."

265

A disembodied voice from beyond the edge: "Kate, the coat's tearing – the seam!"

"It's a good coat; it'll hold. Just climb."

Another disembodied voice from the darkness: *I give you the power over life and death.*

"It's splitting, Kate! Kate! The coat's tearing!"

"Keep going, Joanna; just a bit more…"

Suddenly the coat weighed nothing; flew up over the lip of rock - a freakish bird or giant bat disturbed by clumsy movements on a cliff-top.

Kate fell backwards, while a scream followed the coat up over the edge.

Chapter Twenty

She lay there soaked, her sweat so heavy it stained the sheets.

Every night the same dream, so indistinguishable from her memories that she might have been fooled into thinking it was no dream, were it not for the fact of her waking. Perhaps it had always been his plan to destroy the night for her. She slept with the light on. Was that the setting sun of her nightmares, or simply a way to blank the after-image of his face, which pulsed on her eyelids whenever they closed.

She glanced at the clock - 4a.m - doubted now whether his intention had ever been other than to punish her; reeling her in, fulfilling her needs, showing her a promised land of darkness with skies of black velvet and a contorted stone-scape, before leaving her to abandonment of another kind; worst of all, leaving her prey to the alien sensation of vulnerability.

She was a blank canvas now for the universe to colour in. Heaven forbid a conscience might be revealed.

Kate shook her head, attempting to shatter the destructive images. Night after night they came when she woke, and she found them more frightening than the nightmares. At last, powerless as always, she sat up. Once again she needed affirmation of her existence, another irony of Tom's Curse, which included resorting to a notebook by her bed. She doubted everything each night as she lay alone with her thoughts, surrounded by phantom memories. She asked herself whether she had ever been the strong one of the three friends, or had she in fact been the victim of splitting and projection, rejecting her weakness, her obedience and compliance and attributing it to two companions instead. Had she been an unknown planet, its position only discernible through the behaviour of the stars around it?

Those thoughts duly noted in her book, she was suddenly on her feet. Though it was early she needed to get out; what she called 'finding some pieces of mind' when graveyard wit occasionally surfaced.

* * *

The first stop was indeed a graveyard - Highhill Cemetery; the place where for many people everything ends, but for her it had begun.

It was around five in the morning. There was no-one about as she parked up. She couldn't help but glance at the crumbling crypt, wishing he would step from it, beckoning with a freakishly strong hand, though God knew how she would have reacted. Was it just another part of the curse that she would have to come by here every day for that reason alone?

She headed for a new plot with a fresh headstone.

Strange that there were no more tears to feed the flowers. She read in silence:

In loving memory
Diane Horsham
Beloved daughter of....

She read less each time. Maybe catharsis was hers after all.

Now she turned her attention to a second grave. It was near the one she had visited with the dark man on the night of the poetry reading, in the less well-tended part of the cemetery.

To the casual eye the headstone was unmarked, except, typical of the sad, disrespectful times, there was some minor graffiti. Someone had sneaked in one night to scratch a single word: *Tom.*

It had been a struggle persuading the vicar of St Mary's in Highhill to allow the burial, given that the bones found out on the moor by Kate had not been identified. Of course she had lied about finding them out on open moorland, but had not wanted the search parties to make any connection between them and the death of Diane. She had retrieved them in secret from the mine and then claimed to have come across them one day while out hiking. Carbon dating tests were being conducted – for some reason local historians were intrigued - but the vicar was uneasy. Perhaps this was a suicide; maybe even a Satanist. He had wanted to bury the remains in unsanctified ground, but Kate had kicked up such a fuss that, in keeping with the church's modern philosophy of compromise, otherwise known as hedging your bets, they had agreed to an unmarked grave.

Just a couple of sleepless nights later, she had returned at the dead of night to the dead. Visions of *Pet Semetary* had played in her head as she dug down, placed the object at a depth where she believed it would remain undisturbed and covered the grave again. Rather like the Stephen King tale, she wondered whether she was actually giving the ancient bones new life.

Her lips took a peculiar twist now, somewhere between a smile and remorse as she looked down and thought of the broken plastic watch lying in the soil; time refusing to decompose, frustrating worms and environmentalists alike.

She glanced at her own watch. Time was more important to her now, for many reasons. If it weren't for the exhaustion she would have welcomed the sleepless nights; the extra hours they gave her. Nearly six o'clock. She knew Joanna would not have slept well and calling on her at this time would be no problem.

* * *

She didn't bother going via Joanna's house, guessing she would be at the café already, throwing herself into anything that kept her physically busy enough to silence the clamouring of her mind.

For a while after the cave their times together had proved awkward - they had even shied away from pecking each other on the cheek - until the old, but underused engine of their friendship had warmed up and spluttered into life.

Kate sat now in her Land Rover, parked a few yards down from the Art Café, her fingers thrumming on the steering wheel as she watched the soft lighting fall from the window. She felt the furrow forming between her eyebrows, creating the hardening of features that was becoming so familiar in her mirror on the days when she bothered to look. She shuddered, remembering...

...their arrival back at the Café that morning in Joanna's Prius, which Kate had driven, her friend being in no state to be entrusted with control of a car. Kate had left the Land Rover at the...scene. Astonished by the speed with which her thoughts were making their way through the darkness of her mind, Kate had a plan forming already. She needed to get back to the Land Rover before it drew anyone's attention. There were never many people out on that part of the moor at this time of year, but one needed always to allow for Murphy's Law.

In the staff car park at the back of the café. Kate killed the engine and slumped back in her seat. Joanna remained in the position she had adopted for the entire return journey – slouched forward on the edge of the passenger seat, her fingers interwoven, clenched, the knuckles white as if her mind had not yet released the lip of the drop to which she had clung in desperation when the jacket had split .

Kate had watched her or a moment.

"Joanna, you need to open the café. Hard though it is, you really need to carry on as normal. Really"

No response for a few seconds, and then a tear-stained face had turned towards Kate, though still nothing was said.

"Go inside, wash your face and open for business."

"But..."

"Diane?"

Joanna's eyes squeezed shut.

Kate watched with a peculiar detachment as her hand, powered by an ethereal remote-control, traced a slow path through the plasma which separated her from other members of the species and rested on Joanna's arm. Adding to the alien sensation of another person's mass beneath her fingertips was the slight trembling, though Kate could not be sure whether this was Joanna's fearful shivering or her own trepidation.

"Don't you worry about Diane," said Kate, the reassuring tone coated with enough self-deception for them both to allow its sinuous seductiveness to tempt them to forget. "I will deal with that. What's done is done."

Having ensured Joanna pulled herself together enough to give a performance as the enthusiastic owner of a small business, Kate had taken the keys for Diane's Volvo and set off for the now well-trodden corner of their field of nightmares.

It was still early and she passed no other vehicles or hikers during the final leg of the journey. Parking the Volvo by the gate, she had ensured there were no signs that anyone else had been around in recent times. There were no tyre tracks to speak of as the patch of ground by the gate was heavily overgrown with grass and weeds. Footprints? – well, she wasn't about to trail across the entire route eradicating those, but boot-marks across moorland were about as unusual as rat-droppings in a mill.

She didn't know how long it would be before the searching would begin, but Kate would make sure Joanna was the one to report her friend as missing. She spoke to her most days. After that, it would not take long till the police found the vehicle. As for the body...that was in the lap of the gods, in all senses, but as long as they went the right way, she was pretty sure the police would discover the mine.

The bicycle – that lay covered by a sheet in the back of the Land Rover.

Before she left, she turned and surveyed the scene. It seemed calm enough, but the desolation was all too appropriate. The place had claimed one, probably two lives – only time would tell regarding the latter, but she would know soon enough. She wanted to blame that barrenness for robbing her of her immoral guide, but that would have been to duck the issue; she had made a decision, whether conscious or unconscious, to save a friend at the expense of a mentor. Her eyes took in that realm of darkness for the last time; she would not be revisiting. Most disturbing were the memories – figures dancing just far enough into the fog to frustrate her with their familiar movements and featureless faces.

* * *

It had seemed a wise thing to do, to insist Joanna stayed with her that night. It was not a time for the former to be alone – for either of them, if she was honest. She showed Joanna to one of the spare rooms.

"Here are some towels. It's en suite, so just make yourself at home."

She had given her friend a hug, or as good an approximation as she could, having never offered such support in her life. Joanna had clung to her and was slow to loosen her grip. The sensation wasn't unpleasant; was this how it felt then, to give and receive comfort, rather than the surrendering one's body to the satisfaction of primal urges – one's own or another's?

Or then again...

Joanna's cheek was now pressed against hers and she could feel the dampness of tears. Again flesh rested against flesh, perhaps for longer than seemed appropriate. Was it wrong?

She knew it would be only a matter of time before lips slid across and met lips, hunger overpowering hesitancy.

"Joanna?" Her own voice sounded weak, pliant to her ears.

Joanna had stopped for a moment to look her in the face. Kate had never noticed before the soulfulness of her friend's green eyes. For just long enough she was lost in the beauty of them – long enough for Joanna to ghost through the plasma and place her lips on Kate's neck.

Now Joanna had watched, fascinated by her body's responses to the butterfly kisses which made the hairs stand up on her arms as they teased her down where her neck met her shoulders. She moved sinuously to allow the now open blouse to fall to her waist, brushing her hardening nipples with infinite delicacy.

Nothing was rushed; the love-making seemed to comprise one slow, sensual swirl. Later, Kate would struggle to remember how they reached the point of no return; how her legs came to be wound across and around Joanna's shoulders; how Joanna's delicate hands held her bucking hips firm and her tongue took on ridiculous dimensions in its probing insistence.

Kate's gaze refocused on the present and now she found her knuckles white on the steering wheel. Both of them had sought solace from their troubles and respite from their anguish in physical intimacy. She had felt in the responses of Joanna's body the reason for years of spinsterhood. For a moment, through her own lack of discomfort or disgust at the acts they were committing, she had questioned whether here, too, lay the key to the subsuming of her own soul; to the use she'd made of her first husband; to her desire to be hurt and pleasured by something that was an uebermensch. Yet from the moment the force of her orgasm had released her, it had felt wrong to be lying with another woman's head on her breast. The discomfort must have communicated itself in some subtle, subliminal way, because nothing was ever asked

274

or offered again. Had their love-making been her friend's way of trying to thank her? Back in the cave, when Joanna's hand had appeared out of the dark at the very moment the ripped jacket gave out, grasping at the edge of the drop with every last vestige of her strength, Kate had not hesitated to haul her from oblivion, when there might have been good reason to let Joanna fall. After all, in coming for her friend, Kate had sacrificed something she had always sought. And then there was the question of Diane...or rather there had been no question from Kate and Joanna had not been ready to talk yet.

Even if they had chosen to venture down the Sapphic path, there would always have been two figures standing at the end of the bed, staring with ghostly drowned eyes, pointing with bony fingers, accusing; perhaps just mocking. In the end she had been surprised how easy it had been to move apart; it had caused only a slight wound, which had scabbed over and healed soon enough. Neither of them mentioned other wounds, which would ache and throb forever. Would they ever heal? From where she was sitting, it seemed to Kate that Joanna was a survivor. Perhaps her love-making had not been a way of thanking Kate for saving her life after all. Who knew what other reasons lay beneath.

* * *

Joanna was scrubbing the worktops when Kate arrived.

"Hi there. Come in. Help yourself to coffee."

"Coffee machine already on the go! The new demographic must be working well for you then."

275

Joanna gave a sharp look. "It has to. The old clientele seem to have lost their appetite after the news about Di..." She hesitated. "Let's just say, there are no more readings down in the cellar."

They both looked towards the stairs that led down.

"Still too many ghosts down there?" said Kate.

Joanna continued to scrub; pursed her lips. "Yes, the curious students soon lost interest. Less pretension; more bacon. Suits me. I didn't realise there were so many early crew, but I guess this is a port city and it's paying me nicely. Not the dream I had..." she trailed off again. "But then again, there are dreams and dreams. I can still do my bit for the environment. As for angst, demons – I've got enough of my own to process."

Of a sudden she seemed to become aware of the intensity with which she was scrubbing the spotless worktop and looked up. It was clear the broad grin that followed surprised Joanna almost as much as it did Kate.

"Out out, damned spot."

She laughed; a gentle sound, which nevertheless shattered the air.

"What is Charlie going to do now that you've 'dumbed down'?" asked Kate, only half- serious.

Joanna stopped, rested her hands on the work surface as if considering. "You know, he always was a twat."

Now she burst out laughing.

* * *

The man walking up in a hi-vis waistcoat and donkey jacket saw the figure slumped against the wall. The stranger turned and one look into those eyes was enough to make the workman falter in his stride. Heaven help whoever or whatever they were contemplating, because that black look did not bode well for someone. Nor did the way the watcher, who kept the lower face hidden, turned and made off down the road, disappearing into the gloom of the pre-dawn December light like Jack the Ripper in a London fog.

* * *

Joanna smiled as she busied herself in expectation of the first customers. A glance at the window and her smile faded. Suddenly pale, she hurried across the café and, having fumbled with the latch, threw the door open to look up and down the street. She leaned a moment longer in the doorway, then stepped back inside and closed the door.

"Nothing." She paused. "A ghost."

Still she chewed on her lip, lost in thought, and then rubbed her arms where the goose-pimples were visible, her skin clearly responding to more than the chilly winter air.

As she turned back to her work the door jolted open again, the bell, which was not yet motionless from the previous incident, clattering. Joanna jumped.

"Morning." It was the man in the donkey jacket. "I do not smell bacon."

"Good morning, Bill." Joanna's smile was perhaps too broad, but it was heartfelt nonetheless.

Bill rubbed his hands together. "An early riser please, and

one of those steaming mugs of coffee. Me old bones feel strangely chilled this morning."

* * *

When he had finished his breakfast, Bill buttoned up his donkey-jacket to the top, pulled on his woollen hat and thermal gloves. As he reached for the door-handle, a thought appeared to strike him and he turned to Joanna behind the counter.

"You be careful," he said

Joanna smiled. "You're telling me, of all people? What – are you about to advise me that…" here she put on a spoof West Country accent, "…there be strange folks about?"

"Well actually…." Bill stopped, seemed to think better of something and stepped out.

Chapter Twenty-One

It had stayed with Kate all day – Joanna's laugh.

Something was simmering in the cauldron, just waiting for the heat to be turned up.

Joanna had not spoken about what happened in the cave. Oh the superficial stuff; sure. There had been a search and rescue operation once she had reported her concerns about Diane and someone had seen the Volvo parked on the edge of the moor. As concerned friends, the two of them had, of course, joined the search parties, which meant that the resting place of Diane's body was found with more speed than might otherwise have been the case. No way would they have allowed history to repeat itself; one set of abandoned bones in a watery crypt was enough for anyone. Kate suffered mixed emotions when a more intrepid member of the search party ventured further and discovered the other skeleton. In many ways, this underground kingdom belonged to Tom and he to it. She would have preferred that it be left undisturbed. Having trailed the searcher, she was quick to pocket the plastic watch she found as he wandered off to fetch the others.

Joanna had stayed out of the mine; spared herself the resonance and echoes. Again, Kate's reaction to this vacillated between relief that her friend would not give herself away by some misplaced word or tic, and irritation that, once again, she, Kate, was the only one able to confront this demon, risking the nightmares that would follow.

The nightmares – she had taken steps now to leave them behind. Time would tell.

But Diane's final moments? No mention of them was ever made. They both knew it would have opened a can of worms for which Joanna was ill-equipped. For her some things were best left wriggling in the dark.

Joanna had always worked long hours at the café. Now Kate had observed she was like something possessed. But it was different; less altruism, more practicality; no more artistic endeavour, or themed nights; less organic free range options; more fart trade than fair trade. Egg, chips, beans, bacon – good cheap comfort food served with efficiency. The business was doing well. And yet...surely that cathartic cleaning of worktops was driven by more than a dislike of oily stains and smells. The quote from Lady Macbeth had been more appropriate than Kate dared to mention.

As soon as she had left the café that morning, Kate resolved to return before close of business. She needed to try to slot the final piece into the jigsaw. Sometimes, being unable to save your friend, being paralysed with fear, was not a crime. At worst it was cowardice, but various wise, some would say clever people, had run away from the open, snarling jaws of death. It reminded Kate of the joke about the two wildlife photographers who realised that a lion was advancing on them. As one pulled on running shoes, the other said: "You'll never outrun a lion." The reply came: "That's okay, as long as I outrun you."

But Kate had decided - of all those things left wriggling in the dark by Joanna, it simply wasn't fair that insomniac, nightmare-ridden Kate be one of them; the friend who had not run; who had sacrificed the chance to play the Game of Death to save her. It wasn't right that one woman could cleanse her conscience with cleaning product and a rag, while her rescuer would never be at peace. At the very least, Joanna owed her this – an explanation. She would have to retrace her steps in the darkness, just as Kate had done.

So it was that Kate found herself parking up again in Bath Street around nine p.m. Christmas lights of varying degrees of tastefulness twinkled from the windows of the establish-ments – except, strange to note, from the windows of Jo-Jo's Café. Joanna had rather paid lip-service to the festive season. Illuminated snowmen and stars flashed in a display, which Kate knew bore no relation to the owner's understated taste. But there was nothing now, just a noticeable gaping black hole where the café stood.

As she stepped out of the car, she experienced a moment's dizzying déjà vu. No surprise there, of course – she had called in during the dark hours of that very morning.

The next thing that struck a discordant note was the locked door. Joanna would turn the sign to closed but rarely shut up shop till she left for home. Peering inside brought no enlightenment, so now Kate tried phone numbers; three of them – Joanna's home number, the café and her mobile. She heard the café phone ring three times. All kicked into voicemail. The prickling at the back of her neck was enough to make Kate turn and look up and down the road. She reached into her pocket, produced a key-ring and found the café key, which had been entrusted to her.

In she stepped, closing the door gently and being careful to lock it for a reason she couldn't explain. The closure of the door threw the café into a silence she had never experienced before, accentuated by the humming of refrigerators and freezer units. That buzzing seemed to trigger atavistic dizziness again – as if her body was preparing to protect her from the madness of tinnitus.

Except another sound intruded, uneven against the flat-lining silence. Water. A peculiar confluence - both a lapping and a rushing, incongruous on the ear. And she could hear voices; again a strange juxtaposition of high-pitched shouting, quiet enough not to be heard from the road, along with an intermittent...what? Some sort of muted whining.

Now that her eyes had adjusted, she could make out a flickering light, emanating, it seemed, from the stairs that led down to the cellar.

Kate forced her leaden feet forward. She approached the steps and could make out certain words, whose resonance seemed to materialise in the darkness. One was Joanna's voice for sure, the other less distinct, but there was no mistaking the screams, which would have formed jagged migraine lights if the dark air could sculpt.

Now something about the sounds struck Kate – they were repeating themselves, as if someone was pressing a rewind button over and over. She realised she was hearing something on a loop. At the sudden awareness that the other screaming voice was Diane's, Kate shuddered with such force that she was almost thrown off balance.

And what was it about the sound of the water? The rushing sound seemed distant - part of the loop - but the lapping sound seemed real and present.

CHAPTER TWENTY-ONE

By now, Kate had reached the top of the stairs.

Just a few steps down, she could see that there was indeed water. The cellar had flooded. She moved forward with caution, the thrumming in her head worsening, and started descending the steps.

Now Kate gave an involuntary gasp and almost pitched forward, grasping the handrail to prevent the fall.

In the middle of the dark cellar was Joanna. Light and shade interplayed on her bone structure; a peculiar, ghoulish homage to Hitchcock's *Psycho*. There was despair and pleading in her eyes as she looked up at Kate. She appeared to be sitting, and given that there was duct tape across her mouth, which emphasised the cheek-bones in a corrupt similitude of the dark man, Kate had to assume she was tied up. The water came up to her chin and every time she moved, she caused the lapping, which breached her nostrils while she struggled to keep them above the waterline.

Kate stood paralysed, except for her eyes, which flicked left in the direction of a large plasma screen, once used for artistic presentations, but in latter days more often than not tuned to sports channels for the customers. It was the light from this that danced on the peaks and hollows of Joanna's terrified features.

Rather than a cult classic of horror fiction, what looked like a home movie was playing on the screen; a terrible, short work.

"My God!" said Kate to the night air. "He filmed it."

Joanna renewed her struggles with gagged pleading to her rescuer – the weird buzzing from before. Her eyes were a study in terror. But Kate was transfixed by what she saw. It seemed that the dark man must have placed a camera with its

283

lens focussed on the tiny ledge where Joanna had sheltered from the flooding tide, and there she was in spooky night vision green, cowering while the waters pressed just below.

Also clinging to that small rocky spur, literally by her fingertips, was Diane.

"Please Joanna, help me! I can't hold on!"

"There's no room here, Diane!"

"Give me your hand!"

Joanna grasps Diane's arm, but it's clear she doesn't have the strength to keep that hold as the tide sweeps on.

"Diane, you're pulling me in!"

"Please Jo, there might be room if we both stand! Please pull me up!"

"I can't!"

All the time the water surges, deafening. Diane sways like a reed in its currents.

"Help me!"

"Let go, Diane, you're pulling me in. I can't swim."

"It's so cold, I..."

"I can't!"

"Help me!"

"Let go!"

Joanna starts to slip over the ledge. "I can't swim, Diane! I'll drown!"

Diane's teeth are chattering. "It's so cold...help me for God's sake help me!"

"Let go!"

Joanna brings her fist down in sheer panic on Diane's knuckles. Again.

Again.

Diane screams, sobbing, forced to release her hold. She slips

*back into the water...and doesn't resurface. Joanna hauls herself
back onto the ledge. Her eyes scour the water.*

"Diane? Diane?" She pauses. "DIANE!"

*At last she sinks back cowering against the rock wall, wipes her
wet sleeve across her eyes. She clasps her arms around herself,
shivering.*

"Please Joanna, help me! I can't hold on!"

The loop had started again.

Kate tore her eyes from the screen, her head swivelling back
towards Joanna. The words came back to her:

"I give you the power over life and death."

What issued from her mouth seemed beyond her control,
as if she was possessed: "How I envy you." She saw Joanna
frown and shake her head - a mirror of her own reactions
perhaps, though there was manic incomprehension in the
captive's eyes. "You had the courage to make a decision that
I could not." She paused and felt a hint of a manic smile form
on her lips. "But now I have a chance for redemption."

Her head jerked left and right, eyes narrowing.

"Maybe he's filming this even now; judging me. He didn't
leave after all. He knows I'm his now and he's testing me."

Again Joanna shook her head, muffled sounds of despair
fighting to escape the duct tape, before stopping as the water
penetrated her nostrils, causing her to snort and lift her head.

Kate turned back to her; her smile an obtuse contradiction
to the terrible events she was describing: "The difference is
- you murdered her." She started to come down the steps,
unconcerned by the water, in which she was soon waist-deep.

Joanna was holding her head still this time, but her eyes
widened and bulged as if the pressure behind the gag might

285

cause them to explode. Perhaps she sensed her life was now in more immediate danger.

"I think you might have more trouble living with this one. But you'll always be a survivor." She waded around the back of the captive audience, took hold of the back of the chair and gave it a slight shake, to the accompaniment of a desperate groan from Joanna. Now she came round the front again, put a hand on Joanna's cheek and felt her flinch. "So I'm going to transfer to you the power over life and death."

In the background Diane screamed again and sank below the surface of the water.

"I'm sure you did the right thing, letting her go. Some say it's like falling asleep," here she stooped to look into Joanna's eyes, fascinated by the unadulterated terror she found there, "though personally I think the inability to breathe must be terrifying." She stood tall again, turning to look at the screen. "But then at least it's over – not like the long years of guilt and recrimination." She turned back to Joanna. "I guess, like all good stories, we'll see what, or who the morning brings. Unless, of course, you decide to just let your head drop."

Kate waded back towards the steps. At the bottom she turned again, surveying the scene and shaking her head in admiration.

"So clever," she whispered. "How could I have let him go? I hope I passed the test."

The feeling of relief that swept through Joanna as she watched Kate's boots disappearing back up the steps was the last thing she had expected – but then again, so was seeing Kate again, with that unhinged look in her eyes.

The relief was short-lived.

Chapter Twenty-Two

Thump thump thump...thump...

    She had known that resuming the medication would have an impact on her body...

Thump...thump thump...

...but this pounding was erratic, disconcerting, frightening.

Her eyes opened, rusty shutters rolling back. Now she lifted her head; a slow, creaking process as she eased it away from the backs of her hands, to find herself still at her desk. The hands, in turn, were stuck to the pages of the notebook, from which she started to peel them as if sloughing off dead skin.

Thump thump thump.

She jumped as the beating at her door continued.

Mouth dry, face paining, back aching, but worst of all, stomach churning with a dread for which there was, as yet, no name, Kate got to her feet and scraped her way to the front door, just in time to cut short the next barrage.

Her fears were not lessened by the sight of two police constables, flanking another man in what she assumed, with peculiar subconscious clarity, was the regulation overcoat of all fictional detectives. He seemed real enough though.

"Mrs Sanders?"

She squinted at him. "Miss. Yes?"

"May we come in?"

"May I ask why? Or is that obstructive of me?"

He held up what she took, based on superficial scrutiny, to be a police ID, though he might just as well have been there to read the meter, so little detail could she discern.

From the weariness of his expression she could tell that her words might just have been laden with a touch too much sarcasm, but he remained impassive – stayed professional.

"Of course. There has been an awful, certainly unusual incident at the establishment known as Jo-Jo's Art Café. We understand you may be able to help us with initial enquiries into the terrible event."

"Me?"

"Well, the general consensus seems to be that you and Joanna Kent were close friends."

Her dread had acquired a name, if not yet a personality. Kate felt herself slump as she opened the door wider and turned, allowing the officers to enter behind her. The sense of detachment was disconcerting, in part because she knew it was down to a certain anodyne impact within the medication, but also because she could hear things falling in the mist at the periphery of her vision, which might have been leaves pattering in a sudden frost, or the footfall of demons closing in.

She knew why they were here and yet she didn't.

The detective was speaking again.

"...a warrant. We just want to look around, you understand. We will try to disturb as little as possible."

It was as much a surprise to her when the Kate of old reappeared of a sudden. She threw herself down in a chair, grabbed a packet of cigarettes and, having lit one, made a grandiose gesture with the cigarette-wielding hand as she snorted out an ostentatious jet of smoke.

"Knock yourselves out."

Then she felt all the theatricality drain from her at the sight of a figure in the doorway. She sat up. Was it him? Was he Branwell Bronte in that famous painting – there, but not there? He spoke and all doubt left her, replaced by an almost childish dread – which was more than appropriate when she thought about it.

"Doctor Crabtree?"

He stepped inside. "Kate." The tone was warm, so it was strange how it chilled her.

She drew on the cigarette, feigning calmness; coldness. "Have you brought me back my memories? My past?"

He continued to smile. "I believe you did that yourself." He reached into a pocket and produced a piece of paper. "Your repeat prescription, Kate. Out of date now. But I never forget a patient or fail to check on one. I'm only sorry I didn't spot this sooner. When did you stop taking them?"

"The day I found out what had happened...I think. When I found the papers my parents signed, agreeing to me having ECT. That was when..."

She stopped herself, but knew at once her eyes had betrayed her. Dr Crabtree, who appeared to have stepped straight from Kate's memories, looking the same as he did thirty years before, even down to the suit and the urbane smile, had caught the direction of her glance and wandered across to the desk, where the journal lay open. He pressed down one of the curling pages, started to read and a frown deepened the lines on his still handsome features.

But then, all eyes in the room were drawn to the constable

who was standing across the room.

"Sir, you might want to have a look at this."

The detective walked over to examine the object now being held for his attention; a mobile phone. From where she was sitting, Kate couldn't see the screen. She didn't need to. She knew that movie well enough – the two women shouting; screaming; the dark waters swirling away, draining a life with them.

Like figures on some huge piece of automata, all eyes turned from that image towards Kate.

Chapter Twenty-Three

Doctor Crabtree leaned forward to rest his elbows on his knees, enjoying the stream of sunlight into which his face moved, but noting how it had the paradoxical effect of both warming the room and rendering it more stark. The book hung pendulous in his fingertips.

"I guess this is a classic example of both the benefits and drawbacks of electro convulsive therapy. The plus side was that it dulled your memories -" he paused, "- I was going to say erased, but clearly subsequent events show that they were merely locked away – in that box you found containing your parents' consent form, as it turns out. The downside is, that box seems to represent your conscience. It got buried deep, even though all the time it was just sitting there waiting to be found, while the medication kept you from wandering to that place."

"You mean the ECT dulled my pain, but the medication dulled my wits," said Kate, the steel in her voice clanging around the sparse cell.

"Well, the new pills are not having that effect, are they?" He shook his head. "I feel guilty and not a little ashamed, given the progress we've made in thirty years of medical research, that you were still on that damned lithium treatment.

But the fact that we're sitting here talking, the fact that now you have balanced recall, shows we're going to be okay."

"Okay?" Kate smiled, but it was a wistful expression. "There I was thinking the world was full of groundlings, mired by their petty consciences, while I was bestriding the stage, magnificent in my darkness. All that time, I didn't realise I was just half a person."

"Interesting that you had enough self-awareness to come off the medication in the search for answers."

Kate looked out of the reinforced window across the beautiful gardens which cloaked her prison. "And ironic that they were, as you say, just sitting in that box waiting for me to find them. I wonder why my parents never destroyed it."

Doctor Crabtree gestured with the journal he was holding. "This was just a story as far as they were concerned; the product of your disturbed mind; yours and someone else's. They found these outpourings worrying, but of course didn't know the history – the reason for the fault-lines and fragility of your conscience. Once the treatment had been agreed, they locked this away along with the medical consent forms and – another irony of ironies - it all appears to have faded from their memories too; fortunately, or unfortunately, depending on your point of view. Then along came Pandora."

He observed Kate and she watched him back. "*Fortunately or unfortunately* you say, Doctor Crabtree. Which of those is your professional opinion?"

The doctor felt himself redden and it was one of many reasons he didn't utter a word as Kate reached into her pocket and produced a packet of cigarettes, before lighting up without permission. For six months he had watched her struggling to surface. This nihilist with scant regard for rules was part of the real Kate – no doubt about that – though in the end she was proving to be, perhaps, a sheep in wolf's clothing.

He turned the way-marker slightly, diverting the attention away from her awkward question. "So many people want to forget. You just needed to remember." He referenced the book with his eyes. "So this has turned out to be another form of medication; a hypnotic which took you back to places you had forgotten." Now he pointed to a second book on a table beside him - a similar, if not identical notebook. "So what was this? You've suggested you might be prepared to talk about it?"

Kate dragged on her cigarette, exhaled; stared at the other book. Crabtree continued.

"As I said, I think you're almost ready to step onto the path that leads away from this place. Professionally, I'm delighted." He leaned further forward. "From a personal point of view, and to my shame, I need to know that I have understood correctly. There's so much..."

Crabtree leaned back again; almost a physical manifestation of his attempt to rein in his excitement as he continued.

"I mean, the books look more or less the same, but, despite someone's best efforts to disguise the fact, this one -" he lifted the one he was holding, "- is much older; thirty years, I'm guessing." He looked at her and found features which remained a study in blankness. "It starts off in the handwriting of one child, continues in another and then concludes in yours. That one," here he looked at the one on the table, "which was found in the Joanna Kent's coat pocket, is written in a poor approximation of a child's handwriting and has the first page torn out. It looks..."

He turned back to her – and stopped, noticing a single tear, which tracked a glistening path in the sunlight; a salty harbinger of a new spring perhaps, or at the very least a leak from the well of hope.

He waited.

"I needed him to live on," she whispered.

Again, Crabtree waited. So many doctors did not appreciate the need for silence. He liked to believe he was not one of them.

"Once I saw the full consequence of what we had done – that eddying, soulless mass of stinking water and not a sign of...him except the notebook on the ledge, I just needed to keep him alive."

Now it was her turn to fall silent. Crabtree decided he had to throw a rope; couldn't let her sink back beneath the current from which she had just emerged. "So you took his diary, journal – call it what you will – and invented his escape, recording it in the original journal; continuing on his behalf."

When Kate turned her gaze upon Crabtree again, he was taken aback by the dark intuition in her eyes. "So which one do you think I am Doctor – Tom, or Bones?"

It was apparent she had been absorbing far more of their dialogues, or indeed of his discussions with other psychiatrists, than she had cared to reveal in previous sessions. There was little point in lying to her.

"Both." He could tell the answer surprised her and this gave him a misplaced sense of satisfaction, for which he felt immediate shame. "I think you had a greater affinity with that boy than you knew. From the moment you saw him, you recognised an outsider – a bit like you. There before you was the perfect opportunity to project some of your feelings of self-loathing. In sending him scurrying across the moor and abandoning him, you were shedding a skin you found distasteful. Then, when you saw what you had done, you panicked, believing you had sloughed off the better part of you."

He watched her eyes narrowing, her steady gaze quite in keeping with the snake image, as was the impossibility of knowing what emotions flitted behind it when at last she responded. "What if I was simply just evil; if there was no fresh, clean skin beneath the old discarded one, just my bloody innards?"

"Then why would you have gone back to find him? An evil person would have just moved on."

"To make sure my secret was safe? Instead, I got a nasty surprise when I discovered the enormity of what I had done. I panicked about getting caught. So I covered it up."

"I disagree. Why would you have kept the journal, crying out your guilt for the world to discover? You had committed no crime. According to everything you have told me in the last months, I think you lay the first night, contemplating your actions. The next day, you found nothing but the diary and your guilt did the rest. Going back to my comment, I think part of you is Tom, escaping from the darkness to which you had abandoned him and part of you is Bones – the friend you both needed; or the fragile conscience doomed to be a silent witness. You so wanted him to have substance, you even gave him a back story about smuggling. Were those diamonds and gold coins part of a better world that might be yours one day?"

She said nothing; usually a sign that the truth was knocking on the lid of its box demanding attention.

"So what happened when you found the box in your loft?" he asked, aware of the leitmotiv which had developed in his imagery. She frowned and he added: "I mean, did it have an immediate impact? Did the memories come flooding back?"

Kate gave a wry grin. "Unfortunate choice of words."

Once again, Crabtree felt himself blush. This woman had an undeniable ability to unnerve you by picking at the scabs of your weakness.

She continued: "At first they trickled, as if I was reading someone else's history – which in a way I suppose I was. The images were familiar, but unrecognisable, like walking into a nightclub wearing shades. I needed to remove the glasses. I recognised the author had to be me, but I was someone I didn't know. What helped me was finding the authorisation documents signed by my parents?"

"Howso?"

"It gave me a starting point. Without it, I might have assumed the journal was indeed a fabrication; a project from the grubbier recesses of my imagination. But knowing I had been diagnosed as bipolar, borderline Multiple Personality Disorder, made me realise the writings might have been post-traumatic. I needed to rediscover the person I had been before the trauma. I needed to rediscover the trauma itself. That was when I decided to come off the medication; remove the shades."

Crabtree just nodded; stayed quiet. They were venturing into her loft in all senses. She was reopening the box.

"Of course, at first I assumed the two sets of childish hand-writing were both mine; some extreme manifestation of my various personalities. It wasn't until..." Kate paused, stubbed out her cigarette with greater intensity than necessary and reached for another one. "It wasn't until my head cleared back to its original confusion that I understood what had happened."

She lit up, took a deep draw on the cigarette and continued: "What we had done." Now she looked at Crabtree and he felt the chill. "Who had paid? Who had won? Who had lost?"

"Nobody won, Kate."

The slight curl of Kate's top lip seemed to drain the warmth from the room. "Perhaps - but some people got to live their lives without having their brains fried."

There was nothing Crabtree could say to that, so once again he waited. He knew the anger wasn't done.

"For some people, time applied its balm and they forgot. Their better halves stayed with them."

"But neither of them married..." Crabtree stopped himself as it dawned on him what she meant. "Oh, you mean..."

"They weren't condemned to living life devoid of a con-science."

"Do you feel that has been a negative thing for you, Kate? Isn't a conscience a mixed blessing? How do you know Joanna and Diane weren't haunted every day by their part in Tom's death?"

Kate looked at him and snorted. "Pur-leeeze!" When Crabtree refused to be drawn she continued. "They didn't go back. Oh, I'm sure they felt remorse, but then they just buried their heads in the sand and got on with life. I've seen just what a survivor Joanna is...was."

Now even Kate fell silent and Crabtree watched as the irony of those words struck her.

"You don't feel the universe has balanced things out now? Albeit thirty years later, Joanna did follow her conscience and look where it got her."

Kate snapped back. "You don't think it took my involve-ment for that to happen? As I said, Joanna was a survivor. Her laugh that morning, in the café..."

Crabtree frowned and Kate picked up on this.

"...when she called Charlie a twat. I know now that was the tipping point for me...for him."

"Ah yes – the Dark Man," said Crabtree, "aka your con-science, your avenging angel, your soul-mate. I didn't need letters after my name to work that one out. Transformation: from the caterpillar that was Tom to the death's head moth that was your anti-hero. That was your masterpiece – to begin with. The way you set up his physical presence in the cellar at the Art Café, then his non-appearance at the next function." Crabtree leaned forward. "All very in keeping with your theatrical ambitions. But again, what fascinates me is how he started appearing to you alone." Crabtree gestured with the book. "Your conversations with him are intriguing. They offer a remarkable insight into your conflict, as your newly exhumed conscience battled with your desire for something darker. He became woven into the very fabric of your daily actions."

Crabtree opened the journal, flicked through to what looked like a suitable page and started to read. The words had the power to unite doctor and patient for that passage of shared, distorted time, but for very different reasons.

Extract from 'The Dark Man'

His words weren't registering with me on anything other than a superficial level. I was lost in a world of a thousand questions. Had it taken nothing more than a pair of small pieces of blue membrane in his eyes – his contact lenses – to both intoxicate and dismay me? Did that now whet or blunt the perversity of our acts? Well whoever he was, he might as well have been whistling in the wind that scoured the moor at that moment, for all the sense things were making. It was a perfect storm and it was sending me towards the rocks.

Now I looked up at him again and saw my distaste mirrored in his eyes.

"Let me make this a little simpler for you," he said. Turning to shield his face from the wind, he replaced the blue lenses with great dexterity.

The transformation was remarkable, as if I, too, had put in magic lenses. Though I would need time, at least I could begin to imagine desiring him again. That simple knowledge was almost too much for me. I had heard so often that the eyes are the windows to the soul and though I did not believe in the soul, still I knew what people meant. So what trick was this? Did the lenses bring out the humanity in him, or the lack of it?

He was saying something.

"If that's all it takes, Kate, to rip your heart in two, to make the difference between you loathing or desiring me, then that says everything about humankind to me; confirms everything I ever believed. It also makes you absolutely the person I thought you were – which is what has saved you."

"Saved me?"

"When they read my poem in the café that night, I watched the three of you, Joanna, Diane and you; studied your eyes – I've learnt to read them very well over the years."

"So you were there!" I gasped. "I knew it!"

"Your eyes alone were unaffected by what you heard; there

299

was no stirring of memory, no pricking of the conscience. You were rapt; lost entirely in what and where you thought I might be. I saw your darkness; the void where a soul should be. And as I say, that is what has saved you, for this world tried to tear my soul from me the day I was born. I think it clung to me like a bad smell until I lost it here on the moor one night, thanks to you three she-devils. Oh, you should have heard how I laughed the first time I read Macbeth years later." He grinned for a moment. "Anyway, there is no place so deep or dark as the pit of self-loathing which a conscience forces you to inhabit, and thanks to you I escaped it, so don't punish yourself too much."

He reached out a hand and lifted me to my feet again, where I tottered for a moment.

"How did you find us?" I asked. "Why did you wait so long?"

"It is indeed a long story and only you can choose whether you have time to hear it. As you know I cannot give you eternity, but you have the power to decide how long we do have; you and I as..." he paused, "...well, since we cannot be soul-mates, shall we say cell-mates?"

With a start and a chill of recognition, I found I understood absolutely. The living ghosts of which he had spoken – they were Joanna and Diane. And as his previous words came back to me – the part about there perhaps being only one ghost – I realised that for one of them it might already be too late.

He seemed to sense my hesitation: "But know this; whichever way you go you cannot turn back."

I composed myself. "Before I make a decision, I must know my choices; understand what I'd be losing. I know you're about to tell me your story, but what of them; my friends?"

"Your friends." The last word dripped with the slime of contempt and I realised to my shame that it was for me and my weakness. *"I took them where they wanted to go. It's not a matter of black and white; their fate is tied directly with mine, albeit more than three decades have frayed the rope. However, it is a simple matter of life and death – and at this moment I don't know whether they're alive or dead."* He shrugged; stepped towards me. *"But you do have this in common with them; you have come to a point, much as one of them did this morning, where turning back will leave you dissatisfied and unsettled."*

Now he gave a wolfish grin. *"Which reminds me, I almost forgot my manners. I must thank you for giving Jo-Jo..."* he paused to imbue the familiar name with as much scorn as possible, *"...that final push over the edge."*

It dawned on me slowly. *"You mean..."*

"The dead owl, yes. Joanna was ready to crack from the moment we met. If your heart is made of stone, hers is glass – cold, but weak. That second night in the café, I saw a woman whose darkness matches your own, except unlike the demon-peopled underworld that lurks within you, Kate, hers comprises shadows full of creatures that startle and dart away from the light of her soul. We, or rather you, merely dragged one of those creatures from its hiding place and hurled it into a café window.

"But I digress. What do you want to do?"

He was right; I had to know. In many ways my choice was simple; live out my darkness, or try to save my friends and live with the regret of a passion unfulfilled; a fruit half eaten. Memories would never revive that taste.

"Tell me your tale," I said, knowing in that instant that I had made, for me, the right choice. Yet even that self-knowledge made me fear for my future. Hadn't I always made the choice that suited me best? I had never needed a term of reference or comparison. It was frightening to think that I was in danger of

developing a moral compass. That the life in which I'd always had control might already be gone.

With that, he produced from his pocket a battered notebook. As he started to flick it open I saw a page was torn out, right at the very beginning.

Crabtree stopped, the look in Kate's eyes telling him he might already have read too long. It was time to lead them down another track.

"Why do you think he started appearing to you, Kate? I mean, I can understand why you invented him – a shadow flitting across the moon, disturbing the long-buried memories of your friends – but to you he seems to have become very real."

"You tell me. You're the shrink."

It was what he had feared as he read on, intoxicated by the tale and failing to notice the shadows falling. It was time to search for rivets again to keep the boat watertight, rather than looking too far out to sea.

"OK – but I can't do it without your help. I need you to run through with me once more the timeline of this thing. We've looked at sections of it till we believed we had a semblance of understanding, but we need context. So..." He looked at her and she nodded, the feistiness gone and a sort of weary resignation moving into its seat. "You found the journal and the medical papers. Once the initial curiosity passed, what replaced it?"

"Anger?"

"With...?"

"My parents at first." She sighed. "Misguided as it turned out. They acted out of concern. But it was pretty quickly overtaken by a sense of injustice; indignation."

"With your friends."

"With Joanna and Diane, yes. It seemed to me they had managed very nicely, thank you, to get on with their lives."

"Can you really blame them for the fragility of your nature?"

Kate gave Crabtree a sharp look and ignored the comment. "Joanna was the worst culprit. Diane? She had always ridden on our coat-tails. She was always peripheral. Now I guess she's just collateral damage."

Crabtree hoped the shock didn't register on features trained for years to adopt mask-like inscrutability. "So what happened next? I mean, clearly your plan was to wake the old memories, which you hoped were slumbering in their respective subconscious minds."

Kate's eyes seemed to look into the void. "The story needed to pick up where it left off. Tom needed to take his revenge. What better way than for him to return as some sort of avenging angel? It appealed to me on many levels; in its darkness, its theatricality. I'm not sure I meant for it to go as far as it did, but the whole thing seemed to develop a life of its own."

"As did he, in your mind, once the medication wore off."

"I approached an actor friend in one of the horror theatre groups I'd belonged to. He was able to create the figure in the cellar of the café. I stayed away that evening, unsure whether I would be able to prevent myself laughing." Now Kate did give a little snorting approximation to a laugh. "Funny; it seemed the past wasn't buried as deeply in those two as I'd imagined. When they came to see me the next day, I could tell they were disturbed; Joanna in particular. They didn't need much nudging after that. I knew the poem would have an impact."

Of a sudden, Kate's forehead furrowed and she fell silent. This was the point for which Crabtree had been waiting.

"It goes a bit vague here, doesn't it?" he ventured. Kate said nothing. "This seems to me the point where the contiguous line between reality and imagination blurs."

"No, I remember going to the graveyard on the night of the café gathering." Kate regained some composure and countered, though she lacked conviction.

"But why?" After a pause, Crabtree broke his own rule along with the silence. "I think we have to acknowledge, Kate, that at this point your MPD became, quite simply, more extreme. You went to the graveyard to see the Dark Man, but he was purely your invention; created to provoke your erstwhile friends, but also a manifestation of your guilt and your desires."

There was a pleading, helpless look in Kate's eyes that moved Crabtree. "But what about the tramp at the graveyard. He saw him too."

"Isn't it more likely that he saw your figure moving in the darkness and got scared? His reaction tipped your feverish imagination over the edge at that moment. You fell over, got up again, drove yourself home and then fell into a deep sleep, full of some pretty wild dreams."

"The owl?"

"Mmmm, not sure where you got hold of a dead owl, but in the end it was just a part of your cunning plan." Crabtree tried to inject a touch of Baldrick into the last two words, hoping to inject a lightness to what must have been unsettling memories for Kate. "And it worked perfectly. The rest I

304

know from our previous discussions. After that, the voicemail messages from Joanna told you when she would be heading to the scene of past events. You went and planted the pink watch and the copy of Tom's journal which you had made with its torn out first page. You left the bicycle, which all those years ago you had found yourself unable to dispose of as guilt wracked you. When you left the scene you even drove past the others coming to meet their fates and flashed your beams so they wouldn't recognise your number plate. Then you just turned and followed them across the moor. You watched, waited, untied the rope you had left once they were down in the pit, even filmed the denouement.

"And left."

"So why did I go back?" Kate was no longer looking at him. Her eyes were squeezed shut, though whether to keep the demons out or in was hard to fathom.

"I can't know for sure, Kate, but from what I read to you a few minutes ago, I would say you either passed out once again, or sat in your car. During that period of unconsciousness or contemplation, you had more discussions with the Dark Man. In these, you believed it was him who had summoned you; him you followed onto the moor. Your dialogue with him seems, at a simplistic level, to represent some sort of battle with your conscience. Again you returned to full consciousness, this time caught between a sense of loss and a vague awareness that someone was in danger. My feeling is, that sense of loss was because what we might call your mission was now complete. The Dark Man had fulfilled his purpose, but you still needed him on a deeper, more complex level, which we have yet to establish.

"From this point, the real Kate..." Crabtree parenthesised

the air, "...rescued Joanna without any proper recall of her own involvement in events and proceeded to cover up Diane's death to help her friend.

"There it might have ended. A part of you – a disturbed part I have to say – would have taken satisfaction from a revenge served very cold indeed. Who knows whether the journal of the Dark Man would have continued; certainly you updated it with your later dialogues, which is remarkable when you consider how you passed out and woke with little recall. We have no way of knowing, Kate, whether you wrote the words to fit the actions, or vice versa.

"But of course, Joanna had to go and laugh in the café that morning, showing you once again that she was a survivor; throwing her contempt into the face of Tom, the Dark Man. If her experience had broken her, that part might have lain dormant in you, perhaps forever.

"Instead, you returned to the café to punish Joanna, so far into the darkness that you have no memory of your actions. I think it's fair to say, the reason you believed you had lost the Dark Man on the moor was because he had actually become a part of you, instead of a separate character that appeared to you. A workman came forward to say he saw someone outside the café on the morning of the unfortunate incident, and the look in that person's eyes had shocked him with its intense malevolence. When we showed him a picture of you, he said the eyes had it."

Crabtree had been watching those same eyes, waiting for her to release the tension from her eyelids. At last they unscrewed, but the confusion and horror now showing made him wish he had a better ending for her story. She would leave this place at some point, but what the world held in store for her, he could only guess. Medication would restore balance to her personality, but he feared it would be just a ceasefire; an uneasy truce between light and dark. He would have to make sure he monitored her. Still, at least he would be able to introduce some good news to this session in due course. For now he continued, believing she was in a position to understand and take this harrowing business on board at last.

"Of course, the conflict within you continued; first, when you returned once more to the café, to find the results of your actions; then, when you believed it was none of your doing."

Kate was staring at the floor. Tears rolled down her cheeks and she was shaking her head. There was a deadness in her voice when at last she spoke: "I'm not ready to leave here." She turned to the window. "To go back out there." Now she put her head in her hands. "What have I done?"

Crabtree thought it might be time after all. While it was hard to watch Kate's suffering, it seemed to him to bear out the findings of recent tests. The remorse was coming from a better place, one of sensitivity and emotional, but not mental, fragility.

"Kate, I think you need to rest, but only so that you can feel strong again. The questions you have asked, particularly that last one, have put my mind at ease." He extended a hand. "Come – I'll take you somewhere more comfortable to sleep. On the way, I want you to see something."

He observed her hesitancy, sensed her uncertainty. Reaching further, he waited till she put her hand in his and then helped her to her feet.

They headed along a corridor of closed rooms with reinforced windows in the doors. Stopping by a particular door, Crabtree peered through the window and seeing that it would be safe, gestured to Kate to look as well.

He heard her gasp and, as he had anticipated this reaction, was there to take her arm as she staggered.

Kate turned to Crabtree, open-mouthed. It was almost a comical look. She croaked something which might have been a word, looked through the window again and then whispered: "What? How?"

"It's ok, she can't see or hear you through that door."

"She survived?"

"Amazingly she did make it through that night."

Now Kate's eyes and words betrayed a bewildered anger. "You didn't think to tell me?"

"Kate, you took so long to surface, we weren't sure what your reaction would be; whether it would even push you back under. Besides, she wasn't in a great way – physically or psychologically. A night spent knowing the slightest move-ment might cause you to drown; being visited by someone you believe is deranged and who tied you there; watching a constant loop of yourself killing someone; what effect did you expect it to have? Please excuse the brutal simplicity of my words, but I believe you are strong enough to hear these things now."

Kate turned back to the window. "Can I speak to her?"

"Not sure that's a good idea. She's better, but fragile. Eventually, of course, you'll have to."

"Meaning?" Before Crabtree needed to provide an answer, he saw it dawn on Kate. She was definitely on the mend, albeit she was waking to a world of hurt. "Oh, I see. For every action there is a consequence."

"I'm afraid so, Kate, though in the case of you two, it's a hell of a job to fathom what the actions mean and what the consequences may be. She is here to recover, but she will then have to stand trial for the manslaughter of Diane Horsham. You will be a key witness in that trial, but also, potentially, a conspirator, albeit indirectly, in perverting the course of justice. Then there is the question of your attempted murder of Joanna." He waved a hand. "Oh, I'm sure you will be fine – diminished responsibility etcetera – but you see the complications."

"And what of the original sin?"

"You mean the death of Tom? Ironically, there is no evidence of any crime. There was no record of him anywhere. We have – sorry, would have had – only the word of the three of you to support his existence. Your journal cannot be submitted as evidence."

"But the bones – the ones buried at Highhill Cemetery; the ones I..." she hesitated, "...found out on the moor."

Crabtree smiled. "You mean the ones you brought up from the mine. I think your Machiavellian ways have confused even you. I found it odd that you wanted him to have a burial, but assumed somehow you must have been able in your mind to separate the reality of Tom dying from your imagination's version of events. A nice touch for the poor lad to be laid to rest in hallowed ground." Crabtree raised a finger for emphasis. "Except...the DNA tests showed those bones to be at least one hundred and fifty years old."

Chapter Twenty-Four

Travis Blunt – that was his stage name of course – had been astonished to read about the upcoming case. His initial inclination had been to keep his part in events secret, but with a true thespian's love of the spotlight, he had been unable to resist turning up at the police station to outline his role in the whole sorry affair. Except under the rather bored gaze of the police officer, his part hadn't seemed all that important. In fact, he had started to feel like a bit player. An extra.

That was, until now.

Now, someone had decided to give him a line; to shape, at least, the mystery of the thing.

It wasn't much of a line, but by the reaction of the police officer, it seemed he had, at least, made an impact; as if he had stepped forward and pronounced: *Beware the Ides of March.*

"So let me get this straight," said the policeman. "You didn't do it."

"No, officer. It just struck me, all at once, as a peculiar and, well, rather juvenile thing to do. So when the day arrived... I didn't - haha!" His attempt at a joke elicited no response, so he cleared his throat and continued. "I mean, creeping down an alleyway dressed like something from the Phantom of the Opera, sneaking in through a little-used door and then sitting in the back of a cellar till someone spots you. It would hardly have been my finest hour. Besides..."

He paused for dramatic effect. Again, there was no response other than a resigned, impatient sigh from the officer across the table, so he hurried on.

"...I know Kate - Miss Sanders has a fondness for all things dark, but there had been something about her eyes on this occasion when she asked me to do this, which I found, I don't know – unsettling."

"Well do you know who it was, Mr..." the policeman looked at his notes, "...Blunt."

Travis put his hand to his chest theatrically. "Oh no, officer, it wouldn't have been anyone else. Kate wouldn't have known I was not going to show. It was very much a last-minute decision. It's not like I was being paid, or anything."

The officer scratched his head. "Strange. This sheds a new light on things...I think."

Travis couldn't resist. "Perhaps a ghostly light – haha!"

III

IN THE LAPTOPS OF THE GODS

Copyright © 2006 David Palin

Chapter One - Logging in

"Sir! Dr Phillips, you'd better come quickly! Daniel seems to be having some sort of a bad reaction."

The Director of Research didn't know that he was hearing the technological equivalent of the slap made by the first fin that hit land when life decided it no longer wanted simply to swim. But he did look up with concern from the unimpressive neurological readout he had been scanning. "What sort of bad reaction?"

"Flatlining."

Now the PhD jumped to his feet. "What!?" It was not entirely a rhetorical question, but he didn't wait for a reply, though a thousand silent answers came, most of them initial, selfish reactions to what the future might hold for a scientist whose work may well have turned out the lights in another's cranium. No layman was going to understand what he was trying to achieve; half the time he wasn't sure himself.

Mike, the messenger, and one of his assistants followed him into the corridor.

"Have you attempted to resuscitate him?" asked the director.

The young man hesitated. "There's no need yet."

Dr Phillips stopped and turned to face him. "Meaning?"

"That's the weird part. The cardiograph is flatlining, but he's breathing, blinking, behaving normally, except..."

"Well?"

"Except he's *not* behaving normally. I mean, he's not behaving at all."

The doctor tutted impatiently and turned on his way again. You couldn't rely on the young for rational answers in this sort of situation - *what sort of situation?* It was better just to go to look for yourself.

However, he had some reluctant sympathy for Mike once he arrived in the laboratory. The subject of concern, a senior programmer, was sitting as usual at a huge bank of monitors and display panels in the clean room. Except 'usual' was the wrong word, both for his demeanour and the whole set-up.

It always disturbed Dr Phillips to see his human guinea-pigs wired up, catheters of needle fineness inserted into their heads attempting to read...well, that was just it. You might as well send a submersible to the bottom of the deepest ocean without lights; its pilot would still come back with more information than these sensory catheters were gathering and would have a better idea of what he might be looking for in the first place.

If this had been a medical research project, things could have been given a more positive spin. But Dr Phillips' Unholy Grail, as Director of Research for KompuKraft, was less philanthropic, more radical, hence the need for greater secrecy. He wanted to build the first thought-controlled computer, the next generation of machine, the next quantum leap.

Right from the start, the risk had been that no-one would know what exactly was going wrong if something did; which boundary had been overstepped. There were no way markers in the unknown. That was the problem with the brain. Man had taken the microchip beyond the miniaturisation of his wildest dreams, but nobody truly understood the workings of the mighty machine that conjured those dreams.

So indeed, nothing about this scene could be described as normal. The catheters were connected to a black box, from which emanated a Medusa's tonsure of leads, wires and cables, each in turn leading to a massive bank of myriad dials and monitors. Inside the black box was the world's most advanced microchip, the future cash cow of KompuKraft's already mighty IT empire, a wonder of the modern world, created after decades of research. It had taken as long as the Pyramids to complete, and to the geeks of KompuKraft it bore an importance inversely proportionate to its size. Some companies were still struggling with voice activation, but this tiny chip just about stopped short of giving backchat.

Dr Phillips looked at the monitors. Usually they stared back at him blankly, because their unsuccessful task so far had been to reveal any response from the microchip to cerebral activity. Normally the only screen reflecting any sort of activity was the cardiogram to which the Senior Programmer was attached. Now the doctor's eyes widened. Some of the screens seemed to be filled with snow and static, while others had streams of numbers running down them like rivulets of water, zeroes and ones. In the shard of glass that was the 1500 feet high World Research Centre of KompuKraft, a latter-day Tower of Babel, only one language was spoken, binary.

Phillips looked with even wider eyes at the cardiogram,

317

which was indeed flatlining as Mike had said. Quickly he entered the pre-chamber and donned a sterile suit, his shaking hands struggling with the zip closures. His assistant followed.

They entered the clean room and Phillips went to his volunteer. He looked into the young man's eyes and saw nothing except tiny square reflections of the monitors. He put a fingertip close to one of Daniel's eyeballs; there was no reaction from the eyelid or pupil, but instead a peculiar pulsing filled the air for a few seconds before passing, causing Dr Phillips and Mike looked at each other.

"Catatonic," said the doctor to no-one in particular.

"Dead according to that," Mike reminded him, pointing at the cardiogram. "Yet breathing. I don't understand. What's keeping him alive?"

Dr Phillips turned his head to look at the computer, then shook it as if to dismiss a thought. "I don't know." Beyond the glass of the clean room he saw the project paramedics arriving, a separate team within the company response unit. One was carrying a mobile generator, another paddles. "C'mon, we must unhook him so the medics can at least try to restart his heart."

Gently they started to remove the catheters.

Though he wasn't completely surprised, Dr Phillips felt nauseous with excitement when the cardiogram suddenly leapt into life even as the last catheter was extracted. Was he the only one who had half understood?

Daniel blinked once, then looked around him in surprise and puzzlement. "Um...oh God, did I fall asleep?"

They had witnessed, unknowingly, the first step of the birth of the new gods. Unlike the old deities, these ones did not draw their strength from primitive minds seeking anchorage or reason where there was none. Indeed, they were the result of the sharpest intellects overreaching themselves.

When the children were born, everyone sympathised with the unfortunate parents. Rebecca had fallen pregnant while Daniel, her husband, had taken some sick leave from his job at KompuKraft, where, he told her, he researched connections between algorithms and repetitive neural signals. If it had been just the one child the problem might have been ignored, but triplets, and all of them mutants, meant that even the hard-line boardroom pragmatists ordered a halt to Project TCX. Three children, normal to look at, but devoid of any of the five senses could not be dismissed as an unfortunate accident. The problem was, no-one knew what the problem was.

So, as with all things that cannot be understood, they had to be contained and observed. Daniel and Rebecca took little persuading to give up their freakish burdens, even though the birth, overseen courtesy of KompuKraft's private healthcare programme, produced unforeseen complications, which meant that Rebecca would be unable to have more children. They felt little attachment to these flesh and blood equivalents of a wiped hard-drive and overcame the trauma with a large dose of pay-off, which also bought their silence.

In the meantime, the top floors of The Shard were closed off, which was of no consequence to anyone but the powers that be. Those floors had always been jokingly referred to as 'the gods'. Life was like that.

People had more or less forgotten about Carol Fisher, mainly because she had withdrawn from Project TCX years before. A bored guinea pig at first, she had started feeling uneasy about the ethics of the project, but had sensibly kept that to herself. Also, she had wanted to start a family and wasn't sure what poking around in the brain might do to her, which she admitted was an irrational response for a science graduate. Still, logic dictated that she minimise the risks, so she had asked to be moved to the company IT helpdesk.

Hence she felt somewhat vindicated as she entered the surgery of Dr Penny Thatcher, the medical consultant paid for full time by KompuKraft to look after the welfare of their five thousand employees in the World Research Centre.

"I think I'm pregnant, so I'd like to..." She hadn't expected the concerned look that threw Dr Thatcher's pleasant features into shadow and it stopped her in her tracks. "What's wrong?"

Dr Thatcher got up from her seat and went across to the window. She seemed to be weighing up something, biting her bottom lip. When she finally returned to her seat she leaned forward on her elbows and put her fingertips to her forehead. Carol noticed that the doctor's hands were shaking.

"Doctor, are you okay?" The irony of that question from patient to physician was not lost on either of them.

Dr Thatcher looked at Carol and suddenly she was just Penny, a seemingly vulnerable woman, as she took a deep breath and spoke. "Right, I've just come to a big decision. I've not discussed this with anyone before, not even my husband. Before I continue, I want to ask you something. How much does this child mean to you?"

Carol felt suddenly sick with worry and couldn't help but

put her hands defensively across her stomach. "Everything."

"Seriously? Don't give me any glib answers. This is more important than you can know."

"Seriously, everything. I'm thirty-eight. I never thought I wanted kids, but now I feel I'll only be complete when I have one. Doctor, you're frightening me."

Penny reached a hand out in apology. "I'm sorry." She looked at the ceiling, exhaled then continued. "Well then, if this child, assuming you *are* pregnant, means that much to you I must ask you to do as I say, at least if you want it to spend its life with you."

"Now I'm very scared." Carol looked ready to run.

"Again, I'm sorry. Look, what I'm about to tell you must not leave this room. I must have your word on this. Otherwise your child's future cannot be guaranteed, or rather it can, but not in any way you would want. Yours I couldn't vouch for either."

Carol had had enough. What was the matter with the doctor? Had she been trawling her medicine cabinet a bit too enthusiastically? She stood to go.

"Do you remember Daniel Payne?"

Heart pounding, Carol nodded. "Yes." The word scraped from her throat.

"And I needn't ask you if you remember Project TCX? I looked at your medical file before you came in. Luckily for you I'm the only one who ever sees it. I'll be shredding it when this appointment's finished."

Carol sat down again.

She remained seated in stunned silence. Her eyes were drawn to the ceiling, as if they could pierce a thousand feet of building and see the three mutants sitting like tiny stone idols in the empty white room that had been their prison for the two years of their lives so far. Tears filled her eyes as she thought of them and then they dried as she pictured the newly-forming life in her belly. Something else was forming with it; she could feel the bile and fought it down.

"How could you?!"

Penny couldn't blame the woman for feeling angry. Each time she examined the mutants she hated herself for being a part of the silent conspiracy, albeit a more-or-less innocent party. But now fate had offered her a chance for redemption, one which, as a woman and mother herself, she was determined to take.

Carol saw the sadness in the doctor's eyes and felt a twinge of regret for her accusation, especially when Penny spoke again.

"I ask myself that every day when I hug my own children. And that's why I want to give you the chance Rebecca never had, or at least chose not to take. Carol, don't judge her too badly. If you ever held these mutant children, as I have done, and felt the reflex hug that is your response, knowing that they will never see or hear or smell you or your world, never tell you the simplest things, such as that they love you, you would understand."

"That might well be my lot, from what you've said."

Penny smiled. "Let's hope not. You never entered the catatonic state that Daniel suffered. I'll give you a thorough examination, and with the interactive ultrasound we have these days, I'll be able to give you some accurate prognostications."

Carol looked Penny straight in the eye. "Whatever the

322

results, I'm keeping it. They can't buy me off like they did Rebecca. Nor are they going to get the chance to sterilise me."

The shadow returned to Penny's face, only deeper this time. "Whatever the results, you will need to keep this pregnancy secret. What's more, you'll need to disappear - forever." Carol's mouth opened in shock and protest, but Penny continued with a commanding hand gesture. "Make no mistake, they play hardball. It could be that, as a one-time guinea pig in TCX, you are already under observation, but I don't think so. But if they found out you were pregnant, you...I don't know what would happen."

"But they paid Rebecca and Daniel for their silence. Surely they would do the same for me."

Penny sat back in her chair. She put her hands in her lap and her gaze followed them. "They are certainly silent."

Carol didn't want to ask, but felt compelled. "Meaning?"

"They were involved in a tragic car accident just days after Daniel resigned."

She looked at the doctor and felt the bile rising again. "How could you still work for these...bastards?"

"What choice do I have, as someone who knows too much?"

"But why should I trust you?"

Penny looked at her and smiled ironically. "What choice do *you* have?"

On both counts, Carol had to admit she could see the doctor's point.

"But trust me you can, with more than your life," continued Penny. "Now let's examine you and yours. We can go on from there."

Chapter Two - Passing by

P aul Miller swung the car left at the roundabout and started up the hill through the woods along the road that led to his home. He wished he could accept this early autumn day's invitation to feel wonderful. As if it were being focussed through a magnifying glass, slanting afternoon sunlight turned the changing colours of the leaves to flames against a backdrop of blue sky. It was the weekend and he had spent the day with his family, which had done them all good. Psychologically at least. At first.

Now he could feel the coolness of the shadow that never left them. In the back seat, directly behind the radiant blonde head of his beloved wife Karen, was the reason for that chill, their daughter Miranda. Not that he loved her one fraction of an iota less than the day she was born. It was just that no matter how tight he held her, the sickness held her closer still. Some days were better than others. That morning, down by the river, she'd been like any other little girl, well, any girl that didn't collapse in a heart-rending fit of pulmonary distress while chasing a butterfly, coughing till you thought that frail body would burst.

Cystic fibrosis, eh? They could fit the works of Shakespeare on a chip the size of a pinhead, but some old things just refused to be anything other than larger-than-life. Find a cure for that on Google.

So here they were, smiling till their hearts were breaking to keep her spirits up, heading home from another aborted day out, with a pale little girl behind them clasping an oxygen mask to her face

As they came around the next bend of this steep, winding road, they saw the figure walking slowly ahead of them, seemingly weighed down by a battered rucksack. Paul started to slow down as there was no pavement and he was approaching another bend. The figure was wearing a shapeless green waterproof, scruffy Wellingtons and a battered sou'wester. It was rare to find anyone walking up this tough and dangerous hill, with its steep incline and speeding cars, let alone a figure as peculiar as this one. They couldn't tell if it was male or female, just that it was dishevelled and tired.

A part of Paul was preparing to stop, but on this road it was tricky. Yet he knew that, if he really wanted to, he would find a way. That was the crux of it; no denying. He knew he ought to, but he had a sick girl in the back...*the old person's lungs would be heaving like his little girl's*...and stopping on this road could easily lead to an accident...*in the same way that someone dressed in green could be hit and killed.*

Before he knew it he had passed the figure, which appeared to stumble and lurch as he drove by. A glance back revealed the long, matted beard and filthy clothes of a tramp.

Paul was just about old enough at forty-one to remember the occasional scabby inebriate on a park bench or in a shop doorway in the city centres, but their ilk was so rare now that they had almost passed into mythology and were certainly never seen in this neck of the woods.

But the eyes - it was if they had met his in the rear view mirror, intensely blue, incongruous in the frame of bushy beard and brows, the suffering eyes of a young man grown old. They shocked him.

But not as much as the gasp that Karen gave as she grabbed his shoulder.

"Paul! Look...Miranda!"

He switched the direction of his gaze and felt his stomach yo-yo, then pulled over as best he could to the side of the road.

The girl had removed her mask, revealing a face no longer pale and drawn, but almost blushing with health. Then, following a deep breath devoid of the dreaded bubbling that so often emanated from her lungs, she said, "Mummy, daddy, who is he?" and turned to stare out of the rear window in the direction of the tramp.

They had watched the mutants grow, fed them nutrients to keep them alive. What was the point of providing haute cuisine to something with a less discerning palette than a rat? But no one knew what he or she was looking for or at, and the subjects themselves had no purpose. Even a laboratory rat has a maze to run through. These beings simply sat, like statues in a desert, waiting for time. In their silence they were almost eloquent.

Perhaps that was what stirred Josh. Or maybe it was just pity. He had watched through the glass as the medical team had gone through their routine of replacing the saline and the protein drips, performed the necessary physiotherapy and disappeared. Their procedures were so perfunctory as to appear almost callous.

A wave of empathy washed over Josh, the technician whose turn it was that evening to undertake the stultifying task of monitoring the mutants. He had never liked the way the medics, with the exception of that nice lady doctor, made flippant remarks or thought of supposed nicknames for their wards. Hard though it was to imagine, he wondered whether they desired to communicate. On the off-chance that some subconscious recidivist behaviour might surface, he placed laptops in the hands of the three motionless child-beings.

He knew it was pointless; wasn't sure quite why he did it, but it was an inspired and dreadful moment.

Ping.

The sandwich stopped halfway to Josh's mouth. Frowning, he lowered his magazine and tipped himself upright in his chair so that he could see over the partition and through the glass. Just for an insane moment there, he could have sworn he had heard, through the soundproof room's intercom, a laptop re-activating from standby mode.

His mouth remained open, but not to receive the sandwich.

The twitch of a head and a hand could not have caused more excitement if they had emanated from the mummy of Tutankhamun. The dead fingers of one mutant were moving with bewildering speed across the keys of the laptop, and she appeared to have sent a message to her fellow freaks, because they turned their unseeing eyes towards her - and smiled. At the same time, another laptop emitted a soft electronic chime; the receipt signal for a message.

Trembling, Josh entered into the white room. His arrival appeared to go unnoticed and he watched over the shoulder of the mail recipient as he tapped out a reply. What he saw caused sweat to break out on his forehead and he retreated

327

swiftly to his desk. He lifted the handset.

"Sir, you may want to come up here...right now...sir."

"It's binary all right," said Doctor Phillips.

The mutant was typing line after line at astonishing speed. When he stopped, the message simply disappeared from his screen - and there were receipt tones from his companions' laptops.

It appeared that the engineers had both failed yet succeeded beyond those wild dreams after all. Soon they would be wishing they had not.

The new gods had awoken.

"Doc, I have to stop you there."

Even if he hadn't possessed his big, mid-west accent, Thad Leblanc's use of the epithet 'Doc', his expansive hand gesture and self-confident glances at his fellow board members would have marked him out as American. The others had just about reined him in when it came to a mission statement. This was a British company. But he was dominant by nature, a businessman among scientists, the driving force behind the commercial success this company now enjoyed. He continued:

"Can you repeat all that, but in English this time? My learned friends here may know what the hell y'all talking about, but I'm just a plain ol' farm boy." He looked around again, knowing no-one was fooled by his act and revelling in that knowledge. He was the bad-ass Yank they'd brought in to make them rich and he'd obliged, with his ability to cut through the jargon, or as he put it: "To see what was ham and what was spam". However, he wanted to be sure that he really had heard what he thought he had.

Dr Phillips swallowed his chagrin and started again. "The aim of Project TCX was, from a certain point of view, to create a thinking computer. It would seem that we have succeeded, but not as we intended.

"To use a well worn image, we have a chicken and egg situation. I do not know whether something in the unfathomable recesses of the brain caused a response from the chip or vice versa, but it is my belief that Daniel Payne's cytogenesis was affected and this transferred to his progeny. In essence, the computer started to eradicate what it considered to be unnecessary elements - the five senses. It could only second-guess the requirements, of course. So instead of having a machine that we can control by our thoughts, we seem to have a thinking machine.

"Of course, it isn't possible to tell whether the mutants possess thought processes or not, but they do seem to commune somehow, turning or nodding their heads in response to receiving e-mails from each other. That they cannot read these e-mails makes some sort of ESP seem likely, as is often the case in these relationships."

"Well," said Leblanc, "if they are sending e-mails to each other, they must be capable of thought."

"Those mails simply contain links into programmes. My best men have studied these, but they are astonishingly complex, written at ridiculous speed. Luckily we have the best programme writers and analysts on our payroll, but even they can only sit and watch in amazement.

"There is no chance of communicating with these mutants by normal means. They do not understand the world of flesh and blood, of emotions, frustrations, rhetorical questions, normal questions. Their frame of reference does not exist. How do you explain, well, anything to someone who has no senses? No, they seem to bend their powers inwards towards the consideration of a micro world none of us can reach, though they deign to answer questions framed in the correct code relating to all matters IT."

"A kind of futuristic Ask Jeeves," said Leblanc flippantly.

"If you like." Dr Phillips thought the only way to draw the bumptious prick's sting was to agree.

Leblanc stood and moved to the head of the table, a signal to Phillips that he had heard all he needed to, that the stage was now set for him. The doctor sat down. Though he was the least qualified amongst them, there was something about Leblanc that made his colleagues respect him despite the distaste they felt for him, perhaps because he had made it to CEO via that other oft-referenced cliché, the school of hard knocks.

The American stood thinking for some moments, with his back to his fellow board members, then turned. He gestured with open, down turned palms.

"So, Doc, it looks like these freaks are capable of creating software way ahead of its time."

"Decades."

"Well, some of it may still be state-of-the-art, though you guys have sat on it for so long it's probably redundant by now."

Dr Phillips allowed the insult to wash over him. Like any good researcher he had merely watched for a few years to try to be sure of what he was seeing. "It's unlikely any of it has passed its sell-by date."

"When will you realise, research without an end product is

not research, it's an indulgence. Anyway, we also have some pretty sophisticated hardware. I mean, we are the market leader."

"Yes, but we're not that far ahead of the..."

"So," the raised hand emphasised the abruptness of the interruption and was meant to, "we should do what any world leader would do when he has the most sophisticated weaponry available. What the fuck have we been waiting for?"

From his body language it was obvious the question was rhetorical and the meeting was at an end. Compliantly, the other board members, scientists to a man - the only woman was the Chief Accountant - pushed back their chairs. He could almost taste their hesitation.

"Hey!" The word was as placatory as Thad Leblanc could make it. They turned. "If it makes y'all feel any better I'll change the metaphor. We're master craftsmen, with the best tools and blueprints money can buy at our disposal. Now I want us to build. It's been, what?..." He did a mental calculation, "...six friggin' years you've...we've been sitting on this goldmine. Let's get out there and do it." He looked around at each of them as he spoke, knowing that what he said next touched on their collective raw nerve, their biggest fear. "I want us to be such a market leader, so far in front that we have auditors and monopolies commissions coming out of our asses. I *want* them to make it their business to investigate us. I welcome it, 'cos they'll find nothing. And even if they wander up to the one hundred and fiftieth floor, they'll see nothing untoward, just three intense children playing with computers in a crèche. Just pieces on a board, gentlemen, pieces on a board. No one needs to know how they were carved."

Chapter Three - Counting down

Now the old gods had thundered, raged, complained and finally huffed against the fading of their might. For millennia they had sulked while they lost the fearful hearts and minds of men and through this their potency. They had watched helplessly the arrival of the age of the single deity and took some petty pleasure now from its decline. Yet no door had presented itself for their return.

They had a lot of time on their ethereal hands and though time was a concept they no longer regarded, they could hear the ticking of the clock and knew that, for them, midnight was drawing near.

"There must be something out there." The words came from one who stared into the shimmering inkiness of the night. He preferred and had retained the name of Zeus, since it was under that name that he had enjoyed his greatest triumphs, strength and, as his favourite race would have said, kudos.

"I must confess, I'm not sure I'm up to the challenge. I'm not half the man I was," said another.

"You only ever were half the man you were," said Zeus, referring to his fellow deity's propensity for appearing as Pan, half man half goat, a form in which he had often chosen to indulge his appetites. Zeus guffawed in a suitably god-like manner at his own jest. To anyone wandering among the ancient, ruined columns of the temple that night the sound would have registered, if at all, as a swirling puff of dust in a faint breeze.

"You can talk," said Pan, riled. "Look what happened to your statue."

"At least it was one of the Seven Wonders of the World."

"Till the Romans moved in."

"Ah, but then I became even mightier. Centuries later, people still say 'By Jove'. Whereas you seem to have had a set of pipes named after you."

Unable to think of a reply, Pan fell into a sulky silence. And so too did the Athenian night. Stars winked above them in the dark humidity that these beings had not felt in centuries.

"Why are we still here?" asked Pan of no-one in particular.

"I would say leave musing to the Muses, but they too are as good as gone, my poor daughters."

"So, I ask again, why are we still here?"

"Because men feared us enough. Because in less civilised parts of the world they fear us still."

"But those savages, those tribes that continue to hold us in dread, they have no influence in the world that matters. So our strength wanes. Yet surely we should go to them, to where we still hold sway and humans quail in terror before us, or seek our guidance. Look around you. These walls are crumbling."

Zeus scowled at him. "And yet people still whisper in awe when they come here and see this last vestige of the magnificence we had. As you say, look around you, listen. Feel the imposing silence." Zeus's geist moved on top of a battered stone plinth that once had held his carved image and he assumed the pose again, visible only to his shapeless companion. "The splendour of those times. Can you not picture it still? The apogee of man's achievements as a civilisation and they worshipped *us*. It is still here in the hush of this Mediterranean night."

"Ha ha ha ha ha!" The sound of mirthless, ironic laughter came from behind a pillar. They recognised it, looked at each other and groaned as a female voice said, "Pathetic!"

She stepped forward, her form changing constantly, shimmering and shifting; Venus, Isis, Diana, Juno, Hera, Gaea.

"I knew I would find you here. Listen to you. 'Magnificence, splendour, the apogee of man's achievements'." She snorted contemptuously. "At least in this last one you speak true. For ancient as we are, as gods we were man's creation, Zephyrs, and particles of charged dust, given some limited power through the bodies of men and through their desire to fear us, their need to believe that there was something greater than them, or through the ability of their most ambitious leaders to subjugate others with that thought."

The puff of wind known as Zeus turned to her. "To what do we owe this rare pleasure..." He looked at the polymorphic form in front of him and gave a sardonic grin. "...um, how do you wish to be addressed today?"

"Well, since you ask, Minnie will do for the time being."

"Minnie?"

"Yes, it's their idea of a joke."

"They? Who are 'they'?"

She floated past them to stand by the outer columns of the temple, looking out across the city lights into the night. "While you have been sitting here crying, like mortal men,

335

into your drinks, bemoaning your lot, reminiscing about bygone times, I have searched the planet for a means not only to prolong us, but..." she turned towards them, "...to give us a power that, whether you like to believe it or not, we never had. And I have found such a vessel. A conduit back into the world and consciousness of man."

The other deities looked up suddenly with interest. Pan narrowed his eyes suspiciously. "And why would you share this with us?" he asked.

The she-deity gave a knowing smile and raised one eyebrow. "We gods must stick together." She turned and looked into the night again, her voice becoming momentarily wistful. "The decades of my searching have been lonely." Looking back at them, her smile grew arch. "Then there are those needs which, even in human form, only a fellow god can satisfy. You must admit, Zeus, our previous efforts with humans have not been a great success."

Zeus made to protest. He considered himself to have been quite a catch in earthly guise. But she raised a hand to still him. "Besides which, the number three is a perfect fit."

Zeus sat down again on his plinth. "You have our attention and you have us at a disadvantage...Minnie. So let us start at the beginning. Why the name? It does not seem fitting."

She wasn't listening, but stood instead with her hands pressed against one of the columns, her eyes drawn upwards to the remains of the ornate Corinthian capital. "These ruined stones will be replaced by a tower of glass and steel." The other gods looked at each other quizzically. They hadn't been out much. "Our new temple stretches to the heavens, a true Mount Olympus, taller already than the pyramids."

There was a polite, but impatient cough. "Always the

thespian," said Zeus, "but still you make little sense. Again, why the name?"

She looked at them derisively, then decided to continue. "It started as a joke, as far as I can tell, amongst the humans. They referred to them as 'three blind mice', then gave them three names that they considered appropriate; Mickey, Minnie and Jerry." The other deities furrowed their brows and she scowled. "You really have not been out much, have you?"

Zeus stood, affronted. "Are we then to be mice?!" he thundered in suitably Jovian manner.

Minnie raised her eyes towards their mythical home in exasperation. "No."

"Blind then?"

"These vessels are indeed blind. Nor can they hear, smell, taste nor feel." Zeus/Jove stood, but himself was struck dumb. "But they have eyes and all their organs and we will make them live."

Are they dead?"

"More importantly, they will make us live. And we will be powerful." She raised her hands towards the stars and their reflection in her eyes was both ice and fire. "Truly powerful in the world of men, not the stuff of myths. And those same scientists who demeaned us will call us something more appropriate, such as Oppenheimer." She paused, waiting for the inevitable question, but it never came. Even Zeus and Pan had heard of the atomic bomb. "For we will have in our hands a weapon just as deadly, if not more so, for through it we shall control minds."

Chapter Four - Opting out

Though Carol Fisher certainly meant well, she might have done better to keep the details of the dreadful legacy to herself.

"Why, mother, why tell me now?"

"I made a promise to myself at the time that, even though I would have to run and hide, come your eighteenth birthday I would tell you. You have a right to know and are old enough to make up your own mind."

"But how could you just walk out on...my father?"

She knew it was a lot for him to take in, but that last sentence carried just a little too much teenage self-pity for her liking and she couldn't help the sharpness of her reply.

"I had to make sacrifices too. He was also my lover. I adored him." She cursed herself for starting to choke up. "But I couldn't be sure he would keep it to himself. The only way to keep both of you alive for certain was to do what I did."

"Even when I was born a normal child?"

"Normal?" She looked at him and such was the closeness of the bond that had developed through their life together, giving him maturity beyond his years, he knew his last comment was specious. He continued, regretting his thoughtlessness and hoping the dust raised by his next question would cover the false spoor of the last one.

"How do you know about what became of the - what did you call them - mutants? I mean, that they suddenly showed this amazing ability with computers."

Carol Fisher hesitated before answering, as if even mentioning Penny Thatcher obliquely to her own son might endanger that woman. Secrecy had become such a way of life. "Do you remember when you were little, a lady with black hair and sunglasses driving a pick-up truck came to see me?"

"Of course. How could I forget? Visitors didn't exactly come strolling by on a regular basis over the years."

"Well, let's just say that her hair isn't black, she changed hire cars at least three times during her journey and she took a hell of a risk to come here. But she felt it was only right that I knew what was happening. She believed it was important I was aware of any behavioural traits that could potentially surface in you. It might seem like paranoia, but I needed to be aware of anything that could act as a flag."

He'd never questioned his precocious excellence as a programmer, had always taken for granted his three hundred words per minute keyboard skills, even when his mother had insisted he conceal it - she'd convinced him it would seem like showing off, but now of course he knew better. He'd always absorbed information easily and thirsted for more. In so many ways, what he had just heard made enough sense that he couldn't deny it; the remote backdrop to his upbringing, the lack of friends and formal schooling, above all his intuitive empathy with the computer.

With the new found self-knowledge came despair. These

machines that were his ersatz friends had shaped his fate and that of his parents, and he became determined that they would shape him no more. Watching and listening intently over the following days, he saw what was happening in the world, and marvelled that he had been blind to it before, as blind as his unseeing cousins in their rat-run. Now the invasiveness and insidious control of the microchip became clear, latent and unavoidable through mankind's growing dependence on the computer in every single walk of life. Instant communication and information was as important to the lifeblood of the times as oxygen.

This new insight allowed him to sit emotionless in front of the television and computer and his innate powers enabled him to see the milliseconds of subliminal advertising in broadcasts and games. And everywhere, from advertising hoardings at sports events to product placement in dramas, from the anti-virus in his laptop to the spam e-mails and SMS's, from the plasma screens in supermarkets to the check-out scanners, from the growing number of CCTV cameras to software for holiday snaps, the same message, the same name. Each instance might have represented just a grain of sand, but it was part of a dune that moved unstoppably, enlarging the silicon desert that was the twenty-first century.

And at the centre of it all, like a big, bloated spider sat KompuKraft. Suddenly, everywhere he turned he was aware of the malign touch of its web. Wherever there was a lens or a screen he saw one of its myriad eyes. And people were just insects, flying blind into the silken, deadly stickiness of its trap.

Given his own skills, he could only begin to imagine what an inside track the three mutants gave KompuKraft with their unparalleled abilities. His mother had left the company well before he was born, of course, so he had no proof of this except what his eyes told him. And there was an ability, which despite his peculiar kinship with the three freaks he did not share with them; he could sense things, in this case KompuKraft's ambition for control. Ironically, the rest of humankind seemed to have put their senses on standby in that regard.

His mind would fill sometimes with the horror of imagining their existences, those 'beings', which was the word that sprang to mind. They were not people, just as a bird-of-prey that was hand-reared was not a bird-of-prey. The three were locked in a gilded cage. With a shudder he acknowledged exactly what his mother had done for him, how if KompuKraft had ever found out about his conception they might well have forced his abortion, or if not, kept him like a specimen to be examined, forced him to perform; all hush-hush, of course. It would have been a living nightmare for him, robbed of the insensate oblivion enjoyed by the mutants. And heaven knew what the bastards would have done to his mother to ensure her silence, except heaven would have played little part in it.

Suddenly, he felt as if he were already trapped in the web, bound, suffocating, already a slave to his computer. How he had plagued his mother for a KK250 instead of the old steam-driven pile of crap she insisted he use. Perhaps that was another reason she had decided to tell him everything on his eighteenth birthday, because she knew he was now old enough to go out and do what the hell he wanted.

If there was another way for him in his life he was momentarily at a loss to define it. It was only when he admitted to himself that the world he knew could no longer be his world

341

that an alternative presented itself.

When Carol returned from her job at the village shop, the silence when she opened the door was not the first indication that something was amiss. She was used to that, knowing that eventually the machine-gun typing on the keyboard upstairs would scurry into the margins of her senses. It was as she wandered though into the back yard and saw the twisted skeletons of Will's pc and mobile phone that she panicked and hurried upstairs.

Things looked much as usual, with the bric-a-brac of a boy's life strewn around the room. Except for the empty desk, which had an ominous sheet of paper placed much too thoughtfully and neatly in the middle of it.

Remotely she watched her shaking hands pick it up.

Dear Mum,

Call me a coward, but when it came down to it I couldn't bring myself to say goodbye, knowing that the look in your eyes would tear me apart.

I know now how brave you were, not just in taking that decision eighteen years ago, but every time you started your car, every time I went to the shops, every time the doorbell rang after dark. And finally, in telling me everything, knowing it would change life irrevocably. Only you know why you did the latter, Mum, and though part of me wishes you hadn't, the greater part of me is glad that you have and knows that you had to. In telling me, you knew that, if I was true to being your son I would have to go. Please don't look for me or raise any alarms, though I know even as I write it that's a redundant statement and you would never do that.

So anyway, please don't take this as a goodbye, though I can't promise it's an 'au revoir'. To quote one of those old bands you used to like, I've got to break free. God knows what I'll do now. Maybe I'll work on a farm, go to a kibbutz or just walk the open road for a while – do something that keeps me off the straight and narrow!

I've taken nothing with me that would link me to you. That's for your own safety, but I guess it means that if anything happens to me you'll never know.

Be brave, Mum. Who knows, maybe one day you'll even hook up with Dad again. That would be nice.

Your loving son,
Will

By now Carol had plopped herself down on the end of the bed. Half her tears were for herself and they were bitter, but those shed for her son were not. She had always known that telling him of his heritage would be to open the cage, allow him a freedom that, no matter how tough, would feel like something better than a witness protection programme. Through the tears she smiled.

Chapter Five - Going up

"Damn them! They've put another camera in place." Will withdrew his head hurriedly round the corner before the motion detector kicked in, and leant back against the wall in dismay.

"I tell you, Willy boy, the time will come sooner rather than later when we'll have to give this game up and join the ranks of the civilised," said his partner in grime, in his incongruous Berkshire accent. "It's getting harder by the day to have a good rummage. This is no fun any more."

"It's okay for you to say that, Sparky; this *is* just a game to you."

Sparky put a hand on Will's threadbare sleeve. "No man, I've heard what you've said. They fuck with our minds. It's self-deluding to believe we have free will...hey! Is that why you chose your name?" he asked, with a grin.

"No, it is Will. And remember, don't you ever tell anyone that."

"Like who?" Sparky's smile disappeared. "Who do we ever get to talk to? We haven't seen another brother in a long time." Suddenly Sparky was smiling again. "Do you think they're all hiding in some long-forgotten tunnel underground somewhere, like in The Terminator?"

Will sighed at the younger lad's foolishness. "No, I reckon they've all gone one of two ways; yours or mine. Either way, it's a cul-de-sac."

"What do you mean?" Sparky tried to look affronted, but there was a look in his eye and he couldn't hold Will's gaze when the latter next spoke.

"You see, Sparky, though I personally have lost track of time a bit, my contact with the likes of yourself means that I know I have been on the road for about twelve years. But in the last couple of those I've noticed a sea-change.

"At first I felt strangely liberated. I had a bit of savings with me and I could drift, doing casual farm labour, beach-combing, working in vineyards, construction work. I slept where I could, sometimes comfortably in workers' quarters or in barns, occasionally a bed and breakfast. It was an adventure. Even when it got tougher, became more of a fight for survival, there was always something I carried with me, something no-one else could touch, that stopped me from succumbing and rejoining the technological age.

"And though it went against everything I believed in, I stole if I had to. I got by. It's amazing what places you can find when you have to wash clothes, sleep for a few hours. If I was cold or wet, knowing the alternative kept me strong."

"Well, what was, or is, the alternative, man?" said Sparky. What is it you're carrying with you?"

"If I told you wouldn't believe me, and your own cosy world, which you'll doubtless return to, would never seem the same."

Sparky bridled at this second, less oblique suggestion that he was about to give up, partly because he knew that was exactly the way he was heading. His rebellion was almost over before it had really begun. Will was determined to help him feel better about it as he continued.

"Let's face it, as you said, this is getting almost impossible. We're both starving. More and more of the places where we used to find food are being covered by the cameras, like this skip here." He gestured with his thumb in the direction of the corner of the wall. "There's no loose change to be had as nearly everyone pays by KompuKard these days, and in any case, with begging outlawed we can't be seen to ask. And you?" With grimy fingers he felt the shabby fabric of Sparky's coat. "This is just another version of the rich student's baggy, shapeless, I'm-trying-hard-not-to-look-privileged jumper." Sparky pulled his jacket from Will's grip. "I'm sorry. Look, don't be angry. In twelve years I've seen them come and go - the would-be, angst-ridden anarchists, rebelling against their vision of 1984. I've had more partners than Clint Eastwood. Believe me, you don't know the half of it."

Offended, Sparky bit. "Oh and you do, do you? What makes you so different?"

Will gazed past him at nothing. "Like I said, if you knew, you really wouldn't believe me." Now he looked his companion in the eyes again. "But don't deny that on any number of occasions recently, huddled in a storm drain or behind a tree in a park, as hunger spasms attacked, or as you forced down gratefully the scrapings of melted cheese from a discarded fast food wrapper, you have comforted yourself with the thought that you could return anytime to the life you knew. You're not alone in that. Everyone is nice and cosy as they are and sometimes I get frightened when I realise that escape tunnel has probably collapsed behind me. I have to go on. Look, the bottom line is I can't say any more. It would put other lives at risk."

"That's some pretty heavy duty stuff you're saying."

"Well, Sparky, do yourself a favour - don't repeat it to anybody."

"Okay, okay." It clearly wasn't okay, but the young man was getting the message from his obstinate, perhaps slightly insane companion. "So anyway, this sea-change you were talking about."

"Yeah, a couple of years back it all just seemed to get a bit more serious. Like somebody wanted a homogenised society. It's the Morlocks and the Eloi all over again."

Sparky pulled a blank expression.

"Read your H.G. Wells," said Will with a sigh. "I tell you, sometimes I wonder why I'm bothered what becomes of mankind when they don't care about the basics any more."

"But you're not," said Sparky testily, "you're worried about you."

There was nothing Will could say to that. Adding anything to the truth is usually impossible. "Anyway, that skip back there is typical of the sort of thing that's happening." The skip was where a food-packing company disposed of items that looked less than perfect. The CCTV camera covering that yard was a new addition. "And you've said it yourself: we've not seen one of our brothers in a long time. On the plus side, of course, there seems to be no crime or any sign of it. The police appear within seconds of any offence. The down side is, an offence seems to encompass anything beyond the straight and narrow, which is where I happen to spend most of my time. But even I haven't dared to pinch so much as a sweet from a corner shop in a while.

"And cards - we're in a world controlled by cards - entry

cards, payment cards, exit cards, identity cards, toilet cards, car-park cards. I can't get any casual labour any more; the foremen are scared of lightning raids because they have to prove they've asked for your identity card. And who controls those cards? Have a good look. If you must ask yourself anything when you have gone back, ask that. And be careful."

Will gestured towards his clothes. "I didn't always look this bad, you know. But it's got to the point where I can barely scratch survival from the soil any more. I feel my days are numbered. But still, I don't think I could live with myself if I came inside again, even if there were a way back in for me now."

"Why?" The simplicity of Sparky's question was a sign of both desperation and resignation.

"It doesn't matter why. Just look at me." He put both weary hands on Sparky's shoulders, which sagged. "And I think now is as good a time as any for the ways to part." The lad didn't look up, but simply gave a sad nod. "Look, it's only been a month for you. So go home, tell your parents you have been, I don't know, youth hostelling or in a commune or something, apologise for the smell and get back to your life. And thank you, Sparky."

The lad looked up with tears in his eyes at a face both young and aged beyond its thirty years and felt gratitude for being allowed to retreat gracefully from that fate and his own failure. Still he gave it one last shot. "Hey, why don't you come with me? My parents have plenty of room. You're a clever guy. You could..."

"Thanks," interrupted Will, "but there's no way. Rest assured, if it ever got out that you knew me, there's a chance that both our lives would be in danger. Believe that and be on your way. You're a good lad."

Looking back, perhaps it was a premonition of desperate acts to come, an awareness that he was close to breaking that drove him to that sad goodbye. Maybe he knew the worsening hunger and weakness made his next despicable act inevitable. Did he hope that his reward might be a bullet to end his misery? If so, he made a gross miscalculation. He knew well enough from his own observations that the police arrived within a minute of cameras picking up any acts of scavenging. Even before he had chosen this way in life, legislation just about tolerated tramps if they didn't beg or 'cause distress within the public sphere', though this didn't stop the police from harassing them and moving them on. 'Distress' seemed fairly loosely defined, as indeed did the 'public sphere' and rooting in bins and skips seemed, in the eyes of the authorities, to fit the definition of causing one within the other.

So he should not have been surprised in the slightest that stealing food from that child brought down the full wrath of the authorities, with an impact so great, it might have fallen upon his head from the top of Mount Sinai.

He was starving, prepared to risk all for a bite of that burger, knowing there was never the remotest possibility of escape. While summoning up the courage needed to push his scruples aside, he imagined the Great War. He wondered whether the foot soldiers, after months of skulking in rat-infested trenches, nerves shredded by constant bombardment, caught between the fear of action and the despair of torpor, felt this sense of dislocation and distortion, unable to comprehend time or place as they finally received the order to go over the top, placing their heads at last into the jaws of death. When the parents turned their backs, he leapt forward, snatched the carton from the little boy and ran as fast as his weakened condition would allow. Then he stopped in a side road, only wanting enough time to stuff the manna into his crusty mouth.

In the side-road, blissful silence reigned for a moment. There was only the aroma of the burger, the faint whine of cameras turning to focus on him and the distant sirens, growing louder. No one had pursued him - they all knew that there was no need in this society of omniscient law-enforcement. So he sat, enjoying every last mayonnaise-encrusted shred of lettuce, licking the mustard from his fingers. The police found him with a smile on his face.

They soon wiped it off.

When he came to again, he found himself held fast in plastic restraints, like cable ties, around his wrists and ankles. There was a metallic taste in his mouth and red fluid down the front of his stained T-shirt, which he knew was certainly not ketchup. His body ached, as much from being hurled around on the floor of the van now as from the beating.

The violence had shocked him. Having never seen the arrest of one of his kind before, he had no idea what awaited him.

At last the van came to a halt, screeching unnecessarily to a stop so that the captive in the back slid along the floor and cracked his head. Through the semi-consciousness that ensued Will felt himself being pulled by his ankle restraints from the open back doors of the van so that he fell to the pavement like the proverbial sack of potatoes. Now he was dragged by those restraints, the flagstones scraping his back and hands. Still he was aware enough to notice, before he disappeared down a goods entrance, the towering, needle-like building he was entering, around the very top of which clouds wisped like wraiths. This was no police station, it was The Shard, home of the Three Stooges, his freakish siblings.

But his journey continued downwards along a ramp. He wasn't quite past caring and fear started to replace the pain. This particular journey, which if he had but known it was the easy part, ended with him being dumped in an ominously bare, tiled room. There was a drain in the middle and the silence was emphasised by a slow, regular dripping somewhere. Beyond the door was darkness, above him harsh spotlights, though a toe-capped boot added a few stars as it connected with his ribs, once for each word uttered by the uniformed thug.

"Filthy!...stinking!...fuck!"

He had assumed they were policemen, a lot of whom nowadays were difficult to differentiate from the jackbooted Nazis of history, but why had they brought him here, to the HQ of KompuKraft? For Will, it confirmed his belief that for the last two years, this gigantic company had started to exert a stranglehold on all facets of life and society. No surprise there, when it was clear from his mother's words that it was run by megalomaniacs. In his eyes, it exonerated his increasingly solitary lifestyle, nihilistic view of the world and every decision his mother had made since before he was born. He felt a flicker of pride through the pain, but he was like a tea-light in the darkness of night's cathedral and it seemed that he would soon go out.

He did not consider himself a tramp, merely disenfranchised, but he wondered if all the vagrants and homeless, noticeable by their decreasing numbers in the last couple of years, had ended up in this room or its like.

"Right, let's get 'im cleaned up."

The uncouth voice barked an order and suddenly Will was hit forcefully again, only this time by a power-hose, as brutal and shocking in its own way as the boots. He watched the mixture of blood and dirt wash down the drain. Then he was hauled roughly to his feet.

"Right, let's get 'im dried off. Don't wan' 'im dripping on the carpets."

The thugs released his ankle restraints then stepped back, and from vents in the walls and ceiling came blasts of hot air. Of all the experiences in the last hour it was the least unpleasant, but by the end of it he was aching and dehydrated.

What followed was surreal in the extreme. From the harsh, terrifying basement area he was bundled into a goods elevator, from which he emerged into a different silence, the imposing stillness of KompuKraft's reception lobby. It was Saturday, so this area was empty except for two guards, who still asked the two cops for their Ids before waving them through. Beyond the smoked glass Will saw the outside world going by soundlessly. If it hadn't been for the noise of his and his captors' feet on the marble, he might have believed he had gone deaf. Looking up, he saw cameras in the top corners following their movement across the lobby. There were abstract paintings on the walls, Dalis, possibly originals. They seemed to reflect how he felt now, dislocated, only obliquely in touch with reality.

He was thrown into another lift, a carpeted one, so plush and well engineered that the closing of the doors and the journey upward were just rumours.

When one of the thugs spoke it almost shattered the silence.

"What do they wanna see 'im for?"

"Who knows. Maybe it's a freak show." They laughed out of all measure for the wittiness of the comment.

"It's rumoured they never see anybody - just live up there in their own little world."

"Little world, hah! That's a laugh."

If the lift ride had been too smooth to cause his stomach to lurch, this revelation made it flip. It seemed he was being taken to see the three mutants. But why? And what had changed? They wanted to see him? Something was wrong here. According to his mother they were beings deprived of senses, statues. Perhaps he wasn't being taken to them at all. But if he wasn't, and if it was the powers-that-be in KompuKraft who wanted him, that was game over. Had he been tracked down? Was his arrest an excuse? And if so, was his mother still alive?

Chapter Six - Moving in

For both gods and mutants their union was almost orgasmic in its painful, intense ecstasy. But for the mutants it nearly broke them, a sensory overload, too much data to compute, as their bodies were invaded and all systems suddenly switched on. They lay writhing on the floor, by turns spasming into the foetal position then stretching out. Their various drips and catheters either pulled free or brought equipment crashing down.

Even for the gods it was a new experience. Previous attempts to invade human bodies had always met with resistance and they had needed to machete their way through a tangle of emotions. Here they had slid into virgin territory without the encumbrance of a personality to fight against and the purity of the experience almost overwhelmed them.

They had chosen to make their move at night; though the mutants never slept the staff were less alert after a vigil that had lasted twenty-eight years. Their wards were part of a production process now, running like a machine on the one hundred and fiftieth floor. But the birth pains of the new gods brought them running, though they could only stand and stare helplessly. The full extent of the metamorphoses hadn't yet struck home - it was a soundproof lab and the

354

intercom, through lack of diligence, wasn't switched on, so the guttural moans that accompanied the writhing escaped the onlookers.

At last all was still. As the technicians looked in they noticed a haze in the white room, as if something was smouldering. Dr Phillips, who it seemed almost lived at The Shard now, had been summoned by an emergency alarm. He strode in and looked through the glass.

"What the hell has...?"

He broke off as the three figures twitched, stirred then started to push themselves to their feet. Given the wasted state of their muscles, which apart from those required to use a keyboard were only activated by physiotherapy, this was an act that many would have considered beyond them. Dr Phillips signalled to the other four technicians to follow him and they rushed into the white room to help the mutants. As he held one of them by its skeletal arm, Phillips imagined he felt a peculiar pulsing beneath his fingertips, though he dismissed this as his own racing heart.

"They seem undamaged," he said. "So what the hell happened here?" There was a collective silence broken by somebody's "don't know". Phillips turned on his team. "Don't know? This is your shift." He gestured around him. "And look at the bloody equipment!"

As Phillips stooped and started picking up pieces of machinery he missed what the others saw, though they couldn't believe their eyes. The mutants seemed to be looking around and the one nearest the doctor was watching what he was doing with that cocking of the head typical of a curious dog. Phillips, suddenly aware of the inactivity of the others stood up and started to reprimand them, but his words died in his throat as he saw the team looking past him.

If the three siblings had had a purity of creation and purpose, like water, then the sulphurous nature of the old gods had polluted them, turned them into something much more corrosive. If any immediate proof of this were needed, it was the awesome blow that not only knocked Dr Phillips senseless, but also sent him flying off his feet across the room.

The mutant, twisted his head left and right as if freeing up a stiff neck, then looked at the hand that had delivered the blow, clenching and straightening the fingers.

"By Jove!" said Jove, "I was never able to do that before."

"Just imagine," said the goddess next to him, also examining her wasted body, "what will be possible when we are at full strength, some hours from now."

She turned the previously unseeing eyes towards the technicians, who stood slack-jawed. As one they turned, colliding with each other in their desperation to get away. But the she-deity simply stepped across to one of the undamaged laptops and typed with unnatural speed. The research team came to a crunching halt as they collided with an exit door that should have opened.

"Whoooh!" gasped the goddess, "look what I just did. And I didn't even have to think about it."

"What did you do?" asked Jove/Zeus.

"I believe I just overrode the programme for opening the doors. She turned to her fellow deities, ignoring the commotion amongst the scientists. "We are going to be so powerful."

The members of the board of KompuKraft looked around at

each other in the pregnant silence. There was a mixture of apprehension and curiosity in the air, as well as irritation with being summoned at what they foolishly believed was an ungodly hour. There was also an element of self-consciousness and embarrassment, as they had been told to come straight away by Dr Phillips and none of them was looking as spruce as usual. Even Thad Leblanc, the power-dressed clothes-horse, had greying stubble showing. The fact that Dr Phillips was not yet present in the boardroom added to the irritation. The question was asked once again by Dr Melvyn Biggs, Director of Programming, as he sipped tentatively at the steaming coffee-to-go he had picked up en route: "Doesn't anybody know what the hell is going on?"

"Roger certainly sounded agitated when he called," replied another.

"Yes, but in a strangely constrained way," said Biggs, "like someone who knows their phone's being tapped."

Just then a door opened at the far end of the boardroom. There was rustling movement around the table, as if everyone had been stirred by a breeze like leaves in a gutter.

In walked Dr Phillips. There were gasps, but he gave an urgent little hand signal to everyone for their silence and then took his place along with them at the table. At first everyone's eyes were fixed on the ugly bruising on the side of his face, but then there was another gasp, more like an involuntary, half-stifled cry from Barbara Jaeger, the Chief Accountant, and they all looked towards the door.

"What the fuck...?" said Thad Leblanc, inelegant but succinct as ever. His jaw hung open in common with everyone else's.

They were still in their white, loose-fitting garments as

357

they had been for the thirty years of their lives so far. The invading forces now within them had given them some colour already, but still they had a preternatural look about them, not least their eyes, which were hideously compelling and were the windows to something other than a soul.

As they came in and stood at the head of the table, shaven-headed and homogenous in appearance, like ethereal acolytes, Dr Phillips seemed to shrink back from them. But when they spoke, it took all the will-power of the other board members not to cower as well, so dreadful were the voices, grating on unused vocal chords, yet powerful and commanding. The female, who stood in the centre, had the aura of leadership and she spoke first.

"How ironic that we now speak and you are struck dumb." Her comment elicited no response. The awe felt by the scientists amongst them, in other words all except Thad Leblanc and Barbara Jaeger, was being held in check by Dr Phillips's miserable demeanour. There was nothing but dismay on his face. The female mutant continued. "Well, we called you here at this time because we could and we wanted you to get used to that because things are going to change around here."

Now Thad Leblanc found his voice. "Meaning?"

When she looked at him, Leblanc was amazed to find that he both flinched from her gaze and experienced a massive surge of testosterone in his loins.

"Meaning exactly what you are already fearing subconsciously. Yes, we're taking over."

There was subdued yet outraged murmuring around the table.

Leblanc stood. "Says who?"

"Says you," the male mutant to the right of the female said. Now they all noticed to their amazement that he appeared to be more powerfully built than upon his arrival. "That is once you realise the price all of you would have to pay if your dark secrets ever came to be public knowledge."

Leblanc felt his knees buckle and he sat down. My God! In one fell swoop he had been defeated.

Now the female spoke again. "This does not have to be a conflict; no need for internecine warfare. Let us combine our strengths and we can make this the greatest empire since the Greeks." She looked across to the mutant containing Zeus and gave a slight smile, which he returned.

"What do you mean?" said Biggs.

"It's quite simple really. We continue to provide the genius, the inspiration, the Muse, and you provide the technical know-how. Together we can rebuild the pyramids."

"And if we refuse?" The voice was Leblanc's.

Zeus looked at him. "I don't think you want to do that. Besides this is a win-win situation, to use the jargon of the late part of the last century. You as a company will be continuing along a path you have already taken. In return for your compliance and..." here he looked at his white clothing, "...a few long-overdue luxuries, you will all become rich commensurate with your wildest dreams.

"I doubt," said the third mutant, which contained Pan, "given that they are scientists, that their wildest dreams were very wild. He sniggered while looking lustfully at Barbara Jaeger in a way that made her feel unclean.

"More important," said the female mutant, "you will have our silence."

Leblanc may have been terrified, he may also have seen

that there was no alternative, but as he was the guy used to showing people that they had no choice, he recognised in these power-crazed oligarchs his own demise and the bitterness was evident in his voice. "So that's it, huh? Situation normal. Just carry on towards world domination. Well we've shut people up before and we can do it again."

The other board members cringed. When you had kept a lid on something for so long, hearing it alluded to, even within an inner sanctum, was shocking. They all knew what he meant

The goddess-mutant looked at him and it took all his resolve not to shrink away.

"We have absorbed much in the few hours since our, shall we call it awakening, including everything ever held in your...our system's memory and databases. Let's face it, we redesigned most of it in our lifetime. So I can only assume you are talking about the fate of our parents." Leblanc lived up to his surname now and went completely pale. "That is why we know that you, Thad Leblanc, have the special skills, are exactly the calibre of man needed to ensure the success of our joint venture. You see, we have a plan, a simple but devastatingly effective one. And human nature being what it is, it's not going to make us very popular. So we're going to need all the winning qualities in that greedy heart of yours. People will not like KompuKraft. As you can see, our appearance wouldn't exactly win us lots of friends either. We need a front man, and that is you, Mr Leblanc. Our feeling is, we need to remain your little secret."

Barbara Jaeger spoke up. "What about your team, Doctor Phillips? Haven't they seen what's happened?"

Phillips seemed to flinch yet again before replying. "When

I saw what was happening I dismissed the team for the night. They're unaware. I shall," he hesitated, "tell them that there's been a change of protocols.

"They have been silent thus far," said Zeus. "I'm sure they shall remain so."

But Leblanc's mind was already racing ahead. What was done was done, if not forgotten or forgiven. "So, you said you had a plan. What is it?"

The female deity leaned forward and put her hands on the table. "Ah, yes, Mr Leblanc, as the public face of KompuKraft, you may wish to head home and tidy up, for in a very few hours you will be facing that public."

"Whaddaya mean?"

"I mean that in a few short hours panic will be setting in within a couple of major corporations and undertakings that rely even more heavily than others on their computers. Even now there is a virus at work in their systems and we, KompuKraft, can provide the only effective anti-virus." The other board members saw Dr Phillips look up. This was evidently news to him. "We will wait for these other bodies to announce their problem, then reveal that the same virus has attacked our system also, yet has been brought under control."

"Let me guess," said Leblanc, his voice full of suspicion and knowledge. "We created that virus."

"Well, we had a little time," Zeus hesitated before continuing, "to kill."

Dr Phillips leapt in. "But...but surely that virus will be traced back to us!"

"You underestimate our skill," said the goddess. "We are way beyond anything yet dreamt of. It will be as if our footprints have been washed away by the tide."

"What if other anti-viruses work?" said Melvyn Biggs.

"Trust us, they will not."

"But," said Leblanc, "just how is the sale of an anti-virus destined to make us so powerful? And surely the authorities will be as suspicious as hell."

Now Zeus stepped forward. "That, Mr Leblanc, is where you come in. We are providing here the golden opportunity to make KompuKraft *the* power in software and hardware. We are giving you the weapon; you must use it." Leblanc was struck by the echo of his very words, back when the mutants' special ability had been brought to his awareness.

"In the short time since our metamorphosis we have done our best to absorb and understand the workings of this modern world," said the she-mutant taking up the argument. "My feeling is, our initial choice of victims will cause enough panic; that others will not stop to argue the rights and wrongs. They will want what you have to give. Whether they suspect you or not, the authorities can do nothing. Sooner rather than later they will be eating from the palm of your hand."

"And who exactly did you single out as guinea pigs?" asked Leblanc

"Parts, but not all, of the air traffic control system at Heathrow Airport, some Metropolitan Police forensic records and certain National Health Service systems." There was a hum of reaction around the table. "Enough to give doubters a foretaste of what their inaction might bring."

"Jesus," said Leblanc, "you'd better be sure that this thing is not traceable."

"Leave that to us," said the Pan-mutant. "Meanwhile you'd better hurry along now and think about what you're going to say."

Taking orders from these creeps wasn't easy for Leblanc. "What if I just blow this whole little scheme of yours apart?"

Zeus made to advance menacingly towards him, but the she-mutant held up her hand to stop him and turned her black, shifting eyes on Leblanc. "That of course is your choice and you will have plenty of time to reflect on whether it was the right one in prison, which is where a number of this company's actions will land all of you." She looked at each of them in turn then back at Leblanc. "As for us, we are only beginning to understand the kind of hellish jail in which we have been trapped all our lives. A common prison would be freedom in comparison. But no-one would be able to prove our collusion. We are simply three mutants, products of your devilish machines." Silence ensued. "Be here at nine o'clock to present your statement. Do not fail us."

Leblanc and Phillips exchanged glances. "I won't," said the American.

9.05 am. It had been an unusual presentation by Thad Leblanc's standards, devoid of PowerPoint slides, videos, statistics and sound-bites. Yet in a perverse way it had given him one hell of a buzz, like breathing pure oxygen. He'd been given the ultimate PR task, much as he resented the circumstances. There were lives and global market domination at stake. What more incentive could a man in his position want?

The demographics had kind of concentrated his mind and by the time he had returned to his office, shaved and put on the fresh set of clothes he always kept there he'd come up with the solution. A simple one, but devastatingly effective.

With balls of steel he would face the press and point out to them that, altruism to one side for the moment, this was a classic case of supply and demand. A company like KompuKraft invested millions in research, in the hope that it would develop something unique. It could not now be expected simply to surrender its advantage for the benefit of the more myopic. Of course it would seek to profit from it while at the same time providing a service to all.

He had realised that the mutants were absolutely right. Popularity was not the issue here. Thus it was announced that anyone wanting to take advantage of KompuKraft's sophisticated anti-virus would "...have to enter into signed, long-term agreements for the supply of hardware, software, technical support and upgrades."

There were cries of disapproval from the gathered press-men.

"Mr Leblanc," shouted one journalist, "ethically how do you think this makes KompuKraft look?"

"Well, I know that, from a touchy-feely-warm-and-fuzzy point of view it don't look great. But this is business, my friends. There'll be those among you and out there in the market that will raise your hands in uproar. But hey, tick-tock-tick-tock. Our systems are doin' just fine."

"Mr Leblanc, there are planes circling up there, being talked in using old back-up systems that will doubtless fall prey to this virus any time. Other flights into Heathrow are being diverted or cancelled. How do you think folks feel about someone holding lives to ransom in that way?"

"Probably the same way they feel about companies that have a virus attacking their vital systems who haven't invested millions of pounds into research to make those systems secure and are now too tight-fisted to reach an agreement with someone who could solve their problems."

Thad Leblanc's performance that morning was so good, he almost convinced himself. It wasn't until he returned to his office and saw his clothes from that morning hanging there that he remembered: he was just the messenger boy now. He looked at his chair - it was no longer the seat of power.

He stalked across to a mahogany cabinet, poured himself a large Jack Daniels, downed most of it and looked at the clock. 09.45. He put the drink down in disgust.

Chapter Seven - Cleaning up

The seemingly impossible had happened: they'd become bored with power.

Over the course of two years they'd watched nearly everyone bend to their will. Institution after institution had fallen. Using inherent skills they did not truly understand they'd hacked into banks, intelligence agencies, military defence systems, the world's financial institutions. Everywhere they had planted their angry little seeds and watched them grow into big, bad bastard sons. And people had soon forgotten KompuKraft's seemingly mercenary attitude at the start of the crisis. They were seen instead as providers of unquestionably efficient and almost impossibly advanced software and hardware. Their systems were the most secure there had ever been and when, for some inexplicable reason, a new, untraceable virus appeared, anti-virus upgrades could be loaded with the minimum of fuss. It was global hegemony with two capital K's.

When they were not toying with the nerves of IT directors around the globe, Juno, Zeus and Pan, which were the three names they appeared to have settled on amongst themselves, indulged their senses up in the clouds, satisfying their hybrid appetites. The novelty of this had not yet worn off, but still one afternoon Juno stood by one of the penthouse windows looking out across the shimmering city below. From the couch, where his magnificent, muscular body lolled, Zeus admired her nakedness and felt his softening penis start to twitch again.

"Does my love-making now make you sad?"

"No, Zeus my love, but standing here does."

"How so?"

"I see a world that we dominate that does not know of our existence."

"I've been out there many a time," said Pan, who was lying stretched out on the floor, also naked.

Juno looked around and the impatience was evident on her face. "I'm not talking about sneaking into some night-club, where the music drowns our otherworldly voices."

"Oh, you don't know what you're missing. They positively welcome the weird in these places. And the things they have to offer. Potions, pills and gases, which would make you come so violently, this latest frenzied orgasm of yours would seem like a Greek tragedy in comparison."

"Pan, for you eternity is just the chance for a long fuck."

Pan opened his arms in faux innocence, then rolled onto his side and looked at Juno over the top of his designer sunglasses, initially worn to cover his disconcerting eyes, but to which he was now so attached he wore them during sleep. "You're forgetting MTV." Juno turned back to the window. "But what I am saying, dearest goddess, is that there is nothing to prevent us wandering out among the prolls."

"It is you who are forgetting something." Juno's eyes wandered to the very back of their luxuriously appointed penthouse, towards what appeared to be a room with blacked-out windows, incongruous in the opulence. "We cannot afford to stray too far from that which keeps us strong. We would soon weaken, magnificent though these bodies have become."

"And you certainly are magnificent, my darling Juno," said Zeus.

Pan pointed to the black windows and said, "Hopefully the ability to harness that power won't remain beyond us for very long. I've been to some clubs that would put the old Roman orgies to shame."

Zeus got up and crossed to the window and addressed Juno. "Standing there gazing out across the city, you remind me of how you were that night in the balmy Mediterranean, when you first told us of the possibility of being here. And how right you were. We have come so far. Don't let it get you down. It is always the nature of absolute power that it is ultimately unsatisfying."

"I know, I know. But I just want to," she hesitated, "lash out somehow. We own these people, but no-one quails before us."

"The board of directors does."

"Yes, but we can hardly condemn one of them to push a boulder to the one hundred and fiftieth floor for the rest of eternity."

"I see, I see. Yes, you're right. We need to create another Tantalus or Prometheus, create some sort of a punishment in keeping with our mythological status."

"What about Thad Leblanc?" said Pan. "Maybe he could be condemned never to look in a mirror again." He laughed at his own joke.

"Oh pipe down," said Zeus

"Hah!" Pan giggled, then wandered off to the fridge to get a beer. "Very good. Pipe down." Zeus frowned at him. "D'you get it? Pipe. Pan."

Zeus raised his eyebrows and looked despairingly at Juno, but she smiled indulgently. Pan always won her round in the end, which was an irritation to Zeus, especially when Juno invited the former to join their lovemaking, and particularly as Pan's tastes were exotic to the extent that he didn't mind who he made love to.

"We have already punished Leblanc," said Juno, "by taking away his power, making him our lapdog. In a way there is a strange parallel with our situation; materially he has all the things he ever wanted, but something is missing, in his case control."

"Well, for someone to defy us," said Zeus, "realistically they would need to be outside our sphere of influence. And that narrows it down to a very few people. The bulk of the world's most powerful figures are in league with us, willingly or unwillingly. There's very little that doesn't feed back into our server, one way or another."

Suddenly Juno slapped her forehead. "Of course!"

"What?" said Zeus.

"Really we need to pick someone of no significance. In this world of instantaneous data flow, hurting someone of importance would draw attention and let's face it, if the world decided as one that it didn't want us here, well, let's just say we can't control bullets. So let's trawl the security cameras, find someone who doesn't approve of our sanitised, safe world and who won't be missed."

"To be honest," said Pan, "the world we've created in-volves most of its citizens sitting at home like couch potatoes.

369

They know that outside on the streets it's virtually a police state. That's why the clubs are so popular. There's an understanding that anything goes, but never leaves." He stepped forward conspiratorially. "There's this one place where they piss..."

Zeus raised his hand. "Enough."

"There must be someone," said Juno, absorbed in her idea. "Someone who's breaking the rules."

"Well, we've wiped most of the homeless from the files of mankind."

"Never mind," said Juno. "Put the word out with the police. We want to see anyone they catch who can safely be deleted from the records. Whoever that is will wish they'd never been born. And," her eyes gleamed as she had another idea, "they can trial the control chip."

She turned to the window triumphantly. Then she became aware of Zeus' hot breath on her neck.

"Do you feel better now?" he said as he nibbled on her neck, stiffening her nipples.

"Much."

Then his hands were on her breasts, squeezing. "You see, there are compensations to our lives in these bodies."

She closed her eyes, enjoying the pressure, reached behind her and applied some of her own. "Oh there are," she said, "enormous ones."

Chapter Eight - Chipping in

As he was bundled out of the lift he could see through the windows that they were only about halfway up the building. They marched him the few feet to another set of lift doors, by the side of which were retinal scanners. There were also cameras above, but he noticed that these didn't follow their progress like the ones in the lobby. The policemen looked into the scanners and after a few seconds the doors opened. These ones didn't move silently like the others, but lumbered under the weight of what appeared to be armour plating. Will realised that the thugs must have belonged to the higher echelons of the police; God only knew what the rank and file comprised.

As the lift rose Will was now sure he had been singled out. No way would every common-or-garden offender be brought here. But how had they found him? Had Sparky gone and blabbed? Had he been actually working under cover for KompuKraft? He was really scared now. What were they going to do to him?

Will was rising through seventy unpeopled floors. The Shard had never been fully occupied and had been built with the company's expansion in mind, but when Project TCX had misfired the empty levels had been seen as a perfect barrier between the quick and the dead. So the lift could not stop between floors eighty and the top. Even the exalted ones, such as Thad Leblanc and the other board members had never ventured this far once the new gods were installed.

And suddenly he was there. In a peculiar moment of detachment he realised the doors were about to open onto the one place he had avoided or been kept from all his life.

He was hurled into a sort of ante-chamber, smashing helplessly with his hand still tied behind his back into what was presumably bullet-proof glass. He fell to the floor and as he tried to look up a boot on the back of his neck prevented him. Something dropped beside his head - it was his battered rucksack. He'd forgotten about that since his arrest.

There was a voice. It made his skin crawl; human, but not quite. Yet it was not robotic like electronic voice boxes. That it was female made it somehow worse.

"Release his hands and send him through here."

"Ugh, disgusting!" said another. He looks worse in the flesh than he did on camera."

"Yes," said yet another, "and this is the cleaned up version."

"Get up," said the woman. "Oh, you officers can leave. We'll call you when we're ready." He didn't hear the boots on the carpet, but the doors rumbled shut.

He rose with difficulty on shaking legs. He had been prepared for a shock, but not quite this.

Perversely his eyes first scanned the room, as if avoiding looking at the owners of those unnatural voices. 'Eclectic' hardly did the place justice. Then he realised that if these creatures had only recently come to their senses, they would have drawn their influences and ideas from a wealth of sources. There'd have been no guiding hand or style guru up here in this penthouse.

But the dominant feature was a wall covered with flat screens, perhaps fifty to sixty of them, each containing different flickering images which in themselves changed every few seconds. He realised that these were not television programmes, but rather pictures from everyday life. At first he thought they showed only footage from security cameras, but to his astonishment could see that mixed in with that was what appeared to be scenes from the homes of ordinary people. How had they done it, achieved this level of intrusion?

Suddenly all the screens went blank and he could avoid his captors no longer. He turned to face them and received his second shock.

His mind had prepared him for figures from the old films, when psychics and beings of higher intelligence were invariably portrayed as pale skinned, smooth-headed ethereal creatures in white robes - ironically the reality that had confronted the board members of KompuKraft two years before. Instead, Will saw three very beautiful and different creatures, the one common feature being that they wore highly fashionable sunglasses, which appeared almost to be welded to their faces.

There was a muscular man whose very bulk threatened and seemed ready to burst from the beautifully tailored casual blue shirt, open to quite low on his smooth, deeply-muscled chest. The other man was slimmer, his stance slightly affected, though it went well with his looks, which were handsome in a louche, debauched way. He wore leather trousers, slung low on his snake hips, a black shirt open almost to the navel and a string of beads. His hair was long and he reminded Will of someone, an actor or singer from decades before.

But striking though these two men were, the woman dominated the room. Indeed the others seemed to cede centre stage to her. She exuded sex and cunning, mother and lover, in equal measures. Her beauty might have been overwhelming had it not been for the sunglasses. Pale skinned, black haired, cruel cheekbones, voluptuous lips and a figure that appeared almost defined for the white shirt and blue jeans she wore. It was the type of body that would enslave its lover for eternity.

But Will had also heard her voice and knew that it could never be seductive.

"Do you not fear us?" rasped the voice of the muscular one.

"I fear only what I think you have become." Will was astonished to hear this, at a loss to explain his sudden courage. Perhaps it stemmed from his sense that there was no humanity here; that his cause was lost so he might as well go down fighting.

"How dare..." started Zeus, but Juno interrupted.

"And just what do you believe we have become? Who do you think we are?" she asked, moving a couple of steps closer.

"Who knows?" Will responded. His fear, astonishingly, was mixed with anger now, remembering the beating he had taken, and this strange new strength seemed to have infused him since he had entered the room. He was not going to give them the triumph of his submission. "The Three Stooges perhaps." This was greeted by frowns. "Before your time, I guess," he added laconically.

"Nothing is before our time. We *are* time," said Pan, one knee bending in a defiant but camp gesture.

"You speak bravely," said Juno. "Enjoy your strength while you have it." She now stood directly in front of Will. There was a scent in the air, like smouldering sandalwood. He became aware of her voluptuous cleavage. "Do you want me?" she said suddenly, her mouth curved ever so slightly in an indolent smile. He heard the sharp intake of breath from the muscular man and a snigger from the other one. Will swallowed hard, but did not reply. "And now?" she continued removing her sunglasses with a swift movement.

Will couldn't help but react, wanting to look away, but compelled not to. "My God!" he said, as he looked through the enlarged pupils into something far darker and deeper.

"Actually not your god," said Pan mockingly. "He had his chance and failed you all."

"What the hell are you?"

Zeus stepped forward. "Three blind mice that have grown into three fucking great rats." He guffawed with laughter, then looked at Juno and frowned. She had not stopped gazing intently at Will. "What is it, my love?"

She kept staring, but shook her head. "I don't know. There is some...knowledge in this man." She paused. "Some disturbance." She broke away uncomfortably, replaced her sunglasses and crossed to the window.

It was a moment of variegated relief for Will. Not only had those eyes gone, but also it seemed his true identity remained a secret after all. So just why was he here?

"I'm not sure now," said Juno cryptically, looking out across the city.

"Well I am," said Zeus. "It's been so long since we were able to punish anyone, you're naturally feeling a bit uncomfortable."

Suddenly something he had heard clicked with Will, struck him like one of Jove's mythical thunderbolts. Despite the circumstances the realisation caused an alien sensation to start surfacing in him. At first he didn't recognise what was coming, but here it came nonetheless, for the first time in some immeasurable years, a laugh.

"Hah! I get it." The three looked at him in unison. "I mean, I don't know what you are, but I know what's happened."

Juno's dead voice contained something approximating trepidation as she said, "And that would be?"

"You are something," he struggled for the right words, "some force, some beings that we humans could not even begin to comprehend, and you've settled in three empty bodies, and you think - maybe have always thought - that you're some sort of gods." His last words were accompanied by an incredulous smile.

Zeus couldn't help himself, but strode forward outraged, hand raised to deliver a blow. "Worm!" he bellowed.

"Zeus!" Juno's voice checked him, the name she used proof to Will that his theory was correct.

"I cannot stand here and take such insolence!" raged the erstwhile father of the gods.

Juno had crossed the room and put her slim hands on one of his bulging arms. "You will not have to. He's our guinea pig, remember. He can face an eternity of punishment."

Will was shaken, despite his bravado. The one whom the female had addressed as Zeus had been fearsome to behold, the effect enhanced by an apparent smouldering in the air, and the dread intensified by the woman's ominous words.

But Juno had not sought merely to calm Zeus's temper. She was intrigued. There had been a connection between her and

376

the prisoner. She had sensed it and now she stepped forward again, removing the sunglasses once more. To everyone's surprise she placed her hands on either side of Will's head, forcing him to look into her eyes. She felt him shake, but held him firm.

"What else do you see?"

Will spoke as if hypnotised. "Age. Time - time back to the very essence of itself. Darkness before the light. Anger. Sadness."

Now both of them realised that he was not the only one shaking. Juno released him.

"You see much." She replaced her sunglasses and stepped away again.

Will had become aware of an energy in the air, some sort of a charge and he could have sworn that it came pulsing in waves from a set of blacked-out windows at the far end of the suite. Juno saw his eyes flicker in that direction. As if breaking the mood, she pointed hurriedly at the wall of screens and they came on again, except now they all showed the same image, a dishevelled man snatching a takeaway carton from a child and running. The deed looked as shameful as it was, and Will hung his head.

Juno spoke again. "The mighty seer is not so mighty that he will not steal food from a child. But unlike imagined gods, we do see all, for which you will be punished in a fitting manner."

The pulsing from the black windows had stopped and now all three of the gods exuded power. Zeus spoke. "We have sought to rid this world of ours of crime and evil, but always there will be people like you." Will knew well enough what type of world these control freaks were creating, but now he was scared and stayed quiet. It was clear that, by whatever means, they did have power. Zeus continued. "So as befits gods, we will mete out appropriate punishment. Know now that every time you interact with a child, even if it is just that your eyes meet, the evils or sickness that would attack that child in its life will, from that moment, be carried by you in that battered rucksack, a suitable vessel I'm sure you'll agree. Of course it will weigh heavier each time. You may never put down that burden. Great will be your pain if you do. And as someone who shuns respectable society, you may never stay more than one hour in any one place. Should you try to do so, more pain will be yours. Nor may you return to anywhere you have been before. You are doomed to wander forever. And we will be watching." Zeus waved a hand in the direction of the screens. "This is our judgement on you."

Will had been fearing imprisonment, the type of life the mutants had led before, so through this grand pronouncement he felt the hysteria rising. He managed not to laugh, but his face must have showed his incredulity.

"You doubt our powers," said Juno, "but know this, they are very real, not the stuff of mythology any more. There was once an experiment in this building, known as Project TCX." She was indeed powerful; she had turned the blood in Will's veins to ice, though he tried to conceal it. She continued. "It was an attempt to produce thought-controlled computers."

"Juno!" whispered Pan urgently, "tell him nothing."

"Calm yourself Pan. Even were he to talk to someone, they would think it was the ravings of a madman."

"But if he does - suppose they believe him."

"Who will he turn to, the police? We own them, likewise the government. And if some maverick investigator were to come, where would he look? What would he look for? Who would admit their guilt?" She turned her attention back to Will. "Yes, my ragged friend, the purpose of Project TCX was to develop the next generation of computer. As with most people who probe where they do not understand, the researchers didn't know what they were dealing with and accidentally allowed a highly developed, intelligent machine access to man's thought processes. The microchip absorbed them. Years later, three brilliant technical minds discovered this information and they believe they have harnessed it, programming a microchip that will enable them to control the thoughts of others, or at least pre-programme them, given certain stimuli."

The hysteria had long since departed and Will felt his legs shaking again. Still he could say nothing.

"Say, for example," continued Juno, "the creators wanted someone to believe a certain fact each time he encountered a particular trigger." Juno saw the comprehension in Will's eyes and nodded. "Yes, we are way beyond subliminal advertising now." She bent to a small table and picked up a syringe. It contained a colourless liquid.

"What is that?" asked Will

"You see, if you choose to go around avoiding any interaction with civilised society, you can't keep up with the latest developments in computer technology." Juno held up the syringe and looked at it with pride. "The competition is till stuck with sand. Our liquid research is the sea that will wash them away. For now we call it the fish."

Pan laughed. "It's our little joke. It can't be called a chip any more."

Juno signalled to the other two. They moved either side of him. Will knew it was pointless to struggle.

"I would recommend that you do not put up a fight," said Juno. "This fish will be injected straight into your spinal cord and while it is state-of-the-art, these hands are not. "Once in your spine, the fish will receive signals from and deliver them to the brain." She put a hand beneath Will's chin and lifted his head in an intimate gesture at odds with the cruelty of her next words. "What makes this such fun is that you will know precisely what we have done to you, yet be powerless to prevent your reactions. To use the jargon of these times, that really will be a mind-fuck. Oh, and one last feature of this little fish is that it will enable us to track you." She turned to Zeus. "Make sure you hold him still."

"Happily," said her fellow deity.

Chapter Nine - Moving on

The heavy blow to the back of his head was the last thing Will could almost remember before waking face down on a hard concrete surface. He was aware of light ahead of him and lifting his head painfully saw that he was lying on the ramp leading down from the goods entrance of The Shard.

Will got to his feet and lurched drunkenly from the combined effects of malnutrition, dehydration, shock, fear and brutal beatings. He was struggling to recall everything, wasn't sure whether it was all a bad dream. But as he struggled into the daylight, then looked up at the towering structure of The Shard, the memories flowed back as painfully as blood returning to a numb limb.

A family saw him and crossed to the other side of the road, urging their two children along as they hurried by. Suddenly something pulled at Will's shoulders and he staggered, heart thundering as he became aware that his rucksack appeared to have grown heavier.

"No," he said, shaking his head in a refusal to believe. "No, no, no." But his face started to sweat at the implications. "It can't be real."

He reached behind him and patted the rucksack. It col-

lapsed, empty beneath his hand. Whatever meagre possessions he owned had been taken. So how could he explain
its weight on his shoulders? What had they done to him? It
couldn't possibly be true, yet he knew already that it was.

A car went by and a little boy looked out of the back window
at him in curiosity. He staggered again. It felt as if someone
had dropped a couple of bags of sugar into the rucksack from
a height.

He had to get out of the city, and by the least populated
route.

As he turned down a side street he was aware again of The
Shard looming over the city like a totem to an evil god, which
of course was precisely what it was.

Part of him couldn't believe that he was walking free. There
was an innate celebratory tingle in his skin at the feel of the
air. But the tingle in his spine caused him to question the
price of that freedom.

The battery in his watch had run out months ago and he could
only guess at how long he had walked through the valley of
the shadow of death. His one consolation was that, no matter
what powers they did or did not possess, they could not cheat
him of death.

He had toyed many a time with the idea of simply lying
down in a field somewhere and allowing the reaper to come
and harvest him, but he feared the pain. From those days
when his watch was still working, or he could see the hands of
a clock somewhere tick past the hour, he knew what agonies
would wrack his body.

In many ways this was the purest of existences. Seeking
at all times to avoid humanity, his food was berries from the

hedgerows, fruit from overhanging trees. He drank water from streams. He had found one isolated grove in the early days where he would have been content to stay, knowing the burden on his back would grow no heavier. So he tested the gods and stayed where he was. Sure enough, as the hour came to a close the pains commenced and he had to move on.

He had been lucky, found some waterproof clothing in an old barn and avoided being hunted down for the theft. Then there were items of abandoned or lost clothing, a glove here, a scarf there. On warm days he shoved them into his pockets. He had tried once to remove the rucksack and place them inside, but his fingers were numb and swollen from helping to support the load and the straps of the rucksack had pulled tighter, restricting him, reminding him that the load was his forever. He knew it couldn't be true, couldn't be happening, but he was powerless to prevent it.

Despite his best efforts, he had encountered children, camping in the woods with parents who abused him and drove him away, as if he wasn't already trying to make his escape, or driving past when he had not been quick enough to get off the road. Thus the load continued to grow.

There was also the mental torture that befalls a proud man who no longer has even his dignity. His motley assortment of clothes, his smell, the ragged, increasingly matted beard and hair, the dirt on his hands and face, meant that he was despised and feared. How his perspective changed. He was overjoyed one night to find a tiny, unmanned railway station with a toilet that had a working hot tap, the remnants of a bar of soap and a lukewarm radiator. He had thought back momentarily to the tantrum he had thrown on his sixteenth birthday on finding that his new computer was a Titan 20, not the KK250 his heart desired.

After taking a rest in the relative warmth for what he believed was probably about half an hour, he had stuffed the last of the toilet paper into his pocket as if it was currency of old and carefully wrapped up the soap.

Mostly he endured jeers and suspicion when he was forced into small villages; well-founded suspicion of course, because his intention was to steal. Always there was the risk that he would encounter a child. When it happened the straps of his rucksack would bite, almost pulling his ever-weakening body to its knees.

One glorious autumn afternoon, the beauty of which mocked him as it burrowed beneath his filthy skin, seeking the shrinking corner of him that remembered the happiness a turning leaf could bring, he found himself on a forest road, which decided to transform into a winding, uphill slog. The sack on his back appeared to have doubled again in weight. He was weary beyond description, barely able to put one foot in front of the other, but capable of summoning beneath the layers of clothing a sweat that chilled as it cooled.

He became aware of the sound of an engine behind him round the bend. Looking to either side he saw that the banks of the road were quite steep as they climbed into the trees. He was at the point of mental and physical surrender that precluded caring any more, so he stayed on the road.

The car's revs were high as it came up the hill, and he heard it slow behind him. As it went by, the few threads of his shredded soul that still bound him to humanity dragged his gaze towards the windows. He glimpsed a little girl, pale, with shadows both under and in her eyes that matched his own. And as they met his, he felt a force hit him every bit as hard as the police boots that had kicked him on the day of his capture. He staggered and continued looking through the rear window, past the face of the little girl, seeking desperately the eyes of the driver, knowing it was impossible, but hoping for compassion.

At the same time, it seemed the weight in his rucksack trebled. It dragged on his shoulders. Finally, he could take no more and was driven down, first to his knees, then face downward onto the tarmac.

The moments between his head striking the ground and unconsciousness taking him were almost sweet in their abandonment.

Paul brought the car to a screeching halt.

"Miranda!" screeched Karen Miller to her daughter. "Put your mask back on sweetheart."

"But I don't need it, mummy! I can breathe fine."

"That's because you had it on, honey. Put it back." Karen was fighting. Her mind didn't want to accept that some sort of miracle had happened. That was a dangerous road to take, one full of hope. "Tell her Paul."

Paul was sitting in a daze, looking by turns at the back of his daughter's head as she stared agitatedly through the rear window and at the figure lying in the road.

"Perhaps he needs my mask now," said the little girl.

Somehow, for an impossible instant it seemed that Paul's and the tramp's eyes met. He wasn't sure what he saw there; some kind of gruesome knowledge, a reflection of suffering.

"Paul, tell her!"

"She's fine, Karen. Aren't you, honey?"

The little girl turned around. Her face was pink and full

of health. It had never looked like that, even when she was free of her illness. She came and put her hand on her father's cheek. "Yes, daddy, I'm fine, but the man isn't, and he made me well."

"Miranda, baby, that's nonsense," said Karen in a voice trembling with all manner of emotions.

"It's not, mummy. He looked at me and made me well again. I felt him take my sickness from me, and then it went to him and now he's not well."

Karen opened her mouth to protest again and then realised that she had no grounds. And even if everything were pure coincidence, then she was going to be grateful for that coincidence. Oh boy, was she!

Nevertheless, she couldn't help feeling a little uneasy as Paul started to reverse the car.

"What are you doing, Paul?"

Miranda answered for her. "We're going to get the man, aren't we daddy?"

"Yes we are, baby."

"Paul?" Karen started to say something, but he cut her short.

"Don't even think about it, Karen." Looking at the road behind him he continued distractedly, "There are more things in heaven and earth than are dreamt up by IT technicians."

"What?"

"I don't claim to be a hippie or a happy-clappy," he stopped the car, then looked at Karen, "but if there's the remotest chance that man lying in the road healed our daughter, I want to know and I want to help." With that, he got out of the car.

Both he and Karen had to check their instinctive desire to stop Miranda as she pushed open the door and skipped down the road ahead of them. Then reality kicked in and Paul called his daughter back. "Hey sweetheart, let me go ahead and suss this out. You two stay back."

As he crouched by the body, Paul got the strong stench of ripe sweat. Carefully he turned the man over, saw the bleeding cuts on his forehead and nose, and the stains on his clothes.

He stood. "Okay, I'm also a practical guy. I've got some plastic sheeting in the boot of the car. You two spread it over the seats, then I'll get him in."

"Paul, are you sure?" Karen looked concerned, but also guilty that she felt disgusted.

"No, but I don't want to die wondering."

He knew that he was going to have to move the tramp on his own, so to lighten the load he lifted the man's top half and eased off the rucksack. That was when he noticed what should have been glaringly obvious – the sack was flat. It was empty. Something wasn't making any sense here. Perhaps Karen was right to be wary.

Was it a dream, or death? This sense of firm but gentle hands leading him, warm rain washing away his pain, lying finally on soft grass to sleep.

He woke to the most complete disorientation. Sunlight fell in gold bars across him through wooden blinds. For a long time his eyes could not adjust, nor stay open. Everything was unfamiliar, from the scent of soap to the soft pyjamas. There was no panic. He felt he could lie here forever, but grew melancholy because he knew it could not last.

At last a door opened, and in walked a couple. He didn't recognise them, but knew beyond doubt who they must be.

"You came back for me." The sound of his own voice shocked him. Had he really given up talking, even to himself? Or was it the acoustics of comfort that threw him?

"We did."

"Why?"

"We were hoping you could tell us."

He frowned and they smiled.

"How long have I been asleep?"

"Umm, just under two days."

Jolted, he tried to sit up, managed to get halfway. "I must go. You'll be in danger."

The woman looked worried immediately, but the man put a calming hand on her arm. "Tell us what you mean," he said.

"They put a tracker chip inside me."

"Who's they? The police?"

"No." He looked around wildly. "I can't say any more."

"Well this...tracker chip can't be much good if you've been under our roof for forty-eight hours and no-one's come for you."

It was all starting to come back to him. "My rucksack, where's my rucksack?"

"We threw it out," said Karen. "To be honest it stank. Not like you..." She blushed and raised her hand in apology. "I'm sorry, I didn't mean it that way."

Will managed a half-smile. "Oh, I stank all right."

"I just meant it didn't smell of dirt." She looked at Paul for affirmation. "Just...wrong somehow. Bad."

The man came forward and held out his hand. "My name's Paul, by the way. Paul Miller." The proffered hand was taken tentatively, the physical touch another sensory shock after all this time.

"Will."

"And I'm Karen."

Will sank back again, still weak. "I'm sorry, I'm forgetting my manners. I want to thank you for what I can see you've done for me. There's so much I don't understand."

Paul sat on the edge of the bed and laughed. "You and us both, mate. But look, try to get some more sleep and we'll talk more later."

Will reached out and caught his arm, the jerky movement causing Karen to gasp involuntarily. "No, let's talk now. There are important things for both of us to know and for me to do."

Paul sat now in a chair in the corner of the room. His arms were folded and there was a strange look on his face that Will couldn't interpret.

"I know it's hard to believe. You probably thinking you're listening to a lunatic's ravings."

"No," said Paul very deliberately, "that is what I would have thought if it weren't for the fact that my daughter is fit and well, and hasn't needed a respirator in two days, which is a first, believe me." Paul leaned forward. "But I knew there was something about you when I looked into your eyes as we drove past." He leaned back again. "So if I have understood correctly, you think that your curse has somehow been broken." He glanced across at Karen. Her face was a mask.

"Not just broken. It has proved to be multi-faceted. It's turned on itself, eaten itself somehow. They said that I would have to take from every child I interacted with the evils latent in it. They programmed my thoughts to believe that. Despite myself, I felt it happening. But as I said, these beings do have powers and through some," he groped for the words, "conjoining of universal forces that I, and apparently they, do not understand I took the illness from your daughter. They said that I could never put down my burden and I didn't – you took it from me. You felt a rucksack that weighed nothing. To me it was like carrying the world on my back. They also programmed me to believe that I could stay no longer than one hour in one place. At first I made sure I complied, because I had felt the power and the pain of my curse; terrified, I kept moving. But now, having lost all track of time I have come through. I didn't wilfully disobey. I don't know whether what was injected into me was indeed a tracker chip, or perhaps they have simply got bored with their game."

Karen spoke. "You do understand how difficult this is for us to take in?"

"With all my heart, yes. But there is one last thing I have withheld from you." Karen and Paul exchanged glances again. "I will tell you because I trust you, but please, swear to me you will tell no-one what I am about to tell you, at least until I say that you can."

"Go ahead," said Paul. "You can trust us."

"The bodies that these beings invaded were the mutated results of an experiment that went wrong in KompuKraft." He heard Karen's intake of breath, saw Paul's jaw muscles clench. "I believe I am partly a result of that experiment." Now Paul's jaw muscles gave up and fell open. "But I was luckier. My mother withdrew from the project, but I seem to have developed certain advanced computer skills, which make me the only man who can fight them - bring them down."

"How the hell are you going to do that?" said Karen.

"I had a few crazy ideas before total exhaustion took over from anger. I must remain hidden from them for a while longer, but I have to do something."

Just then there was a tap at the door and Miranda came in. Will's instinctive reaction was to back away and tense, wait for the pain. He knew it was programmed into him. But there was nothing. He realised that this in itself proved nothing, as he had already taken from her what he could. Yet instinctively he knew the programmed curse, and its unexpected side-effect, had passed. Even the would-be gods didn't know what they had given him. It added a further dimension to the shape of the plan even now emerging from his muddied thoughts: the possibility that something good could yet come of this. What had happened to this girl was so overwhelming, it had to be worth a shot, albeit a long one.

"You've got a look in your eye," said Paul with a faint smile as he sat his daughter on his knee.

Will returned the smile. "That's because I have a feeling of purpose for the first time in...twelve years, I think." He looked embarrassed. "I have another favour to ask."

"Not till you do me one," said Karen.

"Anything."

Her face broke suddenly into a smile. "Please shave off that disgusting beard. You may be a prophet, a voice in the wilderness, a hermit, but you don't have to have a beard."

"Never thought I'd be asking to borrow one of these things."

"You can have it, as far as I'm concerned," said Paul. "Totally bloody ridiculous the way technology dominates our lives now. I used to work in IT myself, but I got out while I was still human. You're lucky it was us that drove past you. Correction." He put a hand on Will's shoulder in sincere apology. "We were the lucky ones. What I meant was there are enough people who are happy in their ignorance, who would have driven past." He remembered he had done exactly that. "I mean...oh shit, I'm just digging myself deeper, aren't I? I don't know what I'm saying really."

Now Will was the one with the reassuring hand. "Hey, don't worry about it. There's been rather a lot for us all to take in. And you're right, there are more than enough people who are happy slaves to these things." He waved the identity card he was holding.

"Couldn't have put it better - which I guess I illustrated." They both laughed.

"I'm a bit out of touch, to put it mildly," said Will. "Will this get me into the records office without the need for any fingerprints or retinal scans or photo ID?"

"Absolutely. It's just a library. Once you're in just slot it into the computer. Here, take my KompuKard as well. The records are huge. I think you'll be there for hours so you might want to get a drink and something to eat."

"Are you kidding!? Try stopping me eating and drinking. You have no idea how good your food tasted today."

Everything had novelty value that day: walking without the burden of the rucksack; hateful glances; passing family groups without cringing; or gaining access to buildings and food. He was careful to wear a baseball cap, and wherever possible, to keep his face averted in as casual a manner as possible from any cameras. Luckily, he realised that Karen's insistence he shave had a side-benefit: the gods had only seen him with a beard. All in all, however, he experienced the seductiveness of conformity.

In the records office of the library he took the first tentative step along the hazardous path of his plan. Will knew that, in keeping with many of the giant corporations, KompuKraft would monitor its website assiduously, and he didn't want Paul or Karen involved any more than they were already, so he had to be careful how he researched when using Paul's card. Like all good hackers, he was going through a back door. He sought out back copies of the broadsheets going back three years and ploughed laboriously through them seeking any reference to KompuKraft.

He struck gold. On the same date, just over two and a half years ago, all the major newspapers were dominated by news of a computer virus attacking several major networks and corporations, among them KompuKraft, who claimed, unlike the others, to have an anti-virus that was coping. Two and a half years ago, thought Will, was probably around the time society appeared to become more Draconian.

From his oblique perspective, as he read on, he saw that the anti-virus invaded ever-increasing areas of public and private life, directly and indirectly. He knew KompuKraft had to be at the centre of it, and had probably created the virus, injecting the poison to create the antibodies. Except they'd have created the antibodies first.

The more he read, the more he saw now that that company had inveigled the leaders of mankind on a massive scale. It was astonishing to contemplate that they had covered their tracks. Surely someone must have suspected them.

They had to be stopped, but it was obvious that could only happen from within.

Paul and Karen had been relatively easy converts, but even they had seemed incredulous at first. If he hadn't cured their child...and he couldn't roam the earth seeking out the parents of sick children, even if the power had not deserted him, which remained to be seen. Without it, who would believe him? And indeed who would want to? Hadn't he felt for a moment today how comfortable life could be within KompuKraft's embrace?

There was only one way to bring them down. Literally or metaphorically, he had to hack his way in.

There was an added complication - did he want to bring them down at all? The one doubt that assailed him wasn't borne of any concern for global systems, not even those in hospitals. His years as an outcast and the recent months of torture had left their mark on him, like shadows on an x-ray, and he could not waste too much sympathy for others. After all, most corporations doubtless had some primitive back-up to which they could resort, and if they didn't have it, more fool them. No, it was rather that, having experienced the wonder of curing a terminally ill child, he had felt the power for good that also lay within the grasp of the would-be gods.

He didn't know whether the anti-virus was the brainchild of those invading powers, but assumed it had to be, since the mutants in their original form seemed to have been around for some years before the virus surfaced. If he could only convince the self-styled deities that they could be eternally worshipped for all the right reasons.

He was racing ahead of himself. With an ironic twist of theologies he realised that one thing was unavoidable: he was Daniel and he was going to have to enter the lion's den to prove it.

There followed a wave of despair. How the hell was he going to do it? But as he continued to flick through the newspaper pages for the rest of that day, an answer came to him in a recurring image. To confirm his suspicions he started to go back further. The image continued to appear and the subtle change he thought he had noticed seemed increasingly apparent: Thad Leblanc.

Those beings might have thought of themselves as gods, but they could also prove to be like Achilles in having one vulnerable point. It was obvious in press reports from earlier years that Leblanc was the power in KompuKraft, giving that vast, cumbersome organism direction and purpose from the day he joined as a ridiculously young CEO twenty-nine years before. But in more recent times, namely since the start of the virus catastrophe, with the exception of his press conferences on the day it all kicked off, he gave more of an impression of a puppet, a thing of discordant words with sound-bites instead of dialogue. There was something in his manner, particularly in his eyes. Had he lost power? That wouldn't sit well with a wunderkind like him. He was probably no longer the acid-tongued decision maker, just a big bag of sugar sweetening the bitter pill that was KompuKraft, unable to kick the Three Stooges up the arse for fear of the company's big secret coming to light.

Will knew he would have to approach cautiously, like any wounded beast. Besides which, revealing himself to this man, someone capable of sanctioning murder to safeguard his interests, was a risk in itself. He thought of Daniel and Rebecca Payne.

Will couldn't help wondering why Leblanc hadn't simply had the mutants killed. The dirty secret would have been wiped out forever. He assumed it was because all the wheels set in motion by those three now had a momentum that would be unsustainable if they were no longer around. Where would that leave KompuKraft and its board of directors except with egg on their faces? According to his research, the rest of the directors appeared to be men, of science, and a woman of accounts, probably lacking Leblanc's deviousness and still to some extent in thrall to the technological wonders unfolding before them. He noticed how there had been no changes at boardroom level in thirty years. They were trapped, all of them, with their guilty secret.

Subtle changes in Leblanc's rhetoric led Will to believe that he was no longer the one who guided the ship. Indeed, he seemed sometimes to be simply hoisting the sails, his words no longer the driving winds, just so much bombastic hot air. He noticed that Leblanc now sometimes read his press announcements from a script, which had not been the case in bygone years. Their content was often highly technical and complex. Maybe Leblanc didn't trust himself, felt out of his depth, though it was clear he still loved the limelight.

"You are definitely my man," whispered Will. "You too are disenfranchised."

Yet even as his plan formed, Will had to acknowledge it was hanging by the slenderest of threads, because the question he couldn't answer was why someone of Leblanc's ambition was still there.

He took the opportunity of the resources at his fingertips to scroll through a few years worth of IT magazines, using as a pretext the need to know the enemy, but in reality simply enjoying some vicarious pleasure. It did nothing to lessen the magnitude of the job ahead.

Despite everything, he had still not fully appreciated the extent of KompuKraft's hold on mankind. There was nothing any Monopolies and Mergers Commission could have done about it, since it had been achieved through sheer applied brilliance. Even Will had to marvel at what was on offer in terms of software and hardware. They were streets ahead of the competition, if the Pacific Highway could be called a street at the wrong end of which stood Seattle. Will began to doubt himself even more. What if he was wrong about the virus? Surely the best minds in IT would have tried to address that particular issue. But no, he had to cling to the belief that those three super-advanced minds had covered their tracks. He had to hope that he was half as good as he thought he was, although untried in twelve years.

Slender threads.

Part of him was tempted to try to hack in now, but he knew that even before the rise and rise of KompuKraft, system techies had developed extremely sophisticated defence and detection warnings, which made KompuKraft's achievement in breaching the world's most secure systems all the more incredible.

Or unlikely?

On returning to the Millers, Will returned the cards with gratitude.

"Find what you were looking for?" asked Paul.

"Actually, yes."

Paul raised one eyebrow. "What exactly is your plan?"

"You wouldn't believe me if I told you." From the look in his host's eye, Will saw that trying to close him out was unwise. "Look, I want to offer you the option of plausible deniability. Please don't be offended."

"You mean so I won't talk under torture?" Will looked at the floor as a momentary shadow passed behind his eyes. "Sorry buddy, that was thoughtless. I didn't mean..."

"'Sokay." Now Will smiled. "Could I ask you another favour after that last asinine comment?"

"Of course."

"Do you happen to have a laptop I could borrow?"

"I have the corpse of one in my workshop and probably enough bits and pieces to make it work, but if you want to borrow my new one that's no problem."

"I don't want anything linking me to you. A recon hybrid will do very nicely thanks."

As they walked through the house towards the workshop it had a weekend family feel to it that Will had never experienced through all the lonely years his mother had been forced to endure. Images came to him, flashed before his eyes in bursts of a few seconds. They stopped him in his tracks.

He looked up at the top corners of the lounge.

"Hey, Paul," he said, causing his host to stop in his tracks, "do people tend to have cameras in their homes these days?"

"Cameras? You mean hand-helds, cine-palms, that sort of thing?"

"No, I mean more like security cameras."

"Not in their homes, I wouldn't have thought. I don't know of anyone. Why?"

The images came flashing again. There was something peculiar about them, a distortion, like looking through a fish-eye lens.

It came to Will with a jolt, but he decided for now to leave his sinking feeling submerged.

"No reason."

With the detritus of Paul's former IT existence Will put together a functioning laptop.

"So is this here the transmitter?" he asked, pointing at a gismo he didn't recognise.

"Transmitter and receiver."

"And it enables you to connect remotely to the server."

"Within reason, yes. Or should I say within range. Even KompuKraft haven't been able to alter the basic nature of radio waves."

Will whistled. "Way beyond anything that was available to me twelve years ago. No more dialling in." He looked at the gadget in question again, smiled and slotted it into place.

"That's true on the modern laptops," said Paul. "But that one there is about eight years old."

Will looked it over once more before snapping it shut, ensuring he had everything he needed. "It'll do for my purposes," said Will.

And suddenly it was time to go.

He wasn't aware that he'd been putting it off in any way, but the week he'd spent with the Millers was the happiest time since he'd left home. They had built him up again, not just with the wonderful food, but with affection, which he'd not experienced since he was eighteen. His gratitude was matched by their own, which he both understood and didn't, because it had been pure chance that had enabled him to help them, whereas they had made a conscious decision. Still, one way or another he had given them back their daughter.

So, after a hearty breakfast the four of them stood at the

door.

"Look, are you sure about the card? With your skills I'm sure you could adapt one of my spare ones. Otherwise how are you going to eat?"

Will patted the new rucksack and smiled. "Believe me, in the past, what you've put in there would have lasted me a month. Mind you..." here he patted his stomach, "...I'm not sure you've done me any favours." They laughed, and Paul said:

"Well, we didn't want you thinking about getting into those smelly old clothes of yours. Now you're larger you have to borrow some of mine."

Then Will's face grew serious. "If I succeed in what I want to do, I hate to tell you this, but those cards will go out of the window, and a lot of other things with them. And I'll be able to walk into a shop and buy food again."

Paul reached out and put a hand on Will's shoulder. "Good luck to you, fella. I don't know exactly what your plans are, but I do know you're resourceful enough."

"Hey." He put his hand on Paul's arm. "If I'm successful you will see me again, and sooner than you think."

Chapter Ten - Reeling in

He heard the whining of the camera as he approached the huge iron gate. It took him back several months to the alleyway, where he had sat licking mayonnaise from his fingers and awaiting arrest. He shuddered. Somewhere behind the house and beyond the extensive grounds was the eternal, unconcerned murmur of the sea.

He wasn't fooled by the lack of security guards. He'd seen the tiny pinpoints of light recessed in the gateposts, which he knew could eviscerate him. But as with so many things now, he'd ceased to be scared.

Will pressed the intercom button.

"Yes?"

"I can make you the power in KompuKraft again." There was a long pause.

"What the fuck are you talking about?" The expectorant voice was menacing, but tiny particles of uncertainty had wafted through with it.

"I'm not prepared to discuss it through an intercom." Another long pause. Then a clunk as the gates started to move.

Under other circumstances Will would have admired the

statues and original Henry Moore sculptures as he wandered up the azalea-lined path towards the massive frontage of the residence. But Will's eyes were fixed upon the figure in beige chinos and a blue golf shirt, which was striking golf balls from the cliff top a considerable distance into the sea with what was literally practised ease. The man didn't stop as Will drew nearer and the latter had to admire the former's control. Despite what had to be curiosity verging on fear he was insisting on giving Will a lesson in one-upmanship. Having received a shock to his system he was still striking a masterful ball.

Let him have his moment, thought Will. I'm about to utter words that will shatter his glassy world.

He saw that his arrogant host was late middle-aged, tanned, toned and perfectly coiffured, as only a bored billionaire can be. Will stopped about ten yards away and waited. He saw the walkie-talkie on the ground by the golf bag with which Leblanc had responded to the intercom. In the bay of the driving range was a CCTV screen.

Thad Leblanc still had ten balls to hit and he didn't break off till they had all followed a perfect parabola into the waves. He then strode towards Will and jabbed a finger in his direction. "You'd better tell me quickly who the fuck you are, before I wrap this club round your head." The last word drawled to a mid-west close.

Will tried his hardest to stand his ground without flinching. "Since we appear to be dispensing with formalities, I guess I'll need to grab your attention."

"You did that at the gate. Now get on with it."

"How's about if I say 'Daniel Payne'?"

Leblanc actually dropped the club. He couldn't prevent

himself glancing around, as if a fellow actor had said 'Macbeth' instead of 'The Scottish Play'. When he gathered his wits he said, "Come into the house."

As they marched through into Leblanc's study, Will had to admire the tastefulness of the decor. The furnishings were minimalist, clearly expensive and very masculine. It looked as if Leblanc got his own way here at least, though Will found it difficult to imagine the man involved in something as sensitive as setting up home. Still, there were pictures of Mrs Leblanc and two children, boys of course. He wondered whether the man had ever suffered a moment's regret for the fate of the Daniel and Rebecca Payne. Obviously he was forced to spare the odd thought for their freakish brood.

In the study Leblanc gestured Will towards the leather chair by the desk. He wandered across to a drinks cabinet, poured himself a Jack Daniels and then sat in the captain's chair behind the desk without offering his guest anything.

"You've got about a half hour before my wife and kids are back from church, so shoot. Who are you?"

"Someone who knows all about Project TCX."

Will saw that it was possible for a tan to go pale and enjoyed *his* moment.

Credit to Leblanc; his face almost managed to remain impassive, but there was an undeniable ripple beneath the surface. "Project what?"

"Don't insult my intelligence, Mr Leblanc. I've been through too much. But believe me, I'm not here as your enemy. I want your help."

Leblanc took a sip of his drink and, still holding the glass, pointed a finger at Will. "You want my help. You come in here uttering words that people have avoided in thirty years.

I know you're not wired - the gates check all that, but I think you'd be too clever for that. Still, I'm guessing this is blackmail."

"Actually, no." Will looked around him. "Although this is an impressive place you have here I don't want part of it. I want my own. I want a piece of the action."

Leblanc reached down and started to open a drawer of the desk. Will stiffened.

"I should warn you, Mr Leblanc, you were right when you said I was too clever. If I don't return from here in one piece there are instructions in place, which would make it pretty certain that you wouldn't have a piece of this action much longer."

Looking aggrieved, Leblanc continued to reach into the drawer and pulled out a cheque book, which he slapped on the table. "As you know I'm a very rich guy. How much is it gonna take for you to go away and do your thing?"

"Put your cheque book away. It's not that easy."

Leblanc leaned back in his chair and picked up his glass. "It never is. Look, we don't have a lot of time. Why don't you take it from the top?"

"Very well. I know you're a man who no longer has control of the company that he initially made successful."

"There you go again with that. What the fuck do you think you know that I don't?"

"It's obvious. Gateposts can only do so much. If I had really wanted to ram the gates and take you out with a machine-gun or grenade launcher, I could've. It's like you've given up, like you feel you're not important enough to be a target any more. You're not making enough enemies, rubbing people up the wrong way away from the cameras."

"Setting that aside, I know you were the man who put KompuKraft on the road to success. But then two-and-a-half years ago you became the figurehead on the prow. Someone else was sailing the ship."

"Oh, someone else," was the mocking reply, which nonetheless lacked conviction.

"Yes, three mutants to be precise." The glass of Jack Daniels was placed carefully on the desk. "They suddenly came alive like something out of Frankenstein." Will was having to make some assumptions, but Leblanc's narrowing eyes showed him he had hit home.

"And you know this how?"

"Daniel Payne was scared. Despite the money, he didn't trust you guys, wisely as it turned out." Leblanc simply stared back at him and said nothing. "Nor had he given up completely on the idea of having children. So he made a little deposit at the sperm bank. Perhaps he was riven by guilt at having given the triplets away. Wanted to find out in secret, I guess, whether his next attempt to have children would have the same results. It didn't. I'm proof of that."

Leblanc leaned forward, openly incredulous. "You're...the son...of Daniel Payne?"

"Yes, but not of his wife Rebecca. And as you can see, I was a bit luckier than my three siblings."

The host leaned back again. Once more his eyes narrowed suspiciously. "So why'd you turn up now? After all this time."

"Because, I don't know how, but those three freaks found out about me and they brought me to The Shard a few months ago." Leblanc's face was that of a man who had given up being surprised by surprises. "They tortured me. So now I want revenge. I want to knock them off their pedestal. Take

405

what they think is theirs.

"What I saw in The Shard and what I see here are the fruits of work at which I would excel. I saw something that should also belong to me. Enough of being the outsider, the computer genius who scrapes a living. I want the good life. I want acknowledgement. And I want those freaks working for me directly. Every day I want them to regret what they did to me as they see the power they once had, but in my hands."

"Why should I believe you?" asked Leblanc, almost atonally. "What proof do you have?"

With this Will reached behind him and started to take off his rucksack - an action that still brought a dislocated pleasure after his recent ordeal.

Leblanc made a defensive gesture. "Go careful there."

"It is a weapon, Mr Leblanc, but not a conventional one. It's the only one in my armoury." From the rucksack he produced his hybrid laptop, which was on standby. "I have something to show you."

"Well, I can't say I ain't curious."

Will started to type on his keyboard at a ridiculously fast speed. Despite the wilderness years, he had lost none of his innate ability. He spoke as he typed.

"Would it be fair to say that your laptop is state-of-the-art, artificially intelligent, with random encryption via a radio-controlled link to KompuKraft's impregnable server?"

"Yup."

"Verified only by fingerprint scan on the mouse-pad combined with retinal scan on log-in?"

"Yup."

"So there's no way that within half a minute I should be able to read this."

He turned his laptop around so the screen was facing Leblanc and placed it on the desk.

Leblanc looked in alarmed amazement at the screen then reactivated his own with a flick on the mouse-pad to confirm what he thought he was seeing. The information on both was identical.

"How the shit did you do that?"

"In some ways I don't know. Call it an acceptable birthright from Project TCX. I'll pass on the other ones, like deprivation of all senses, turning into a mutant and being locked away like a dirty secret for thirty years."

Leblanc got up and poured himself yet another, even larger Jack Daniels, but this time offered Will a drink. He took a soda water.

"Okay, you've got my attention well and truly now. I don't know where you got all your gen, fact is you've got it, whether you are who you say you are or not, so it don't much matter. I believe in looking forward, except for payback, which is something to look forward *to*, but also requires you to look back. You've also clearly got some ability, which might well be of use to me. I think we can work together on this one. Except I don't understand why you don't just take this skill of yours and go make yourself that fortune you desire. It's a big world out there. We might have suckered it once, but it don't mean you couldn't too."

"Because I'm thirty and I want everything now. I don't want to waste years begging for financial backing. Kom-puKraft is already there, top of the tree, and I want to sit on the...well, next to top of branch. I'm a gun for hire."

"And you think I'm your open sesame?"

"We could be good for each other."

The American lifted his glass. "What makes you think I'm not a 'glass is half full' kinda guy, happy with my lot?"

"You?" Will started to laugh.

"Okay, I give you that one. Thaddeus Leblanc could never, ever be accused of that."

Will suddenly turned serious. "You want your company back, Mr Leblanc. It's why you're still there."

Will knew he had Leblanc, from the moment it had dawned on him during the train journey down to the coast that Leblanc wanted KompuKraft so badly he was prepared to wait through all the ignominy, like a snake in an s-bend, for the right moment to strike. The American didn't know how or when that moment would present itself, but when it did he wanted to be ready and he wouldn't let go once he had bitten. To the mutants though he had probably been as conspicuous as a rattlesnake and they had outmanoeuvred him so far.

Will had taken some chances in lying, but since he knew he had to act swiftly, he would be leaving Leblanc no chance to make any immediate investigation of his claims. Later would be too late, for both him and Leblanc alike.

Suddenly the moment of truth arrived.

"So what's your plan...what's your name again?"

"I never gave it. And it's not important." He didn't want this man knowing any more about him than he had to, for his mother's sake, above all, if things went wrong.

He had to hide from Leblanc the fact that the latter was just the key to the door, not to Will's future.

"May I use your laptop?" asked Will, who saw the wary look in Leblanc's eye. "Oh, you can log off from anything you're doing, just not from the system. I don't want to trigger any alerts."

"Okay." The word drawled cautiously. "But go careful. What are you looking to do?"

"I want to show you something."

He was winging it, having to trust his ability to do what he thought he could do. But about half a minute later, giving Leblanc no time for deep thought, he said, "Look here." He knew the screen would mean nothing to the man more attuned to profit and loss accounts. He continued. "The clever part of what your three pals did was hacking into the other systems." Leblanc feigned incomprehension. But Will wasn't fooled. The man was no longer the snake: he was a trapdoor spider, and Will was about to tread on dangerous territory, very close to the lair. "The virus they planted, on the other hand, is pretty simple." Here he looked Leblanc straight in the eye. His host was a man of implacable will and looked straight back. Will couldn't help but feel a repulsive respect. There was an unspoken understanding between them from that moment, a shared secret. That was good, that helped Will's cause. The spider had seen just how much venom his intended prey carried and decided he was better off on his side. "You see, the anti-virus is based directly on the virus, it literally picks it apart thread by thread. Every now and then, to keep the world interested, and paying for the latest downloads, the mutants alter one thread."

"How come you alone have found it so quickly? Surely other companies and corporations have top men who could do that."

"That's the other clever part. It takes genius to create something so simple and still more genius to find it." Will was deliberately portraying an arrogance alien to his true nature. He needed to be the type of guy Leblanc wanted on his side. "Just never forget what KompuKraft has created here: thought processes that are a couple of generations ahead of the best minds; skills in covering footprints."

"Yeah okay. Now get to the point."

"The point is, your three friends didn't reckon with somebody like me. I can mutate that virus."

"Meaning?"

"Make it a bucking horse, that the handlers have trouble dealing with."

Leblanc stopped looking at the screen and shifted his frowning gaze to Will. "If I'm understanding correctly that would mean it starts attacking KompuKraft's system."

"Yup." He mimicked his host's earlier responses. Leblanc looked aghast.

"Why in God's name would I want that?" Something dawned on him and he pushed Will's hands. "Get away from the goddamned keyboard!"

Will stood and backed away, hands upraised in a calming gesture. "Hey, like I said it's known in the trade as a bucking horse. You can get it under control again."

"Are you crazy?"

"No. Listen, all it does is buy you some time."

"Explain."

"I set it to mutate every three seconds. No one can deal with that except the mutants. Pretty soon they'll see that the only way to fix it is to switch it off temporarily."

"What?!"

"Yes. Around the world all the systems dependent upon you and your server and your technology will start to be affected."

"How the hell does that get me anywhere?" Leblanc was on his feet.

"They, the mutants, will need you. Think in the here and now. As things stand you control nothing. You're their front man in this situation. Scientists are never enough to calm people. In fact they, the other board members, would tell it as they see it and just make it worse, because they'd see nothing. They've no evidence and a scientist without evidence is a blind man. It's your bargaining chip with the mutants. Without you to spin things KompuKraft's reputation will go down the tubes. With you there to say 'hey world, nobody's perfect, but we're here to protect you', the world will accept that these things happen and you're trying to put it right."

Half of Leblanc's mind was already standing in front of the press. He took a nip of his drink and frowned into it. "I dunno. It sounds fraught with danger to me."

Will seized his chance. "So it's a risk. Since when was Thad Leblanc scared of a risk?" He could almost see his host inflating in front of him.

"What if they don't wanna negotiate with me?"

"They will. They'll know I'm behind this."

Leblanc looked at him with curiosity. "As you're potentially such a thorn in their sides, I'm surprised they didn't kill you when they had the chance."

"They only wanted me broken. Death proves nothing. Anyone can kill a man. Not everyone can claim to have crushed someone, have them running scared for the rest of their life." For a few moments he was lying on a tiled floor underneath The Shard, lights hurting his eyes and the ominous drip-drip-drip sound eroding the last of his free soul. Then he was wandering, unable to rest or shed his burden, weary beyond enduring. As he climbed from these memories back towards the light he wondered what he would do if all went according to plan and he found himself face to face with those who had so nearly taken his spirit. He looked up and into the face of Thad Leblanc and realised if his features reflected even a part of his pain, he had probably allayed the American's suspicions. He continued, "They'll know because I intend to be standing right in front of them when it happens."

"So that means..."

"Yeah, that's right, I'll be doing the negotiating."

"Again, what if they just don't wanna know?"

"Then everything comes crashing down."

Leblanc was once more true to his name – he went white. "It's crazy. I can't let it happen. It's..." He took a pace forward in frustration.

"I admit it's the worst case scenario." Will stood his ground. "But again, I really am your secret weapon. Trust me, if you are capable of trust. There's more to this than you know, but now's not the time to go into it."

Something occurred to Will and he reached toward the laptop.

"Keep your fuckin' hands to yourself," shouted Leblanc, darting forward.

Will gave the cursor a deft flick and logged off.

Leblanc was angry with himself now. He'd allowed this stranger too much time and latitude already and things felt suddenly like they were spinning out of control. He'd held back because the guy clearly knew stuff he shouldn't, which had thrown Leblanc off balance. He'd wanted to assess the exact nature of the threat posed. Then there'd seemed to be some advantage to be had after all. But now the guy's words and behaviour were making the American edgy. He didn't like mysteries. And he certainly didn't like having to trust anyone.

"What have you done?" he barked

"Looked after your interests. I figured if the three stooges noticed Thad Leblanc poking around in the anti-virus programme then, no disrespect to you, they might get suspicious."

Leblanc raised his eyebrows and then gave a little appreciative nod. The thinking behind that move both met with his approval and calmed some of his fears. 'Hmmm.' It was a non-committal sound, one that both his opponents and allies over the years had come to recognise, but never read. Then a light seemed to twinkle in his eyes. "I guess you're right - about the system crash. Shit happens. If there's one thing I've learned in business it's that shit happens. It's how you clean it up that counts. With your obvious abilities and the skills of my technicians we could build things up again, with or without the freaks. Of course my preference would be without them "

Inwardly Will breathed a huge sigh of relief. "Precisely. With you in power and me earning fat wads of money in support."

Leblanc took his seat again and pointed a finger at the computer. "But what if they agree to co-operate, let me back into the seat of power again? Where does that leave you?"

"Still your second-in-command."

"Why should I agree to that?" The question was not aggressive.

"I think it's a small price to pay for what I'm giving you. And look at it this way: what choice do you have?" Will gestured around him again. "Yes, you have all this, but as I've said already, it's empty wealth. Without me as your deputy you'll never have control of the mutants or your company. As soon as you've calmed the world's fears they'll just push you aside. But with me there, you'll always hold an ace. They can stay trapped in their tower as far as I'm concerned, still sending down the ideas. I'll be there to put them into action, filtering, controlling. I'm their equal and I'll be on your side. Without me, you're no better than a shareholder, than any of your fellow directors. Someone else pulls the strings."

There was a long silence, during which Leblanc fought the temptation to punch Will in the face. At last he managed to swallow his anger.

"Okay, where do we go from here?" he asked.

"To The Shard."

The mental image of that monolith brought home the enormity of the task to both of them. Will sensed irresolution in his host.

"What's the matter Mr Leblanc? Has inactivity dulled that famous appetite for action?" Leblanc looked up at him, stung. Will needed to strike now. "I need you to get me in there. You're the key."

Leblanc raised a hand, almost in resignation. "Hey, they haven't requested my presence for a long time now. I certainly don't have access above the eightieth floor."

Will had guessed as much. "No, but just get me past the goons on the front door."

"Why d'ya need to go in? We could sit outside. I'm sure you could hack in using my laptop."

Will thought fast. "True enough, I could, but your anti-virus looks like it has a very swift response alarm. I can delay its response, but not kill it. In a matter of one or two minutes from the moment I trigger the virus mutation I need to be in there distracting those three, so they don't see the first system flag, don't get the chance to respond immediately. I want them to have a taste of just how destructive this virus could be."

Leblanc stroked his chin. It had always been his way to question everything. One of his strengths as a businessman had been to give the impression of acting rashly. It caught people off guard time and again. But he rarely left loopholes. "If they don't play ball, how are you planning to bring everything crashing down, as you put it?"

"You'll still be in the server room. All you'll have to do, at my signal, is hit the return key again. I'll have set things up to re-install the anti-virus, which as I said before, they'll have switched off in panic, and that will trigger the mutating virus again. They won't even know it's happened. I noticed you had a walkie-talkie outside and I assume you have another handset somewhere. If I'm in any trouble, I'll switch it on, and you'll start to hear the dialogue. That's your signal."

Leblanc swallowed hard. Once again he felt things like a novice skier who'd stepped on to a black run. Nevertheless Will had been right. The former power-player could not resist this sliver of a chance to be the man again.

Will knew that he had to keep him on track, stop him from thinking too long. "Can I assume the server room is below the eightieth floor, so that technicians would always have access for routine maintenance?"

"You can. But what if we're seen wandering around near it?"

Suddenly Will had a horrible thought. "Are there cameras in the server room?"

"No, only in the corridors."

He breathed a sigh of relief. "Okay, leave the corridor cameras to me. Just get me through the front door. I don't think anyone wandering in with Thad Leblanc is going to be regarded with suspicion."

"But you said they'd brought you in once already." Leblanc's eyes narrowed. "What if they recognise you? Or maybe you were lying to me."

"I looked a bit different then. You're being very cautious, Mr Leblanc."

"Oh well, there's only control of the world's largest and most important company at stake." He accompanied the sarcastic response with a suitably exaggerated gesture of indifference. "Every successful man is careful. And another thing: I don't normally go in on a Sunday."

"Again a risk – a chance we'll have to take. Look, just get me to the server room. I won't need long." Will wished he felt as confident as he was preparing to be. But now was not a time for doubting his abilities. He closed his laptop emphatically. "Come on, Mr Leblanc, as your fellow Yanks would probably say, let's go and kick some mutant ass."

Chapter Eleven - Loading up

They set off for the city in Leblanc's gleaming Mercedes. It was the strangest sensation; Will's first proper ride in a car since he'd left home, if you discounted the Millers' mercy dash, of which he had no recollection.

His eyes scanned the dashboard, particularly the satellite navigation screen. Nowhere could he find the tell-tale double K symbol. Good old Germans. At least one major company hadn't sold out.

The two men rode in silence, lost in thoughts of their very different agendas.

The Shard was visible from miles away, an ominous slash in the canvas of the horizon. In the car, two hearts thumped as one. Soon the gargantuan splinter of glass and steel towered suffocatingly above them. As they drove down the ramp into the car park, the memory of his last journey below this building caused bile to rise in Will's throat. Despite the highly engineered, luxurious cushioning of the impact, the car doors boomed threateningly in the enclosed space when they shut.

As they rode a goods lift to the lobby Leblanc broke the silence. "If we're confronted, let me do the talking. How good's your American accent?"

"I thought you didn't want me to talk."

"Yeah, but if you're pressed."

"I dunno. Passable, I guess."

"Well then you can be a friend of mine from NASA. We're brokering some sort of a deal in private. But leave it to me if possible. I'd been planning to say you were just a technician, but those freaks would know if there was something wrong with the system, or at least there's a chance they would."

They stepped into the silent lobby, the circumstances so different from Will's last visit, but his destination the same. The first guard approached them, then stepped back almost deferentially when he saw the identity of the visitor, trying to move his hand back away from his gun butt as surreptitiously as possible.

"Um, good morning, Mr Leblanc." He nodded in Will's direction. "Good morning, sir."

"Good morning, John," said Leblanc. This was no great feat of memory since John was wearing a nametag. "How's it hanging?"

Clever, thought Will. Mateyness usually ensures no questions are asked. But this was the largest company in the world and a question did follow.

"Very well, sir, thank you. Could I ask your guest to sign the book sir?"

Leblanc smiled conspiratorially. "John, this is one visitor I'd rather not advertise, if you get my meaning." He tapped the side of his nose. He saw the hesitation in the guard's eyes and the curious glance from the other guard behind the desk.

"Okay, sir. But you know how you're always telling us to allow no deviation from security etiquette, everyone to sign in and be searched?"

Leblanc reached inside his jacket and the guard stiffened slightly. He was confused. What Leblanc drew out was his wallet, turning his back to the cameras as he did so. "Okay, I'll just get out my ID." The ID appeared to have a picture of King William on it and a large number. The guard's eyes changed from frowning to bulging, as did those of the reception guard when the same ID was pushed into his pocket. Leblanc clapped both of them on the shoulder. "Well done for your diligence."

"A pleasure, sir."

They got into another lift and started heading up in a whisper of movement.

"Let's hope our freaky friends were otherwise engaged and had better things to do than look at pictures of the lobby," said Leblanc. He opened his laptop case and handed the machine to Will. "Get moving."

The lift stopped at the fiftieth floor and they got out. As they walked along the corridor towards the server room Leblanc looked nervously at the camera. Unlike the ones in the lobby it was fixed and looked down the corridor in both directions. Nothing would escape it.

"I don't like this," said Leblanc. "My being here is a big warning flag."

"No need to worry, Mr Leblanc," said Will and walked alongside the big man holding the laptop open, showing him the screen. On it was a picture of an empty corridor.

They walked to the server room door and Leblanc said, "Okay, I give up, what's with the empty corridor shot?"

"That's the fiftieth floor, where we were just walking."

The American opened his mouth in disbelief. "Are you

sure?"

Will pointed to the top right-hand corner of the screen where the number fifty showed. "It was simple. When we were in the lift I went into the control programme for the cameras and looped it. It's going to show thirty seconds of footage from two minutes ago over and over."

"Clever. But surely they're gonna notice if some action footage keeps feeding repeatedly."

"The cameras are on twenty-five different circuits. All the ones on this circuit are corridor cameras, and it being a Sunday, they were all blank when I checked. Lucky I guess, but not surprising. If there are any guards who are dedicated enough on a Sunday to somehow notice the loop, they'd be pretty unique."

Though Leblanc had a key, the door to the server was unlocked. Will looked around and took it all in. The very ordinariness of the room seemed, its sterility seemed, designed to deceive, yet somehow it was appropriate, for it was the stony heart of the monster, the centre of the web, and all analogies seemed appropriate. There was something he could only feel, not see, a thrumming in the air, as if a bass string was vibrating at an incredibly low resonant frequency. It had a peculiar quality to it. Will could think of no other way to describe it - what was emanating was not sound, but darkness and wrong. Were they twanging a thread of the web, warning the spider of their presence? It sent a shudder through him. His mind scrabbled back and he realised that it might be the same energy he had felt up in the penthouse, issuing from behind the blacked out windows.

"Can you feel that?" he asked Leblanc.

"Feel what?" The distracted thought went through Will's

mind that perhaps you had to be some sort of freak to experience the sensation. "What I do feel is cold, and I can tell you now it won't be long till we trigger some sort of alarm in here."

Will knew he was right. There was air-conditioning to keep the massed ranks of equipment cool, but now it was common practice to have alarm systems that detected increases in temperature caused by heat sources such as unauthorised personnel. They had to work fast.

Will plugged the laptop into a power socket. Radio-controlled or not, he didn't want the computer to power down for any reason.

And then he was away, his body almost overwhelmed by the data at his fingertips, surfing a wave of information that brought him crashing ashore into the tangled roots of the world's most advanced computer system. It was a rush he could barely control; that he managed was pure instinct. He was the pinball wizard in the old song, playing by intuition.

Suddenly, he'd done everything he needed to do. Then it was as if he flew backwards through a firmament of white numbers against a dark sky and he was sitting with his finger poised above the 'return' key. He looked at the time on the screen - two minutes had passed.

"Okay, I've done all I can. The lift doors are on manual. Have you got your walkie-talkie set?" Leblanc showed him it. "Keep the channels open, but whatever you do don't try to contact me. As soon as I hit this key the virus will start to load. This is it, Mr Leblanc - we're going to get your company back."

"Hey, wait a minute. Whaddya mean, the virus begins to load?"

"You know, like we agreed, the preliminary attack. A shot across the bows to get their attention. But if things don't go well, on my signal you hit 'return' again. That'll really set the guns blazing."

Leblanc gave him a strange look, then said, "You know, I really don't know if I can do this. It'll feel like cutting off my own leg."

Will had been standing by the server room door, but now he strode back towards Leblanc with such a look in his eye that even that bully backed off a pace. "Sounds to me like they already cut off your balls. Hit the button, Mr Leblanc, otherwise maybe I'll just go and strike a deal with them myself. Then you'll really have nowhere to go."

Leblanc wasn't a guy to take insults well, just like Will wasn't one to dish them out - this hard-nosed act drained him to the point where he shook.

"How do I know that ain't what you've got planned any-way?" said the American.

"Because if anyone wants revenge on these fuckers more than you it's me. Enough. Look how easy it is."

With that, Will hit 'return' and ran from the room towards the lifts, having set in motion a process that no amount of 'Ctrl Alt Delete' would cure.

Included in this was the deactivation of the lift-controlling programme. He saw that the manual override panel by the side of the lift doors was now backlit, which would only ordinarily have happened in the event of building systems failure. Otherwise, even during a normal working day, ID cards were required, or as he had seen before, retinal scans in high security areas. He pressed the up arrow and stepped inside.

As his journey began, or ended, depending on one's point of view, the machinery of his heart was louder than anything propelling him upwards.

He was travelling between the devil and the deep blue sea. He thought of Leblanc. Would he push the button? Probably not, but then Leblanc didn't trust him either. He was right not to, but for all the wrong reasons.

He stopped at the eightieth floor, got out and crossed to the penthouse lift, relieved to see that it too had a backlit panel. There was no time to mark the symbolism of this moment with a suitable apophthegm, as he didn't know whether the feed from the camera above this lift was being observed. That was something he would only find out when the doors opened at the destination.

Which they did now.

About halfway to the penthouse Will had been aware of a noise coming down the lift shaft, which he'd assumed came from the generator. But then he'd recognised it as pounding rock music, which assaulted his ears with a tenfold increase in volume as the doors opened. He had the feeling he wasn't expected. That was more than confirmed, firstly by another series of rhythmic sounds, which filtered to him through the music, and then by what he saw as he stepped out.

None of the three was in a position to see him, but they were certainly in a position. Zeus lay on the floor, the soles of his feet facing Will, who still stood behind the bullet-proof glass. Straddling Zeus and also facing towards the lift, with her sex sliding frantically up and down the length of his magnificent phallus, was Juno. Her face was hidden from Will's view by the lean body of Pan, whose buttocks her fingers kneaded

423

as she rocked her head backwards and forwards towards his hips. The ecstatic moaning of all three parties provided the back-beating rhythm Will had heard. On a small table to the right of them was a mound of white powder.

Though the wall of screens off to the right flashed its myriad images, Will realised to his delight, that it was unlikely anything he had done in the last few minutes would have entered the consciousness of these three would-be gods indulging their transcendent appetites.

Whether she sensed some change or scent in the air he didn't know, but Will saw Juno's hands tense. If it weren't for the menace in her black eyes, there might have been something faintly comical about the way her face appeared around Pan's buttocks. A gasp escaped her, and the others followed her gaze. The frustration on their faces turning to rage, but fear also surfaced.

Juno rose, her eyes never leaving Will's. In them he thought he saw recognition. Not so her fellow deities, who now looked absurd and oddly vulnerable, as she discarded their glistening erections, which started to wilt. But there was nothing absurd about Juno. Her awesome nakedness moved across the room towards Will, the music beating a backdrop to her advance, her hips matching the beat and her swaying breasts counterpointing it. She was magnificent, the more so because it was obvious that she was wary, a stalking lioness, not knowing Will's purpose here, only knowing that whatever it was, she would confront it, dealing the card that she alone held - the ace of spades, its blackness mirrored between her legs.

Will felt himself being drawn, his heartbeat starting to match the pounding music as he swayed. It took all his self-possession to remember his shield: the memory of what they had done to him; and the knowledge that she had wanted it. Yet he felt he would surrender it all for one kiss.

She stood before him, so close he could have reached out and touched her naked body. She almost willed it, and asked him once again the question, "Do you want me?"

Did he want her?! The question was a reflection of her, on the surface naïve and innocent, yet underlain with an ancient, elemental, dangerous lust. Yet her eyes promised something else; she was offering more. He knew this suddenly because she had recognised him. He looked so different now and they could not have been expecting his return, yet from across the room she had known him. On their previous encounter the offer of her body had been mocking. Now, an instinct that perhaps they shared told him she viewed him, if not as an equal, then as a worthy opponent. He believed if he had reached out to touch her, she would have welcomed him to her body.

"You know I want you, as every man has always wanted you, but I do not fear you. And you, I think, more than the others, need to be feared as well as loved."

She nodded, a simple, eloquent gesture.

Now Zeus thundered forward, still naked, fist raised. "How dare you come in here?" He made to strike Will, who stood his ground. But as in their last encounter Juno raised her hand to stop him.

"It would be unwise to destroy our saviour." Zeus looked at her aghast, whereas Will watched in admiration. "It is the Seer."

Zeus, with fist still clenched and mouth open, looked at her, then at Will, then back at her. "But..."

425

"Yes," she said, "he survived. And the fact that he stands here means that our defences have been breached. We have been complacent. Which in turn means that if he meant us harm, he could simply have planted a bomb and left."

All this time, Juno's eyes never left Will's, and he saw there was more behind them than he had seen or imagined. For a start, there was wisdom. If any of these creatures could claim to be a god, it was she.

"Indeed you're right," he said respectfully, "I'm here to bring KompuKraft down, one way or another. And there is already a bomb ticking." He pointed to the screens. They turned and saw how the pictures were breaking up and going blank.

"What's happening?" asked Pan of no-one in particular.

"Hoist with your own petard, I'm afraid," was Will's response. "There is a virus attacking your system."

Pan raced across to a laptop and started tapping keys at a pace too furious to follow, his eyes darting backwards and forwards at an increasingly frantic rate from the laptop to the screens, until at last he slammed his fists on the keys and turned to the others.

"He's loop-mutated the virus. We'll have to disable it."

"I suspect it is pointless," said Juno, still holding Will's gaze and with even a trace of a smile brushing her sensuous lips. Will looked at her questioningly. "This was meant to get our attention. He has something to tell us, or he would not be here. But whatever the reason, KompuKraft as we know it is doomed."

There were immediate howls of protest from Zeus and Pan, and the latter turned back to the laptop, muttering, swearing and hitting keys in a frenzied attempt to outthink the system.

Juno waved a hand in the direction of a small steel cylinder on a glass table and the rock music stopped. She too stood silent, acutely aware that what could only be described as a barely audible throbbing filled the gap, pulsing in the air, as it had in the server room. Will felt it. She knew he did as she saw his eyes glance around and fix on the blacked out windows in the far corner. They both knew the time would come when he would ask, but it wasn't yet that time.

He addressed her. "I'm surprised you're taking this so calmly."

" 'Calmly' is perhaps the wrong word. I had doubts even as I meted out your punishment. The old vengeful goddess in me sentenced you nonetheless, but the moment I saw you standing there today, I knew that something was about to change forever. That was why I offered myself to you. On your first visit here it was a taunt, this time an acknowledgement."

Zeus was stung. "This is intolerable. Why can't we swat him like a fly? This virus is not beyond our powers, we just need time. We can call Leblanc to buy that for us. We are geniuses. The world needs us."

"Kill me and there are others," said Will.

"But none with your powers," answered Juno. "I know that much." She turned to stand square in front of him and asked, "Who are you?"

"The spawn of the same devil that bred these bodies you inhabit."

Zeus looked at him in astonishment. "Liar!" he bellowed.

Juno merely nodded. "That explains much. I don't under-stand everything and this is probably not the time for long explanations. Perhaps later."

"Later be damned. We should kill him and take our

chances," said Zeus, "for if we're not the sole possessors of these powers, then we are nothing."

"Well, I'm here to tell you that you are the possessors of unique powers that you yourself perhaps don't fully understand. I'm not here just as a destroyer. I bring you a gift for the future, if you can just see your way out of the past. Harness these powers properly and they will earn you the love and respect of all mankind."

"Our power comes from fear and respect," said Pan, who had given up his impromptu helpdesk in frustration.

"Because that is all you've tried to know," said Will. "But surely there is a greater strength to be found in love."

"That is unlikely," said Juno. "Love is weak, a spindly branch on the tree of lust."

"Look where fear has got you," said Will. "Trapped in your gilded cage, behind bullet-proof glass and steel doors, two thousand feet away from the rest of humanity."

"Humanity, " snorted Zeus.

"You dismiss us," retorted Will, "but we appear to have been your preferred vessel for materialising."

"Because you are weak," huffed the would-be god.

"Found a way in here though, didn't we?"

"This getting us nowhere," said Juno impatiently, raising her hands like a mother silencing two rude sons. "And the Seer has a point."

"Your punishment failed," continued Will, while Zeus bridled at the lack of support from the woman he had been pleasuring not ten minutes before, "and another of your empires is about to crumble, as they have always crumbled. On the other side of the world, even as we speak, systems are failing."

Not knowing what to do next, the deities stood so still they could have been the statues of which they were once so proud. He pitied them in their nakedness. He spoke again. "But I'm here to offer you a way out; no, not just a way out - a way to even greater power." Will walked past them and crossed to the windows that stretched from floor to lofty ceiling. "To be out there and to be loved and revered."

Juno followed him and stared over his shoulder at the city stretching like a spillage to the horizon.

"And you would share this with us because...?" asked Pan, while Juno's mind was taken back to that balmy Mediterranean night as she had stood in another decaying temple looking out at the twinkling lights, and ever-doubting Pan had asked her a similar question. "We who tortured and punished you."

"Because unbeknown to you, through your curse you gave me the power to cure a child, a terminally sick child. I saw the effect of that miracle reflected in the faces of her parents, felt it in their gratitude."

"How did that happen? I don't understand," said Juno, for once losing the air of command her sexuality gave her.

He looked at her. "I wouldn't expect you to. For you are simply stardust like the rest of us, only in a more complex form, subject to the whims of the universe even as you, like us, try to control it. You thought you had reached the pinnacle of your achievements with the thought-programming 'fish'. What you couldn't know or comprehend, what none of us will ever understand, is the elemental nature of your powers, which, combined with the great unknown at the centre of man's brain and amplified by the technical genius of your mutant bodies, caused your curse to come to fulfilment in

429

the form of a blessing."

Juno looked at him wonderingly, before saying, "Have our powers also caused you to become an orator." She smiled and Will felt a blush tingle on his skin for the first time in years.

Zeus and Pan had now joined them and stood also staring out across the recesses and grooves of the city, rendered orthochromatic by distance and pollution.

The air throbbed again.

"It wouldn't be easy for us," said Pan. "We can't simply step away from all that has made us strong."

"How strong are you? Out there," Will pointed to the city, "you're not feared, not directly, only through your agent, KompuKraft. How can you be feared if no-one out there knows of your existence.

"Anyway, I'm afraid you have little choice. I will destroy KompuKraft." He looked at them over his shoulder. "But we can build it into something better. I'll take you out there." He turned again to the windows. "We can simply walk out of here today. Who can stop you? The creators of Project TCX? When it went horribly wrong they killed your parents and kept you prisoner, using your talents in the most unethical way possible? They won't dare to talk. And who would believe or forgive them if they did? You're merely the victims.

"You have created something astonishing and unique in your liquid chip – it's all in here." As she was the nearest, he pointed to Juno's head. "Constructing it won't be beyond the world's finest scientists, with your guidance and instruction. If it's used properly, ethically, you can become such a force for good. We can build another empire, greater than anything seen for the last two thousand years. And you'll be honoured like a story two thousand years in the telling."

"You speak of the single deity, the second coming," said Juno.

"Call it what you will - no pun intended - but you cannot hide in here. Do you know of the events that came to be known as 9/11?" The mutants looked suddenly, fearfully out of the window. "Death finds a way."

"Not to us," blustered Zeus unconvincingly. "We are immortal."

"We are," said Juno, "but these bodies are not." She looked through the window again, both wistful and angry. "Oh why did I overreach myself? I became greedy for adulation and acknowledgement. Up here amongst the clouds, close to our..." She stopped, but Will saw the direction of her gaze. "We could have been safe, perhaps not forever, but for now. But it had been so long since I had been worshipped, made sacrifice to. I needed to be feared and adored. And now look at us." She turned to Will. "People are doing what they will always do when they fear. They tear things down. But for my arrogance in singling you out for punishment, we could have replenished these bodies indefinitely."

"For what it's worth, I forgive you." Juno smiled, reached out and took his hand. Her touch was paradise. "The world can still be yours, but you must not look to rule it. Be instead the most amazing force for good. Harness your powers to those of technology to fight sickness and evil. You will find all the worship you ever sought. Do it here, if you must, but make a fresh start."

Juno looked again towards the black windows, then back at Will. "That cannot be, unless good really can thrive in the midst of evil. But..."

There were three sounds, like three stifled sneezes.

431

Juno's hand tightened in a reflex. She looked at Will. "Perhaps I could have loved you," she said, her face registering some extreme of emotion. What was she saying?

Then suddenly knowledge and despair were his in an awful, languid clarity. There was a trickle of blood from Juno's mouth, her grip on him loosened, and then she fell forward, followed domino-like by her siblings. They hadn't even had time to register shock before they went. And as always the immutable dirty fact of violent death lacked any glory or elegiac beauty.

Will spun round to see Leblanc standing there, his silenced pistol still pointing its finger of death at the space that Pan, the last of his victims, had occupied.

"That's for all the times you pissed me off," he said to the corpses.

"Leblanc, what have you done?"

"Taken back what was mine – wasn't that the plan? Seemed to me like it was taking too long." He looked through narrowed eyes at Will, who felt the first flakes of fear settling on him.

"But...you killed them." It was all he could think of to say. He was stunned.

"Let's not forget, I'm Chief Executive Officer of KompuKraft, and I just made an *executive* decision – pun intended." Will wondered whether those last two words were a taunting indication of just how much Leblanc had overheard. "Anyway, didn't seem like you were getting anywhere fast, so I thought I'd check for myself."

Will was sure he would have heard the lift. "How did you...?"

Leblanc gestured with his gun towards a disguised door in

432

the far corner of the room. "Health and safety, boy." His accent was edging further towards Ohio and the cadences of the cattle markets he had known as a boy. "Huge building like this, there's a fire, you can't use the lifts. But hell, I just could never get past the eightieth floor before. That's where those stairs start. I could've got in before, I'd have blown these assholes away long ago and taken my chances."

Will followed Leblanc's gaze back to the three mutants. That's all they were now, no longer gods, as he noticed with astonishment that their bodies appeared almost to have deflated, returned to their former emaciated state.

Above them was a shimmering, like a heat haze. I wonder, thought Will, but he felt nothing, no change in his body. He was just left to wonder how it might have felt, but knew that they would never have separated, having been together since time began, those three...well, what were they? Forces of nature. As he looked at the wasted corpses he knew at last that one's definition of gods depended on a number of things. Perhaps turning ugliness to beauty might have been one of them.

So, it hadn't gone as planned.

Before he could turn his mind to taking in the situation, there was a question that he needed answered and his attention was drawn to it again. There was still a faint, but perceptible throbbing in the air and there was no doubting its source. There was a door and he went to it.

"Where ya goin'?" demanded Leblanc.

"Can't you feel it?" It was a redundant question. If the guy hadn't noticed it in the server room, there was no chance now.

With his gun still in his hand, but pointing now to the floor,

Leblanc joined him at the door. "I guess. Kinda vibration or somethin'"

So there were still wonders in the world.

"I don't know," said Will. "This seemed to be some source of power for them. Perhaps it gave them the strength to maintain those bodies, even enhanced their powers. To me, it seemed to change in frequency somehow with their moods."

"What the fuck are you talkin' 'bout?" The farm boy was definitely in control now he had a gun in his hand.

"Like I said, I don't really know. But when they brought me in here they told me they were gods, that they had taken over the bodies of the three mutants."

"Bullshit."

"You saw their appearance just before you...shot them - their sheer physical beauty. Look at them now. Whatever the explanation, clearly something happened to them to transform them."

Leblanc thought back to that take-over meeting a couple of years back. Then he shook his head and looked at the blacked-out room. "This here was the old research laboratory for Project TCX, place it all started." He put his hand on the door handle and turned it.

Almost anticlimactically, it wasn't locked.

"Well, after all, they never had visitors," said Leblanc, his humour a subconscious attempt to combat the tightness in his chest.

Chapter Twelve - Winding up

D arkness hung in that room, in every possible facet of its meaning, from the inky blackness of a moonless night to the shadows of concealment that lurk at the edge of one's reason. Will felt it at once. This was a container that Pandora would have balked at opening.

Both men hesitated at the door, with even Leblanc sensing that some manifestation of hell prevailed. There were shapes in the room, which appeared to move spasmodically, jerkily, causing something to creak. Peculiar but faint sounds confused the ear, impossible to identify without any context. And here and there in the blackness winked lights, which might have been eyes looking out from hiding places in the pit of night.

When at last the light from the doorway started to win its battle with the gloomy interior, Will wished it hadn't. As the dreadful scene unveiled itself in all its monochrome horror, Will suddenly understood what he was sensing if not what he was seeing.

"Oh my God! Fear, to the power of four."

"Jeeezuss!" groaned Leblanc taking a step back.

Will, however, stepped forward into the room. There were four large tables, on each of which lay a body. Except they were not corpses. As he drew nearer he saw the occasional twitch. What was left of each emaciated figure was clothed in what appeared to be overalls, which hung on the skeletal forms.

Will's need to see the gruesome details of evil overrode his better judgement. But while he may have thought that he was resolved and fully prepared to face whatever was there, he was wrong.

In the dim light he could see that something about the faces wasn't right and he approached the first table. As he bent towards it he recoiled suddenly, in horror, and vomited. That there were no eyes, only empty sockets, which would have been bad enough, but the nose and ears had also been sliced away crudely.

Leblanc stood frozen, shocked by the other man's stricken response to what he could not yet see. He stayed there, like a timid archaeologist at the mouth of a cursed tomb. Will remained doubled over retching for a few moments longer. Why? Why had they done this?

And then the horrific simplicity of it hit him, and he retched again, partly at the thought of what he was about to do, but also through chest-tightening pity for what these people had endured - were enduring still. *Could he still call them people? - he thought it would be better not to.*

He had to know for sure and returning to the first table he reached out tentatively. The facial skin was like parchment, barely concealing the bones beneath. He pushed the lower jaw downwards. It was tough, as if the terrors endured had fixed that jaw in a rigor. When the mouth opened there was a dreadful sound like a death rattle, accompanied by a twitch of the head. Will pulled his fingers away hurriedly, though not before he had confirmed that there was no tongue. His stomach ached from the convulsions, but that was nothing to what these poor souls suffered.

Distractedly, he noticed there was an ID badge attached to the top pocket of the overall. He removed it, but couldn't read it in the darkness. Leblanc saw him peering at it.

"You want more light in there," said the American in a shaky voice.

"No, I can see more than I want to." He put the badge in his own pocket.

There was one more trial and he would go through it, for their sakes and souls. He allowed his eyes to wander down towards the nearest hand. Sure enough the fingers had been removed. Will noticed the catheter inserted above the stump of the second finger and his gaze followed it back towards the head of the table, where it was attached to a regulator, an early twenty-first century improvement on the clumsy drip feeds rolled around in hospitals before. They had been kept alive.

The four regulators provided some of the winking lights that he had seen upon opening the door. The rest belonged to a large square box from which leads snaked towards each table. He stood staring at it. The cables seemed to disappear into the base of the victims' shaven skulls.

That was another almost eccentric feature; despite the carnage, the bodies had been kept shaved and groomed. The toenails of the one he could see had been cut. Will thought he understood.

He turned his attention back to the box. He didn't know whether his presence in the room had caused it, but the throbbing in the air had grown slightly stronger. The box was

437

its source. That and the blinking lights held Will hypnotised. He felt himself starting to sway slightly. What was this thing?

Leblanc's voice broke the spell, as if he'd read his mind.

"That was Project TCX, the source of everything that's happened in the last thirty years. My God! They didn't know what they were doing when they started that one.

Will turned and left the dark room on distinctly shaky legs. "But you knew about *this*," he said angrily, as he walked up to Leblanc.

"No I didn't."

Will reached into his pocket and produced the ID. He read it, then waved it in front of Leblanc's face. "Joshua Jones, Senior Project Assistant." He paused. "Why, Leblanc?"

Leblanc stared past him into the room. "He was certainly one of the four technicians unfortunate enough to be here when the mutants came alive. I'm not going to collect the other name tags."

"So you did know. For fuck's sake, what kind of...creatures were you?"

Leblanc gestured with his gun hand towards the room. "I swear I didn't know this was going to happen." Then he hung his head as he continued. "The freaks told us that we just couldn't afford to have junior people who had witnessed their, let's say metamorphosis running around free. Dr Phillips was a different matter. The project was his brainchild - unfortunate choice of words I know - and he could be trusted to keep quiet. The mutants told us they would 'take care of the problem' if we could take care of the peripherals. It wasn't difficult. There were a select few people looking after these freaks at the beginning of the project and we chose them very carefully. They needed to be qualified of course, but also

438

have few ties; maybe orphans, no siblings, that kinda thing. Plus with our technical know-how we could expunge their records from just about anywhere. It would be like they'd never existed. It also helped that they lived in rooms on one of the lower floors and were sworn to silence about their work." Now he looked Will in the eye. "But I swear by my children's lives, I thought they would just be...removed. I didn't know this was gonna happen. In fact, I don't even know what *this* is. What exactly did you see in there?"

Will looked at Leblanc with total contempt, the taste of bile still thick in his mouth. "Well let's just say death would have been preferable. I think I know what this is. But first, how many bullets do you have left in that gun?" He wasn't going to spare Leblanc.

Leblanc nodded. "Enough." He walked into the room. Will lurched into the penthouse. He heard the words 'Oh my Go...' cut off by a retching sound. There were four more stifled sneezes and the American re-emerged, pale, into the daylight. The thrumming had stopped.

"Now can you tell me what..." he pointed towards the room, "...what that shit in there was?"

"It was death and life, revenge and homage."

"Let's just cut the riddles, shall we?"

Will turned and looked at the mutants' bodies. "Okay, but I'm not sure the truth is any easier to understand. You see, although every fibre in your pragmatic body wants to deny it, the mutants were possessed by some sort of ancient, elemental forces." Leblanc frowned sceptically. "Well how else do you explain what's happened. Their bodies were useless empty shells, their brains computers enclosed in dura mater, and then suddenly - or are you going to deny this?

- from what I've seen they developed into these beautiful, powerful people with thoughts and a mind of their own. Did you ever look into their eyes?"

Leblanc remembered that first meeting in the boardroom and the effect the woman had had on him. "Yeah, I did."

"Then you'll know that something preternatural was lurking there. Those beings may have been around since the nothingness at the beginning of time and through the millennia, from time to time, they've been worshipped, in one form or another, as gods. I'm guessing of course. But in front of me they called each other by the names of deities. They needed, thrived on the power that came from our fearful obeisance." He pointed to the charnel house behind the blackened windows. "That was a battery, if you like, that gave them strength. I wouldn't be surprised if that box in there was tapping into their darkest fears and playing them back, over and over."

"You mean they kept those poor bastards alive and terrified for kicks?"

"That's one way of looking at it, but a simplistic one. I think the terror was being amplified in some way and they were feeding off it by a means beyond our earthly comprehension. Oh, I don't know, this is so much conjecture. Damn, why did you shoot them? There was so much I could have asked them."

"We weren't in the asking game, case you've forgotten. Besides, d'ya really think you could have worked with things capable of creating that house of horrors over there?"

Will looked Leblanc in the eye. "You mean people capable of sanctioning death?" They stared at each other for a moment. "The answer is yes. Because do you know what that terrible room shows me? That it wasn't just the massive egos of the deities driving this whole thing. I said it was revenge. I said it was homage too. The possibility that I am right makes me feel sick."

"What possibility?"

"That the mutants somehow, for thirty years, despite their sensory deprivation, were aware of how they were being held and treated. Then when they were possessed they took revenge on the project technicians. Lashed out if you like. They created images of themselves, thought it was poetic justice to deprive them in the crudest, cruellest way of their senses. Who knows? Maybe when thirty years were up they would have released them as a symbolic gesture. Did you see how they've kept the heads shaved, the nails cut? They're doing what was done to them. If it's possible to look past that savagery, then yes, that very consciousness makes me believe we could have worked with them. Who am I to judge whether they were right or wrong? And once it was done it was done. They couldn't take it back. That's where the gods came in. They believed, misguidedly, that they needed fear to survive, to keep them strong, and they had it on tap. The universe is a place of darkness, for sure."

"Why didn't they do the same to Phillips? He was the project leader."

"As the project leader they had him where they wanted him. He would never talk. The other four might've. And he was a conduit to the rest of the team that was going to realise their vision for them."

"And me?"

"You know what you were, their link to the outside world. And they had you over a barrel too."

"I always knew I'd get back at the mother-fucking freaks." He looked at Will and a peculiar look came into his eye. "And how do I know they're not in you now?"

"You'll just have to take my word for it, they're not."

"But you have a kinship with them. Mmmm." The grunt conveyed uncertainty and suspicion. He looked at the mutants' corpses. "They should've possessed me. They, we, could've had it all."

Part of Will knew that he should hang around to try to keep a rein on someone like Leblanc, but the greater part of him wanted nothing to do with that poor excuse for a human being.

"So where do we go from here?" said the CEO.

Will shook his head once. "It's your mess."

Leblanc puffed out his cheeks and looked around him. "Sure is a mess, and eight's a bigger body count than I was allowing for. What to do, what to do."

"Like I said, it's your mess, Leblanc"

Then Will frowned, just before Leblanc shot him in the stomach. "MISTER Leblanc to you. I see from your face you just got the math. And you're right, it's *my* mess. I'm in charge."

Will sank to his knees, feeling blood seep through his fingers. Not lots of it. It had been a clever shot to the stomach, which meant a slower death, giving the American time to gloat.

"I'd like to thank you for getting me in here. It'd proved quite beyond me by any subtle means since these freaks took charge. Now, since I told the guards to clear the building, with the lift malfunction being a safety hazard and all, I've gotta bit of time this fine Sunday to sort things out."

442

Will had fallen onto his side now. He could feel his insides being eaten away by acid.

Leblanc continued. "You didn't really think I was gonna launch the full goddamned virus did you? Let me tell you something: our top guys are pretty fuckin' good. They may be a couple of generations behind the mutants, but I guess we've gotten ourselves a bit of time to catch up now. And don't forget, at least not before you die, we're the ones who invented the technology that created those fuckers. We're still a few generations ahead of the competition. Shame you can't come on the ride with me, but hey ho. In the meantime you can ride the pain train."

With that he shot Will in the kneecap. "That's for calling me no better than a shareholder."

The trilling of Leblanc's cellphone at that moment was both incongruous and surreal. He answered it as if it was any other day in the office, recognising the number.

"Yo Phillips, whadya want?"

The wave of pain from the first wound had taken Will back to the agony of his curse. This time he knew there'd be a quicker end. But the memory of the Millers' kindness that had brought his punishment to an end, just a week before, brought him some warmth now too. With it came thoughts of his mother. One day during his burdened wanderings he'd found himself close to the town where he was born. Though in a dilemma about it he'd gone past his old home. It had had an air of neglect. He'd wanted to see if she was there, hoping she wasn't. His burden would have prevented him from staying and he would have wanted nothing more. Nor had he wanted to bring suspicion and gossip, which would have inevitably followed the appearance of this mad, dishevelled traveller.

During his early years away from home he had always sent money, made phone calls, being careful not to tell his mother anything she could reveal to KompuKraft under...he shut the thought out of his mind. But as times had become tougher, he'd been unable to make phone calls, leaving his mother nobody to contact if she were to move on. He had no idea whether she still lived here.

He'd wandered down the alleyway alongside the house and looked into the back yard. It bore a similar look of disuse. Then he had wept, wanting to be young and innocent again and feel comforting arms around him. He hoped she had moved on with her life, having achieved her aim of raising him to manhood...

A fresh wave of pain as the bullet struck his leg, then through that the shrill noise of a mobile. He had to hang on, stay alive just a bit longer. Because something about that call, that mobile ring, its timing, told him that they had done it: he and his mother had beaten KompuKraft.

To say the news coming down the airwaves was bad was like saying the captain of the Titanic had a leakage problem.

"Leblanc, have you been watching developments? Or are you more troubled right now about whether the green reads left to right?" They weren't on the best of terms, hadn't been for thirty-two years. They were puppets in the largest marionette show of all time

"Cut the crap Phillips. What's goin' on?"

"What's going on? Just one or two helpdesk issues from across The Pond."

"Whadya mean?" Leblanc turned his back on Will's dying

figure. It was a Pavlovian response to taking a critical call.

"Oh. The Pentagon, the CIA. For fuck's sake Leblanc! Don't you monitor anything?"

"Course I do. And you mind your tone with me. Information, please."

"There's a major virus attacking their systems as we speak." The sentence was purposely delivered with heavily ironic calmness that barely concealed the hysteria beneath.

Leblanc turned and looked at Will. "Whadya mean 'major virus'?" The muscle groups that form a grimace and a grin are very similar. There's a fine difference, but it was apparent on Will's face.

"We've had no contact from the mutants," said Phillips, "but I can't get hold of them, and, of course, they never believed in phones with those freaky voices of theirs." The mutants had only ever communicated with the directors by e-mail. They had disliked interruptions, and, as Dr Phillip rightly surmised, they had never liked the effect of their own voices. "You'd better get over to The Shard now. I'll meet you there after I've phoned everyone in. Get hold of those three. We need an emergency meeting, whether they like it or not."

Leblanc felt sweat forming on his brow. "Hey, whoa, wait, wait. This virus - has it shown any sign of stopping?"

"It's gorging its way through the CIA's criminal records as we speak. Take charge Leblanc. Get this sorted." The line went dead.

"Hope you've got a disaster recovery plan in place," groaned Will, dying, but determined to enjoy the moment.

Leblanc spread his hands, palms upwards. "What...?"

"You didn't think I was going to trust you. I launched the

virus, full stop. You hitting the 'return button' would have done absolutely nothing. There was never a solution to a virus mutating that quickly. The mutants knew it."

Never had a man felt such deep regret for firing a shot while at the same time wanting to empty several more into his victim. "I gotta get you to a hospital."

"How're you going to explain that one?" Will's voice was growing fainter.

"I'll think of something. And you're gonna help me."

"Oh yeah?"

"Yeah. Or, by God, I'll find your mother, and the pain you're suffering will be nothing compared with hers."

"I don't think so, arsehole. She outwitted KompuKraft for more than thirty years, and if it weren't for the fact..." he broke off as he was hit by a surge of pain in his chest – the end wasn't far away, "...the fact that you're already history, she'd carry on. I said you needed me. You've killed the only person – people – who could help you, Leblanc. And you know what, I never would have risked my soul by helping you." His voice was no more than a whisper, but it was enough to say his piece. There was no throbbing in the air, but the fear and despair on Leblanc's face gave him strength. "It's your mess, Leblanc. You're in charge. And everything certainly points to you as the trigger of this global meltdown. Think about it and then wonder; how many bullets have you got left now?"

Will's grin was the last thing he had strength for, and he was dead before the final vengeful bullet struck his head.

Leblanc looked around him. Boy, oh boy. But he wasn't finished. It's just that there wasn't as much time as he'd hoped for. He thought he'd covered the bases, but he had to get down to his office, have a drink and think things through. Ah, forget the drink. He'd done too much of that and he wasn't thinking clearly, that was obvious. He got into the lift and went down.

Point 1 - why did you order people to leave the building for health and safety reasons when the lifts could still be operated on manual?

He tried to shut out the questioning voice for the prosecution, but as the lift descended his spirits and chances seemed to go with it.

Point 2 - why were you, against all your usual practices, in the building on Sunday, the very day this all kicks off?

Point 3 - why were you in the building with a stranger?

Point 4 - why did you bribe the guards?

He knew if the finger of suspicion and guilt was pointing at them, no amount of money would make them take the blame.

Point 5 - where did your guest disappear to?

Point 6 - where are the mutants, and why did their disappearance coincide with your most irregular visit to the building?

Okay! Okay! Okay! A step at a time.

No, no step at a time. You have no time.

Yes, he had people who could clear bodies away with no questions asked, but godammit, he hadn't thought things through. The prospect of returning to power had blinded him, as had the demon called Jack Daniels. If he got out of this, he wouldn't touch another drop of the stuff till the day he died.

He'd been so out of practice of having to make major decisions for himself that he'd fucked it up when he'd had to step up to the plate.

Of course, nobody went up to the penthouse, but that didn't mean they wouldn't be expecting directives from

447

there. He'd so wanted to be rid of those freaks that he hadn't really stopped to consider how others would react to their disappearance. When the ball was lost over the fence two and a half years ago, the others had got on with using another one. But that ball had been his and he'd felt the loss more keenly than anyone else. He was the only one prepared to climb over and get it back.

Now the likes of Phillips would be wanting technical answers to technical issues. Shit, with the lifts on manual there was nothing to stop Phillips going to demand them, since he too was a man pushed to the limit.

And that led to the great big fucking Point 7: there was a global system meltdown that the world at large would expect him to address. They'd only ever known *him* as the face and driving force of KompuKraft.

He was back in his office now, the inner sanctum where he hoped to find just a little pocket of time in which to breathe. On his desk was his laptop, which he'd removed from the server room back in those wild, halcyon days of a few minutes ago, when he'd thought he was covering his tracks. He noticed that the screen was telling him he had mail. In a daze he brought up his Inbox. He had mail? He had about thirty e-mails, all of them timed within the last half-hour and he recognised with a sinking feeling the names of most of the senders. It seemed some people never slept.

They were companies, corporations and institutions using KompuKraft's systems, hardware and anti-virus. With a shaking, sweating hand he opened the first mail. It was simply a receipt acknowledgement, but with his guts turning runny Leblanc went to his own Sent Box and looked to see what e-mail he was supposed to have sent. The offending mail was blank, but with an attachment. An mpeg.

Opening it, he recognised his study, saw himself holding a discussion, one he knew had taken place that very morning. He heard the voice of his unexpected guest in the background.

"The clever part of what your three pals did was hacking into the other systems. The virus they planted, on the other hand, is pretty simple. You see, the anti-virus is based directly on the virus, it literally picks it apart thread by thread. Every now and then, to keep the world interested, and paying for the latest downloads, the mutants alter one thread."

"How come you alone have found it so quickly? Surely other companies and corporations have top men who could do that."

"That's the other clever part. It takes genius to create something so simple and still more genius to find it. Just never forget what KompuKraft has created here; thought processes that are a couple of generations ahead of the best minds; skills in covering footprints."

"Yeah okay. Now get to the point."

He closed it down and looked at the circulation list, which could probably be summarised as everyone KompuKraft had conned with its anti-virus scam.

Leblanc was now so on edge that he almost jumped when the laptop chimed to tell him he had another e-mail. He didn't want to look, but what the hell, he did anyway. He noticed it was from an unknown address, but with a symbol indicating it had been sent with a deliberate delay. He opened it with a fatalistic sense of detachment.

If I've read you right, Leblanc, this is an e-mail to a dead man.

Who knows, it might even be from a dead man. I knew you wouldn't have a clue what I was doing in the server room. Or should I say, what I am doing, since I can see you even as I'm writing this. You should get it in about half an hour, by which time the game will be over, one way or another.

It's amazing what address books you can find when you're rummaging around. Hope you like the mpeg. It's possible you didn't know about the tiny fibre-optic cameras in your company's laptops, so strictly speaking you're not being hoist with your own petard. Those cameras, by the way, would be enough to see your company in serious trouble when word got out. I hope very sincerely that you don't find your way out of the mess that you're probably in. Have a good death, because I don't think there'll be much else to enjoy where you're going."

Leblanc closed the laptop with unusual gentleness. Just then his cellphone rang. Phillips again. He cut off the call. Fuck off. He looked around at his office. Boy, he had had dreams when he took over this company. Unfortunately, literally, the dreams of others had brought him down. He took the gun again from his inner pocket and checked to make sure that he hadn't wasted his final suicide pill on that other freak upstairs. Then he removed the silencer.

"Why not go out with a bang?"

He looked to his right, towards the drinks cabinet.

"Now, what was the last thing I said about Jack Daniels?"

Chapter Thirteen - Logging off

A few minutes after Will sent his e-mail to Leblanc, Paul Miller received one. At first he was highly suspicious, seeing that it originated from KompuKraft. Then he saw the title, 'Cystic Fibrosis'.

"My God, he's in!" He laughed out loud enough to bring Karen running. She looked towards where he was pointing and her face also broke into a big grin.

"Go, Will, go!" she shouted.

Then Paul opened the mail.

Hi, Paul, Karen and Miranda, I don't have a lot of time, but what time I do have you bought for me. Attached are some very complex macros. Paul, you used to be in IT. I've simplified them to keep you above suspicion. They hold the key to an incredibly advanced anti-virus. Sell them well, be rich, enjoy life and don't forget your favourite charity.

The tone of the e-mail struck Karen. "Do you think we'll see him again?"

"Sure we will," said Paul. "In our daughter's smile if nowhere else."

On the day KompuKraft died, Del Palmer heard a knock on the door. As an attractive man in late middle age, who had been widowed a couple of years before, he wasn't unused to answering the door to attractive, later middle-aged women. This one was different, familiar, and something about her caused a peculiar stirring in both his stomach and his loins.

Of course, the familiarity was because she lived locally. He'd seen her in the area a few times, though closer up she was more striking.

When she spoke it sent a tingle down his spine.

"Hello, Del, pardon me for disturbing you. I have mixed emotions about the news I'm bringing."

"I'm sorry?"

She shifted awkwardly on her feet, but he was not yet inclined to let her in.

"Firstly, may I say I'm very sorry about your wife's death."

No, couldn't see a good reason yet to invite her in. "Would you mind telling me where this is going? Who are you?" He felt defensive and confused.

"I wanted to get in touch before, but didn't have the courage. Nor did I think it would be right so soon after…"

"Excuse me, you're talking in riddles. Would you mind getting to the point. I don't mean to be rude, but…"

"That's quite okay." She raised a hand, which she had just taken out of her pocket. "You're absolutely right. But would you mind if I come in? I've come to tell you about your son and many things that need telling."

"What? Yes. No!" The door swung back then forwards again in his hand. Was she mad?

"There are things the world will discover after today. I want you to hear them first from me."

He opened his mouth to speak, but she again raised her hand and cut across him. "I'm sorry I ran from you all those years ago, but I did it for your sake too. Please give me the chance to tell you why."

"Carol? My God! But...we presumed you were dead." He stood open-mouthed. "And, I know it's so many years on, but...you don't look like you."

"Amazing what a good plastic surgeon can do."

Del stepped back and very slowly raised his arm, gesturing into the house. "Please, I think you'd better come in. Forgive my manners." He looked distracted and sought some anchor for his thoughts. "I'd offer you some coffee, but I'm afraid I'm all out. I was going to nip down to the shops, but this damn thing," he picked up a card from a small table and waved it, "won't be any use. It looks like all things KompuKraft have crashed world-wide." He paused as a thought struck him. "I wonder if they'd accept money."

His rheumy eyes lit up when he saw it. A bit battered, but quite a prize, certainly the pick of today's crop. He scrambled his way up the pile of refuse in the dim light of the recycling centre and grasped a strap, then held it aloft like a prized pheasant.

"Beggars can't be choosers," he said, cackling as ever at the old joke as he rode back down the rubbish slope like a demented scree runner, the rucksack swinging from his flapping hand.

A vagrant like him always had a few treasured possessions to carry around and this would be perfect for the job.

Someone else might have noticed the peculiar smell that issued from the sack as it was opened. But Wally hadn't

453

washed in ten years and his olfactory senses had long ago given up in protest. So he continued to shove in old socks, gloves, the battered remnants of a book and other things that did not bear closer scrutiny. That done, he decided to pull on the rucksack, test it for fit.

"Nice, very nice," he said approvingly, hefting it on his shoulders, then pulling the waist straps shut. "Maybe a bit snug." He reached for the strap adjuster and pulled it. "Must be the other way." It had got tighter. But not just the one around his middle. The shoulder straps seemed to be biting now as well. He tried to open the waist strap again. It was stuck fast.

He was starting to panic now, pulling at the rucksack in different directions, like a child stuck in a jumper that was too tight and wouldn't come back over its head. That was when he noticed that it seemed to be getting heavier.

Issuing a series of guttural sobs and gasps, Wally staggered off into the night.

SHUTTING DOWN

About the Author

David's dark psychological thriller novels have led to interviews on BBC Radio and in the media. He's intrigued by the things that hide, often in plain sight, in the shadows beyond the light of our everyday lives. A fluent German speaker who studied English and German literature, he believes we have always been drawn to darker tales and imaginings.

When not writing or being distracted by his other time-consuming loves of sport, music, the theatre and travelling, David loves to encourage and support creativity in others, editing and co-writing for various authors, plus running writers' workshops from Berkshire literary festivals to the far north-west of Scotland!

You can connect with me on:
- https://davidpalinauthor.com
- https://twitter.com/DPalinAuthor

Also by David Palin

Let The Game Commence is a dark and twisted thriller out now as an eBook, hardcover and paperback.

Let The Game Commence

Arthur Du Fuss, bitter, alone, and ignored by his neighbours, has two secrets: one dies with him when he commits suicide; the other is the vast wealth he amassed through the creation of a cult board game.

Now his erstwhile neighbours receive a post-mortem invitation to the offices of a charismatic City lawyer to play a final version of the game; the prize - Arthur's fortune. As they dice with the devil, the game first exposes the fragility of their relationships, and then tears them apart, with tragic and horrifying consequences. But Arthur, too, must pay for his revenge. The old man learns that outstanding debts can still be called in, even when you are dead.

Printed in Great Britain
by Amazon

27081202R00255